Beach Breeze

ALSO BY JOANNE DEMAIO

The Seaside Saga
Blue Jeans and Coffee Beans
The Denim Blue Sea
Beach Blues
Beach Breeze
The Beach Inn
Beach Bliss
Castaway Cottage
Night Beach
Little Beach Bungalow
Every Summer
–And More Seaside Saga Books–

Summer Standalone Novels
True Blend
Whole Latte Life

Winter Novels
Eighteen Winters
First Flurries
Cardinal Cabin
Snow Deer and Cocoa Cheer
Snowflakes and Coffee Cakes

beach breeze

A NOVEL

JOANNE DEMAIO

This is a work of fiction. Names, characters, places, and incidents are either the product of the author's imagination or are used fictitiously. Any resemblance to actual persons, living or dead, events, or locales is entirely coincidental.

ISBN: 1543115276
ISBN-13: 9781543115277

Joannedemaio.com

To the Connecticut Shoreline

For its gentle beach breeze,
ever a part of my summers,
ever inspiring my seaside stories.

one

ONLY A YEAR AGO, JASON Barlow considered his life fortunate. Home was his family's weathered cottage by the sea—a gabled house sitting on a stone bluff, the waves breaking down below. He'd promised to be there for his new wife, always. Standing at a church altar last summer and watching Maris, his beautiful bride, walk down the aisle, every star finally aligned for him.

But didn't he know, didn't he somehow know. A fortunate life? Experience taught Jason otherwise, and now he's mad as he drives along a dark road. Mad because, in his happiness, he'd been foolish enough to forget one important lesson: On any given day, hour, or minute, life can spin out from under you. It happened nine years ago, when he lost his brother, and Jason nearly didn't survive the day. So it's important to be wary and not trust happiness, not too much.

And this past summer had been blissful. From Maris finally being by his side, to his cottage-architecture career kicking into overdrive with his biggest job yet—designing Stony Point's first beach inn—it was all good. There were moonlit seaside walks, nights fishing on the rocks with the guys, Sunday mornings in bed with his wife, summer shindigs and easy times.

If nothing else, Jason should've known it was all, well, it was all *too* good. Especially after meeting Salvatore DeLuca, Maris' cousin. Sal, who rolled into town like a cool summer wave, who charmed all the beach friends, whose ready smile had everyone spilling secrets. It was Sal, after all, who unexpectedly stepped into the boat shoes of the brother Jason had lost.

So, yes. Jason knows as he steers his SUV on the winding road leading away from his Connecticut beach life. Yes, he knows that for the past year, he had it all. All the happiness a man could want. That's right, a fortunate life. And it was a warning he didn't heed. Happiness.

Because now, mere hours after giving Sal's eulogy, here he is—alone. Alone and driving away from his cottage on the bluff overlooking Long Island Sound, the stars surely shining above the salty water. Maris is no doubt worried inside that stately home, with lamplight spilling from the windows, framed paintings hung on the walls, hurricane lanterns and her conch shell on the mantel, a sea breeze lifting the curtains as she holds the note he left behind—his penned words telling his wife he has to leave, to find a way to get through this unbearable grief. To not let her see him come undone, again.

So with each passing mile, each passing town, Jason's beach life diminishes. The seagulls crying, the silver-tipped waves lapping along the sand, it all ebbs until he has to tilt his head and strain to imagine it. Sal's wooden rowboat creaking against the old dock, the sea sloshing into the bluff, the grasses whispering in the lagoon, everything goes silent as he clocks the miles away from it.

The shingled cottages, the painted bungalows, the seaside sunrises and sunsets, they all wane with each rise and curve of pavement beneath his vehicle's tires. The sandy boardwalk, the rocky ledge at the end of the beach, his brother's beloved driftline, all of it fades to nothing as the stars above taunt him with their glimmering hope. Stars he will not look at, will not trust, will not believe in. What was it his father used to say about his Vietnam soldier days? *The darker the night, the brighter the stars.*

When the dog whines behind him, he glances over his shoulder. Madison seems as unhinged as he is, the German shepherd panting and fidgeting on the seat. Jason's suitcase sits on the back floor, and his crutches lean in the corner of that seat. The dog steps past them to put her muzzle to the open window and snort the night air, visibly upset at not sensing the salty breezes of home, the damp of the sea.

As Jason's eyes tear up, he leans forward to see through a mist hovering over the night road. The dog will adapt, just like he will. It's better this way. They'll find someplace new to start over, with no reminders of sadness, no memories of beach happiness. A clean break.

Driving through these coastal New England towns, swaying marsh grasses and bait shacks and ice-cream huts give way to cornfields and white split-rail fences and tall trees looming around each bend. A bead of perspiration skims along Jason's face as he drags a hand through his usually unkempt hair—now cut and manicured, all for Sal's funeral. For this day.

Headlights glare when occasional oncoming cars

approach, then pass him in the night. Each one signifies another mile driven further away from Stony Point. Meanwhile, the dog grows more distressed behind him as she sniffs in noisy bursts. Jason knows just what she's doing. He inhales a long breath and misses it already, too—that sweet scent of salt air filling his lungs. Madison paces across the backseat from one open window to the other, desperate, such that Jason quickly turns to her. "Settle down, Maddy. Sit, now!"

It's a sudden car horn blaring through the darkness that has him spin back around, wrenching the steering wheel to veer his SUV onto his own side of the road, nearly losing control of the vehicle as he hits the brakes. "Shit, shit, shit," he's saying while throwing a glance at the rearview mirror. The car he almost hit head-on skids and weaves as the driver tries to keep a steady course, before continuing on with a second enraged blare of its horn.

And it's enough, all of it: the thought of crossing over the centerline at a high rate of speed and nearly causing a head-on accident; the angry sound of the other car's relentless horn; the anxious German shepherd panting heavily behind him; his own heart pounding; the narrowly escaped vision of passengers being pulled from two mangled cars as an emergency helicopter hovers close by.

Yes, it's enough to make Jason steer his SUV onto the shoulder of the road, the heaves of the ground jostling the vehicle—which comes to a stop at the bottom of a long driveway near a country shanty. A hand-painted sign propped in the yard advertises garden-grown tomatoes for sale.

"What the hell am I doing?" Jason asks. He drops his

face into his hands, then drags those hands through his hair again, afraid at how he can't see clearly through those damn burning tears that he can't blink back, that won't stop coming.

So he breathes: one breath, shaking, then a longer one—more steady. Because he can't make the phone call like this. When he lifts his cell phone from the console, his hand shakes enough for him to light a cigarette and take a few drags before flicking the butt out onto the road. He lifts his phone again, and after a few quiet seconds, dials and listens through the rings until she answers.

"Maris?"

two

SALVATORE DELUCA ONCE TOLD JASON that second chances were God-given. *Molto speciale*, Sal added in Italian—very special. What about third, fourth and fifth chances? While waiting in his vehicle parked roadside, the dog settled down in the backseat, it's a thought that won't leave, the thought of Jason somehow having, in his life, the grace of chances.

He had a second chance to live when his brother, Neil, died nine years ago, in the accident that Jason survived.

Another second chance, this one to walk again after the wreck, happened with the help of a prosthetic left leg, below the knee.

Then came a chance at love two years ago when Maris unexpectedly returned to Stony Point, and his life.

And he grabbed his chance to marry her one year ago.

Which brought Jason to this summer when he had the chance to be a brother again. Fishing on the rocks with Sal, talking construction on job sites, paddling through the lagoon while telling his father's Vietnam war stories, having a brew on hot nights. It felt like Neil had returned, in the guise of Sal. Sal, whose eulogy he'd given just this very morning at brunch.

Do we ever run out of chances? Does some power above say, *Okay, that's enough now. Your quota's depleted, guy.* To find out would mean looking up at those stars still glimmering high in the night sky, stars Jason swore he wouldn't look at—not until he can, one day, find his way back to the sea.

So instead his sight falls on a crumbling stone wall ahead, the stones pulled long ago from a field and set around the perimeter of some farmer's property. The SUV's headlights shine directly on it, and after a second, he shuts off his engine and lights, then sits in pure darkness, hearing the clicking of the cooling engine, the slow chirp of lazy crickets in the brush.

Knowing all the while that another chance—maybe reluctantly—has been doled out to Jason Barlow. And to the poor soul he nearly drove into head-on: some guy, or family, who he's sure had to pull off the road, too, just to gasp at the narrow escape they'd been granted. When he looks in the rearview mirror wondering if they've collected themselves yet and driven on, headlights approach, slowly, on a vehicle that also pulls off the road behind him.

Before he can even move over a duffel on the passenger seat, Maris is at his open window, leaning her body inside and embracing him, then setting her hands on his face, her thumb stroking his cheek and running along the scar on his jawline.

"It's okay," she whispers. "Oh, Jason, it's okay." She kisses him, then wipes another tear from his face. "I'm so glad you called me," she still whispers. "I'm here, I'm here."

With that, she opens the back door, leads Madison out of the SUV and brings the dog to her sister, Eva, parked behind him now.

Exhaling a long breath, Jason closes his eyes and leans on the headrest. When he looks to the side-view mirror, he sees Maris standing at the vehicle behind him, still talking to Eva. Finally, her sister pulls onto the street and drives toward Stony Point, taking the dog with her.

Then he waits, hearing the approaching footsteps of his wife. She opens his door and helps him out, hugging him in the darkness for a long, long moment. "I was so scared for you," he hears in his ear. And what it does—that worry, that love—is it simply chokes him up.

"Jason. Are you all right?" Maris steps back and searches his face. "I have to know that you're okay."

He looks at her brown eyes, her long dark hair, the star pendant and braided gold chain on her neck. It's not possible to talk without breaking down, and he's sure from the look on her face, she knows it. So he just nods, then walks around to the passenger side as Maris settles in the driver's seat.

"Come on," she says, reaching over and squeezing his hand. "Let's go home."

~

Not a word is said. Maris drives along the Connecticut country roads, and Jason feels almost impatient to get back now, to the very place he'd fled only hours ago. His eyes stay on the road, anxious for the barns and picket fences and farm stands to revert to lagoons and buoyed bait shops and ice-cream huts illuminated with fluorescent lighting, vacationers in shorts and sandals lingering there with one last sundae or cone this Labor Day weekend.

All the while, he takes silent, deep breaths, waiting for that salty scent hinting at the nearness of the sea. They don't talk, and there's a sense of relief in the silence enveloping them. Finally, Maris steers the vehicle around a gentle curve and turns off the main drag to the narrow beach road leading to Stony Point. She drives beneath the stone railroad trestle and waves to Nick on duty at the guard shack, where he nods to them as she continues by.

The sandy beach streets look achingly familiar. Golden light spills from screened-in porches; painted bungalows sit on stone foundations; overgrown hydrangea bushes cascade alongside front walkways; folks sit inside shingled cottages with paned windows—folks playing cards, having a drink, laughing and living as summer wanes. As Maris drives toward their home on the bluff, the tires close the gap Jason had created.

"Want to walk on the beach?"

They're the first words Maris has spoken since she got in the driver's seat. And Jason knows why she asks. The beach, the salt air … oh, how it cures what ails you. But maybe he's afraid this September night—afraid to learn that his brother's mantra might not be true, after all. So he tells her no.

"How about something to eat on the deck? There's leftover grinders."

"Maybe later."

She turns into their sloped driveway and pulls up alongside the backyard. "Sit out on the bluff, on your father's bench?"

"No."

"Let's go inside, then. We'll have a glass of wine." Her voice is soft, and accommodating, as she unclips her seatbelt and they get out of the SUV. "Is your leg bothering you?" she asks when he stands still in the driveway.

Jason glances to their house rising in silhouette against the moonlit night sky. From here, he can see part of the front porch, shadowy in lantern light. Low limbs of a maple tree sweep the side of the house, where some of the windows are dark, except where Maris left on a kitchen light, and maybe a table lamp in the living room. He looks past the curtains into the scarcely illuminated rooms of his home, seeing faded walls, seaside paintings. Rooms where he grew up with his brother, together plotting crabbing outings on the rocks, or rowboat rides through the marsh; where he's held Maris in his arms while slow dancing to the jukebox; where he's thrown a glass of Scotch against the hearth. Rooms filled with whispers and shadows, spirits and memories.

"Jason?" Maris asks, waiting for his answer.

He takes her hand as they climb the stairs to their wraparound deck. It sits on a stone foundation, along which solar walkway lights shimmer. "I'm fine now, sweetheart."

Though he's not, and isn't sure when he will be again.

three

DO YOU THINK ANYONE WILL show up?" In the silence that follows, Kyle Bradford stares at the ceiling over the bed. It's white-painted beadboard, and actually very nice, as far as ceilings go. Funny how this is the first time he's noticed it since they checked in here at their rented vacation bungalow. It's hard to believe that was only a few weeks ago; it feels like a lifetime. His hand nudges Lauren dozing beside him beneath a cool sheet.

"Show up to what?" she asks, not opening her eyes.

He reaches over and strokes her blonde hair. "Sunday breakfast. I gave the open invitation yesterday, after Sal's funeral." Sunshine is edging the window shade, warning him it's getting late. "I closed the diner to the public, in case the gang wants to get together there. Or wants to talk about Sal." He reaches for his cell phone on the nightstand.

"Any messages?" As she asks, Lauren pulls the sheet up to her chin, eyes still closed.

"Nothing."

The window shade lifts in a slight breeze, so Kyle steps out of bed and flips up the shade to feel the cool, salty air.

He leans his hands on the sill and looks out at the dilapidated lawn swing and overgrown horseshoe pit in the cottage yard, then settles back on the bed.

Lauren turns on her side and watches him. "You did put the offer out there, so I guess we better get to the diner, in case anyone shows."

He checks his phone again. "Your parents don't mind having the kids today?"

"No. It was Mom's idea. I brought over a few of their things when I had dinner there last night. And at least we have the long weekend to pack up here."

Kyle flicks through his day-old voicemails. "I haven't heard from Jason."

"Didn't you see him yesterday afternoon? How was he?"

"Quiet. A little off." Kyle remembers how Jason started up with those damn smokes again, not that he wouldn't mind one right now, too, lying in bed on a late-summer morning. He sets his cell phone on the nightstand. "This is our last day at the cottage, Ell."

"Maybe forever, Kyle." Sitting up and leaning on the headboard, Lauren looks around the bedroom with its vintage cottage décor: seashell-filled lamps, framed lighthouse paintings, mismatched dressers. "If we can finagle buying our own house here at Stony Point."

"Please. If I have to look at one more run-down money pit." He's kept an open mind; accepted there aren't too many year-round places in this beach community; added an outdoor patio at the diner to make extra house cash; adjusted his budget; and still, not one property on the market suited their needs.

"It's just a sad weekend." Lauren slides back down on

the bed and closes her eyes. "First with Sal's funeral, and now leaving this little cottage to go home to our everyday lives."

Kyle turns his head on the pillow and watches his wife. Her hair is sleep-mussed, her face lightly freckled from a few weeks of beach sunshine. "So let's end it on a happy note," he says while slipping his arm behind her and settling her into the crook of his shoulder, then tipping her face to his and kissing her.

The surprising thing is the way she kisses him back, deeply. No small talk, no playing around, just her kiss opening to his, her hands lowering his shorts, such that he brusquely pushes up her satin nightshirt and lifts himself on top of her. As though they can't get back to happiness soon enough.

~

From where he's waking up, Cliff Raines can see the fireplace. It's an ideal fireplace for a beach inn, with a garland of white seashells draped beneath the driftwood mantel. Beside it, faded buoys of red, blue and yellow hang on the wall. He sits up on the nautical-striped sofa where he spent the night and sees how Elsa started working on her future inn's décor right when she moved in last year.

He straightens the tee and canvas pants he'd slept in, then lifts his button-down shirt off a chair back and slips it on. All the while, he remembers the last time he was here at Elsa's, when they'd kissed in her garden. Lord knows he'd never planned on spending the night yesterday. But during an evening patrol of Stony Point Beach, he noticed one single lamp shining in her paned window, and it struck him as lonely. Almost as though Elsa was leaving a light on for the son she'd said a final goodbye to that morning. His heart broke at the sight of that lamp, so he went to the door and overstayed his welcome, even when she'd later tried to whisk him out.

"Let me first close up some windows," he'd said, biding his time to keep her company. The last thing he wanted was for her to be all alone as the day of her son's funeral came to an end. So he methodically went into each room of her cottage and closed some windows, while adjusting the others to all the same height. On his way through the kitchen, he then washed the random plates and cups in her sink, spritzed her little herb pots and wiped off the countertops.

"Clifton! Leave things be," she'd called out from the living room where she sat in front of the television.

He'd seen the flicker of the TV screen, but heard nothing. When he walked into that room, he saw why: The volume was off as the news anchors silently mouthed facts and reports. "I'd love to catch the headlines, Elsa. Here," he said, taking the remote control from her. "For a few minutes." When he sat beside her and turned up the volume, she thanked him for all he'd done and said she was going to turn in; he could let himself out after the news. Which gave him the perfect chance to instead fall asleep on the big sofa so that she wasn't alone in the house.

Now, as he turns on the coffeemaker, Elsa walks into the room wearing a long robe and terry slippers. In her late fifties, she's striking—even through her veil of grief. Golden highlights lighten her thick brown hair, which she's tucked behind an ear as she peers around the corner.

"I thought I heard you here! What time is it?"

"Early," Cliff tells her while pouring water into the coffeepot. "Are you going to The Driftwood Café for breakfast?"

"No." She walks to the window over the sink and opens it a crack. "Wait. How did you get in here?"

"I never left. Spent the night."

"What? Where?"

"You shouldn't be alone these days. I slept on the couch."

"Oh, Commissioner Raines," she says, sitting herself in a chair. "I'm fine. Honestly. Sad, but that certainly does not violate any of your beach ordinances."

"Okay, but you can't start the day with an empty stomach. What can I make you?"

Moments pass … moments that turn into long seconds, then a minute. It's enough of a silence to get him to look over from the open refrigerator to see Elsa's moist eyes staring out the window, toward the distant sea.

"Jason left," she says.

Cliff pulls out a fruit drawer in the refrigerator, then looks at her again. It's as though she hadn't even heard his breakfast request.

"Yesterday. He just up and left my niece." She looks at him, finally. "He wrote a very sad note for Maris, which we discovered over dinner. Maris, her sister, and me."

"What are you talking about, Elsa? Jason left his wife? You didn't mention that last night." Cliff closes the refrigerator and walks to the table.

"Yes. He was actually more distraught with Sal's passing than anyone realized."

"They were close, those two. Almost like brothers."

"Exactly. So I guess Jason felt like he lost his brother again, and it was too much. He's gone."

"Where?"

Elsa shrugs. "I'll call Maris later to see if she heard from him. Now I have to get ready. I'm driving to the Cross Sound Ferry this morning. Might as well close up Sal's New York apartment."

"Today? So soon? Elsa, the funeral was only yesterday!"

"And it'll be good for me to keep busy." She stands abruptly and wraps her arms around herself.

"I'll drive you to the ferry. So you can rest."

"No, I'm fine. Really. I need some quiet time to think, that's all. The drive will help."

Cliff stands, too. "But I insist," he says while pushing in his chair. "I can even come with you to New York. With September here, this beach community can do without its commissioner for a bit."

"No, no. That's very nice of you, but I'm not sure how long I'll stay in the city." She presses back her uncombed hair and gives him a slight smile. "Most of the week, I'd imagine. This way, my own car will be parked at the ferry and I can get myself home without bothering anyone for a ride."

And he knows. He just knows. There's no arguing with Elsa DeLuca on the day after her son's funeral. She's going to do whatever she sets her mind on to get through this sad, painful time.

"If you're sure," he says.

"I am."

"But you still can't start the day on an empty stomach."

He opens the wrapping of a loaf of bread and drops two slices in the toaster. When he does, her chair scrapes the floor as she slides it back out and sits again, as though it's too much to even get ready this Sunday morning. To brush her hair, to pick out an outfit to wear. When he glances back on his way to the fridge for butter, she's gazing toward the window again, where a seashell wind chime clinks in a light breeze.

"The Hammer Law is ending, now that vacation season is over," he tells her. "I'll be removing the notices from the community bulletin boards."

Nothing from Elsa, then. Not a word, not a nod.

"It's good, Elsa. You'll be able to move forward with your inn plans. Get that renovation going. With Celia, too." He sets the butter on the counter and pulls a knife from the drawer. "She'll help with the decorating, I'm sure." While waiting at the toaster, he silently looks over his shoulder at her. "Salvatore would want that for you."

Elsa still doesn't say a word. Instead the toaster pops up the bread, which he butters and jams. Once the plate is set in front of her, he stands there until she glances at him, then lifts a piece of bread and nibbles a bite. If he can just keep her eating a little, maybe sip some orange juice, too, she'll keep up her strength. So he pours her a small glass, then fills the watering can on the counter and carefully lifts it to each of her red herb pots, looking back at her after watering each one, just to be sure she's nibbling and sipping enough to sustain the day.

~

The bed is empty beside her, the pillow cold. When Celia looks at it, when she reaches her hand from her side of the bed, there is no smile this time. No listening for Sal pulling a pan from the cupboard out in the cottage kitchen, to make scrambled eggs. No Sal walking into the bedroom with two steaming mugs of coffee, telling her *Buongiorno, bella. Time to rise and shine.* No Sal hitching his head to the dock outside, where he'd set their two Adirondack chairs in the sunshine.

So that's gone now ... Sunday mornings lingering in bed. Now, she throws back the sheets and gets herself up as soon as her eyes open. Last night hadn't been easy. Her guests were gone, the funeral over, and an eerie silence set in. After pressing one of Sal's shirts to her face and inhaling deeply, she'd slipped her arms into the sleeves, folded back the cuffs and slept in it. In the kitchen at dawn, she pours a mug of coffee and, cupping it close, stands at the slider.

Then she does exactly what Sal would do. Opening the slider to the deck, she grabs a lawn chair with one hand, her coffee in the other, and drags the chair across the lawn. Her terry flip-flop slippers get damp from the dew; Sal's shirt billows behind her in a sea breeze. And that's fine, all fine.

It's the tears that upset her, the way they blur her destination, making her stop and lift the soft fabric of his shirt to blot her eyes. While silently weeping, she sets the chair on the center of the dock's rickety planks and sits herself down. If she closes her eyes, it's just like the summer mornings when Sal sat with her.

But she doesn't keep her eyes shut. Instead, she looks at the scenery. Sal's rowboat is still moored to the dock, the little wooden vessel creaking against the dock piling. Beyond it, cattails sway on the marsh banks, the brown spikes reaching high to the September sky. Sweeping grasses along the marsh are tinged with gold as summer days tick past.

But it's a blue glimmer she finally can't stop herself from looking at. The sea-glass engagement ring hasn't left her finger since he'd slipped it there. All Celia thinks of, touching it lightly, is being in New York with Sal, just over a week ago. His surgery was days away when he cleared his mother and two visiting friends out of his apartment for a while. It was obvious that he wanted time alone with Celia before his valve-replacement operation; it was that serious of a matter.

"Yes," Celia had whispered as the door finally closed when the apartment emptied.

"Come closer," Sal told her, reaching out his hand from the sofa.

She took slow steps, saying the word again. "Yes."

"What are you talking about?" he asked as she stopped beside the gray sofa and ran her fingers along the nail-head trim.

"Yes," she whispered once more, looking down at his brown eyes. "Yes, to the question you're going to ask me."

"Question?"

Her finger-fidgeting shifted from the nail-head trim to his hair, wavy and overgrown after a casual summer at the beach. She sat with him then and looked around the room, taking in the black-shaded table lamp, the painted chest of drawers, the mounted brass sculpture of a bull's skull—a reminder of Sal's life on Wall Street, working the bull markets.

"Yes," she told him again, turning to him and drawing a

finger beneath his chin. "Yes, I'll marry you."

And he took her face in his hands and kissed her. Kissed her long. It was painfully obvious that he'd drawn out the kiss until he could get his emotions in check. Because she felt it, felt him fight back a sob in the midst of the whole romantic mess. When she pulled away, silently touching his lips with her fingers, he put his hand in his pocket and pulled out the ring box.

"You know me well, pretty Celia." As he said the words, he lifted out the platinum ring with a blue sea-glass stone surrounded by diamonds, and placed it on her finger. Sea glass, of course, after they spent much of the summer beachcombing at Stony Point.

Their engagement lasted two days. Two magical days filled with hope, two optimistic days before Sal never woke up from his heart surgery.

Celia looks at the blue ring now and runs a finger over the smooth stone. "Oh, Sal," she whispers, her words taken up with the September beach breeze. The marsh grass sways; a seagull flies low; the rowboat rises and falls on the gently flowing water. "Tell me what to do."

~

The seagulls are feeding out on the bluff; the sea breeze brings in the sound of their cawing. It's how Jason wakes up every day. He lies in bed now, eyes closed, an arm flung across his face. Maris is beside him, her body shifting beneath the sheet. She may be turning on her side, facing him, but he can't be sure. Somehow, he can't lift the weight of his arm off his face, doesn't want to see the light of day.

Not yet. Because behind this darkness, it's safe to wonder where he'd be today if he hadn't called Maris from the roadside last night. Would they both be better off apart, for a while? He in a hotel room inland somewhere, getting a grip on his life's twists and turns while leaving the sea to her?

Instead, he's aware of her closeness as the weight of his arm presses over his eyes. They're both unmoving in the bed—still as a tide about to change. Minutes pass like that, filled only with awareness.

Until her fingers stroke his palm on that arm flung across his face, the touch a feather against his skin. Her fingertips circle his open hand, then silently move along his arm, up to his hair, softly touching the strands.

"Time to get up," Maris says, so close. "We're going to the diner for breakfast. Kyle's expecting us."

"You go." Jason doesn't move his arm. "I'm staying in to rest."

"No, no," she murmurs. "I'm not going without you." She lifts his arm then and kisses his lips, once, twice. He feels her long hair brush against the skin of his face, but his eyes remain shut. "You had your chance to be alone yesterday." Another kiss behind his closed lids, then her fingers stroking his jaw. "But you came back to me." A kiss on his ear, his neck. "Now?" Her voice is hushed. "Now I decide your day."

Jason opens his eyes and turns his head toward her, surprised at what he finally sees. Her deep brown eyes are simply worried; her gold chain glimmers on her neck; the lace strap of her nightshirt slips off her shoulder. "Okay, sweetheart." He keeps any resistance, any regret, out of his words. He loves Maris too much to worry her even more, not after what he put her through with his departure yesterday.

Her eyes watch him, taking in his face, his hair, his mouth, upon which she leaves another soft kiss. "Where were you headed last night, anyway?"

He does it then. Closes his eyes again, drapes that arm over his face and takes a long breath. She doesn't move, and he knows she's waiting him out. "As far away from the sea as I could get."

four

KYLE LOOKS UP FROM THE big stove, toward The Driftwood Café's entrance. How many of his friends has he seen walk through those diner doors, over the years? Jason, always alone in the past. Especially after the motorcycle accident, adjusting to his life with a prosthetic leg—a life that no longer included his brother. Maris swept through those doors two years ago now, returning to Stony Point from a Chicago fashion career to settle her father's estate. Since then, she and her reunited sister, Eva, have shared countless cups of coffee at their favorite window booth, making up for lost time together. Then came Elsa, last summer, tiptoeing into life on the Connecticut shore for Maris and Jason's wedding. And Matt, heck he stops in for a snack after his state-cop graveyard shifts before going home to sleep. Seriously, Kyle witnesses the lives and happenings of Stony Point just by who walks through his diner doors.

And this is the first Sunday ever that the CLOSED sign hangs there. He waits to see which of his friends will walk in for Sal's memorial breakfast. Lauren crisscrosses the diner, setting down silverware and coffee cups. He imagines appetites will be light, in sadness: bacon and eggs picked at, pancakes poked at, muffins nibbled. But coffee will be poured aplenty.

"We'll have to pack up the cottage fast after this, Kyle." Lauren straightens a stack of white coffee mugs behind the counter. "Head back home to Eastfield and get the kids ready for school."

"I can't believe all that went down in just the past week. Man, no one could've predicted the way this summer turned out."

His wife walks toward the wide windows and looks at the empty parking lot. "Do you think we should set up on the patio?" she calls over her shoulder.

"No. It's too hot today, and the yellow jackets are fierce this time of year."

She bends to take another look down the busy street. "Have you heard from anyone? Jason? Nick?"

"No one."

Still at the stoves, Kyle lines up his tongs and turners, whisks and weights, then helps Lauren push a few tables together—all while glancing out the window toward the parking lot, squinting through the sunshine to decipher any cars.

~

"Wait a second." Maris tugs Jason's hand in the silver diner's parking lot.

Jason stops and looks back at her. "What's the matter?"

She pulls him to the side, out of view of the windows.

"Just this." She gives him a quick hug and kisses him on the cheek, too. "You okay?" she asks, dabbing a hint of lipstick off his cheek.

"I'm good, darling. You don't have to worry."

It's the best she'll get from him, she can tell. Clip sentences, nothing extra, his grief keeping him quiet. So when they walk through the diner doors, she's glad that Kyle's approaching them, wiping his hands on his white chef apron.

"Hey, guys," he says, giving Jason a hug first, then Maris. "I knew you'd show up. Come on, sit." He leads them past the red-cushioned counter stools to a window booth, asking over his shoulder, "How're you guys doing?"

"I still cannot believe that Sal's gone," Maris says as she settles in beside Jason. "Just gone."

"It's hard to think the Italian won't be breezing through that door again, stopping in—as he'd put it—on the road of life." Kyle nods to the diner entrance. "Man, he'd get this place jumping when he pitched in and waited tables." He briefly clasps Jason's arm. "You'll miss him on your job sites."

"No shit. Already do. How's Elsa holding up?" Jason asks Maris. "Did you call her?"

"When you were in the shower. Oh, she's so sad," she adds. "My poor aunt."

Kyle leans back in the booth and straightens a silver napkin dispenser on the table. "She coming here today?"

"No. She's actually headed to New York to close up Sal's apartment."

"So soon?" Jason asks.

Maris reaches the back of her fingers to his whiskered

cheek and nods. "Sal's good friend in the city is helping her out. Michael."

"What about Celia?" Lauren asks when she stops at their booth with a pot of coffee. "Have you heard anything?"

"She walked the beach with us last night," Maris explains. "Her father and neighbors from back home were at the cottage with her. Got the feeling she was ready to leave, too."

"I doubt she'll come then," Lauren says, pouring hot coffee into their mugs. "Too bad."

Maris nudges Jason's cup closer to him as Lauren scoots into the booth, fussing with her maxi dress as she sits beside Kyle. Maris adds cream to her own coffee, stirs it, taps her spoon on the mug rim and sets it on a folded napkin. When she looks up, Lauren gives her a sad smile and reaches across the table to squeeze her hand.

Right as Kyle elbows his wife and points out the window. They all take a look, but it's Lauren who nearly knocks over the coffee as she rushes out of the booth, hurrying past the glass pastry case overflowing with blueberry muffins, toward the door.

~

Celia Gray can't help remembering. It's that kind of day when every memory will run through her mind like a movie reel, as though she's playing the lead in one of those romantic flicks that steal her heart. By day's end, she's sure that every scene of her and Sal's love affair will be thought of, mentioned, talked about and wept over. If only the day could have a made-for-the-movies happy ending. But alas, it's never to be.

Celia approaches the diner now, imagining the director would be off to the side while an assistant raises a clapperboard. It would identify the film as *Celia's Summer Romance. Scene: Final. Take: One.* The black-and-white clapsticks would snap together then, and the camera would roll.

As though on a director's cue, Celia takes a few steps across the parking lot, remembering back three months to when she walked into The Driftwood Café for the first time: sitting with Elsa and discussing her inn renovation; meeting Kyle, the diner's owner; starting her summer at Stony Point—recently divorced and catching her breath while staging a few cottages and strumming her guitar. Elsa took her under her wing that day, offering her a grand beach-inn decorating job so that the furnishings would be ready after renovations wrap up next spring.

And now, instead, a post-funeral-day breakfast for Elsa's son and Celia's fiancé. Shielding her eyes from the morning sun, Celia looks up at the silver diner seeming like a ship docked on shore. Maybe this is wrong. Maybe she doesn't want to rehash everything that happened between that first promising day and this dark one.

But it's too late. Suddenly Lauren, wearing a floral-print maxi dress, appears in the diner's doorway—her arms wide open as she hurries across the pavement to Celia and takes her up in a long hug.

"Oh, Cee," she says, stroking Celia's hair and embracing her. "How *are* you? I didn't know if you'd make it today."

Celia pulls back with a small smile. "Here I am?"

"And I'm *so* glad. We're packing up the cottage and leaving tonight. I hoped I'd see you to say goodbye. Come on," she insists, taking Celia's hand and leading her inside. As soon as the door closes behind them, Maris, Jason and Kyle crowd over. They hug her, talk to her, touch her hand, her face, offer her coffee and food. All the while, Celia fusses with her sea-glass engagement ring, feeling like a new widow. When Maris and Lauren both huddle close and usher her to a booth, Kyle puts his arm around Jason's shoulder.

"Want to show you my new grill out on the patio," Kyle tells him. "Come on, the ladies won't miss us."

Just as they head outside, Jerry walks in to help man the stoves, followed by Matt and Eva, who is carrying a bouquet of wildflowers in a vintage jar. But Eva pauses in the open doorway and calls out over her shoulder, "Jason! Good to *see* you," before hurrying over to Celia with the flowers, and a hug, and tears, too.

Celia's not sure what to make of the commotion in the diner now—her friends arriving and milling around with sad smiles, the cook prepping the griddle, the scent of bacon and eggs filling the diner. But the movie director would surely want to rein in the focus, and he might stand and draw his open, flattened hand across his throat, yelling, *Cut … Cut!*

~

"Give me a smoke. Quick."

Jason looks over at Kyle as they approach the outdoor patio. "What?"

"You heard me. I need a cigarette. Hurry up, guy."

"Christ, you had one smoke yesterday and now you're hooked?"

"That's right. Come on, come on!"

So Jason pulls a pack of cigarettes from his cargo shorts pocket and they both light up. Kyle cups his cigarette and motions him further back on the patio, out of view of everyone inside.

"Ah, sweet Jesus," Kyle says after a long exhale.

"You kidding me?" Jason asks. "Kyle, it's a cigarette, already."

"Quick. Give me one for later. I'll put it in my pocket." He holds out his hand.

"You've got a problem. You're too easily addicted." Jason hands Kyle an unlit cigarette. "That's your limit. Then you're done, you hear me?"

"Yeah, yeah. You, too. We'll quit together, man." Kyle takes another drag of his cigarette, holds it up and eyes the burning ember. "Hey, so Elsa's inn reno will be picking up again, no?"

"Guess so. Hammer Law's done now. My crews are due at the inn next week. They're finishing up another job first."

"Good, good. It's important for Elsa to get back to the business of her business." Kyle flicks an ash and snags another puff of the cigarette. "She'll have things to do to occupy her thoughts. Maybe it'll help."

"Jason!"

Kyle and Jason both look over to see Eva rushing closer. She's wearing a loose tunic tank over capris, and the tunic flutters as she semi-trots to them.

"We really need to talk," Eva says with a glance over her shoulder, before taking Jason's arm and yanking him aside.

"Whoa, Eva. Slow down," Jason tells her.

"Listen." She leans close and lowers her voice, which

only makes her anger more apparent. "Don't you *ever* pull that stunt again. Do you hear me?"

"Stunt." Jason drops his cigarette and steps on the butt. "You mean last night?"

"Of course that's what I mean!"

"It's okay, Eva. Relax, would you?" He glances toward the diner windows. "It's not what you're thinking."

"How many times do I have to tell you?" She hesitates, then whips off her sunglasses. "You are *not* to walk out on Maris again. My sister is the best damn thing that ever happened to you. Right, Kyle?"

Kyle, who had stepped back when Eva stormed over in barracuda mode, nods as he takes another drag from his smoke. "Damn straight."

"And what about Elsa?" Eva turns to Jason again. "Reading that note last night, it was too much for her. The poor woman, after the day she had."

"Elsa?" Jason asks.

"Yes, you jerk! You weren't there. But Maris had me read your note out loud—all that crap about leaving and needing time, and, and coming undone—you didn't see how painful it was for everyone. Especially Elsa, after losing her son. Ooh, I'm so mad at you."

"I'm sorry, Eva." Jason checks his watch, thinking Maris will be looking for him. "I didn't know Elsa heard, too."

"You're so selfish. Don't you remember your wedding vows? *Always*, Jason? *Always?* Don't you know that when things get tough, you don't just pick up and *leave*? You're *married*, now. To *my* sister."

The whole time, Jason's aware of Kyle silently nodding, apparently intrigued with Eva's wrath.

"And always means always, *not* always except when shit happens."

"Wait." Kyle manages one last drag from what's left of his cigarette butt. "Did I miss something here? You left … your *wife*?"

Eva reaches over and takes Kyle's arm in her iron grip. "I thought you knew!" She looks at Jason while still holding onto Kyle. "You didn't tell Kyle?"

"I wasn't thinking straight, Kyle. I was fucked up, man."

"*Gesù, Santa Maria*," Kyle says. "Left Maris? What's wrong with you?"

A sharp noise interrupts them, when Jerry gives a loud whistle from the doorway. "Yo, Captain! It's getting crowded, everyone's here. Let's get cooking!"

Eva's iron grip shifts to Jason's upper arm as he begins walking across the parking lot. "We are so not done with this, Jason, with the way you're always out the door."

"You left Maris?" Kyle repeats, walking close behind them.

As Jason simply shakes his head, Stony Point's beach commissioner, Cliff Raines, is getting out of his car and approaching with a wave, so they wait for him.

"Jason?" Cliff asks, raising his sunglasses and squinting at him. "I thought …" He looks over his shoulder, then back at Jason. "Didn't you leave? Elsa said something—"

"Never mind, Cliff," Eva assures him while looping her arm through Cliff's. "He's back now. And how is my aunt Elsa? Is she holding up okay?"

It's the last thing Jason hears Eva say before Kyle yanks him aside and mouthes to him: *Dude, you left your wife?*

~

It's surprising how the diner filled up in the short time Kyle took to grab a smoke. His main cook, Jerry, already got the stoves going. Jason's sister, Paige, arrived with her husband, Vinny. Nick, and Cliff, and, well, the whole gang's here now.

So Kyle heads to the counter and taps a fork on a glass. "Can I have your attention?" he calls out. "Yo, Vincenzo, that means you, too."

Vinny grabs a red-cushioned stool at the counter, giving a spin before quieting down and saluting Kyle.

"I want to thank you for coming today. You've all got busy lives, but you know, sometimes a friend trumps everything. And today, we're missing a great one. Here's to Salvatore," he says, raising a coffee cup and taking a long sip, watching as every cup in the diner is raised high before sips are managed from each.

Jerry steps out from the kitchen and begins delivering plates heaping with pancakes and scrambled eggs, muffins and sausages, all as Kyle continues.

"This breakfast is the least I can offer in Sal's memory. I'm sure his spirit is here, wanting to tie on his waiter apron, grab a pencil and pad and walk around taking your orders, chatting as you stop here, as he put it, on the road of life."

Celia stands suddenly and interrupts. "I'd like to say something, Kyle. Do you mind?"

"Please. Be my guest." Kyle motions for her to take the floor.

So she does, walking to the diner's counter and turning around to face the beach friends gathered there. Her tear-filled hazel eyes contradict the smile she gives them before beginning. "Sal spoke so highly of each one of you."

Forks clink on dishes as the friends eat and listen. Juice glasses are sipped from, salt dashed on eggs, while all eyes watch Celia.

"So I'm glad you're here today, and that I get to see you one last time. To say thank you for a wonderful summer, and goodbye."

"What?" Lauren asks.

Celia nods at her. "I'll be leaving in a day or two. As soon as I get my things packed. It's really too difficult to stay on, with the memories I have."

"Celia! Are you sure?" Eva calls out.

"Yes, Eva. I'm going back to my job in Addison, this week. So after the sweet summer shindigs we had this summer, this might be the last time I see you all together." She presses a napkin to her eyes then. "And I genuinely thank you, again, for the very best summer of my entire life."

The room buzzes with low talk among the friends as Celia returns to her seat. But Maris is the first to go to Celia, to bend close and put her arm around her. And though Kyle can't hear what she says, he can see from her posture, from her concern as Maris brushes back a strand of Celia's auburn hair, that this is not right. Then Eva and Matt pull two chairs up to her booth, with Eva taking Celia's hand and stroking it as she shakes her head and tries to convince her to stay.

Kyle sees it all—sees Cliff lean over from his seat and mention how Elsa needs Celia at the inn; sees Lauren's tears brought on by her friend's decision; sees the atmosphere meant to celebrate Salvatore DeLuca take a turn to sadness. So there's only one thing Kyle can do.

He clinks a knife, sharply and rapidly, on a glass.

"Friends, friends! First, before anyone," he says, glaring at Celia, "before *anyone* leaves, a toast. A toast to honor not Sal, but to honor everything that he stood for." When he stops talking and eyes them all, they quiet down. "Lauren, if you wouldn't mind, can you refill any coffee cups for our toast?"

And she does, with Jerry helping her as they both cross the room carrying carafes and topping off big mugs with the steaming brew.

"A death is one of the biggest stressors," Kyle announces as the coffee is poured. "It's been psychologically researched and proven. Studies also show that you are not to make *any* life choices in the throes of grief, after a loved one's death. And it's only been days since Sal left us. We're all grieving, *all* of us, in our own ways." He glances at Jason, then. "And so, here's the deal. Right now, we're going to make a pact with this toast. Every one of us." He raises his own coffee cup high and waits silently until every cup in the diner is held aloft.

"To Sal," a voice calls out, probably Nick, tagalong of the group.

"*No*," Kyle corrects him, walking along the length of the counter, his cup still held high. "A toast to *us*. We're making an unbreakable pact with this toast. A solemn vow. Right now. *Whatever* happens," he says while constantly watching them, "be calm, for God's sake! There will be absolutely *no* moving, *no* leaving, *no* hasty decisions, Celia. Jason."

"Jason?" someone asks.

"That's right," Kyle answers. "We have each other. We can work things out. There are lots of shoulders to cry on here, lots of coffee to drink together, or a beer to swig. We have beach walks, diner booths. Anything you need to not make *any* sudden, grief-motivated decisions that you *will* regret in time. No major decisions will be made for the next six months, at the very least. Agreed?"

"I know," Eva says, standing up with her raised cup. "We can have, well, *Meet and Eats*. Yes. Yes, Meet and Eats—dinners together, every week or two."

A few people start clapping, and someone gives a whistle.

"We'll regularly check up on each other and make sure everyone's okay," Eva suggests. "That no one's making hasty decisions that will clearly be wrong, wrong, wrong."

"Perfect," Kyle says. "Sal would want it this way, everybody getting together over food, and leaning on each other—our Stony Point *famiglia*." He paces the diner, and when Cliff gives him a thumbs-up, Kyle reciprocates, nodding. "Okay?" he asks. "So no life choices made alone! Absolutely *no* rash decisions."

When he raises his cup again and takes a long sip, they all do the same.

"And our first Meet and Eat is at *our* cottage. This Friday," Eva says, standing and motioning to her husband, Matt. "For Sal." Then a silence as she presses a napkin to her eyes, before continuing. "*Salute!*"

five

TUESDAY MORNING, IT'S NOT JUST the breeze blowing in the sliding window that wakes up Cliff. It's the power saws, and banging hammers, and warning beeps of lumbering, backing-up trucks. One day after Labor Day, that sea breeze is the wind of change—changing this coastal vacation hot spot into a noisy, industrial mess. He gets out of bed and walks to the metal-framed window to survey the street. There's no denying the Hammer Law has expired. At the crack of dawn, construction workers apparently descended like vultures on the cottage carcasses.

So he slides the window, gritty in its tracks, closed; it's hard enough keeping this trailer clean without dust filling his makeshift bedroom, living room, kitchen combo. After snapping shut the futon mattress and getting dressed for the workday, he heads to the closet-sized alcove in the back, where he combs his hair and brushes his teeth at a tiny sink. All the while, his mind is bullet-pointing highlights for the monthly newsletter. If he's learned anything about the Stony Point residents this summer, it's that they get impatient for local updates and reports. Already his inbox is filling up with emails seeking the next newsletter issue.

Well, they can all wait for his coffee to perk and bagel to toast in the countertop toaster oven. Once he's slathered cream cheese on the bagel, he brings the breakfast to his desk in the trailer's main office and gets going on the newsletter, typing between bites.

A roundup of summer activities comes first—from the Golf Cart Parade to the Clamshell Toss Contest. Next up? The top Stony Point ordinance violations: golf cart speeding and food on the beach. Which brings him to a side note: Many complaints were filed about the recent aggressive nature of seagulls. With a little detective work, it's been determined that sunbathers bringing illicit snacks provoke the seagulls' appetites and assertive behavior—from ruffling their feathers to charging at children on beach towels—all in pursuit of potato chips. So he gives fair warning now: Food fines will be doubled next year.

He then adds a near-drowning update, typing: *Little Timmy is fine and starting fourth grade this September. His mother sent along this photo of him floating on his shark raft, wearing new swimmies, too.* Which gets him to thinking of the day that Sal actually swam out and rescued Timmy. It's because of Sal, who is gone, that Timmy lives on.

With a heavy heart, he continues to the In Memoriam section of the newsletter. *We lost one of our own*, Cliff types. *Salvatore DeLuca, 36, beloved son of Elsa DeLuca, who is renovating the old Foley's cottage and market into a beach inn. Sadly, Sal passed away in early September. For those of you not aware, he suffered from rheumatic fever as a child growing up in Italy. All these years later, residual heart damage required him to undergo valve-replacement surgery, which he unfortunately did not survive. Though his summer stay at Stony Point was brief, Sal will be dearly missed by everyone here.*

Cliff looks at his computer screen then, but all he thinks of is Elsa's painful loss, and how he wishes he could lessen her sadness. So he saves the newsletter for later and golf-carts to her cottage, knowing she's still in New York cleaning out her son's apartment. Maybe tending to the grounds and flowers she dearly loves, while she's away, will help.

The problem is, there's not much more to do than putter: pick up a construction bucket and set it near the scaffolding; move aside a sawhorse; deadhead the red geraniums. Working his way around the rambling cottage, he turns the corner to her backyard—and there she is, sitting at her little patio table!

Elsa's back is to him, her hand resting on a coffee cup, her gaze directed at the distant sea. She wears a light sweater over her shoulders and a rolled paisley bandana on her thick brown hair.

"Excuse me, miss," Cliff says when he approaches, brushing the geranium debris from his hands. "I believe sitting alone in sadness is in violation of Ordinance S1?" With a wink, he pulls out the chair beside hers. "Your fine is spending a few minutes with me."

"Oh! Clifton!" Elsa dabs at her face with the balled-up napkin in her hand. "You weren't supposed to see me!"

"I thought you were in New York this week, closing up Sal's apartment."

"I was. I really was, Cliff." She pulls her sweater closer. "But, oh, I couldn't stay there. Not yet. It was too painful going through Sal's things, so I'm taking some time to just think about him. Here, at the beach."

"What is it the kids always say about this place? The salt air … it cures what ails you?"

"Sal believed that, too. The day he arrived here from Manhattan, back in June, we took a beach walk together." She looks out at the distant sea again. "He told me the words he'd heard in a dream. *Portami al mare*," she whispers while glancing at Cliff. "It's Italian, of course. Take me to the sea."

"Maybe he sensed he needed to rest."

Elsa nods, inhaling a long breath of the salt air. In her pause, a light breeze lifts off that sea, bringing the soft sound of waves lapping onshore. "He'd hoped that taking a break from his hectic Wall Street routine and spending the summer seaside here would be a tonic. A magic tonic. That he'd gather enough strength to handle the surgery." She gasps then, and presses her balled-up napkin to her mouth. "But the way he fell in love with this place, and with Celia, he couldn't leave." Silent tears run from beneath Elsa's sunglasses. "His heart was set on staying at Stony Point permanently. But his own heart was failing him," she nearly whispers.

Cliff reaches for Elsa's hand. From here, the sunlight flickers like stars on the distant rippling waves.

"We had so many *plans*," Elsa continues. "Salvatore was going to get my beach inn off the ground! He was going to marry Celia! He was a godsend to Jason! And then? Then he had to go and *die*—with all that to live for."

Elsa's sobs rise without restraint, so Cliff pulls his chair beside hers, takes her in his arms and leans close, reassuring her, touching a wisp of her hair while feeling her body go limp with sadness.

"Please, Cliff," she eventually manages as she presses her napkin beneath her sunglasses to dab her face. "Please don't tell the others I'm back."

"They don't know?"

She shakes her head.

"Maris? Eva? But your nieces, they'd want to visit you."

"Exactly. And they're so busy with their own things."

"One of which is you, Elsa," he says while squeezing her hand. "They love you very much."

She gives him a small smile. "Just let them get on with their lives without fussing over me. We'll all feel better soon enough, in our own ways."

"I'm not sure about that. *Everyone's* upset about Sal, *and* you."

"Please. Do it for me, so that I can have this quiet time with thoughts of my son. Promise me you won't tell them I'm here."

"Okay, then. For now, I guess." He sits back; in the distance, the sea moves, and the motion of the water is somehow soothing. It reminds him of time passing, always, seconds and minutes and hours. Elsa must sense that as she thinks of Sal's life. "It's good you have the inn renovation to keep you busy. It'll help. And having Celia work on it with you, well, it's what Sal would've wanted."

"I'm not sure, anymore. There's simply too much to do here." Elsa tucks a wisp of hair beneath her bandana and glances back at the shingled cottage.

Cliff looks, too, seeing peeling paint on some of the window frames. Thin white curtains hang in the windows, puffing in the breeze, and in some windows, a lone white starfish is propped on a pane.

"What a handyman's special," Elsa says, looking away from the building then. "Stalled all summer long."

"But the good news is that the Hammer Law's expired, so you can finally move forward. A little at a time."

Elsa stands and pushes in her bistro chair, surprising him with her abruptness. "Thank you, Cliff, for stopping by and looking after things."

"Oh, sure. Maybe you'd like to go out for a bite to eat later?"

"No." She glances back at the big old cottage again. "No, I'm busy all day. There's so much to be done ... I have phone calls to make on Sal's behalf and need to get moving with those things. You know."

Cliff pushes in his chair. "Sure, I get it. Listen, Elsa. Do you mind if I take a picture?"

"Of me?"

"Not necessarily, unless you want to be in it. I need a shot of the side of the inn where Jason will add the turret. Before-and-after pictures would be interesting for the Stony Point newsletter. Folks like seeing that sort of thing."

"Cliff." Another small smile from Elsa. "I'd rather not show this mess, with all the construction debris." Then, a glance at her thin gold watch as she backs up a step. "I better get going."

"Okay." Cliff backs up, too, eyeing her in the bright sunshine. "Okay, then. But I'm always here for you, if you need anything, Elsa." He reaches out to clasp her shoulder and give her a quick kiss, but she turns her face away.

So he nods and walks along the side of the cottage, looking at the weathered shingles, some nearly black with age. The scaffolding has been there all summer on this one side, rising along the wall behind Elsa's kitchen window. The metal poles and wooden planks conceal the beauty of the grand cottage beneath it all. Cliff passes a pile of rocks covered with a blue tarp and figures they're for the stone wall to be built on the sea side of the inn. *To remind my guests it's a safe harbor here*, he recalls Elsa saying. Still worried, he backtracks to sneak a look at the little bistro table he'd just left. It's as he suspected.

There's Elsa, sitting alone at the table again, putting up scaffolding around her heart, walling it up so no one can get in.

~

Jason sits on the boardwalk and looks at the sunlight sparkling on the blue water. He remembers the day this summer when Elsa described that twinkling sunlight as ocean stars. Months have passed since then, months of easy days.

And one week of days have passed since Sal died—since complications from his heart surgery were too grave for his weakened state to withstand, though he hid that well. And so Sal's last and final day washed over him, a quiet wave taking him away.

Elsa must be distraught today, thinking that only one week ago, her son was here. Now she's at his Manhattan apartment, going through his things while sorting through her thoughts. Maris hopes to meet up with her while in the city for Fashion Week, which should help.

But it's a week since something else, too. Since hearing Neil's voice. Whether real or imagined, Jason had grown accustomed to hearing whisperings and words in the sea breeze, in the rustle of the lagoon grasses, in the cry of a soaring seagull. Then it got even better this summer, when it felt like he got his brother back through Sal: tagging along on job sites; having a brew at The Sand Bar; fishing; bullshitting in Foley's back room—the old teen hangout in Elsa's soon-to-be inn.

And now? Nothing. No Sal, no Neil. How many more people will he lose at Stony Point?

"Hey, guy," a voice calls out.

Jason looks over and sees Nick, dressed in his spiffy security uniform—epaulets and all—crossing the boardwalk. "What's happening, Nicholas?"

"Sheesh, Barlow." Nick sits beside Jason. "Only my mother and my boss call me that." He looks out at the empty beach. "Man, what a ghost town after Labor Day."

"No shit. It's nice."

"Makes my job easy, that's for sure. What's up with you? Working today?"

Jason points to the drab, gray cottage on the hill. Dumpsters sit in the yard, and a work crew is in and out of the cottage, removing last-minute debris. "Demo stuff first at old Maggie Woods' place, starting up on the teardown. Then out to a new job, a Nantucket-style redo, and back to the Woods dump at the end of the day."

Nick glances up at the eyesore. "You're involved with the demolition? As the architect?"

"I'm also project manager on this one. Have to meet with the demo foreman. And that's my cue," Jason tells him. "Got to get to work." He starts walking in the direction of the Woods cottage, surprised when Nick tags along beside him. "What are you doing? Babysitting me? Go to work, punk."

"Eh, it's dead here today." Nick motions to the deserted beach. "I'll make sure you're not breaking any violations at that Woods rattrap."

"Get lost. Had enough of people hanging around me this summer when Maris was away on business." They step off the boardwalk and head to the footpath leading up the hill. "Shit, you'd think I didn't know how to feed myself the way everyone here hovered. Don't need you hanging around me now, too."

"That's not what Kyle said Sunday at breakfast. We have to stick together. Where is Maris, anyway?"

Jason checks his ringing cell phone and lets it go to voicemail. "New York. She's director of women's denim for Saybrooks Department Store. Maris runs their whole show, man, and is killing it with her team, designing their next line of jeans. So everybody's busy, except for you. Don't you have classes or something? How long have you been working on that degree of yours?"

"I'm almost done, don't worry. Taking night classes this semester, so I can get a few more hours in patrolling here."

"Well, get to work then," he tells Nick. "I'll see you when I see you." It's so obvious Nick's up to something, the way he backs off, but his shadow falling on Jason gives away his persistent presence. So Jason whips around and turns up both hands.

"Okay, okay." Nick stops in his tracks. "Kyle told me to keep an eye on you."

"What?"

Nick shrugs and walks beside him when Jason continues

up the winding footpath. "No secrets here at Stony Point, so what the hell, you'll find out sooner or later. Kyle's paying me to check up on you. He wants a report. You know, if your house is dark at night, if you're around and doing all right."

"Now that's God damn creepy. A peeping Nick looking in my windows?"

"Kyle wants to be sure you're okay and not messing up. You know, since you left your wife the other day?"

Jason gives him a shove. "Get lost, I'm telling you."

But still, Nick keeps step with him, just out of shove-reach. At the top of the footpath, past two barrel-planters of impatiens, they take a right onto Hillcrest Road. "So hey, man. Is the wrecking ball really swinging on that dump? Neighbors have been telling me they can't wait for it to be gone. Their property values will finally go up again."

"Pretty soon. The interior has to be dismantled, followed by glass and window removal." The surprising sound of shattering glass—a window being tossed into a dumpster—breaks the quiet. "That all starts today." With Nick right behind him, Jason climbs the weedy hill of the Woods yard. "But seriously? There's zilch worth saving with that one. Ain't nothing but beach blight, dude."

~

Celia unplugs her coffeemaker, then empties the crumb tray of her toaster. A slice of toast was all she could get down this morning. That and a few sips of coffee. A week ago right now, she sat with Elsa in the hospital, waiting. Waiting. Elsa said she'd be in New York this week at Sal's apartment, so Celia gets her phone and texts her a message. *Just checking in, Elsa. Hope you're feeling okay this sad day.* She glances out her slider toward the lagoon, at the dock where Sal's wooden rowboat is still tied. *Thinking of you and Sal, always.*

In the shed behind the cottage, she remembers seeing a little red wagon this summer, when she'd haul out the bicycle for a ride. Her eyes move from the shed in the yard, to a carton on the kitchen table. A carton filled to the brim with white lanterns, sandpiper statues, a nautilus shell, and driftwood wreath. Today seems like a good day to get rid of this coastal clutter. So she takes the box outside to the shed, brushes away cobwebs and rolls out the dusty wagon. It'll do just fine for her mission.

Because if she doesn't start to move on with things like this, her grief will feel too, well, too big. So once the box is secured, she pulls the wagon behind her to the street, the wheels gritty on the sandy pavement. She walks slowly, breathing the salt air, passing cottages that have emptied out now that workaday September lives have resumed.

It doesn't take long to walk the few blocks to Eva's cottage. The two-story Dutch colonial sits on a spacious yard, with the marsh spreading out behind it. Celia knocks at the screen door.

"Hey, you," Eva says from the front porch. She holds a paper and pen as though she'd been working, maybe monitoring the new real estate listings.

"Eva." Celia motions to the carton in the wagon. "I thought of you when I packed this."

"What is it?" Eva asks, stepping outside and lifting a wooden sandpiper.

"My staging things. Maybe you can use them in cottages you list, when I leave."

Eva whips around at her words. "Oh, no. Don't you remember Kyle's breakfast? No hasty decisions. You can't leave."

Celia lifts out the box and sets it in Eva's arms. "It's not hasty. That was always my original plan, to close up my best friend's cottage and go back home after Labor Day. There's lots of staging jobs waiting for me in Addison, before the holidays."

Eva glances inside the box, then hands it over to Celia's arms. "Same here, Celia. So many renters want to buy a cottage after their summer vacations. I'm going to need a stager, it's a very busy time."

"Well, that friend I mentioned? Amy? I'm supposed to go to her daughter's birthday party soon. She'll be four." Celia sets the carton back in the red wagon, then sits on Eva's front step. "Okay." She takes a long breath. "Okay. It's just that there's nothing here for me." She squints up at Eva in front of her. "Everywhere I look is a sad memory. So I'm going to follow my original plan."

"But what about Elsa?" Eva sits beside her on the stoop. "You were going to work with her!"

"That was before Sal died. I just can't, now."

"But we all made a pact. No rash decisions. Wait a week or two, spend a little time with Elsa." She takes Celia's hand in hers. "You were going to marry her *son*."

"And I'm sure seeing me will only remind her of her loss." Celia shakes her head and stands. "No. It's all too much, no matter how I look at things." Again she walks to the wagon and picks up the carton.

"Listen." Eva stands, too, and opens the screen door. "My daughter Taylor's back to high school, so we can talk."

Knowing Eva will not take no for an answer, Celia carries the box to the enclosed front porch. She sets her box on the floor, then reluctantly sits in a white wicker chair.

"Let me get us some pastry," Eva calls over her shoulder as she heads to the kitchen.

When Eva returns to the porch, setting a plate of raspberry Danish on a small end table, Celia knows. Oh, she knows she'll have a very difficult time extricating herself from this beach town and the wonderful friends she made here this summer. It's not Eva's kind smile that does it, or her light words saying they'll have some nice girl-talk as she sits down across from Celia.

No. It's the way Eva discreetly moves her foot and nudges Celia's carton across the floor, slowly, right back beside Celia, as though Celia is *not* leaving here and the décor box belongs with *her*, because she'll be staging *Eva's* listed cottages. Done deal, decision made.

Eva's one, slow foot-nudge says it all—in no uncertain terms.

six

BY THE END OF TUESDAY—one day back to his work routine—Jason's life resumes its new normal: fatigued, with slivers of pain bothering him. Right at the *moncone*, he thinks—Sal's term to soften the reality of his left leg ending just past the knee. *Mon-cone-ay*, Sal had explained. *It's Italian, for stump.* There's not much pain, but enough to warn Jason to rest, or take off his prosthetic limb soon and switch to crutches. Something, after an exhausting day.

He pulls into The Sand Bar's parking lot and finds a vacant space. There's no smoking in the bar, so a quick call to Maris in Manhattan gives him time to grab a few drags in his SUV. Between her words about trying to reach Elsa at Sal's apartment, and about missing home, he hears her worry.

"Since Sal died, it feels wrong being away from Stony Point," she tells him. "So I'm pulling an all-nighter finishing sketches for next fall's line."

"Don't work too late."

"Whatever it takes. I want to be home by dinner tomorrow, and then just work in the barn studio out back. To be close to everyone there."

"I get it." Jason tamps out his cigarette and gets out of his truck. "Listen, I'm going in for a beer and a sandwich."

"At The Sand Bar? Why not stop at the diner? Kyle will give you a good meal."

"Nah. Don't feel much like shooting the breeze with him today. Miss you, sweetheart."

"Me, too." Then, her voice drops. "Let Maddy out later?"

"Will do. Love you."

In the silence that follows, Jason knows how badly she's missing home. Over the miles, the cell phone holds no secrets. She's fighting back tears, or a lump in her throat preventing her from speaking.

"Love you, too," she barely whispers as he walks across the parking lot to the bar.

Inside, he sits on a stool, hands clasped in front of him as his thumb finds the scar along his jaw. It's impossible to not think of Sal sitting in here all summer, bantering his Italian, Wall Street brand of jive talk, getting everyone smiling. Jason really feels his loss tonight. After ordering a sandwich, he bullshits with the bartender, who's wiping down the bar with a damp rag. It's one of those sultry September evenings when the outside door is propped open to the hazy salt air. Rays of the low setting sun lighten the dusky space. Jason glances over at the small dance floor, where a microphone is set up and some dude is taking a seat on a stool behind it.

"Yo, Patrick," Jason says to the bartender. "What's up over there?"

Patrick checks out the staged dance floor and when he hits a switch, a ceiling spotlight illuminates the microphone area. "Open mic night, guy. Been doing it all summer, every Tuesday." The man on the stool taps the microphone. "Brings folks in on what would otherwise be a quiet night."

"No shit." Jason looks over at the apparent poet who is adjusting his black-framed glasses and reciting a verse, something about finding desire in the September moonlight.

When the second poem starts, Patrick sets down a draft beer and turkey club sandwich with chips, a pickle spear on the side. "Got anything, Barlow?" he asks, crossing his arms and hitching his chin in the direction of the microphone. "You want to sing a song? Tell a story?"

Jason waves him off with a quick laugh, then bites into his sandwich, the dressing dripping from the roll onto his plate. He turns on his stool and watches the reciting poet for another minute, then turns back to his food, takes a swallow of beer and simply eats.

~

Her guitar case is propped on the booth seat across from her. Celia thinks that in the dark bar, the case is shadowy enough that it could look like a person sitting there. If only ... if only it were the man she's missing. She lifts her cell phone and scrolls through old text messages from Sal, looking for a particular one while still not believing he's been dead a week. She pauses when the waitress sets down a drink—her third, maybe—then looks back to her phone. There, that's the message from last month, and it makes her sad enough to take a long swallow of the liquor in front of her.

Ciao, bella. Open mic at The Sand Bar tonight. Bring your guitar?

Celia smiles, reads it twice, then takes another long sip of her drink. Sal loved listening to her play, and maybe somehow, somewhere, he'll hear her tonight. The nightclub is busy, with several tables and booths filled, along with a handful of regulars sitting at the bar. The poet wrapped up his session a few minutes ago, and the patrons are conversing, a few friendly laughs rising from the tables, now that the recital is done.

So before her performance begins, she'll first have to quiet them and get their attention. Which brings a flutter to her heart as she looks around the dim room, glancing at the jukebox off to the side, at the glasses hanging over the long bar, where several men watch a baseball game on the mounted television. Doubting herself now, she fusses with the shoulders of her peasant top and eyes the propped-open exit door.

"Up next," a waitress announces into the microphone while squinting out into the shadows, "acoustic singer-songwriter, Celia Gray!"

Someone whistles and random applause halfheartedly breaks out. Celia downs every last drop of her drink, then takes a deep breath. Lifting her guitar from its case, she winds around the tables toward the stool and mic. When she stumbles, an arm reaches out in the dark and steadies her. "Easy does it," a man's voice says. She continues to the stool and settles the guitar on her lap as her fingers toy with the strings.

Voices still chatter in the bar, and passing traffic sounds come in piecemeal through that open door. Oh, why did she come here? For God's sake, why didn't she stay at the cottage and just cry on the couch? She couldn't, though. It's not a night she can be alone.

So Celia leans toward the mic. "Hello," she says, then clears her throat. The microphone is a little high for her, so she lowers it, then gives it a light tap. "I'm Celia. It's nice to be here with you tonight."

Positioning her guitar, getting it comfortable on her lap, dragging her pick lightly across the strings and adjusting her blouse's shoulder once more … what it does is buy her time. A few seconds to see if the crowd in the shadows will settle down and stop talking. Will even listen to her tune.

But she supposes that she's here, really, for only one person. For Sal, she reminds herself with a glance upward. She clears her throat again and begins singing her first song of the night, her fingers strumming the guitar, her voice hesitant—drifting a little, like Sal often did in his rowboat—as she lets her emotion carry the song to the booths and tables, now quieting in the dark.

~

Jason spins his stool around and leans his elbows on the bar. He's surprised to see Celia and watches her, unsure if she's feeling her liquor, or if grief is unhinging her song. The guitar interlude she plays between verses loses its momentum, until she leans to the microphone, eyes closed, head tipped to the side, and sings the final lines. When she finishes, she places a hand over the guitar's sound hole and bows her head while the crowd politely claps and a whistle rings out.

After that, a cautious silence fills the space. Celia adjusts the guitar on her lap and presses back a strand of hair that fell over her face. Her legs are crossed, and he recognizes her silver-flecked skinny jeans as a pair from Maris' denim line. When Celia's silence continues, he stands, wondering if he should help walk her off the makeshift stage.

But just then, Celia raises a hand to shield her eyes from the spotlight and looks at the scattered tables, so Jason settles on his barstool again.

"It's a beautiful night outside," Celia says, swaying slightly as her eyes glance around the dark room. "So make a wish on a star." She plays a few leisurely chords, her pick drawing them out one string at a time. "I hope it comes true," she adds then. Her hand, still holding the pick, rises to her face to blot away tears. "Sometimes they do, sometimes they don't."

And Jason knows. She's devastated on this one-week anniversary of Sal's death. Still, he only watches as she begins strumming a familiar tune. Everyone here tonight must recognize it, even when Celia brings the music to a slow, evocative tempo. Her fingers move over the strings, and as her other hand skims the fret, she works the slide noise of her moving fingers right into the song. What she's doing is obvious to Jason: She's capturing every bit of her grief in that sound. Until she leans forward and sings.

Twinkle, twinkle ocean star … How I wonder what you are.

The words come so gradually, with sad strums between each phrase, that it takes her long moments to finish each line. There are pauses that may or may not be intentional, but that suit her mood. As she sings, a warm breeze brings the distant sea dampness through the open door, and she turns her face toward it, a scarce smile on her face.

Floating on the sea, so light ... Like a diamond ...

In this pause, the silence is so profound, Jason figures every eye in the bar is on her. Celia raises her hand to her mouth and stifles a sob.

"It's okay," a man's voice calls from the dark as sporadic handclaps rise in encouragement. "Don't be nervous!"

She closes her eyes, her peasant blouse baring her tanned shoulders, her sea-glass engagement ring glimmering on her finger. Then she looks out at the tables and booths, and nods before straightening her posture and strumming once more, her gaze dropping to the guitar.

Like a diamond ... shining bright.

A voice woots from somewhere in the back. When Celia lifts her foot to the stool's footrest, she misses it and nearly falls off the seat. Her hair swings forward—which she quickly presses back—her blouse sleeve gets twisted on her shoulder, and the tears run freely now.

So Jason sets down his beer and rushes to the spotlighted area. "It's okay, Celia," he says into her ear while bending and putting his arm around her. "Let's take a break."

The applause begins then, such that Jason grips the microphone and squints around the room. "Thanks, everybody," he says with a wave before taking Celia's guitar from her and leaning it against the stool. With an arm around her waist, they walk back to her booth.

The three empty liquor glasses sitting there don't escape him as he helps her sit.

"You okay, hon?" a waitress asks. She's brought over the guitar and sets it on the booth seat.

"She's feeling a little sad tonight," Jason assures her as he hands Celia a napkin. "Missing someone."

"Poor thing," the waitress says quietly to Jason. In no time, she's back with two drinks. "On the house," she whispers. "Courtesy of Patrick." She motions to the bartender and hurries off with a worried glance back at Celia.

So much for his quick beer and bite to eat. Instead, Jason settles across from Celia and clasps her arm.

"Oh, Jason, thank God you're here." Celia presses the napkin to her eyes.

"Tough day, I know," he says.

"It's the worst. I thought this would help," she explains with a wave to the staged microphone platform where a woman now plays a tambourine, long ribbons fluttering from it as she sings a carefree song. "Sal loved open mic night." She dabs her eyes, then slides her drink closer.

"You feeling better now?" Jason asks.

"Better, but really embarrassed. I had a few drinks earlier," she says, lifting her glass and taking a sip. "To get me through this."

Jason watches her, then drags the back of his hand across his unshaven jaw. The day's been eternal, this first one back to work since Sal's funeral, and he's feeling every minute of it, so he takes a long swallow of the drink. "What is this, seven and seven?"

Celia nods. "Sal liked to have one here."

"And how many have you had?" he asks.

"A few. Three, maybe?"

Okay, so she's lit. Jason watches as she cups her glass with two hands and manages a long sip of the whiskey and

7-Up blend. He joins her, taking another swig of his own and feeling the iced liquor wash down his throat, washing away the edge of his suppressed grief. So yeah, he thinks, eyeing the glasses—a few potent drinks and everything's feeling better.

"Maybe it was one of those rash decisions everyone's talking about, coming here by myself. But Sal and I came to open mic night all summer, and he watched me sing," Celia whispers. The tambourine song stops and the bar gets unusually quiet as Patrick disconnects the microphone and removes the stool. "You know, it's been one week since he's been alive, and I wanted to remember him tonight." She takes another swallow of her drink. "And now I just want to forget. Like the summer never happened."

Jason's had those days, too, years ago. After the motorcycle accident that claimed his brother's life—and Jason's own leg—how many times did he pray, beg, plead with the powers above to just wake up and have it all be a fucking nightmare. To open his eyes and feel *both* his feet beneath the sheets. To check his cell phone and see a voicemail from Neil. Damn it, it all comes back to him now, the way he'd lift his phone to his ear, press it there and wait in silence for a miracle that never came.

"I've been there, Celia. Believe me."

"So how do I get through this, Jason? It hurts so much, I don't think I can take it."

"And I'm not going to pull any punches with you." In a small copper globe on their table, a candle burns. Its low light flickers in the dark space, casting soft shadows on Celia's face. "Dealing with Sal's death will be the farthest thing from easy. Nearly impossible. But you'll do it."

"How?" She leans across the thick wood table, her peasant-blouse neckline slipping further down her shoulder. "Please tell me something, *anything*."

"How?" He reaches over and lifts the blouse fabric higher on her arm. "One hour at a time," he says when he sits back. "After you get through one hour, try for another."

Celia does it then, recaps every hour she made it through today: from sitting out on the dock this morning with her coffee, hearing Sal's voice in the whisper of the marsh grass, to talking with Eva—who adamantly refused to let Celia even think of leaving. "That rash decision thing, she told me. We all made a pact."

"And with good reason." He motions to the passing waitress for another seven and seven, raising his glass to her. "Any decision you make now, trust me, you wouldn't have made looking back on it in a year."

"Maybe." Celia spins her sailor's knot rope bracelet on her wrist. "Then when I left Eva's and wondered what to have for dinner, I missed having Sal plan dinner *with* me. So I decided to come here and sing his favorite song. In his honor."

"I understand. Some days will be hard, like this one, but the next will be better. You'll see."

"Thanks, Jason." Celia gives his hand a squeeze and holds it for a long moment. "I'm sorry to prattle on like this. I really haven't had anyone to talk to these days." When she leans over the table to say more, her words slur. "And being alone in silence makes everything feel worse." Finally, she releases his hand, lifts her glass and tips it up to finish the drink. "No one to talk to until you walked in here."

"Elsa?"

"No."

"How about your friend from home? The one whose cottage you're staying at."

"Amy? I really don't want to bother her with my story."

"What about Lauren?" he asks as the waitress sets down his drink.

"She left. And she's busy with her kids and their school stuff now. So no." Celia shakes her head, a little too quickly. "No one."

Jason imagines what he'd feel like if he suddenly lost Maris. He'd be done, all done. So when he sees new tears line Celia's face, he reaches over and brushes them away.

"Oh, this darn crying!" Celia says. She digs in her handbag and pulls out a tissue to press against her eyes. All the while, she's also pulling out coins, one at a time, and setting them on the booth table. When she suddenly stands, she wavers, unsteady on her feet.

"Where are you going?" Jason asks, grabbing her arm.

Celia looks over her shoulder at him. Her face is tired, but he sees how she had dressed as though going on a beach date with Sal, those tanned shoulders exposed, her jeans faded and fitted in the right places. Hopeful, and ruined at once.

"It's too quiet in here now," she says, tottering toward the bar's jukebox. "I'm going to pick out a song."

~

Between her tears and the liquor, Jason's sure the song titles are blurring before her eyes. By the way Celia braces her two arms on the jukebox while studying the selection, she's clearly feeling the alcohol. But he waits, cuffing his sleeves, sipping his drink, giving her the space and time to collect herself.

Except, it's obvious she's beyond that now. After fumbling with her coins, she presses enough into the jukebox to pick a song or two, then turns back to their booth and stops, one hand holding that jukebox for balance. Her eyes scan the room and Jason sees how the liquor's taken hold; she's not even sure where she is.

So he leaves the booth and hurries over, holding out his hand to guide her back. Once her hand takes his, it must be the sense of touch that does it. That has her pull herself against him on the small dance floor, folding her arm between them as the slow song begins. They stand together in the glow of the jukebox, Jason starting to object until Celia begins swaying, her smile so sad, it's overwhelming. So he wraps his arm around her shoulder and pulls her close, feeling how badly she misses Sal. There's no mistaking it; it's in the way she leans her body into his, shifting her feet in a dance that keeps her hips moving against him. So he goes with it, for her, and his hand that's reached around her shoulder? It strokes her auburn hair, the strands soft beneath his fingers.

As the jukebox song plays on, the singer questions sailing through ocean tides, and Jason knows. The power of those tides can take you down, and Celia's grief might as well be just that: an ocean tide. Without some footing, some anchor, some navigation, it'll unmoor her.

So when she laces her hands behind his waist and pulls him closer to her swaying body, Jason's hand slides down from behind her neck, where it had been stroking her hair, to her exposed shoulder, grazing the tanned curve of it before slipping along the front neckline of her peasant blouse, his finger tracing a line across her skin there. If he keeps her moving, he tells himself, maybe she'll work off the liquor and get this grief out of her system.

But something about the dance soothes him, too. Moors *him* to this sad woman sharing his same grief. Because isn't Jason *also* reeling from the loss of Sal, who'd been like a second brother. It's precisely that pain that drove Jason away from his seaside home just days ago—the same pain that Celia runs from tonight. On some level, they're in this together, both running.

When Celia rests her head against his shoulder, her every curve presses against him, soft curves he should never be feeling against his chest, his hips. She lifts her head, then raises her hands to his neck and glides her fingers through his hair, toying with thick strands of it while her moist, hazel eyes watch his.

Touch. He's well aware of the elixir of touch. The touch of a salty hitching breeze calming him; the touch of scalding towels on his stump curing phantom pain; every slight touch of Celia's fingers on his hair loosening the knotted nerves of his spine.

The jukebox song continues, with Jason's hands dropping to Celia's waist as together they barely move on the bar's dance floor. There's just enough pressure of her body against his to feel more like a caress, easing his fatigue, his own melancholy. But when Celia's fingers trace along his neck up to the faded scar on his jaw, he takes that hand in his, feeling a change in the dance.

"We need to sit down," he quietly says. "Now."

She looks at him, her eyelids heavy, her smile still slight, and tips her head. As he tucks back her hair and whispers in her ear, "That's enough," she turns her face to him.

"But this helps," she says, her fingers stroking his whiskered jaw as she leans close and kisses him.

Though his first thought is to pull back, Jason doesn't. In the warm bar, as he breathes the scent of alcohol and summer, with the damp night air glancing his skin and the bluesy song playing on, he gives in. His eyes drop closed and his hands run up along the side of Celia's body, his fingers skimming the curve of her breasts beneath that sweet blouse sitting too low on her shoulders. He brings his touch to her bare shoulders until his hands cup her neck and his kiss, slow and deep, becomes too necessary to stop. Her mouth is sensuous and needy, taking his touch without hesitation. And her body, moving to the music while pressed against his, makes him want only more as his hands drop to her hips and pull her against him.

"Jason," she whispers between now-desperate kisses.

Hearing her voice say his name like that stops him. He steps away, pulling his mouth from hers and holding her back by her shoulders. Those God damn rounded, soft shoulders that she wants only to lie beneath his; there's no mistaking that.

"Celia. Get it together," he says then.

"What?" Her confused, gentle eyes stay locked on his. "But I thought—"

"Never mind." He takes her arm and pulls her back to the obscure darkness of their booth, pointing at her seat for her to slide in and stay there.

"Jason," she says, leaning across the table. "I'm sorry if—"

"Let's forget about what just happened," he says, nodding toward the jukebox.

But her eyes tear up. "It felt so nice, dancing with you. Sal used to hold me the same way, kissing me while we danced." Now, those tears spill out, lining her cheeks as she tips her head. "Like we did."

"Sal's gone, Celia. And we, hell, we got caught up in a moment, that's all. A really sad moment at the end of a long, difficult day. It was nothing."

"Nothing?" Her tears come faster now. "You comforted me, Jason, and it worked. It felt so good." She presses her hands to her face, unable to stop that flow of tears. "Oh God, what have I done? What am I even doing here?"

"Don't say anything, okay?" He leans close across the table and drops his voice. "Comb your hair, pull yourself together." He wonders if she even hears him, so he gives her arm a shake. "Celia, *listen* to me, and I'll get you home."

Celia grabs her purse and clutches it close as she stands. "I have to use the ladies' room," she says, then quickly makes her way through the dark bar to the restrooms in the back.

Jason watches her go, wanting nothing more than to get out of this place. To not wonder who might have seen what, to get her to her cottage—and, really? To not see her again. Okay, so they both loved Sal, but they can't lean on each other. Celia has to handle her grief in her own way.

Which he figures she must be doing ten minutes later when he checks his watch and she still hasn't returned to their booth. He cuffs his sleeves again while glancing toward the bathrooms. Couples sit close at tables; guys line the bar, eating and laughing and bullshitting over a beer; and no Celia. Not a sign of her, tugging up that blouse neckline or pressing back her hair or weaving her way back to him. Nothing at all.

So he tosses back the rest of his drink and hurries to the ladies' room. First he gives only a knock, then opens the door. "Celia?" he asks. When there's no answer, he closes the door and turns around to see Patrick approaching.

"Hey, guy," Patrick calls out.

Jason looks past the bartender for a glimpse of Celia somewhere, anywhere.

"Jason, my man," Patrick says as he pats Jason's shoulder. "Everything okay?"

"What do you mean?"

"It's just that, well, normally I don't interfere with patrons' personal business, but we go way back, my friend. I saw you with the lady."

"Oh, that," Jason says, taking a long breath.

"Yeah. *That.*" Patrick eyes him closely. "Where's your wife tonight? At home? Because if I can help out here in some way—"

"It's not what you're thinking, bro. Seriously."

"You're telling me that you and Maris are solid?"

"We are." It's the way Patrick doesn't move, not one bit, not one glance away from Jason, that gets Jason even more riled. "This," he says, nodding toward the dance floor, "it was … Shit, it happened. The lady—Celia—she's upset, lost her fiancé. Sal, man. He died a week ago. You met Sal."

"DeLuca?"

"Right. And things just got out of hand here."

"You sure?"

Jason nods. "You see where she went?"

"Outside to the patio. I figured she needed some air."

"You kidding me?"

"No. She's a bit of a wreck."

Jason looks quickly to the side door, then back to Patrick. "Absolutely. And thanks for asking, guy. I'm okay. But *she's* on some collision course tonight," he says before rushing back to the booth and grabbing Celia's guitar, then running out to the patio. Umbrellas are open over black mesh tables, and twinkly lights line the spokes within each umbrella, casting a soft glow on the tables.

Tables where no Celia is in sight. Jason spins around and double-checks, squinting through the darkness, trying to decipher some women from behind, leaning to the side to see who a few guys are talking with. But none are Celia.

So he rushes to the parking lot and glances into the September night. There, she's at her car, beneath a streetlamp. It looks like she's trying to get the car door open, her body moving from side to side as she stumbles, then regains her footing.

Guitar in hand, Jason quickly heads her way. "Son of a bitch," he says.

seven

THE LIGHTS STREAKING PAST IN a wavering, bright line seem fluid. Celia watches closely as more approach, her body rocking with the motion of the moving vehicle. Each towering streetlight, every set of approaching car headlights, they're all soft and misty around the edges.

Did Sal suffer? Was he trying to hold on in some way during his heart surgery? Before anesthesia took hold, did he see a glimpse of white lights shining on his beautiful chest? Lights that might have blurred as the surgery's drugs coursed through his veins. Did they fade, then, those lights? Or did he simply black out into unconsciousness?

Her eyes drop closed for longer and longer, but Celia manages to force them open each time, the effort strenuous as she lifts her heavy lids. Every now and then, a familiar sight registers with her and she relaxes, until panic sets in when the lights blur again.

Finally, finally Jason swings off the main road onto a left fork to the stone railroad trestle. They're back. She glances at him driving, then leans forward, squinting through the tunnel. "A ring, a baby, or a broken heart," she whispers.

"*What?*" Jason asks as he drives beneath the trestle.

Yes, the cottages she loves to watch at night, they're here. Everything's still here. Her life, her friends. Some of the cottages are aglow with lamplight drawing her eye. It's her favorite thing to do: steal glimpses inside the summer homes. There—there's a piano in that one, up against a white wall. And a television glows from another, a television she'd loved to have been watching all night, instead of, well … Her eyes drop closed again, until she forces them open. Twinkly lights looking so happy outline a screened front porch.

"Take me home," she says. "I want to sit outside near the dock."

Jason drives past her street without slowing.

"Wait." Celia whips around and looks behind them. Trying to keep things steady, her hand grips the door.

"I'll make you a coffee first." Jason's voice comes to her in the darkness. "You'll feel better that way."

She sits back with a sigh as the vehicle drives a long, sloping road. A crescent moon shines in the hazy sky, far above the distant sea. "If I could just sleep …"

"No. You'll sleep later. Coffee now, Celia."

The SUV turns into a driveway with towering trees on one side keeping it in shadow, a dark cottage on the other.

"Where are we?" she asks, turning in her seat. "This isn't my house."

"It's mine," Jason tells her while parking close to the back deck. "You wait in the truck, you hear me? I'll go put on some lights so you can see where you're walking."

After fumbling with her seatbelt, which she cannot for the life of her figure out how to unlatch, Celia instead watches the light show. Yellow lamplight fills some windows in the foreboding house, then the deck is bathed in light, and at last a bright spotlight shines on the driveway. Jason, looking like an apparition, walks toward the vehicle.

"Let's go," he says when he opens the passenger door and she's pulling on her seatbelt strap. "Come on, hurry it up." He waits, then turns up his hands and quickly leans across her lap to unbuckle the seatbelt.

"Thanks," Celia whispers as she slides out of the SUV and her feet hit the pavement.

Jason reaches behind her for her handbag, then slams the door shut. "Go on," he says, motioning toward the deck. But when she stumbles, he catches up to her and puts an arm around her back. Because now, she really feels out of it. If he doesn't prop her up with each step, she'll crumble right to the ground. This way, with his arm holding her close, she leans into him, her hand grabbing his arm when the driveway shifts beneath her feet.

"Slow," he tells her, hoisting her straighter and letting his body support hers. He turns his face to her, talking so close. "You going to make it?" he asks.

Celia nods and lets her head drop onto Jason's shoulder as they weave across the yard, up the stone steps to the deck softly illuminated with solar garden lights. He leads her through the slider and finally inside the house.

~

"Make some room." Lauren pushes aside a newspaper *and* Kyle's legs stretched out on the sofa. So Kyle sits up and she drops the newspaper to the floor, then squeezes onto the end cushion. "The weather on yet?"

"I don't know. I fell asleep." Kyle lifts the remote and turns up the volume. "If we were at Stony Point, there'd at least be a sea breeze cooling things off." He glances across the room at the open windows, windows framed with limp curtains. "I'm beat."

"It's late." Lauren gives his leg a pat. "Go to bed."

"I want to see the weather. If this heat holds on, the diner patio can make us a lot of cash."

The news anchor's voice drones, then goes quiet. Until Kyle feels Lauren swat his leg again. "Wake up! Leo Sterling's on."

Kyle pushes himself further up on the couch. "I can barely keep my eyes open."

"Folks, don't put away your shorts and tees," the chief meteorologist declares while pointing to the weather map. "Because it looks like this summer … will not cease!"

"Perfect," Kyle whispers as his cell phone dings. He picks it up off the end table.

"Is it Jason?" Lauren asks.

"Huh." Kyle scrolls a message. "No, it's Nick, texting me."

"Nick? What does he want at this hour?" Lauren swoops over and grabs his phone. "What are you guys up to?"

Before she can steal a look, Kyle snatches the phone back. "It's nothing. Nick just clocked out from keeping a watchful eye on that beach community where I cannot find a house to buy. He wants to go fishing Friday." But he says it while riveted to the sparse report Nick is slowly typing in.

"Fine," Lauren tells him. Kyle only glances at her as she gets up from the couch and leaves. He's completely engrossed in Nick's words, until she snatches the phone again, this time from behind the sofa. "What the hell?" she asks.

"Ah, shit," Kyle whispers, looking back at her in her nightshirt and slippers, a sleep mask on the top of her head as she backs away and scrolls through the text messages.

"According to Nick—his words now," she adds with a one-handed air quote, "*Trouble in paradise, man. Your best friend's looking like a world-class prick.*"

Kyle extends his arm behind his head. "Give me that."

"Jason? *Jason's* a prick, is that what he's saying?" She drops the phone in Kyle's open hand.

"Let me get to the bottom of this."

"On speaker, please." Lauren scoots in beside him and hits the Speaker button as Kyle dials Nick's phone.

"What's happening, guy?"

"Oh, man, Kyle. You won't believe what I saw."

"Try me," Kyle answers, shrugging to Lauren, silent beside him.

"Jason and Celia," Nick explains. "All over each other, seriously."

"Wait. Did you say *Celia*?"

"I did, dude. Now listen up, would you? They went inside the Barlow love pad and shit, she couldn't keep her hands off of him."

"No way," Kyle says.

"No *lie*, man. And the way he had his arm around her, I'm telling you, it was hot and heavy. I mean, the touching and hugging was intense."

"It had to be Maris you saw." Kyle raises his finger to Lauren's lips as she's about to defend Celia.

"Nope. The wife's in New York. And apparently, when

the cat's away, other cats move right in, all purring and lovey-dovey. From the looks of things, they were really going at it."

"Well, did you stop them?" Kyle asks, standing then and walking to the window. He glances out, not believing Jason would pull this stunt.

"Hell, no."

"Why not?"

"I am *not* about to interfere with Jason Barlow's nighttime antics. Final round of my shift, too. I'm out of here."

"Go back, Nick. Ring the bell or something."

"No way. I'm already gone, man. And Commissioner Raines does not pay overtime. Just reporting in to you, like we agreed."

"Agreed?" Lauren asks. "What?"

Kyle simply takes a long, tired breath as Nick ends the call and says, "Put it on my tab, boss."

As soon as he gets Celia in the house, Jason dumps out the morning's cold coffee grounds and makes a fresh brew. He fills the decanter with water, seeing the unopened mail on the counter, the dirty dishes in the sink, and yes, unpacked wedding gifts still lining the hallway floor. It's enough to get him to shut off the bright overhead light after slamming the glass decanter on the coffeemaker. Madison hovers nearby, venturing close and nosing his hand every few moments, until he shoves her away.

"Get out, just go outside," he says, opening the screen

to the slider and slamming it shut behind the dog who simply turns around and watches through the screen, her ears tall, her eyes locked on him.

The faster he gets coffee into Celia to sober her up, the faster he'll get her out of here. So he grabs two mugs from the cabinet, dropping one on the counter when Madison whines at the screen. "Damn it," he says, picking up the mug and running a hand over the new chip in it. Then he lifts the coffeemaker's decanter and pours hot coffee into the chipped cup.

"Celia!" Jason calls. When there's no answer, he half turns while pouring. "How do you take yours?" As he asks, coffee hits his hand, nicely scalding it and getting him to put back the decanter and throw the mug in the sink—where it promptly cracks in half before he runs the cold tap and shoves his burned hand in the water.

God damn it, is he mad. Mad that Sal went and died on all of them; mad at the dog whining on the other side of the slider screen; mad that when Celia came in she tripped on the dog's water bowl, and now he almost slipped on a puddle of water left on the floor; mad at Celia.

"Who am I kidding?" He shuts off the water and gives his hand a shake before looking toward the living room. Yeah, it's Sal, and it's Maris. If Sal hadn't died, if Maris were home today, this wouldn't have happened. Another glance is tossed back at the silent living room where Celia surely sits, that blouse dropped low on her smooth shoulders, those jeans fitting just so.

Right now, it's not possible for him to walk in that direction, not after what they did in the bar, so he sits at the kitchen table and straightens the salt-and-pepper shakers, tucks a loose napkin into the napkin holder. Okay, it was one kiss, but he knows damn well it went on far too long, and he knows damn well where that kiss was headed.

Shit. He gets up and grabs another mug from the cabinet and attempts pouring coffee again. Celia completely got under his skin tonight, swaying like she did on that dance floor, making him feel good for the first time since Sal died. Getting Jason to forget his sadness—the same way she was, too, moving like that. Shit, shit, shit. Moving like she wanted him right on top of her and slipping that blouse off completely, running his hand over her body, lowering his mouth to hers.

And now, she's here? In his home? Is this part of her plan, then? Pulling that stunt when she snuck out of the bar and he chased after her?

"Cream or sugar?" he calls out. "Celia!"

When she says nothing, he sloshes in a splash of cream and takes her mug, calling her name again while turning the corner into the living room, but before seeing her curled up on the couch.

"Oh, come on," he says. "Celia." He nudges one of her bare shoulders, his fingers grazing the fabric of that peasant blouse low on her arm. "Have a coffee and let's get going." When she doesn't move, he puts the mug on the end table and gives her shoulder another shake. "Drink up, then I'll bring you back to your cottage."

It's a little scary how the liquor finally knocked her out cold; she's deep asleep, saying nothing. Could this night get any worse, when all he wants is Celia gone, and to forget that it ever happened? He paces the room, glancing at her before going to the kitchen and pouring another coffee, this one for himself. When he walks past Celia again, he gives her leg a nudge. "Celia. Come on!"

All he remembers, watching her, is the way her auburn hair fell forward earlier, right as she tipped her head down, with her eyes raised to his, her body moving subtly against him, undulating with each beat of the jukebox. He sits in the upholstered chair in the corner now and sips his coffee while she sleeps in the dusky light. Maris' sketch pads are on the coffee table, beside an empty water glass.

The last thing he needs is to spend the night in a chair, so he walks to the fireplace mantel and stops where his father's pewter hourglass once was; the hourglass he'd given to Sal for his thirty-sixth birthday. Odd how he'd given him a form of time, when the grains of sand were actually running out on Sal's life.

Jason checks his watch, then sits in the chair once more, this time pulling his cell phone from his pocket. He calls Maris in New York and lets her know that Celia's passed out on their couch.

"What happened?" Maris asks.

"Went in to The Sand Bar for a sandwich, right after I talked to you earlier," Jason explains, his voice low. He tells her about open mic night, but not about Celia's sad, breathy singing. He tells her about the glasses of seven and seven Celia downed, but not about his own drinks. He tells her how Celia sang about the ocean stars, but not how riveted he was to her raw performance beneath the lone spotlight. He tells Maris how he helped Celia off the stage, but not how Celia helped soothe the pain he's been feeling lately, with her own intimate touch on the dance floor.

"I don't know what to do," Jason says, glancing at Celia

on his sofa. "I wanted to sober her up and now she's sound asleep."

"How bad is she?" Maris asks.

Shaking his head, Jason blows out a long breath.

"What?" Then Maris goes silent, until, "Jason?"

"Today's the one-week anniversary of Sal's death. The reality of *that* hit her tonight. Head-on, Maris. She's wrecked."

"I can't even imagine," Maris whispers.

"Said she's had no one to talk to. No one, until I walked in tonight. So how do I get her home?"

"You absolutely don't, Jason. Leave her there."

"On the couch?"

"Well, yes. Yes."

"Overnight?"

"She can hurt herself home alone. She'll try to get into Sal's rowboat docked at her place and fall in the water, for all we know. She could drown."

"But all night?" Jason looks again just as Celia shifts her position, stretching out one denim-clad leg while on her side, her hair falling partly over her face. "I have to work in the morning. My day's already overbooked."

Something about Maris' silence unnerves Jason, so he stands and walks to the banister.

"Jason," Maris finally says. More silence, then, softly, "Sal meant the world to you. Do it for him, okay? Don't be mad at Celia. Just do it for Sal. Put a blanket over her and let her sleep."

He resists, first. Not to Maris. But when they're done talking, he first takes the two coffee cups to the sink, rinses them and loads all the dirty dishes and mugs into the dishwasher. It continues, this resisting tending to Celia, as he cleans the entire kitchen: the counters and table get wiped off; junk mail gets pitched; the floor gets a quick sweeping; Madison finally gets let back inside.

When there's nothing left to do but cover Celia with a blanket, he sees something of himself in her, in the way she's sleeping off some biting pain. So it's with gentleness that he drops the blanket over her body. And when he slips off her sandals and tucks her bare feet beneath the blanket, it's with regret that the night even came to pass.

A regret still there when he clasps her exposed shoulder for a long second before shutting off the light and going upstairs in darkness.

eight

BEFORE SHE OPENS HER EYES Wednesday morning, Celia listens. She can't be absolutely certain, but she's pretty sure this is Jason's house. So she doesn't move on the couch, but instead remains still beneath the blanket clutched to her chin. Okay, so her shoes are off; it's obvious by the way she wiggles her toes. And with a quick pat-down, it's apparent that her clothes are all on: blouse, jeans, even her jewelry.

When she opens her eyes, the first thing she sees is the massive stone fireplace. Tin stars lean on its rough-hewn mantel, near a carved seagull mounted on mini-roped pilings. There's a hurricane lantern on the end, with a framed photograph beside it. It's of Jason and his brother Neil, in their twenties, leaning on the railing of Foley's deck. Beside the brothers' photo is a wedding photograph of Jason and Maris, waltzing on the golden evening sand at their Stony Point reception last summer. The sun had set, and the horizon was violet over the water; tiki torches and candles in Mason jars illuminated Jason in a black tux, Maris in a vintage gown.

So far, so good. Nothing bad's happened by orienting

herself in the Barlow house. She turns her head and sees the infamous, original Foley's jukebox tucked into a living room alcove; the upholstered chairs and dark end tables filling the room; and what looks like wedding gifts—from the wrapping remnants—lining the hallway floor. There's a breeze, too, so she props herself up on her elbows and glances toward the kitchen, catching sight of the open slider door letting it in, along with the sound of cawing seagulls.

But she drops back down and closes her eyes when she hears a sudden strange sound. It's a repetitive creaking, followed by a thump, over and over again. The sound approaches, gets louder, then passes her. That's when she takes a peek and sees that it's Jason, walking past using forearm crutches. He wears a dark tee and cargo shorts; his prosthetic leg is not on. She gasps when a blur runs by—it's Maddy, chasing after him as he quickly goes up the stairs. Jason's crutches hit first, then he lifts himself a couple steps past them. With each hoist, the dog nips at the crutches as though she's upset by them. Jason ignores the German shepherd and finally disappears into the upstairs rooms. Overhead, the rhythmic sound of his crutches hitting the floor continues.

Which is precisely when Celia hurries off the couch and finds a half bathroom where she can freshen up. If only she could just bolt from the house, bolt beneath the dark, stone railroad trestle and bolt home to her yellow country bungalow in Addison, far away from every painful memory here in Stony Point.

Instead, there's a mirror over the sink, with lighting bright enough to make her squint. Or maybe it's the lingering effect of too much alcohol. Either way, she winces at her reflection while leaning close to the mirror. First she lifts a hand and slowly strokes the skin of her exposed shoulder. Her eyes drop closed with a hazy memory of slow dancing with Jason Barlow. But it takes only seconds to be so utterly embarrassed by the thought that she lifts the fabric of her peasant blouse to cover both shoulders. Then her hands press back her messy hair, pulling her skin taut on her face at the same time.

"Seriously?" Celia whispers to herself. "You're thirty-two years old, divorced, practically widowed, and now waking up in a stupor in a married man's house?"

To stop the tears from coming again, she drops her hands to the faucet and scoops up cold water, bends close and tosses it on her face—two times, then once again—before grabbing a towel and holding it pressed to her eyes, not really wanting to see any more of herself, or of reality, either.

~

"Go." Jason lifts a crutch at the top of the stairs and motions downward. "Now, Maddy." There have been too many times when the darn dog nearly catapulted him down the stairs, the way she nips at his crutches as though it's a game. He follows her down, taking the stairs two at a time, then stopping abruptly at the bottom and leaning on those crutches.

"You're up," he says, seeing Celia standing behind the sofa. Her blouse and jeans have been pressed out and straightened, after sleeping in them. "Let's get going, then. It's late."

"Jason." She lifts the blanket he'd placed over her last

night and begins carefully folding it. "I'm sorry about what happened yesterday."

Jason takes a few steps with his crutches, pauses to glance at her, then sits in an upholstered chair in the corner.

"I'm actually mortified," Celia continues, dropping the blanket in half over her arm. "It's just that Sal and I used to go to open mic night, and since it was one week since he died, I wanted to go somewhere special to remember him." She stops mid-fold, watching Jason, then looks away from his steady gaze. "That's all."

Jason reaches for the prosthetic liner on the end table, and raises the liner up to the light for a quick visual inspection. After pushing back the fabric of his shorts, he rolls the liner onto the end of his left leg, where it's amputated below the knee. Then he smoothes a sock on over it all—silently, as he methodically prepares to walk.

"Should I go in another room?" Celia asks, her voice a near whisper.

Jason looks up at her standing there, holding the folded blanket close to her chest. "Why?"

"Your leg." She nods to his prosthetic limb leaning against the end table. "It seems personal, the way you're putting it on. I don't know," she says, glancing away with a nervous smile. "Private, maybe. I feel uncomfortable."

All he thinks of is Maris then, and the way she tenderly removes his prosthesis sometimes, particularly when it might be bothering him, or when he's feeling down. Her every slow touch is gentle, her voice a murmur, her massage of his leg loving. "Uncomfortable?" he asks. "How do you think I felt, last night?"

"Oh, Jason. Please." Celia takes a step back, her eyes

tearing up. "Thank you for letting me sleep it off, but I never meant to drink like that."

"That's not what I'm talking about." He inserts his stump into the socket and attaches his artificial limb. "You made a move on me at the bar. I spend time with a lot of people there. Kyle, Nick, Patrick. Good friends."

"I know."

"They'll think I'm having an affair, I'm sure of it."

"No." Celia shakes her head. "Nothing happened."

"Do you even *know* what happened? What do you think they saw?"

"I know what they saw." Her eyes briefly drop closed. "But I didn't mean it. I'm not like that, things just got out of hand … with the drinking, and the sadness."

Jason stands, straightens the fabric of his cargo shorts, adjusts his stance and grabs his keys from the end table. "Let's go."

"Go?" Celia glances to the kitchen slider, then back at him. "I don't need a ride. I'll walk to my cottage."

He hurries past her to the kitchen. "We left your car at the bar."

Never before has a ten-minute drive taken forever. Celia looks over at Jason. He didn't shave this morning; it's apparent by the whiskers on his face. But the dark hair at his collar is damp, so he somehow managed a shower—though how he does so on only one leg, she can't be sure. There must be all kinds of amputee routines in his house, for both him and Maris, which Celia is clueless about. Routines accommodating his mobility.

When they walked along the driveway to his SUV earlier, Celia noticed the barn behind his house. Weathered buoys hung on the outside barnboard walls. Sal used to tell her about Jason's significant architecture studio inside, about the shelves of Neil's leather journals, and the skylights allowing Jason a wide view of the sky over the sea. Jason also added a state-of-the-art loft studio for Maris, so she could work on her denim designs from home.

Celia had never been in the barn; had never known that part of the Barlows' lives. And for certain, never will now. She discreetly adjusts the shoulders of her peasant top and watches only the road. Finally, *finally*, Jason turns into The Sand Bar's parking lot and pulls up beside Celia's car.

"You really need to leave."

"I am," Celia says.

He turns then, and looks directly at her. "You don't belong here, Celia. You had something with Sal, but he's dead and gone. It's time to face that now."

Does Jason know it's only been a week? Does he know how her heart is still reeling? Does he realize how very sorry she is about last night? She says nothing, but reaches for the door handle instead.

"I have my own demons here, and it's not easy."

The darkness of his voice stops her, but Celia does not turn back to Jason. She freezes, though, and listens, having fallen under its spell.

"Shadows, whispers," he says. "In this place, they're so damn real, you think you're going crazy."

There's undeniable anger in his words, and she's afraid to move, to speak. Is he mad at her? At his own demons? At himself? She still won't look, and squeezes her eyes shut for a long moment.

"I have Maris," he continues. "Two years ago, she walked back into my life when I was in a bad way—like you are—and she turned my life around. Maris is my reason for living, for everything. Do you get what I'm saying?"

"No," Celia whispers, finally looking at him over her shoulder, and what she sees is enough. In his expression, in those eyes, there's a turmoil—an undertow—she knows not to engage with.

"There's no one here who will turn *your* life around, and what you imposed on mine in a few hours' time is unacceptable. Go home to Addison. That's where your life is."

Celia's not sure she's ever seen darker eyes. It's all there, in his: rage, sadness, regret. "If I could go back and change last night—"

"You're God damn lucky I *was* there last night. What would've happened to you if I weren't? Some stranger would've moved right in on you, and then what?"

"It was a mistake, Jason." She glances out at her car, wanting only to be in it, putting the key in the ignition. "All of it."

"That's right. And one that screwed up *my* personal life. So here's what you're going to do. Right now. Take your guitar," he says, hitching his head to the backseat, "and go home. Get the hell out of here."

She'll take that as her cue, thank you, and fumbles with the handle, opens the door and practically falls out in her rush. When she opens the back door and reaches in for her guitar, her eyes reluctantly meet Jason's as he watches her every move.

"I helped you out last night," he says. "And now? Now I don't want to see you at Stony Point ever again."

nine

FROM HIS TRUCK, KYLE GLANCES up at that imposing Barlow house. Rays of morning sunlight break through the tall trees, glancing off the gray-shingled, Gothic cottage. Kyle parks his pickup on the street and leans over to see out the passenger window. It's hard to tell if Jason's around, so he gets out and trots up to the front porch, looks at the dusty wooden bench there, at the black lantern sitting on a round table, at a pot of overgrown begonias, then knocks on the door. He waits, wishing he had a smoke as he does, then hurries down the porch steps toward the backyard. Twigs snap beneath his shoes and the grass could use a mowing. Around back, he sees that Jason's SUV is gone, but still … Kyle walks up the stone stairs to the deck and lifts a mug with dregs of coffee in it, before tossing the liquid over the deck railing—which could use a coat of paint. What is it they say about the carpenter's house? It's never done? At least there's only one mug here: Jason's. Hopefully, Nick got it all wrong and Jason was alone last night.

But it's impossible to know what's going on, especially

when Kyle leaves to drive past Celia's place by the marsh. Her car is gone, too. He passes the cottage with its silver-shingled peak, drives to the end of her street, through the turnaround, and continues on.

It's quiet this Wednesday morning, an unfamiliar September sight to Kyle—who's usually here only on vacation in the busy summer months. So he drives down a few more winding beach roads to see if any FOR SALE signs have gone up. On the way, Elsa's rambling inn catches his eye. Scaffolding rises along one side. But with Elsa still in New York, her place is buttoned up tight, idle before the reno resumes.

A block away, there's a familiar FOR SALE sign at the little cottage, Summer Winds. Its paint is peeling, and the front porch is looking shabby. Though the bungalow's small, the lot's decent, so maybe with an addition, it could work for his family. When he drives closer, though, he sees a banner across the sign saying the cottage is UNDER DEPOSIT. Celia's staging must have done the trick.

"Yoo-hoo!" he hears while distracted by the cottage and driving slowly past it. "Ahoy, Kyle!"

So he stops and sees Eva holding a dripping watering can in the side yard. He shuts off his truck and steps outside, taking a deep breath of that salt air.

"What are you doing here today?" Eva asks, her sunglasses propped on top of her head.

"I could ask you the same question." He nods to Summer Winds, still wondering if he and Lauren should've made a move on it.

"Oh, I'm just tending the plants for the new owners, until they move in. Realtor obligations." She points to geraniums and ferns spilling from flower boxes, and to a hydrangea bush with blossoms faded to violet now. "Elsa kept everything watered all summer, but with her busy in New York, I'm helping out."

"Have you talked to her?"

"This morning, I called her on her cell. She's still packing up Sal's apartment. And hey," Eva says, hitting Kyle's arm, "what about you? What are you doing here?"

"Me?" Kyle motions back at his truck. "I brought a nice dinner for Barlow, all packed up from the diner."

"Dinner? But Maris will be home later today."

"Exactly. So I made them something romantic. Lobster-noodle casserole. Ready to heat and eat."

"Oh." Eva glances to the truck seat where Kyle left the insulated case holding the meal. "Usually they go out somewhere, so that'll be a nice treat!"

"Yeah, well." Kyle presses his arm to his forehead. "I don't know if I should say anything, but I heard some news."

"News? Good news, I hope."

He shakes his head. "Nick saw something. I'm not sure I buy it, but he *swears* it's true."

"What's true?" Eva steps closer, squinting at Kyle.

"Okay, I guess Jason was with Celia last night? Nick saw the two of them headed into Barlow's digs …"

"Are you suggesting that Jason Barlow cheated on my sister?"

Kyle shrugs. "Between Maris working in the city, and after Jason's breakdown Saturday, you know, when he left—"

"He left for forty minutes!"

"I know … But maybe Jason and Celia found comfort together while missing Sal?" What Kyle doesn't say is that he *could* kind of get that. After learning last year that his son is actually Neil's, didn't Kyle do the same thing—mess around with another woman? It was Barlow who put a stop to it and helped Kyle get his marriage back on track. "The way they're both grieving, together, you know? I guess you can understand."

"Understand?" Eva sets down her watering can. "Absolutely not. Jason would *never* do that to Maris."

"And I'll bet you never thought he'd drive away from her either, right?"

"That's different." She stamps her foot and looks past Kyle, in the vague direction of the Barlow house on the bluff. "Nick had to see it wrong."

Kyle looks, too, while wiping his forehead again. A lone couple walks past toward the beach, sand chairs in tow, their flip-flops flipping on the sandy road. Kyle waves to them and waits until they're out of earshot before saying more. "According to Nick, what he saw last night seemed very intimate. Arms around each other, ready to roll. Hell, Eva, it could've been a crazy rash decision. So I thought," he explains, turning to Eva then, "well, I'd help Jason and Maris with their marriage. You know, a candlelit, romantic meal for two. But Jason's gone. Celia, too. I went by her cottage."

"You don't think they slept together …"

"I don't know *what* to think. All I know is what Nick saw. Period. And remember, Jason took Sal's death hard. He tries to hide it, but man, he's grieving all over again, just like for his brother. And I read that's when people screw up their decision-making—when they're all emotional. It's a bad time, psychologically. That's when the whole rash decision thing happens."

"I'll give *him* a rash decision. I've had it with Jason lately. If he hurts Maris like that, well, he'll have to deal with me!" She shakes a fist toward the Barlow house. "Maris is my sister, after all."

"Will you tell her?"

She whips around to Kyle. "Not yet. First I'll get to the bottom of this, that's for darn sure. I'll track that Jason Barlow down. Where do you suppose he went?"

"Got to be working. He can't keep up with the jobs lately."

"Wait. Do you think the two of them are still together somewhere?"

Kyle lifts Eva's watering can and pours cold water into his cupped hand. "Don't know," he answers while splashing the water on his face and neck. "Shit, it's hot out."

"But she's not a tramp like that, not Celia."

"Maybe Jason put the moves on *her*. Or maybe I shouldn't have said anything."

"No!" Eva reaches over and clasps his arm. "I'm glad you did."

Kyle pulls his buzzing phone from his pants pocket, then reads the text message. "Hey, do me a favor?" he asks, looking up at Eva.

"Sure."

"It's Jerry on the phone. The diner is mobbed with the lunch crowd and I won't be able to get back here." He walks around to his pickup's passenger door. "Any chance you can deliver this romantic feast?"

~

If there's one thing Elsa DeLuca has gotten good at this past week, it's lying. She evades emails, returns brief text messages and voicemails, and talks on her cell phone as if she's in New York. Not as if she's holed up in her big old beach cottage.

Which she is. When the seashell wind chime clinks outside, she takes her coffee cup from the table and looks out the kitchen window, right to the spot where Jason planted himself all summer with their junk-food breakfasts. Oh, they were so sinfully divine: cinnamon crullers and cheesy ketchuped egg sandwiches and glazed doughnuts. She leans further and sees the scaffolding that's still up, a few sawhorses, a pile of rocks for her new stone wall—all of her renovations stalled this summer by the Hammer Law.

Only Cliff knows she's here at the cottage, and only because he stumbled upon her whereabouts. So she lies to everyone else who calls or emails, telling them she's busy packing Sal's apartment so that they won't fret over her. And it's not as though she *hasn't* been packing Sal's things.

"I have been," she insists to herself before sipping her hot coffee. "Here." She started with Sal's clothes from his bedroom upstairs and couldn't stop. Next thing, there were boxes packed with her belongings, too: linens, mementoes, knick-knacks. Entire closets were emptied.

A sudden motion outside the window catches her eye and makes Elsa quickly duck. She straightens a tiny bit to take a peek. From the edge of the window, she watches, holding the curtain aside and nearly knocking over a starfish propped on the ledge. Silently, while pressed flat against the wall, she spies.

Her niece Eva waters Elsa's geraniums, then walks to the stone patio area around the side and—wait! Elsa hurries to a dining room window for a better spying view. "*What?*" she whispers. Eva picks up a fat piece of chalk and bends down low. Seeing her like that, doesn't Elsa see her own younger self, from years ago? The memory comes right back of the mornings she'd write an inspiration message on the walkway outside her Milan clothing boutique. It's a tradition she hoped to bring to her inn, too.

"What *is* she writing?" Elsa murmurs now. Her niece's grip on the chalk is fierce, her posture rigid. If Elsa didn't know better, she'd say Eva's steaming mad about something. The way she presses the chalk so hard as she writes a sidewalk message, the chalk breaks in half at one point.

Elsa squints and leans closer to see the message, then runs to another window for a better angle. Aha! She can finally make it out: *Seas the day!*

"And that's exactly what I'm going to do," Elsa quietly declares while watching Eva toss down the chalk and leave. "I'm going to *seas* the day, oh yes, and get this packing done. Once and for all!"

So Elsa ties her hair back in a bandana, hurries to the hallway and kicks an empty cardboard carton close to a narrow closet. There, she grabs an armful of old tablecloths she brought over from her villa in Milan last year. After dropping them in the box, she turns back to the closet and stops, glancing to the kitchen while brushing back a wisp of hair.

Something draws her attention again, so she returns to the kitchen window, then goes out the side door, down two rickety steps, and sits, just sits at the little bistro table in the grass—where she'd sat with Jason discussing inn designs on so many summer mornings. It's the same table Sal sat at and read a newspaper while having his morning decaf.

Elsa sits there and looks at the distant blue water glistening in the sunshine. And looks, and looks, and looks, all alone. Like she's done so many times this week.

~

Jason can tell the days are getting shorter by the way the light changes in his studio. Wednesday evening, he sits at his drafting table beneath the skylight, through which the setting sun casts a golden hue on the side wall. When the phone rings, he rolls his stool across the wide-planked wood floor, over to his big L-shaped desk—where invoices are spread out and a calendar is open on his computer screen. At the last second, he lets the call go to voicemail. Customers haven't stopped calling since the Hammer Law lifted; they see construction, and then they want it, too.

But he's got to get started on this latest job, first. So he rolls back to his drafting table and drops a sheet of tracing paper over the current plan. He bends close, his pencil working out lines and angles, pausing to enter dimensions into a calculator, working right through the knock at the door—a knock that gets Madison running across the space to investigate as the barn door opens.

"You're finally home," Jason says without looking over his shoulder, his pencil methodically shading and outlining. "How's it going?"

The voice gets him to spin around. "Eva. I thought you'd be Maris."

"She's not back yet?" Eva asks while patting the happy dog prancing at her feet.

Jason cuffs his sleeve and checks his watch. "Maybe another hour still."

"Oh." Eva walks in slowly, wearing a cropped denim jacket over her tee and black board shorts. Her arms clutch some sort of sack close to her body. As she walks, she glances to Maris' loft studio above. "So how're you holding up, all alone again?"

"I'm good. What do you have there?" He nods to the sack, then turns back to his design. "Something for Maris?"

"Kyle dropped this off for me to deliver," she says from behind him. "A dinner, for you and your wife?"

"Dinner? Something I missed here?" Jason rolls his stool back across the wood floor to his computer and scans the calendar open on the screen. "Some special occasion?"

"I'll say." Now Eva walks toward the shelves of Neil's journals. "It's funny, Jason," she muses while her back is to him. "I've lived here in Stony Point all my life. And I'm finding you hear things you really wished you hadn't."

"Okay, so you're going somewhere with this surprise visit." He glances at the phone, ringing again, then switching to voicemail, before he opens a desk drawer to find a certain architectural scale.

"That's right. Because I don't know who you are anymore. You're not the same guy who married my sister."

Which gets Jason to slam the drawer shut, turn around on his stool and give Eva his undivided attention.

"First," Eva continues while glancing at the framed photos of his completed cottage renovations, "you leave Maris on Saturday. Okay, it was only for forty-five minutes, but still, you left her. And that letter you wrote?"

"It was to *explain* why I left, Eva. You know that."

She takes another few steps, looking at images hung on the far wall while pondering something. "And then, after everything Maris has been through in her life. Settling her father's estate two years ago. Finding out we were sisters after thirty years apart. Thirty years! Almost not getting married last year. To you. So ..." Now she whips around and glares at him. "Are you ever—and don't you dare lie to me—*ever* going to commit to Maris, or not?"

Jason draws his knuckles across the scar along his jaw. "Always."

"You know," Eva says, her voice low as she steps closer to him, still clutching some dinner concoction. "I stopped at Elsa's earlier to water her flowers while she's away. And I wrote on her *inn-spiration* patio, with her chalk? Do you know what I wrote?"

Before he can answer, she raises one hand and waves it brusquely, all while still clutching her package with the other. "I'll tell you," she says, moving closer. With each step she takes, her voice drops even lower. "*Seas the day*. And all I wanted to do was seize your fucking neck! That's right, I said it. I *said* the F-word, because that's how *mad* you make me."

"*I* make you?"

When she nods, tears begin streaking her face. "My sister is the best damn thing that ever, *ever* walked into your life."

"I'm not arguing that." Jason rolls his stool over to his desk then. He takes with him the designs from his drafting table, just in case his irate sister-in-law gets some idea about messing those up in her rant. "And this seems to be a recurring conversation of ours lately."

"You're right." Eva quickly swipes her cheek with the back of her hand. "Because I *know* everyone's upset about Sal. I *get* that." She walks closer still, tightly clutching that dinner sack. "But now I'm even *more* upset about Maris. She's my sister, after all, and this morning I hear you're having sex with *Celia*?"

Jason nearly falls off his stool when he suddenly pulls back—okay, in shock. How the *hell* would last night's Celia episode have ever gotten to Eva's radar ears? He grabs the edge of his desk to stop his tumble. "Eva, Jesus Christ."

"Well? What do you have to say for yourself, Jason?"

"Nothing. Except to ask if you've even *talked* to your sister?"

"No."

"Then where do you get your information?"

"I'm not supposed to say." She looks toward the moose head mounted high on the wall, then back at him. "But it's Kyle, okay? Your …" She shifts that darn dinner in her clutches and manages a one-handed air quote as she says, "*best man.* Kyle and Nick."

Finally, Jason slowly stands and motions to his big, comfortable desk chair rather than his stool—which he's not sure she can manage in her anger. "Come here."

"What?"

"Sit yourself down for this one, and listen up." He points to his chair. "*Now.*" He hears it, as she scoots past him to the chair, the way she whispers *Oh, shit.* "Damn right," he tells her. "You *should* be saying that, and with *fear* for pissing me off like this!"

What she can't see is that her accusation unnerves him.

Just *how* perilously close did he come to permanently screwing up life with his beautiful Maris? The thought alone scares the hell out of him, enough for his hand to tremble as he draws it along his chin. He looks at that hand, shakes it out, then begins talking.

Eva sits straight as a board, watching him with her eagle eyes. But with every sentence of his explanation of the night before, from stopping in at The Sand Bar for a quick sandwich, to Celia coming undone during her drunken performance—which is as much as he reveals—Eva's demeanor softens. She finally sits back in the chair and brushes aside invoices on his desk to make room for that dinner package.

"So she spent the night here, on my *couch*, Eva. To sleep it off, the alcohol and her sadness both."

It happens so fast, Jason doesn't even see it coming. Doesn't see *Eva* coming, such that she nearly knocks him off balance with the way she leaps from the chair and hugs him tightly. "Oh, thank God, thank *God*," she whispers. But then he feels her freeze and quickly back up. "You're *really* not lying to me?"

He can only roll his eyes, first. "You have to believe me. *Ask* your sister, she knows all about it. I called Maris last night and *told* her Celia was three sheets to the wind. And actually, Maris figured it was a good thing I did cross paths with Celia, to keep her out of some other dude's path. Or from hurting herself." He steps closer to Eva. "Which is why *Maris* insisted Celia stay here, for her own safety."

"Oh." Eva gives him an apologetic smile. "Maybe I should go see Celia, then? Poor thing."

"No," Jason tells her quickly, just as his cell phone dings

with a text message. "Let it be now." As he's talking, he reads the message on his cell. "It's from Kyle," he says with an astute look up at Eva. "This is what my *best man* says." But to give Eva a hard time, he walks across his studio floor and lets her sweat it out. "Kyle's asking, his words here, *Friday night fishing this week? Or are you busy?* And the word *busy*?" He holds out his phone for Eva to see. "He typed in all caps, his wussie way of accusing me of having some tryst."

"Oh boy. We goofed, didn't we?"

"Goofed? *That's* what you call it, accusing me of cheating on my wife?"

"But we meant no harm! We're trying to protect your marriage, you're practically newlyweds. And Kyle was so worried about you two! That's why he cooked you a really romantic dinner—to save your marriage. Here it is, with my apology, Jason." Eva nudges the insulated package across the desk. "Lobster-noodle casserole. Already made—oh, Kyle was *so* upset—you just have to heat it up."

Jason reaches past the meal, grabs a few tissues from his desk and gives them to Eva.

"It's just that I'm overprotective of Maris right now," his sister-in-law explains. "All summer, she's been telling me how as soon as she boards the train for New York, she misses everyone here." Eva pauses while dabbing a tissue to her damp eyes. "It's hard to be apart, so I *truly* hope you guys are okay, especially after you left her. On Saturday."

Suddenly the barn door slides open and Maris breezes inside. She's wearing a white blouse with a fitted denim skirt, distressed in all the right places—a frayed patch at the thigh, a shredded tear over her knee. But the beauty of the moment is the way that setting sun shines behind her, casting some sort of halo around his wife's long brown hair.

"Hey, my two favorite people! I'm home!" Maris says while dropping her leather portfolio on a table, all while bending to pat Madison at her feet as the dog circles her and wildly wags its tail. "What'd I miss?" She looks up, first at Eva, then to Jason.

"Nothing, sweetheart," Jason says while walking to her. He tucks her silky hair behind an ear, strokes the back of his fingers along her smooth cheek to beneath her chin, drinking in every molecule of her. That's when he takes her face in both his hands and kisses her deeply—once, then again—deeply enough to catch his own breath before he pulls away and drops his fingers along her gold chain necklace. "Nothing at all."

ten

IT HITS HER, THE NEXT morning.

To step outside and say goodbye would break Celia's heart. Because stepping outside would mean walking on the rickety dock; seeing Sal's rowboat still tied there; hearing the dock post creaking as the wooden boat rises and falls on the flowing water; seeing lingering yellow finches perched atop the cattails lining the banks of the marsh; hearing whispers in the swaying lagoon grasses, which have faded from green to gold; would mean remembering. She had the thought, though, to do it—to bring her guitar out to the backyard dock and softy sing one last song there.

Instead, she puts on her sunglasses and slips on a light cardigan over her long tank top and faded jeans before *closing* the slider to the deck. That's right, it's time to head in the other direction, so she turns and scans the cottage kitchen: toaster and coffeepot shining on the counter, chrome chairs pushed close to the Formica-top table, bowl of faux peaches on that table. After giving a touch to the sea-glass engagement ring on her finger and the sailor's knot bracelet on her wrist, she lifts the last suitcase and carton of decorations before hurrying through the kitchen and living room, straight to the front door.

But the wind chime dangling in the living room window catches her eye. It's strung with ridged white seashells and topped with an entwined, delicately threaded star. Elsa had found two identical wind chimes in the old Foley's cottage, so Sal brought one to Celia. He hung the wind chime there months ago, and the beach breeze got the shells clinking and swaying. *Serenata le stelle*, he told her before waltzing Celia across the room that evening. Serenading the stars.

Her eyes drop closed now, her body slightly swaying with the memory. It suddenly feels that with *every* step through this little cottage, there'll be a sweet memory begging her to stay. To cry. To thumb through photographs with a sigh.

So she sets down her suitcase and box, unhooks the wind chime from the window frame and drops the strung seashells into her carton. Quickly, without looking around to spot a new memory, she tucks in the carton flaps, picks up her things again and makes a beeline for the door. Because right now, her only memory is of Jason's words telling her to get the hell out of here.

Which is why she hurries—stepping outside with her arms full, finagling the door's lock and rushing across the lawn to her car, dropping the suitcase and box into the trunk, then walking to the driver's door.

Where she finally stops, lifts her sunglasses to the top of her head and looks back at the silver-shingled cottage. Only three months ago, she'd hesitantly unlocked that front door with the intention of rethinking her future, beside the sea. She'd wanted only to find some personal happiness after her divorce, and to strum her guitar and search for sea glass on easy summer days. Then, she believed love would only lead to more heartache.

"Isn't that the truth," Celia says as she hikes up her tote, then gets into her car, missing Sal and the cottage already. Funny how her life went and changed from a romantic comedy to a melodrama. From summer rowboat rides and shindigs on the beach to quiet hours alone. From shared super-duper hot fudge sundaes, to only misty photographs capturing fleeting seaside moments.

Oh, she can just see it, a film crew assistant holding that clapperboard indicating the movie—*Celia's Summer Romance*—nearly drawing to a close. Yes, *Scene: "Goodbye," Take: One* would announce this shoot as the clapsticks snap together, cameras rolling.

And … Action! the director would call now on this nostalgic Thursday morning.

So Celia throws the car into reverse and quickly backs down the stone driveway, anxious to get to the final credits and be done with this. A blaring horn stops her, though, and with a pounding heart she slams on the car's brakes.

"*Gesù, Santa Maria,*" she says under her breath while glancing to her rearview mirror. Cliff Raines' golf cart sits half on the lawn, half on the street, as he rushes over.

"Celia! What's going on? Where are you headed so intently?" He stops beside the car as she's opening her window, which is when he also looks at her backseat, where luggage and boxes are stacked roof-high, with blouses and jackets from her closet—hangers included—strewn on top of it all. "You're leaving?"

"Yes. Goodbye. Goodbye, Commissioner Raines."

"Wait. Wait! I thought you were staying. Eva lined up staging jobs …"

"Oh, Eva. Yes, if you wouldn't mind." Celia unsnaps her seatbelt and gets out. "I'm in a hurry," she says over her shoulder while heading to the trunk, where she shoves aside the suitcase and lifts out the box of home decorations, then promptly turns and drops the carton in Cliff's surprised arms. "Could you please give this to Eva? I won't need seaside décor in Addison, and maybe she can use this in her realty business."

Cliff picks up a wooden seagull, looks at Celia, then tenderly sets the bird back in the cluttered box.

"Take it," Celia insists. "If there's anything *you* can use, please be my guest. I'm running late, so if you could mention to Eva, well …" Celia backs toward her driver's seat. "Tell her I had a change of heart. Please?"

"But it feels like there's some misunderstanding here, Celia. What about the pact we all made in Kyle's diner, not to make any rash decisions? Are you sure about this?" He motions with one arm to her over-packed car.

"I'm sure, yes. Goodbye, Mr. Raines." Oh, darn it, won't she miss even this testy beach commissioner? So she gives him a quick, apologetic smile before getting in her car. "Clifton."

As Cliff walks closer, Celia imagines the director standing further away. He'd hold his viewfinder to his eye while framing this farewell shot to capture the sad September marsh beyond. There's such a goodbye, too, in that scenic image of golden grasses against a heartbreaking-blue sky.

"What about Elsa?" Cliff is saying, shifting the stuffed

carton into his other arm. "Aren't you collaborating with her on decorating the inn?"

"No." Celia lowers the sunglasses from her head and puts the car in reverse. "It won't work out, I'm afraid. So I'm going home. And Elsa's in New York still. When she gets back," Celia begins, clasping Cliff's hand that is on the open window of her door, "look after her?"

As she very slowly backs up, Cliff takes hold of that one hand and trots alongside the car, box in tow. "Don't you want to talk to Elsa? I can get her."

"That's okay," Celia says with a glance at his hand still holding hers. "She's in New York."

"Well, no. She's," he says, pausing when he looks down the street. "She's …"

Here, well, the scene is going on too long. So the director would surely roll his two hands over and over, frantically motioning for the actors to speed things up.

"Goodbye, Mr. Raines." Celia pulls her arm back into the car and steers out of the driveway. "Goodbye!" she calls.

While driving along the beach road, she looks in the rearview mirror and sees Cliff standing there, simply watching her while holding her carton. A lobster buoy and decorative lighthouse stick out of the box.

But there *is* no looking back. No, only forward, which she now does. The film crew might have marked her route by placing strategic X's along the road, to keep her in the camera's focus. So she holds her eyes steady ahead, driving toward the railroad trestle over imagined X's on the road. Focusing on leaving. Imagining the view through the camera lens—the arched stone train trestle small in the distance, but getting larger and larger as Celia approaches it, until its dark, damp tunnel is upon her.

"*Goodbye*," she whispers while driving beneath the shadowed archway, the camera now capturing only her diminishing car, and the tap of her brake lights, as she leaves Stony Point behind.

~

Cliff doesn't remember peeling out like this since he was in college. Who knew you could get golf cart tires to actually make a skid? He tears down the sandy street, wildly taking the curves before screeching into Elsa's driveway at the inn. His mad rush doesn't stop there. Getting out and stomping around the construction mess, he abruptly turns back to his golf cart to retrieve a bag there before knocking on Elsa's side kitchen door, promptly opening it and walking into her house.

"Elsa!" he shouts.

"Cliff?"

When Elsa reaches the kitchen doorway, she stops short, wearing cuffed jeans and a knotted-front blouse, with a bandana on her head, rubber gloves on her hands and a worried look on her face.

"What are you doing?" Cliff asks. "*Cleaning?*"

"Yes, actually," Elsa answers while peeling off her gloves.

"But why? It's just going to be a dusty mess once the renovation starts. Won't the workers be here next week?"

"Is that why you barreled into my house? To tell me not to clean? For crying out loud, I heard your squealing golf cart tires a block away." She pulls out a chair and sits at her kitchen table. "Am I breaking an ordinance? Because *you* certainly are!"

"The reason I'm here, Mrs. DeLuca, is to tell you that you have to stop this charade." He slaps his bag on the table beside her and pulls two cheesy egg sandwiches from it, along with a handful of foil ketchup packets.

"What? What charade?"

Cliff pulls out a chair and sits, too. "You can't let people think you're away." He waggles a finger directly at her. "Stop pretending you're *not* here, where you obviously belong."

"Oh, Clifton. It's just for a few days." She gets up and pours two mugs of coffee before returning to her seat. "To think about Salvatore, and to grieve. *Privately*."

Cliff goes to her refrigerator and peers inside. "I doubt you even ate today," he says when bringing cream back to the table. "Aren't these the sandwiches Jason buys you from the convenience store?"

Elsa nods while tearing open a ketchup packet with her teeth.

"Elsa." Cliff adds cream to his coffee and stirs quickly. "Good people are leaving." He tells Celia's story while squeezing ketchup onto his own egg sandwich, then patting the croissant top down flat on it. Between savory bites—when they both quiet at the exquisite, warm, soft mouthfuls of this miracle sandwich—he gives all the details … from the overloaded car, to Celia's tired, tear-stained face, to the box of décor she dropped in his arms. "If she knew you were here, she might not have left. I think she made one of those bad grief decisions."

"And it's for the best, Cliff," Elsa says around a mouthful of egg.

"But you had plans. She was going to decorate the inn ... and help with its vision."

Elsa manages to shake her head while still chewing. "Celia needs to live her own life. To move on now and not dwell in memories."

"She couldn't stay temporarily? Even in a room here, upstairs? Or in that little guest cottage out back? I can clean it up for her ..." Cliff washes down the last of his sandwich with a long sip of hot coffee. "Because you can't manage all this alone," he says over the rim of his steaming cup.

"I can't be her reason to stay here." Elsa lifts the remaining sliver of her croissant and squeezes more ketchup on the bit of gooey cheese and yellow egg, then adds a dash of salt. "Celia was going to marry my son," she's saying. "And he's gone forever now."

Cliff lifts his coffee mug, sets it down, then lifts it again, cups it close to his face and sips, watching Elsa through the steam. She presses that last hunk of sandwich into her mouth, then looks away while dabbing her lips with a napkin.

"But you weren't there." Cliff's voice is quiet. "Her cottage was buttoned up tight, and the way she'd keep crying." He looks over his shoulder, out a window facing the direction of Celia's cottage. "It just doesn't seem right."

~

Fond Adieu. Yes, that's what this next scene would read on the clapperboard of *Celia's Summer Romance. Fond Adieu.* Her dear beach friend, Lauren Bradford, waits outside The Driftwood Café. She wears a long dress with a high-low hem, and her sun-bleached blonde hair hangs straight from beneath a floppy straw hat. But it's the way she's smiling as Celia pulls into the parking lot, waving her over toward the outdoor patio, which gets Celia thinking *fond adieu.* What else would you call a farewell to a summer friend? It's all Celia can do to not start crying as she parks and walks over.

"I'm so glad you could meet me," she tells Lauren, mid-hug.

"I haven't see you since our breakfast, Sunday." Lauren steps back, leaving a hand on each of Celia's shoulders as she scrutinizes her. "It's been a few days. How are you holding up?"

"I'm not. I'm actually leaving. That's why I called you."

"What?" Lauren tips her head to squint out at her from beneath that floppy hat.

"To say goodbye." Celia motions toward the parking lot. "My car's all packed."

Lauren looks out at Celia's car, then back at Celia. "Are you kidding?"

"No."

"What about Elsa? You were going to work on the inn with her."

"I don't think anyone knows where that beach inn stands now."

"But *we* were going to work together, too. You and me. Coordinating the décor with my driftwood centerpieces and staircase mural."

Celia shifts her tote on her shoulder. Beyond Lauren, a distant harbor with sailboats bobbing on the blue water catches Celia's eye. Wouldn't the movie camera be panning there to capture that view in this emotional scene? A scene she must keep moving. "Everything's different now, Lauren. So I changed my mind, that's all. I'm going home."

"But this is so sudden, Cee. We made a pact, no rash decisions!" Lauren takes Celia's hand and tugs her along to a patio table where muffins and a carafe of coffee await them beneath the shade umbrella. "And Eva set up more cottage staging jobs for you," she says over her shoulder, her long dress fluttering in the wind.

"You don't understand." The problem is, Celia really *can't* explain it, not fully. Not including Jason's unmistakable words to her yesterday, words that followed a kiss too intimate, too wrong. Words that got her quickly packing: *You don't belong here, Celia ... Take your guitar and go home ... I don't want to see you at Stony Point ever again.*

Instead, Celia keeps things vague when she sits at the table while Lauren fills their coffee cups. "Without Sal here, my heart's not in it. In *any* of it."

Lauren sits, adjusts the gauzy fabric of her dress beneath her, sets her straw hat on an empty chair, pours cream into her coffee—does anything, it seems, except talk. Until she finally does, and then, okay, Celia *gets* the delays.

"Does this have anything to do with Jason?" Wire bracelets on Lauren's wrist jangle as she nudges over a blueberry muffin.

"Jason?"

After a quick breath, Lauren squeezes Celia's hand. "Celia, there are no secrets at Stony Point. You know that."

"How in the world—" Celia begins, then lifts her coffee cup.

Lauren leans close, whispering, "So, did you *sleep* with Jason?"

Which gets Celia to sputter on a mouthful of coffee. To hear put into words the actuality of what *almost* happened, well, the reality of it all scares the *hell* out of her. Damn this little beach town with its thin cottage walls and close neighbors and prying eyes.

"It's just that Kyle told me something, Celia."

"Kyle?"

"It started with Nick, actually. He drove by Sea View Road on his guard duty, and I guess he saw you and Jason leaning into each other, intimate-like, and headed inside the Barlow house? I was so surprised. I mean, I can't believe you'd do that, you know, mess around with a married man." She squeezes Celia's hand. "With *Jason*."

And what it all is, Celia thinks as she leans back and takes a long sip of her coffee beneath the shade umbrella at the patio table, is this: All the more reason to leave. This will be the one and only time that she'll explain her night with Jason, so that she can then put the *entire* summer behind her.

"I *was* with Jason, but not in the way you're thinking." Her story comes out in classic Stony Point style—between mouthfuls of coffee and warm, buttery blueberry muffins—most of it, anyway. From being alone at The Sand Bar missing Sal, to the several drinks dulling her pain, to her drunken open-mic performance, to Jason helping her off the stage and safely out of the bar. "I'm okay now. Jason had me sleep it off on his couch. Though I can assure you he was *not* happy about that."

"Ouch." Lauren winces. "I'll bet."

"But nothing happened, I swear. He just got me out of a *bad* situation."

"Oh, Celia. That's not the word around town. What a mess."

"And no one has to worry. Jason and Maris are so solid, believe me. Nothing can come between them." She sips her coffee. "And nothing did. But that's not why I'm here. I called you today to say goodbye."

"But this is so sudden."

"Not really." As Celia says it, she's more surprised than she'd expected at the tears escaping Lauren's eyes.

"You can move forward, Cee, past everything. You'll keep busy with the inn, it'll help. And isn't your dad staying at your house in Addison, taking care of it?"

Celia abruptly stands, feeling trapped by the fishnet draped from white stockade fence panels behind them. Trapped by Lauren's questioning eyes. By Jason—his kiss and his words. Celia reminds herself there's no looking back. Only forward. Oh, wouldn't that camera operator move in for a close-up now, as Celia's imminent departure signifies an emotional moment the director wouldn't want to miss.

"I'm sorry," Celia whispers. "I really need distance. And I need to ask you a huge favor, beach friend to beach friend."

"Anything!" Lauren says, standing, too.

"I'm asking that you don't try to reach me. Please."

"But—"

"No. Try to understand it's for the best, Lauren." Well, now … Now, there's no stopping the tears streaking Celia's own face, tears certain to glimmer on her emotional close-up. It might feel better if she could confide about how she and Jason kissed—maybe Lauren would reassure her—but there's no way Celia can reveal the very personal, sexual line she crossed with him. One that put her on the outs here, because there's no possibility of getting back to the *other* side of that line—the memory of their time on a dance floor in a dusky beach bar is just too potent.

"All of our paths crossed this summer," Celia says, instead. "But that's all it was. A summer thing. Maybe we'll meet again one day … on the highways and byways." She backs away while talking, even as Lauren reaches out her hand.

"Celia. We *all* have memories, good and bad. You have yours, and I have a sad love story of my own I can tell you. I've *been* where you are, and *I'm* still here. Still looking for a house in Stony Point. I can help you through this." She pushes in a chair and moves around the table, closer to Celia. "I once lost someone so suddenly, too!"

"You had Kyle to help you. There's no one here for me."

"What about all of us? The whole gang?"

Celia shakes her head, barely able to see through her tears.

"I can't help but think this is a terrible misunderstanding. The inn renovations are starting up next week!"

Celia backs further away, her damp eyes focused on her friend. Everything about this beach town, about even Lauren—with her long, summery blonde hair; and lightly freckled nose; and concerned face; and sunhat; and wire, seaside charm bracelets—all of it reminds Celia only of the happy times she's lost forever.

Lost to a slow song on a jukebox, to Jason's deep kiss

and a lovers' dance that should never have happened. To a few minutes she can no longer face. She desperately glances about for something to say, knowing how she'd so need a cue card to guide her dialogue on a movie set. Words are just failing her.

Lauren nearly trips on a chair leg as she rushes around the patio table toward her. "But what about Elsa?"

"Goodbye, Lauren." Celia leans in for a quick hug, whispering into Lauren's hair, "Goodbye," before pulling herself away and trotting through the bright sunshine to her waiting car.

~

So that's it, Celia thinks an hour later when she turns onto her street in Addison. After this one last scene, *Celia's Summer Romance* will be a wrap.

Quiet on the set! an assistant would first call out as the director orders the cameras to roll. And so the clapperboard snaps on *Scene: "Home Again," Take: One.*

She can envision how the camera would pan this country lane—a far cry from the sandy roads of shingled cottages and bungalows at Stony Point, from the salty breezes ever lifting off Long Island Sound. Here, the lens would capture the curve of the street leading to a red barn, where the swaying, wispy top of a lush cornfield is golden at summer's end, before segueing to her, behind the wheel of her car.

The peaked and rambling colonials gladden and sadden Celia at once; the weeping willow trees remind her of her own recent weeping—both from grief, and from shame. She drives further, seeing the crumbling stone wall reaching down the length of the street. Over the next few days, she imagines she'll sit on the front porch of her best friend's farmhouse. Amy will want to know everything.

But not yet. For now, Celia's headed home. There, on the right. Her yellow bungalow with its white picket fence, and the front stoop she loves to sit on. She turns in the driveway, shuts off the car engine and takes a long breath. Safe. Yes, here in Addison, she finally feels safe.

Safe enough to get out of the car and run up the few steps to her front door, open it wide and go inside.

"Dad? I'm home!" she calls out.

"Celia?" Her father's voice comes from the kitchen, so she heads that way.

"What are you doing here?" he asks while pulling work gloves off his hands. "I thought you were staying on, at the beach?"

Celia gives her father a hug in such a way that he can't see her eyes squeeze back new tears, can't see her take another quick breath to recover. "No. I changed my mind."

The windows are open, and in the wind rustling the September leaves outside, doesn't Celia hear it? The whisper is enough to get her to walk toward the paned window looking out onto the yard, the yard where Sal lined up sparklers on the Fourth of July. She leans her hands on the sill, listening. *Sorridi, my Celia.*

And so she does. She turns with a smile to her father. "It's time to get back to work, here!"

"Are you sure?"

She quickly nods, still smiling.

"I'll help bring in your bags," her father says, taking a step toward the door.

"No!" Another smile—difficult, but it's there. "No, Dad. You finish what you were doing."

"I just came in for some water. I was raking up the acorns, out back."

"That's good. I heard there are so many this year."

"Could mean a bad winter, according to weatherman Leo Sterling."

"Then you finish up and I'll get my bags. It's better for me to stay busy."

He nods and watches her for a long second before reaching over and touching a wisp of her hair. Turning then, he pulls on his gloves and heads outside to the yard, where Celia sees a rake leaning against the deck railing.

It takes a while to empty her car as she lugs things indoors. First, she hefts one heavy armload of her closet clothes. Then, boxes—one after the other, up the front stoop, through the doorway, down the hall—until finally, her guitar. She sets it in her bedroom with the rest of her things.

Her bedroom, with one day's memories everywhere she looks. If Celia lets herself, she feels every touch of Sal's on that hot July night. Oh, that would definitely have been a closed set in her personal movie: no one else allowed but the director, assistant director and cinematographer as the sultry night unfolded.

And doesn't their love scene unfold now as a flashback in her movie. The bedroom windows were open, the air warm. And Sal's fingers—unraveling her French braid, one thick strand at a time as he worked his way through her hair. Fingers that then dropped to the tiny buttons on her seersucker blouse, a blouse gently slipped off her shoulders before they lay on her bed. On the bed where he removed her lace bra, his touch stirring, and unending.

It's enough of a memory to bring her to the bed now, to sit on its edge and see the half shutters on her windows, and the silk scarves hanging from a pegged wall rack, the exact way she saw them that night. That night when Sal first moved over her beneath the cool sheet as the slatted moonlight shone through the blinds, and Sal's kiss, and mouth, and touch, made sure that wonderful wasn't enough of a word to describe the feeling.

The September wind outside blows now and she goes to the window, leaning close, letting it brush tears off her face.

"Celia!" her father's voice calls through the house.

She swipes those tears and rushes to her bedroom door. "What is it, Dad?"

"I'm off to Luigi's for a take-out pizza. Be back soon."

Once he's left, Celia goes outside. She crosses her backyard to the garden shed where items are stored for her home staging. She knows just what she's looking for, and exactly where it is. Second shelf on the right, a large flowered trinket box, which she takes back inside to her bedroom. There, she gently lifts off the box lid.

Because before she can unpack *anything*, she has to empty one particular cardboard carton. After unfolding the carton flaps, she pulls out, first, several pieces of sea glass that she and Sal collected on the beach. She sets them in the trinket box. Frosted sea glass of blue and green, pieces that she'd wrapped in a silk scarf to protect. There's a stick of driftwood, too, from the beach at the secret shack they'd often escape to. And photographs, so many pictures: some Sal took of her strumming her guitar; a few of him alone, his dark eyes always loving; one of him in his beloved rowboat; a couple of Sal sitting with Jason on the boardwalk—Jason's smile ready and true. After seeing those, she can't look at the rest. So she tucks them all back in an envelope and puts them in her flowered trinket box. On top of the photo envelope, she lays the ice-cream stand's menu on which Sal had written his custom-made-up-flavor: *Love Potion by the Ocean.* And then, a dried hydrangea blossom he plucked from a bush beside the bench on the beach dune.

Lastly, Celia lifts out the seashell wind chime, gives it a slight shake and watches the shells clink together beneath the threaded star. She walks to her open bedroom window and considers hanging it there. A light wind might clatter the white seashells, bringing a hint of the beach breeze she and Sal both loved. Is there a way for her to savor the sweetness of their summer? She holds the strung shells up to the window screen so the summer wind faintly jangles them.

And it works; the sound brings her to the sea again as she senses a salt-air caress. A beach breeze bringing every sweet summer memory she shared with Sal.

But there's something else, too. It's what she just ran from, leaving Stony Point behind. With every sway of the seashells comes an overwhelming sadness. Because didn't Sal come into her life much like a beach breeze, touching her heart one moment, then fading away. Every stirring of the dangling seashells will bring her that—sweetness and sadness, together. It's more than she can bear, so she turns and drops the wind chime into the trinket box.

A trinket box holding the special items once intended to

fill Celia's very first happiness jar. But now? Now, she doesn't want these things in a clear Mason jar where she'll see them always. Where she'll be tempted to make the delicate star dance above the swaying strung seashells. Where she'll be so painfully reminded of a love she briefly had in her life.

Instead, the mementoes will stay in this box. A pretty box with a lid, closed up tight.

But first, she nestles her sailor's knot bracelet and blue sea-glass engagement ring beside the dried flower blossom, before setting the lid on top of the box. She carries it to her closet and reaches for an open space on the upper shelf. It'll do. Right there. Always within sight, but not easy enough to look into often. As she raises her arms and slides the box onto the shelf, the house is silent.

Forever imagining her life like a movie, Celia has no doubt even the film crew would be choked up at this point, having filmed her sweet romance in reels and frames all summer long. No one saw it coming—the abrupt ending that turned her exquisite love story into a misty memory already fading. She pictures the director off to the side, regretful that *Celia's Summer Romance* ended like this.

That's a wrap, the director's voice would say, and it would take a minute for the crew to start moving, start talking again on the quiet set, with the story played out.

Suddenly the front door slams shut. "I'm back," Celia's father announces. "Got the pizza. Just the way you like it."

"Okay, Dad." Celia tucks the flowered box further back on the shelf. Stony Point, and everything about it, is history now. She walks toward her bedroom door with only one glance at the closet. "I'm coming."

eleven

FRIDAY EVENING, JASON LOOKS PAST the nautical red, blue and yellow lobster buoys hanging from Eva's deck posts. Beyond them, a dark stream winds through the lagoon grasses. Fireflies flicker beneath a rising crescent moon at the very first Meet-and-Eat dinner, right on Eva and Matt's deck overlooking the marsh.

"Hey, guy," Matt says, approaching with two cans: one beer, the other soda. He gives the beer to Jason. "I've been thinking about that media room you're working on." He snaps open his can and motions it up to the house roof. "Maybe we can add a dormer, to give more space in the attic?"

Jason swigs the cold beer. "Possibly. I'll give you a couple of options, initially, before I get too deep in the design."

"Sup, bro," Kyle says as he saunters over holding a large plastic container of some casserole or goulash he likely whipped up at the diner.

"What've you got there?" Jason asks, nodding to the food.

Kyle cracks open the lid, enough for them to see inside.

"What is it?" Matt leans close and squints in the dusky light.

"Deluxe macaroni salad. Added ground beef, red onion, pickle relish." Kyle grabs a spoon off Eva's teak deck table. "Try some."

Jason snatches the spoon and takes a scoop, which he manages in one mouthful. "Oh, man."

"Good?" Kyle tips his head, waiting.

"Shit. To-beat-the-band good."

"Let me try." Matt grabs a fork from the table and cups a dripping heap. "You cooked this? I could make a meal out of this grub."

"Hey, hey," Eva warns as she swoops upon them and seizes their flatware. "Give me that," she orders. "And that, too," she tells Kyle as she pulls the container from his hands. "You guys will ruin your appetites. Sheesh, we're almost ready to sit down and eat." She sets the macaroni salad on her teak table and switches on the twinkly lights entwined around the patio umbrella spokes before rushing back into her kitchen where the ladies are arranging the buffet.

Kyle leans on the deck railing just as Cliff approaches from the side yard. He holds a bottle of Verdicchio, which he sets on the table. "We could use a nice bottle like that fishing later," Kyle says to him. "Bring a few red cups, then sip and fish."

"Fishing?" Cliff asks.

"We do it every Friday night," Kyle explains. "Cast off from the rocks, usually. Reel in a few, bullshit, have some food and drink."

"Sometimes we grab a boat somewhere," Jason mentions. "Drift out on the Sound."

"That right?" Cliff walks to the deck railing and looks toward the marsh where the low setting sun casts a red-gold hue on the sweeping grasses.

"I can't make it tonight," Matt says. "Working the graveyard shift."

"Too bad," Jason tells him with a shove. "Bones and albies are biting."

"Really?" Kyle asks. "The little tuna?"

"Yup. Water's warm, just the way they like it." Jason raises his beer can toward the distant Long Island Sound.

"Albie." Cliff leans on the deck railing beside Kyle. "Isn't that a big fish?"

"Not off the rocks, near shore. Five, six pounds maybe. Bigger ones out in the deep waters." Kyle makes a whistling sound as he motions like he's casting off.

"Let's go, guys," Eva calls out as the women emerge through the slider to the deck. "Food's on."

They settle at the table, Jason snagging a seat beside Maris. He touches her low, silky ponytail and kisses the side of her head before reaching past her for the platter of chicken cutlets.

"So," Maris suggests, "you're just showering me with affection to get to the food?"

"The good stuff, anyway," Jason admits as she slides the platter closer to him.

"Where's Taylor tonight?" Maris asks her sister.

"Oh, she had a school thing going on." Eva checks her watch.

"Riiight. Convenient excuse." Kyle points his loaded

fork at Eva and Matt. "How old is she now? Fifteen?"

"Yes, and watch it," Matt says. "Our daughter is actually tallying votes from a student council election."

"That's not what we tallied at fifteen." Kyle looks from Matt to Jason. "Remember that time we lined up—"

"Hey," Eva says, cupping her ears. "I don't want to hear it."

"Sorry." Kyle throws her a wink when Lauren slaps his arm. "Tay's a good kid. You guys are lucky."

"She is, and she should be home any minute," Eva says while pouring herself a glass of the white wine. "I'm more worried about Celia, who I still can't believe is not here. I *never* thought she'd up and leave."

"I had coffee with her yesterday," Lauren tells them. "She was so sad, saying there were too many painful memories here. She tried to convince me that there are lots of staging jobs in Addison, before the holidays. But I think she just has a broken heart." Lauren grabs two of Maris' specialty deviled eggs and samples one. "I really miss her," she adds around a mouthful.

"Should we call her?" Maris asks. "It's so odd how she packed everything up like that."

When Lauren and Eva glare at Kyle, he leans back, both hands held up defensively. "Hey, if there was any misunderstanding behind her leaving, it was with good intentions." With that, he grabs a napkin and dabs his forehead while looking to Jason with a shrug. "I give you my word, dude. I would *never* gossip like that. We thought it was true."

All Jason wants to do is evade any talk of that night with Celia. So he leans to Maris and asks her to pass the corn-on-the-cob plate.

"Misunderstanding?" Maris asks the table.

"To put it mildly. Nice job, Kyle." Lauren stands up and straightens the denim vest over her long tee while setting her sights on Jason. "Please let me apologize for my husband. Kyle *did* think he was helping. Because, Jason, you seemed really down after Sal's funeral, and Kyle was worried about you. So when Nick called him that night—"

"Hey, guys," Nick interrupts with a friendly wave as he rounds the back corner of the cottage.

"Oh, the snitch is here," Kyle says.

"What?" Nick pauses in the shadows. "Snitch?"

Lauren sits down and jabs her fork at the air while talking around a mouthful of food. "I'm a witness. Heard the whole conversation on speakerphone."

"Conversation?" Nick asks while stepping onto the deck.

"About Celia?" Lauren then holds up her open palm and secretly points to Jason behind it. "And you know who?"

"Shit. Are you kidding me?" Nick walks around the table and hits Cliff on the shoulder to get him to move over. "Are we still talking about that fiasco?" Nick asks while sitting and running a hand over his goatee.

"Now that Celia ran off and left, yes, actually," Eva assures him. "We are."

Nick turns to Jason. "Hey, I'm sorry, man. I'm telling you it was dark."

"Nice out." Jason spoons himself more of the macaroni salad. "You couldn't give a shout and ask if everything was okay? Because I'm telling you, Nicholas. I could've used a little help that night."

"He was afraid of you," Kyle says as he spears two breaded cutlets.

"As well he should be," Jason adds.

"What?" a couple voices ring out in the twilight, beneath the twinkly lights, forks half-lifted. "*Afraid?* Of *Jason*?"

"Heck, yeah," Nick mutters. Eva hands him a clean plate across the table as Cliff passes him the remaining scraps of chicken cutlets.

"This is about the night Celia was drunk?" Maris asks, leaning close to Jason. "When you called me?"

Jason nods. "It seems Nick saw me help Celia inside, misinterpreted the situation and got the rumor mill spinning."

"Eh, he had good intentions, man," Kyle says. "You know, keeping tabs after you left the Mrs."

"I'm really sorry, Barlow," Nick says. "I just didn't know."

When Maris nudges Jason, he figures it's time to end all this and move on. So he does it; he raises his beer can. "I accept your apology, Nick."

"You *do*?" Nick snaps open a can of beer and raises it, too. "Sweet."

"But someday, I'm going to need a favor. And," Jason says before taking a long swig of his own beer, "I'm just going to *look* at you and you'll know."

"I'll know?" Nick squints across the table at Jason.

"Damn straight. You'll know it's payback time."

~

Maris reaches over and clasps Jason's arm. The past few days have been difficult for everyone. Which is why she's glad they're all gathered *here*, on Eva's deck, on this beautiful

Friday night. If only Aunt Elsa were back from New York; she'd love this, being near the whispering lagoon grasses, seeing the lingering fireflies of late summer.

"Now you see?" Kyle is asking the beach friends gathered around the table. "This is exactly what I meant after Sal's funeral. Rash decisions get made—Jason leaving, and now this mess with Celia—and then *everyone* gets stressed out. So we have to *honor* the vow we made."

"Listen," Maris says. The sun has sunk behind the lavender horizon; the salt air rises thick from the lagoon. "Let's toast to that vow again."

"I'll second that," Nick says.

"Absolutely no more rash decisions!" When Maris raises her wineglass, she waits until *every* drink at the table is lifted. "Our solemn toast … together." She stands with her raised glass, then sips her wine, prompting everyone else to drink from theirs, too. As she sits, Kyle stands.

"*Amici e vini sono meglio vecchi*," Kyle declares, then sips his beer.

A silence falls over them all, until Matt calls out, "Dude, what the?"

"It's an Italian proverb Sal used to say," Kyle explains, "meaning friends and wine improve with age."

"Cheers to that," Lauren agrees.

"Man, do I miss the Italian," Kyle continues as he sits again. "You know that he'd *insist* we take care of our friends, like our wines," he says with a nod to the Verdicchio on the table. "Both bring happiness."

"Look at Elsa!" Eva pipes up. "She should be our role model."

"Elsa?" Cliff asks.

"Yes!" Eva nods vigorously. "She took *control* of the

situation and went straight to New York to handle her son's affairs. She's methodical and *thoughtful* about her decisions. Nothing rash!"

"It's true," Maris says. "I talked with her on the phone all week."

"And how is she?" Lauren asks.

"She seems good. But I've been crazy busy at work and could never find a time to meet up with her in the city." Maris looks at Cliff, who is shifting around the food on his plate. "She *is* okay, though. Right, Cliff?"

"Not sure, really." Cliff fork-slices a cutlet and dips the piece into his macaroni salad before putting the whole hunk in his mouth. "Thought she looked pretty tired."

"Wait." Jason leans across the table and snags another corn on the cob. "*Looked?* You've seen her?"

In the quiet that follows, all Maris hears is the sound of lapping water in the lagoon. Beyond the deck umbrella's twinkling lights, a few fireflies hover as though eavesdropping on their conversation.

Cliff clears his throat, sips some of his drink, then takes a breath. "Hell, I'm not supposed to say anything. The thing is, Elsa *swore* me to secrecy. Even *I* wasn't supposed to know, but I stumbled upon her when I went to water plants at the inn."

"The inn?" Eva abruptly stands, her chair nearly falling to the ground. "She's *here*?"

First Cliff nods, then clears his throat again. "She wanted some alone time and hoped everyone might move on. And not fuss over her."

"But what's she doing home? I thought she was packing in the city?" Maris asks.

"Oh, she *is* packing Sal's things. But here. She's not in New York. It was too sad there, so she came back right away."

"Wait a second." Kyle stands, spins his chair backward and sits again with his hands clasped over the top of it. Then he eyes Cliff. "Are you saying that she's been at Stony Point all week?"

"I am." Cliff adds a splash of wine to his glass and gives a reluctant shrug.

"Cliff," Kyle continues. "This sounds serious, the way she decided to keep it from us."

"I'll tell you what it sounds like." Lauren stands now. "It sounds like a rash decision to me."

"To me, too!" Maris says, standing with the other two women.

"And we made a pact! Lean on each other!" Lauren eyes Maris and Eva. "Ladies? Are you thinking what I'm thinking?"

"Absolutely," they both answer together. "We're going to Elsa's."

Already, Maris is clearing the table. The clatter of dishes and silverware are all she hears now. Gone is the gently flowing water, the sea breeze rustling the marsh grasses, the peace. Now there's an urgency. "Let's clean up and go ambush Elsa with love," Maris insists. "I'll start stacking, you ladies bring everything inside."

"I'll make up a plate of food for Elsa." Eva grabs the macaroni salad bowl. "She probably hasn't eaten right all week."

"Pack something for me, too," Matt tells her. "For a snack later at work."

"Okay. Hurry, you can't be late." When Matt points to the kitchen slider, Eva turns and sees Taylor there. "Perfect. Tay can come with me and the ladies." Balancing a big plastic bowl in one hand, two wineglasses in the other, Eva eyes Kyle and Jason still working on grabbing more food before it's all cleared off. "And why don't you two go along fishing now? We've got this under control."

"I'm fishing, too," Nick chimes in, snagging a handful of potato chips.

Kyle pushes a deviled egg in his mouth. "Yo, Commish," he says while standing up and spinning his chair back into place. He hands Cliff a clean napkin and points to his face. "You might be needing this once Elsa realizes you ratted her out."

Cliff takes the napkin and blots his perspiring forehead.

"Commissioner Raines, of ironclad ordinances?" Nick shakes his head and waggles a potato chip at him. "Your Stony Point secret is no more."

Maris slides a plate away from Jason, and another from Kyle, who resists and pulls back.

"Pack us some of that, would you?" Kyle asks. "To take fishing."

Maris looks from Kyle, to Jason. "I suppose you want dessert, too?"

"You bet," Jason says. "Didn't your sister bake something?"

"Chocolate cake," Eva says, rushing back to the table with an empty container for Maris to fill. "Comfort food. *That's* what this night was supposed to be about." She glares at Cliff. "Not keeping secrets. But about *comforting* each other!"

As Maris slices thick slabs of the sweet cake and wraps them in napkins, she glances over at Cliff, who's been very quiet these few minutes. "My aunt will be mad that you blew her cover. How are you going to explain this to her?"

"I'm not." Cliff pushes back his sleeve and squints at his watch beneath the twinkly lights. Then he gets up, walks to the deck railing where weathered lobster buoys hang from various rails. Finally, he looks back to the guys, hands turned up hopefully. "You fellas have an extra fishing rod by any chance?"

twelve

ELSA'S BEEN CAREFUL TO KEEP only one lamp on at night; a dim one, in her living room. It's the same lamp every night, so that to her nieces, or Jason, or anyone who knows her, it seems like it's a lamp on a security timer, while she's away. It's all a part of her charade.

Tonight, she sits with her laptop in the shadowy living room, reading an email from a neighbor in Milan inviting Elsa to come for a visit. *Buonasera, amica! You might feel better getting away for a few weeks, for a vacanza.* But before Elsa can picture vacationing at her friend's pretty stone villa, she's distracted by a vehicle's tires speeding onto the crunchy stones of her driveway. It must be Cliff; he's been out of control with that golf cart of his lately. Quickly, she sets aside the laptop and hurries to the window, expecting to see him there.

Not expecting to see four *women* crammed in a golf cart: Maris, Eva, Lauren and Taylor. "Okay," Elsa says. "Take a deep breath." She flattens herself along the wall and peers out from the curtain edge. "Maybe they'll go away." But when the women march—that's right, *march*—straight to her door, it's obviously time for a plan. So Elsa scans the room, then runs to the taped cartons near the hallway and slides each box behind the sofa, one at a time, all six of them.

Just as the loud knocking and doorknob rattling begins.

"Maybe they don't know for *sure* I'm home," Elsa whispers. With her foot, she nudges one of the boxes to buy a few seconds. A few seconds more of persistent, okay, *pounding* on the door now. So she moves closer to it, stopping at a wall mirror to tuck back loose strands of hair and pat her face with a tissue from her cardigan pocket.

"We know you're in there, Aunt Elsa!" Eva yells. "Open up, and we're *not* taking no for an answer!"

But Elsa still hides as she presses herself along the hallway wall and sidles to the door.

"Elsa!" Maris calls out. "You open this door. And right *now*!"

Okay, so it's the moment of truth. "Breathe," Elsa repeats. "You can do this." With that, she sweeps the front door wide open. "What in the *world*! What is all this racket, when I just got back from the city?"

"Oh, no you don't," Lauren insists as she pushes in front of the others. "No more lying."

If Elsa had to describe what happens next, she can come up with only one word: avalanche. That's what it feels like she's caught beneath as the four women storm into her cottage like a landslide washing over her. There are hugs, and more hugs, and tears. Someone touches her hair, her cheek, takes her hand. Lights are switched on, illuminating the rooms as everyone bustles around and sets down containers of food. The women's voices are fluid with love and worry about how pale Elsa looks, and how she's gotten thin, and she should come, sit down.

But the entire flurry stops still when her nieces spot the packed boxes, many of them containing *Elsa's* things. They surely can't miss this, not with the way each box has been labeled with a thick black marker.

"Elsa?" Maris points to one in particular. "What is going on here?"

"What do you mean?" Elsa leans over and squints at the box.

"It seems like you're, well …" Maris looks from Elsa to the boxes, then walks slowly to the sofa and reads each labeled box. "If I'm not mistaken, it seems like you're—"

"Moving?" Eva asks, huddled right behind her sister, Maris, but looking over her shoulder at Elsa.

"Oh, those." Elsa, well, what she does is walk to the kitchen. Heck, they have to follow her, right? They're not going to stand and stare at packing cartons. "Think, Elsa, think," she whispers while crossing the kitchen floor to the coffeemaker on the counter.

"Elsa?" Lauren asks, slowly drawing out her name. "Spill it, girlfriend."

"You're fussing over nothing," Elsa replies while doing *anything* but look at them. Instead she brings the coffee decanter to the sink and fills it with water. "I had so many things to move out of the way for, well, for the *reno*. Yes, that's it." She glances over her shoulder. "You know, before the demo crew gets here, and the carpenters. And since I was packing Sal's belongings, it seemed like a good idea to clear the way for construction. At the same time." Then, she does it. Puts the icing on her lie. She simply shrugs and returns to the coffeemaker.

And it works. Behind her, Eva is opening containers of food while Maris lifts a stack of plates from the cupboard. "Well. Okay," Maris is saying. "Okay, then. I guess that makes sense."

With a quick glance, Elsa sees Lauren reaching for wineglasses from another cabinet before opening the silverware drawer. But it's Taylor who innocently *deflects* her lie.

"I'm coming over after school to do my homework *here* from now on, Auntie." She walks to the counter beside Elsa and slides over the big seashell mugs. "To keep you company."

Surprising herself, Elsa tears up at her grandniece's offer. Tears up and runs her hand along Taylor's straight, sun-lightened blonde hair.

"And *I'll* be freezing you ready-to-eat comfort meals, plus you'll come to my place for dinners." Eva shakes a stern finger at her as she says it.

"And, dear Aunt Elsa," Maris adds when she comes up behind Elsa and wraps her arms around her waist. "*I'm* going to stop by and sit in the garden with you." Still behind her, Maris rests her chin on Elsa's shoulder. "I might even sneak over an egg sandwich. You're skin and bones," she admonishes with a squeeze.

Tears continue to streak Elsa's face as she turns and finally faces them.

"What's the matter, Aunt Elsa?" Taylor asks.

Lauren, plucking forks and knives from the drawer, looks back at Elsa.

"Nothing," Elsa manages with a sob. "It's just, oh, come *here*!" She opens her arms wide and Maris, Eva and Taylor crowd close in one embrace. "My beautiful *famiglia*!" Holding them in her arms, what started as tears changes to teary smiles. Because they're all together. Safe, and together.

Even Lauren turns—clutching a handful of silverware—and with her free hand, blows Elsa a silent kiss across the room.

After a little more fussing about where to sit and eat—too cold outside on the deck, kitchen table too small—they settle at the long, wood-planked dining room table. One by one, each woman sits in a navy French country chair, gathered around plates and chicken cutlets and corn on the cob and salads and flickering tabletop lanterns scattering wavering candlelight.

Eva nudges an overloaded dish in front of Elsa. "Eat!"

"*Mangia, mangia, che ti fa' bene,*" Elsa softly says.

"Eat, eat, it'll do you good?" Maris asks.

As she forks a hunk of chicken and macaroni salad, Elsa nods. And smiles, too.

"In the meantime ..." Lauren says in no uncertain terms as she opens one of the dining room windows. "Let's get some fresh salt air in here." Instantly the lace curtain lifts in a sea breeze off the distant water. With a deep breath, Lauren turns to Elsa. "Cures what ails you."

~

Jason's been out here on the rocks plenty of times when the sky is dark; when that slice of crescent moon doesn't drop much illumination on the water. This is when he likes it: hearing the small splash of fish in the water—blues chasing in the minnows—and the gentle waves rushing into tidal pools, then receding with a hiss over the sandy shallows.

"Man, that salt air." Kyle draws a finger around his shirt collar and takes a long breath. "Nothing like it."

Jason looks from Kyle, breathing and fishing quietly, then to Nick, sitting nearby.

"Is that the look?" Nick asks.

"What?" Jason takes his cell phone and a pack of cigarettes out of his pocket and sets them near the tackle box.

"Payback," Nick explains. "You want me to bait your hook for you?"

As if that'd do it. Jason picks up his fishing line and chooses a lure after tossing a dog biscuit to Maddy. "Not even close, pal. I'm not letting you off that easy."

Cliff sits behind them and casts his line. It whizzes past far out into the water. "You all have your fishing licenses?"

"Are you really going to bust our balls over basically shooting the shit on the rocks?" Kyle snags a slice of Eva's chocolate cake from their cooler. "We're practically not even fishing," he says, stuffing half the slice in his mouth, then tearing off a piece for the dog.

"Can't you see, boss?" Nick asks. He snaps open a can of beer and hands it to Jason. "It's more eating and bullshitting than anything else."

"Man, why are you so rigid? Relax, Raines." Jason takes a long swallow of the brew, then sets it beside the tackle box and stands to lean against a large boulder. The Gull Island Lighthouse beam sweeps across the water, catching the big rock in its path.

"Yeah, guy." Kyle presses the last of his cake into his mouth, then reaches for the tackle box. "What's your story?"

After hearing only the waves lapping and sloshing at the rocks as the tide comes in, Jason squints through the shadows at the beach commissioner. That's when Cliff begins, barely.

"Worked for the State."

"For this fine state of Connecticut?" Kyle asks while brushing through the lures.

"That's the one." Cliff pulls on a tug at his line, which goes slack then. "Was a judge. Presided over domestic hearings, enforced the law."

"Is that right? So what landed you here?" Jason asks over his shoulder.

Cliff explains while reeling in his slack line. "Worked in courthouses for twenty-five years. Sitting in those stagnant rooms, I never had a breath of fresh air. Promised myself when I one day retired from the State, I'd work outdoors. Somehow." He casts his line closer to shore now. "This is the perfect way. Enforcing rules outside on a beach."

"Damn. In a polo shirt instead of a black robe," Kyle says without looking up from attaching the lure to his line. Nick is beside him now, shining a small flashlight on the operation.

"Got any kids?" Jason asks, still leaning on a boulder. He doesn't look at Cliff this time. "A wife?"

"What is this? An interrogation?" As though trying to hide, Cliff takes a seat again, shifting onto a cluster of rocks closer to the patch of tall pines beyond. "Thought we were just fishing."

"Like I said, Judge," Kyle reminds him. "It's more BS than fishing. Don't need no license for that." He treads carefully over smaller rocks toward Jason, finally standing to the side of him.

"All right, then, boys. I have a son. In his thirties, about your age."

At those words, Jason glances over his shoulder at Cliff.

"See him here and there. On the holidays."

"Wife, too?" Nick asks.

"Jeez, you guys are really reeling *me* in. What about all of you?" Cliff keeps himself planted behind them, as though he has to keep an eye on their unlawful activities. "Giving me a hard time all summer, breaking the rules. Got some of your own stories to tell, I'd imagine."

Nick sets down his fishing pole and climbs over the low rocks, past Maddy sitting there snorting the air. He makes his way back to where Cliff has cast off. "Let me enlighten you, boss, about this crew." Nick points to himself, first. "You've got me, Stony Point's finest security guard, aiming to be your right-hand man."

"And career college student," Kyle tosses back.

"Eh, I'm almost done." Nick waves him off. "Tuesday and Thursday night classes in Groton this semester."

Jason shifts his stance to grab a piece of cake, giving a sharp whistle to his dog, too.

"Then you got Bradford, there." Nick points to Kyle. "Former steelworker."

"That right?" Cliff asks through the misty darkness as he gives Kyle a salute. "You're a union man?"

"Used to be. Shipbuilding, actually. When the work dried up, I worked as a cook in town. Ended up buying the place a couple years ago. Driftwood Café."

"A coffee shop?" Cliff asks.

"*Gesù, Santa Maria.*" Kyle sets down his fishing rod and snags a cigarette from Jason's pack on the rocks. "It's a *diner*, man," he explains, wincing through the smoke as he lights the cigarette. "Which is worrying me. Because it's not obvious by the name, is it?" He holds up his cigarette and exhales a long plume of smoke. "Sal was hinting at that, steering me back to its old name. That must be why. Shit, I miss the Italian." He looks back at Cliff. "Place used to be called Dockside Diner."

"And then you have Matt," Nick continues. "Absent tonight, because he's working as our resident state trooper. Guy will *never* break a rule."

"Speaking of rules," Cliff warns as he goes back and forth with something nibbling at his line. "No smoking on the beach."

"Except on fishing night," Jason says. He's not about to have this newbie alter their weekly traditions. "Don't like it? You can leave."

"Well what about *you*, Jason?" Cliff asks. "Got to be more to you than those Barlow Architecture signs I see around?"

Jason tosses the last of his cake to the dog, then snaps his fingers toward Kyle, who hands him a cigarette and the lighter. And Jason bides his time in a long silence, lighting the smoke, taking a couple of drags while small waves lap the rocks. "You did a smooth dance there, Cliff." He looks over his shoulder at him when he finally says this. "Sidestepping us with some fancy footwork, evading one important question. You conveniently missed mentioning any history with a wife?"

Cliff stares right back at him. Doesn't flinch, either. "You got me, Barlow. But that's a story for another night."

"Yeah." Jason turns back and casts his line far out,

watching it whistle over the water, then takes another drag of his cigarette. "So is mine, guy." Jason glances at Kyle beside him lighting another cigarette with the embered butt of his first one. "So is mine."

thirteen

THAT NIGHT, MARIS ISN'T SURE which wakes her: Madison's smell or wagging tail. The dog stands beside the bed and rests her muzzle on the mattress, all while her low body sways with her slow-swinging tail. "Maddy?" Maris reaches over and scratches the German shepherd's head. A dank scent permeates the room, and Maris figures the dog took a nice, saltwater swim during the guys' fishing outing. "Go lie down now."

But Maddy stays there long enough for Maris to nudge Jason sleeping beside her. "Hon? Can you let the dog out?" Her hand sweeps across the empty mattress until she sits up and sees that Jason's not in bed. "Oh, I get it," she whispers to Maddy. "Let's go see your master."

Madison prances beside the bed while Maris puts on a light robe. They head to the stairs, which the dog bolts down in one noisy blur.

But Maris stops at her first glimpse of a dim living room light. She quietly descends a few steps, then holds the banister and bends low to see Jason. He's smoking a cigarette in his upholstered chair in the corner; a glass of

Scotch sits beside him on the end table. The dog stops at the bottom of the stairs until Jason pats his chair arm and Maddy walks over. She climbs into her dog bed there, circles around twice, then lies down with her muzzle on the edge of the bed while keeping an eye on him.

Maris still watches as Jason simply sips his drink and takes a drag or two of that darn cigarette. The room is shadowed and he gives no indication of coming up to bed, but instead sits alone. Again. If this wasn't happening over and over, on the heels of Sal's funeral, Maris might let it go. Because she could slip right back into bed, unnoticed, and leave him with his thoughts. Silently, she straightens on the steps.

Or, she can go downstairs and talk to him.

~

Jason shuts off the table lamp. The only illumination in the living room is the glowing ember of the tip of his cigarette. His hand finds the dog-tag chain around his neck as he remembers one of his father's war stories. It was about the times he couldn't even light a cigarette in the jungle. The tiny glow of it would give away his presence to the Viet Cong.

Now, Jason lifts his cigarette and studies the red-tipped ember, thinking of the long-ago night he and Neil sat with their father on the bench on the bluff. Far over Long Island Sound, sheet lightning wavered across the sky, illuminating the night clouds in such a way that they looked like rolling waves. Their father often told his stories at night, with Jason and Neil stockpiling the tales to live out on a hot summer day. As kids, they'd paddle the lagoon or hike the wooded trail to Little Beach while pretending to be in 'Nam. This particular story had them riveted.

We were on night patrol, their father began, *trying to disrupt any ambush the VC might be planning. We walked, dead silent, beneath the rubber trees. It was so black out, I couldn't see, and had my hand wrapped around the ammo belt of the guy in front of me. We all did, to stay together. And though we were blinded by the darkness, that darkness was our cover.*

One night, every now and then there was a flash of lightning. And hell, you'd better be ready for it, ready to scan left and right for any enemy movement in those few seconds of lightness. It was one of only two ways to see, in the illumination from a flash of lightning, which was preferable. Because the only other way to see was in the muzzle flash of the enemy firing on us—in the darkness. That muzzle flash, hell, that was the worst because the explosion behind it was meant to kill, to take us down. In the God damn pitch black of night, that illumination was where we blindly directed our return fire, to stay alive. So darkness, yeah it was our cover. But it was our enemy, too.

Tonight, if he had to choose, Jason would call darkness his cover. Here, no one sees the mistakes he's made in the past week: leaving Maris, and entangling with Celia in one uncontrolled kiss. Here, in the blackness, he can sit in peace as more minutes accrue between those two distressed nights, and now.

"Hey, babe," a whisper comes to his ear. Jason turns around to see Maris bending low, her long hair sweeping forward as she comes up beside him and lightly kisses his face. She crouches then, a hand on his leg. "You're up late. Can't sleep?"

"No, sweetheart."

"Did you go for a walk?" As she says it, in the darkness, her hand strokes his thigh.

"No." Jason tamps out his cigarette in the ashtray and switches on the table lamp. "Being out fishing on the rocks was enough activity."

"Oh." She draws a finger along his thigh now. "Leg bothering you?"

"It's fine."

So she gets the bottle of Scotch from the kitchen and brings it to the living room, pours herself a splash and sets the bottle on the mantel. In a moment, she slides a chair close and sits near him. He listens to her gentle voice telling him about her visit with Elsa, and how her aunt hid out alone in her cottage all week so she could grieve privately.

"I'm sleeping over there with Eva and Tay, to keep Elsa company," Maris says, sipping her drink. "Tomorrow night."

"Don't you have to go into the city Sunday?" Jason asks. "For that early Monday meeting?"

"I do," Maris tells him. "I'll have time."

And then, nothing. They sit there. Together, but silent.

"I get it, Elsa being alone," Jason finally admits. "Sometimes there's no other way." He tips up his glass of liquor for a drink. "To work something out."

"I guess." Maris swirls the alcohol in her glass. "But being alone didn't work for Celia. The way she just up and left, everyone's worried about her. Lauren mentioned she was so upset before leaving."

They quiet again as Maris sips her Scotch before setting it down and walking to the window. Outside, the night is black against the panes.

"Did something happen between you two?" she asks.

Jason looks over to where Maris stands; her back is to him, as she still looks out at the blackness. "Like what?"

She turns, then, and scrutinizes him. "Did you *say* something? Because I know how you can get. And to someone who doesn't really understand you, you can be off-putting." Again she comes closer and crouches in front of him. Her robe hangs loosely open, her satin nightshirt shimmering beneath it. "You saw Celia *drunk*," she reasons in the dim light. "She slept here. And I know you weren't happy about it, so maybe you said something to scare her off?" Maris stands, looks at him, then sits in her chair again. "Is that all it was?"

"Pretty much." Jason takes his empty glass to the mantel and pours in more Scotch. He downs a mouthful. "It was the end of a really long day, my first one back to work since Sal died. And I was beat. So, you know, it was strained with Celia." He brings the Scotch over to Maris, and adds a few more drops to her glass.

"If you're sure that's all it was," Maris tells him. "But I'd imagine Celia was exhausted, too, after everything that happened. So I hope you weren't too hard on her, okay?"

Jason sets the bottle on the end table and touches his glass to hers. In the low light, she raises her glass and finishes the liquor in it. Her dark hair falls back as she does, and her robe slips off one shoulder. When she stands to go upstairs, he instead takes her by the wrist and draws her close. While pressed against him, her eyes watch his as he hooks his arm around her shoulders, his whiskey glass still in hand. There's a sensation, soft on the skin of his arm: Maris' silky hair brushing that arm as he leans in and kisses her, lightly at first. It's nice, the touch of her mouth, the hint of liquor on her lips.

But something happens, something compelling him to lengthen their kiss. Especially after he manages to put down his glass and shut off the lamp, then turn back to her and slip that damn robe right off, all with his mouth on hers, his hand tangling in her hair. The robe drops silently to the floor while his hands stroke the skin of her shoulders, then draw along the top of her breasts as though, yes, as though following the imagined neckline of a peasant blouse—a rounded neckline that slipped too low.

"Jason," Maris whispers into the kiss, trying to pull back, maybe to see where this sudden urgency is coming from.

But he won't let her. The same way he *forced* Celia to stop, he won't *let* Maris stop. Not tonight. No, not as his fingers brusquely undo the buttons along her sleeveless nightshirt and pull that off, too. All while he kisses her mouth, her face, her neck—insistently enough in the darkness that she softly gasps. This time, as he moves her toward the sofa, he's not stopping there. His hands run up along the side of her body, his fingers skimming the curve of her breasts as he brings his touch to those sweet bare shoulders. Finally, his hands cradle her face while their kiss deepens. Her mouth is sensuous now, and impatient as she sinks down onto the sofa, never stopping the kiss while her hands hook behind his neck and pull him down with her.

For Jason, this night's darkness that's been a cover, suddenly becomes his enemy—because it's unclear if it's Maris, or Celia, his mind is really seeing. Within the dark cover of his blackened house rising like a silhouette on the rocky sea bluff, with no illumination from the moon lightening the space, couldn't the shadow of who lies beneath him be either one?

fourteen

BY MONDAY MORNING, JASON'S READY for the distraction of an overloaded work schedule, and so he stands motionless in front of the microwave. He always knows it's Monday by the way his cell phone dings with messages—shit, today even before the crack of dawn. His contractors are early birds, just like him. He glares to the countertop after another ding, then grabs his cell, looks at who's calling and drops the phone in his shorts pocket. "Can't the sun come up first, fellas?" he mutters with a glance through the slider toward the orange horizon.

His day's going to be a juggling act, just like breakfast—hot coffee brought out to deck, plate of apple crisp pulled out of microwave. He's thankful Maris slept over at Elsa's Saturday night, if only for this: sweet leftovers, one of his favorite breakfasts, right after egg sandwiches. Apparently it's Madison's, too, as the dog sits watching him while her tail silently sweeps the floor. Jason grabs creamy coffee-flavored yogurt from the fridge, puts it back, opens the freezer and gets the vanilla ice cream. After dropping three scoops on the warmed apple crisp, he adds two more scoops to the dog's bowl.

Finally, he takes Maddy and all the food outside to the deck, puts his phone on the patio table and opens the daily planner app to review the inn's renovation schedule, which—to everyone's relief—is resuming today. While setting down Maddy's bowl of ice cream, he catches sight of a double sunrise to the east: The red sun climbs just over the horizon, casting gold across the dawn sky above *and* reflecting red-gold on the calm water of the Sound at the same time.

At last, Jason scrolls through the phone app while spooning a heaping mouthful of melting vanilla ice cream and warm apple crisp. On the week's agenda at Elsa's inn: clear out rear yard around guest cottage, prep to rebuild its stone foundation. Elsa's idea to renovate that tiny cottage for guests wanting privacy is genius; it'll look like a little gingerbread house. He switches to the task screen listing details about shingle removal, and specifics on problem areas that need to be addressed before any demo and new construction can begin.

When his phone rings again, Jason continues reading his task list while lifting the last spoonful of now-soggy apple crisp into his mouth. But when he sees on the caller ID that one of Elsa's contractors is on the line, he answers.

"Got a problem, Barlow."

"No, no." Jason sips his coffee. "Everything can be fixed, so no problems. What's up?"

"The lady cancelled. Bailing on the whole job. Ordered us to take down the scaffolding, get rid of the stones for the wall. Wants everything outta here."

"What?"

"I kid you not. She won't let us bring anything—gear *or*

people—onto the property. Except to clear it. Made sure to have her driveway blocked, too, so I've got pickups and a small payloader parked on the street. My whole crew's here, so now what?"

Jason stands and whistles for the dog, lets her inside ahead of him, then grabs his coffee while leaving the food plates behind. "Just wait there, you hear me? And don't take *anything* down!" He tosses back the last of his coffee and grabs his black work duffel, already loaded with the day's paperwork.

"Time is money, guy," his contractor reminds him. "So hurry it up."

As soon as they end the call, Jason's phone rings again. He sees on his caller ID that it's a second contractor from Elsa's and answers it promptly.

"Lady had a change of plans," this foreman says. "She's upset, and won't let the work resume."

"I'm on my way." Jason hoists his duffel on his shoulder.

"Everything all right with her? She's nice enough—Mrs. DeLuca, is it?—but seems a little off."

When Jason passes Maddy's empty water dish, he drops his duffel and scoops up the bowl. "She lost her son, just a couple weeks ago." He turns on the cold tap and fills the bowl, finagling the phone as he does. "Sit tight, okay?"

"Hell, Jason. I've got other jobs lined up. Can't afford delays like this, so I already moved my crew to another site."

Jason looks at the phone, disconnects and sets down the dog's water bowl. With a quick glance at his watch, he grabs his duffel again and heads out.

"Son of a bitch," he says under his breath.

~

The sun still rises and paints a swath of gold across the sea. Jason notices the sight as he drives along Sea View Road and wonders what happened to his quiet breakfast-on-the-deck morning. When he rounds a few curves and finds a spot to park among idled construction trucks alongside Elsa's cottage, the sound of hammering fills the air. So that's a relief; at least Elsa came to her senses and let the work begin. Instantly, his blood pressure lowers, his breathing eases. The last thing this Monday morning needs is a confrontation with his temperamental aunt-through-marriage.

His relief doesn't last much longer than the time it takes to walk around to the front of the cottage. To within view of the hammering that stops his hurried steps cold.

"What's going on?" Jason calls out as he watches a man sledgehammering a post into the front lawn—a post on which a FOR SALE sign is hooked.

"New listing. The old Foley's place is back on the market."

Jason walks closer as the man secures the sign with plastic cable ties. "You the listing agent?"

"No. I just put out the signs for the realty. Surprised to see this one on the market again after only a year." He motions to the disarray of halted-construction: sawhorses, pails of tools, sheets of plywood, construction tape barricading the yard. "Looks like someone ran out of money," he says. "Or had a change of heart, maybe. Blood, sweat and dollar signs can be too much sometimes."

Jason waves him off and walks toward Elsa's stalled inn.

"You interested in the property?" the sign man calls after him. "I can give you a business card."

There's no point in looking back, in answering, in anything, lately. "Bullshit," Jason says under his breath while nearing the entrance. "More fucking bullshit."

After only a moment, he gives a quick rap and pushes the door wide open. "Elsa!" he calls out, then slams the door behind him.

~

A half hour later, Jason sits alone on the boardwalk. White clouds drift across the September-blue sky, and the dark water beneath it sparkles in rays of sunlight dropping down. What it all is, this heavenly sight meant to bring peace, is a ruse. Oh yes, it is. Because he's not feeling any peace at all.

Jason lights a cigarette and leans forward, elbows on his knees. Maybe it would have helped if he and Elsa hashed things out in sand chairs in front of this grand panorama, facing her beloved ocean stars. He watches those sparkles of sunlight wavering on the rippling water, then calls Maris in Manhattan.

"Trouble in paradise," he says when she answers.

"What now?"

"Your aunt is out of control."

"What are you talking about? Elsa was *fine* when I slept over there Saturday night."

"She didn't tell you her plans?"

"Plans? Well, yes. That she's been packing Sal's things, and other stuff, to get out of the way for the renovation."

"She put the inn for sale."

Silence then, as Jason hears Maris close her New York studio's door. "Are you *joking*?" she asks.

"Far from it." He takes a long drag of his cigarette and squints through the smoke. "She completely screwed up my crews today."

"For *sale*? Did Eva list it?"

"No. Someone else."

"I'm coming home. Right now." The sound of drawers opening and closing, of papers being shuffled … all of it reveals her panic. "I'll catch an early train."

"What about Fashion Week? You need to be in the city for it."

"Damn it, I do." Then, nothing but a deep breath. "Okay," Maris finally tells him. "I'll come home tonight, just for the night, and come back here early tomorrow so I don't miss anything. Maybe I can get through to Elsa tonight."

"I'm not sure it's worth it. I just came from there and talked to her for no more than five minutes before she kicked me out. And she left, too. Drove off somewhere in a huff."

"Oh, no."

"Oh, yes. And from what little I got out of her? It's a done deal, sweetheart."

~

"I'm really not feeling this one, Eva." Kyle stands in the cottage front yard as Eva returns the key to the lockbox. He points out to Lauren the paint peeling off the board-and-batten siding.

"It's only paint." Lauren steps closer to examine it. "Maybe the guys could help you knock it out over a weekend or two?"

"Plus, this is a really good spot for the kids," Eva tells them when she turns around. "You're so close to the basketball court and recreation area."

"So instead of seagulls, I'll be listening to dribbling basketballs all summer, which will keep me awake. And I need to get to bed early to open the diner at the crack of dawn." Kyle checks his watch. "Speaking of which, my lunch hour is about up."

"But you can keep an eye on Evan from here." Eva motions to the two-story cottage facing a parking lot, *beside* the basketball court. "Look how the house sits on a small hill."

Kyle watches three cars pass by. "Too busy of an area, lots of traffic here. Hailey could get hit by a car flying through that parking lot."

"I can't do my painting, either, with that racket, Eva," Lauren tells her with an apologetic smile.

"Okay, that's okay! We'll keep looking. More homes always come on the market in the fall."

They climb into Eva's golf cart so that she can bring them back to her house, where Kyle left his pickup. Cottages of every style, neatly tended with trimmed lawns and early pots of fall mums on the stoops, line their route. None are for sale. "How's that sports-shrine addition coming along at your place?" Kyle asks Eva.

"Jason hasn't drawn up the plans yet. I guess he's swamped."

"I'll say." Kyle looks further down the street toward Elsa's. "Especially with that inn renovation starting up today."

"What do you say?" Eva asks, glancing at Lauren beside

her. "Want to swing by and say hi to Elsa?"

Lauren checks her watch. "We can manage a quick hi, just to stay in touch."

"Good idea," Kyle agrees behind them, feeling the sea breeze as they get closer to the water. "Make sure no rash decisions are going on." Kyle says it as they pass more cottage yards with golden plumes of September beach grass, and toppling sunflowers, their blossoms heavy with seed. He takes a deep breath of the salt air while watching the scenery.

"Oh, look!" Eva points ahead. "There's a For Sale sign. I *told* you there'd be more popping up. It's near Elsa's." She picks up speed to check it out.

"Wait." Lauren leans forward, squinting. "That *is* Elsa's!"

Eva cranes her neck to look again, then guns it and drives her golf cart straight up onto a front lawn, before swerving off the grass.

"Watch it!" Kyle calls out from the backseat. He quickly reaches for the grab bar as he half falls out onto the street, then pulls himself back inside while Eva skids to a stop. "I don't have the best health insurance, you know," he says, swiping his arm across his now-perspiring forehead.

But it doesn't matter what he says. Not at all. Because Lauren and Eva are already out of the golf cart and halfway to Elsa's front door.

~

Cliff stands at the community bulletin board at the end of the boardwalk. Wearing a black cap with the word

COMMISSIONER stitched in gold, he tips the brim against the midday sun while holding the latest issue of his Stony Point newsletter. Behind him, in a box on his golf cart seat, there are dozens more, ready to be deposited in the newsletter bin for residents to enjoy.

"Not bad," he says as he scans the page. He changed the header photo to a wide September shot of the beach, included all the necessary ordinance updates and listed personal citizen announcements. The toughest notice to write was the memoriam, and his eyes stop on the thoughtful tribute to Sal. "Not bad at all," he says, remembering how he struggled to word it just right. Which gets him thinking of Elsa, so he glances a block over toward her inn. With a pleased nod at himself, he lifts the glass of the big bulletin board and pins his newsletter beneath it, then grabs more copies for the bin.

"Raines! I've been looking for you."

Cliff turns around to see Jason approaching, his German shepherd at his side. Cliff shifts the armful of newsletters and extends a hand to Jason. "You found me, guy."

Jason gives him a curt handshake. "We need to talk."

"Let me load these into the bin, first." Cliff holds up the newsletters, then drops them in.

"Never mind that. I need to know why Elsa is selling her inn, and I need to know right now. She put my crews out of work with her decision."

"What? What are you talking about?" Again, Cliff looks over to the distant inn.

"You were the only one who talked to Elsa last week, when she *must* have arranged this. What did she tell you?"

"Tell *me*?"

"Hell, all the work I've done on that inn of hers … with designs, contractors, with passing your *countless* zoning stipulations, and now it's all for *nothing*?" When Madison gets anxious, Jason wraps her leather leash around his hand and pulls her close. "What gives, man?"

"I swear Elsa didn't say a word, Jason."

"Cut the bullshit."

Cliff steps back because he's about had it with Jason Barlow. In all his years of being a judge, he's not sure he ever wanted to haul off and belt someone like he does right now, the way Jason's insinuating he *colluded* with Elsa on this development. Instead, Cliff turns around, scoops up the newsletters he'd just put in the bin and drops them back in their brown box on his golf cart seat, then lifts a messy bunch with one hand.

"If I knew Elsa was selling her inn, would I have made *these*?" He shakes the handful of loose newsletters in front of Jason's face, then nods at his big feature announcement. "Read it, that's right. *Coming Soon. The Ocean Star Inn.* Do you know how much *work* went into that photograph?" He looks at it himself, remembering the day he wrote the announcement with a driftwood stick, *in the sand*, and decorated the words with sun-bleached seashells and stones, special for Elsa.

Jason takes one of the newsletters and scrutinizes it.

"I even asked for everyone to extend a wave and a smile to Elsa," Cliff points out, his finger tapping his memoriam announcement on Jason's newsletter. "During this sad time."

"Hey, Raines." Jason looks up from the newsletter. "I just thought …" he begins, glancing at the newsletter again. "Well, I'm sorry—"

"Damn it!" Cliff says, shoving his handful of newsletters into the cardboard box again. "She's *selling* that inn? Now all these have to be scrapped. *All of them!*" He steps to a nearby garbage can and dumps the whole box of newsletters. When some of the papers flutter to the street, he pauses, then keeps walking, straight back to his golf cart.

"Cliff! We can get to the bottom of this, you and me, if—"

"Eh," Cliff says without looking back. He waves off Jason, gets into his golf cart and, that's right, burns rubber for the second time in one week.

fifteen

MARIS TURNS ON THE COFFEEMAKER and checks her watch. At this moment on a Tuesday morning, she *should* be in the city—grabbing a coffee with her assistant, Lily, as they plan their day viewing the latest fashions on the runways. Instead, Maris swipes crumbs off the kitchen counter while the coffee brews, surprisingly happy to be here, rather than there. To be at the beach with her family-in-crisis, instead of with New Yorkers in spring wear. She's really been away too much. Suddenly, a creaking noise comes to her, followed by the tap of Jason's crutches as he maneuvers the stairs. Then, Jason's stern voice warning the dog away from his feet.

"Hey, what are you doing home?" Jason asks in the kitchen doorway as Maris is pouring coffee. Madison skids to a stop at Jason's side, eyes his crutches, then scrambles into the kitchen, her nails clicking on the floor.

"And what are you doing on your crutches?" Maris asks over her shoulder. "Is your leg bothering you?"

"Isn't it Fashion Week? You and Lily should be networking the runways."

Of course, Jason's right, especially since Saybrooks wants to do *their* first show, debuting the fall denim line Maris and her team are working on right now. If all goes to plan, Maris might very well watch her own designs on the runway, come February.

"But didn't you get Kyle's text?" Maris unplugs a cell phone from the charger on the counter.

"Kyle? Do you know how many text messages I've been getting, mostly from pissed-off contractors, thanks to your aunt?" He slips off his forearm crutches and sits at the table just as Maris sets down his coffee, *and* his cell phone, which he takes to read Kyle's text. "Sweetheart …" He looks up at Maris, and his eyes drop from her loose tee to her frayed cutoffs, back to her face. "Please don't tell me you're missing a day of Fashion Week for Kyle's *boardwalk* meeting."

Maris nods while leaning against the counter and cupping her steaming coffee. "If you're coming, too," she says, "don't you need to cancel your early appointment?"

After a glance at his watch, Jason grabs his crutches and stands, stopping for a quick sip of the hot coffee. "My blower's in the shed. I'll get my leg squared away and clear the sand off the boardwalk for Kyle."

Maris walks over to him, sets a hand alongside his face and kisses him. "I've got fresh fruit," she softly says just as two slices of raisin bread pop up in the toaster. "I put your plate out on the deck already." She kisses him again, while running her fingers up his arm, then whispering, "Let's have breakfast, first."

~

Kyle squints at his watch, paces the boardwalk beneath the shade pavilion, glances along the length of the beach, then turns to Jason, Maris, Lauren, Nick and Cliff gathered behind him. "I guess we should get started," he says. "I'm glad you all could make it to our own beach *piazza*—to quote Sal. I know you all have to get to work, and so do I. Jerry's covering the diner for this meeting of ours."

"Wait!" a voice calls out.

They all look to see Eva and Matt, both carrying trays of coffee to-go and a box of cinnamon doughnuts from the convenience store.

"Goodies for everyone," Eva says as she sets the coffee cups on the boardwalk bench. "Sorry we're late."

"I just got off work," Matt explains, motioning to his state police uniform. "Have a bite to eat, guys," he says while holding forth the open doughnut box and walking in front of everyone sitting on the bench.

"What about Celia?" Cliff asks while taking a cup of coffee from Eva. "Anyone try to reach her?"

"No," Lauren explains. "She asked us not to, at least for now. I guess she needs a little distance from everything here." Lauren raises her sunglasses to the top of her head. "Maybe someday she'll come around."

"Okay, then," Kyle begins again while sipping a coffee. In his pause, a wave sloshes gently along the beach, and a seagull swoops low, cawing as though calling order for his meeting. "As you all know, Elsa's inn is for sale. Which was definitely a rash decision. Our dilemma is to get her to change her mind so she'll stay put, here at Stony Point."

"We have to make her feel loved, so she can't leave," Eva says. "Visit her, have dinner with her."

"Take beach walks," Maris adds from where she sits beside Jason.

"Convince her to start the damn renovation, for God's sake, so she can *see* what she's building with that inn," Jason suggests while dunking a doughnut half in his coffee. "It'll be epic, especially with the added turret."

"But how?" Cliff peels the lid off his coffee cup.

"Don't know," Jason answers around a mouthful of food. "But lots of workers depended on her job for their income, too. Men were ready to swing hammers yesterday."

"Hell, she came this far, right?" Kyle asks. "The plans are complete, correct?"

Jason nods, with a slight salute to Kyle.

"Has anyone talked to her?" Lauren asks the gang.

"I tried last night," Maris says while turning to Lauren. "But couldn't reach her."

Eva sips her coffee and leans over, toward Maris and Lauren both. "Do you think she's *really* serious?" she asks them.

"You bet I am!"

They turn then, each one of them, at the sound of Elsa's words.

~

Some say that memories are beautiful. Moments are captured in our minds as though in the soft blur of a camera lens. That blur erases time, so that a smile, or touch, or look from years ago can feel as though it happened hours ago. The feeling from the special moment may fade, or come and go, but memory preserves it, in some way.

Which is why Elsa thinks memories are actually cruel. The last thing she wants preserved is what happened a few short months ago, right on this very boardwalk. She does not want to *see* all the beach friends gathered here on that hot summer morning when she explained the personal meaning of ocean stars—how they're night stars fallen from the sky, regaining their strength as they twinkle atop the sea in the morning before rising back up to the sky later in the day. She does not want to remember that it was her sweet sister, June, who told her that story so long ago. She does not want to remember how Sal hurried off the boardwalk during her gathering this summer so that he could help Kyle in his diner. She watched Sal trot away, keys in hand, while hoping she'd see him again—her secret lifelong vow *any* time he left her, given his heart condition.

And she does *not* want to remember that it was at that sunny meeting when she assembled her stellar business team of Jason, Celia and Lauren before announcing the name of her future beach inn: The Ocean Star Inn.

Now, Sal is forever gone, never to return. Celia has left. And her dream of a beach inn has evaporated into the sea's mist.

So Elsa promptly moves forward in time, to this Tuesday morning in the middle of September, the sun shining as brightly as then, twinkling on the ripples of the sea like, yes … stars.

"I need to begin," Elsa says as she steps slowly past the boardwalk bench where everyone sits, "by assuring you all that though my inn's plans have been cancelled, I will pay each of you for any work already done."

"This isn't about the money," Maris insists. "We just

want you to stay put and not make any decisions right now. Aunt Elsa, your grief is clouding your judgment."

"It's a huge mistake, deciding to sell your cottage at such an emotional time," Lauren adds. "You'll sell it and then go where? Do … what?"

Elsa shrugs. "I'm not sure yet, but am considering a few options."

"What can we say to convince you to take your cottage *off* the market?" Eva asks as she takes Elsa's hands in hers.

Giving Eva's hands a squeeze, Elsa simply tells her, "My mind is made up." When she pulls out of Eva's clasp to continue walking, Eva sits again, beside Matt.

"But you showed up for my wedding last year, in place of my mother." Maris lifts her star pendant. "You've given us *so* much, and now you're leaving us?"

"Nobody wants this, Elsa," Jason says when Elsa passes in front of him with her hands clasped behind her back.

"You *are* like a mother to us, Elsa."

Elsa turns at Eva's words. "But I'm *not* your mother. I was Sal's mother. And he was going to partner with me, so we would run the inn together."

Cliff stands and faces Elsa as she paces the line. "I heard from Maris and Eva that during your ladies' sleepover this past weekend, you shook on our pact to not make *any* rash decisions. So can't you just *think* about selling for two weeks, at least, Elsa DeLuca?" He steps closer to her, hands turned up. "Or a month?"

"No, Cliff. I can't. No."

"What about the studies proving you need an entire *year* before making any decisions?" Kyle looks at everyone sitting, circling his hands for them all to agree with him. "We don't want you to be one of those regretful statistics. You know, making a grief-decision and then wishing you'd waited."

A chorus of voices rises, and Elsa hears it—their urgency, and frustration, and love. None of it can alleviate the sad pain in her heart as she deeply misses her only son.

So what Elsa does is this: She bows her head, raises her open hand up high and keeps it there until everyone goes silent. When they do, she glances at each of them sitting on the boardwalk in the golden morning sunlight as a sea breeze lifts off the water. "Please know this was not an easy decision for me. Maris, Eva … I didn't mention it during our sleepover because I didn't want our special time together to turn into one long argument. *And* I did not want you to change my mind. Because here's the thing … I still must go back and forth to Sal's apartment, all while tying up *many* legalities of his estate. What it does, all of it, is it makes his absence very final, breaking my heart over and over again. So it is no longer *in* my sad heart to continue with the inn. I cannot bring that desire back, not without my son here. Everything's changed."

As she says her words, her eyes connect with all of them, one at a time: Cliff, her nieces, Kyle and Lauren, Matt, Nick and finally, Jason.

Nothing could have prepared her for his reaction. Jason stands up, looks long at her, then turns and silently walks away. Just leaves—his footsteps quiet on the boardwalk, as, if she's not mistaken, he slightly favors his prosthetic leg.

"Jason?" Maris calls, standing and looking from him, to Eva, from whom a sob escapes.

"Oh, what a mess," Eva says, pressing her fingers to her crying eyes.

Lauren sweeps Eva up in a hug. "It's okay, hon. Shh."

Elsa watches this emotional disintegration carry on, then looks toward Jason as he continues walking away.

Suddenly a blur passes Elsa. It's Maris, in her frayed shorts and tee, running after Jason. But she stops, just stops, and returns to Elsa. Taking hold of Elsa's hand, she steps close with a concerned smile.

"Do you see what you're doing?" Maris points with her other hand to Jason, then to everyone gathered on the sunny boardwalk, sitting, standing, fretting—their coffees cold, their cinnamon doughnuts untouched and getting stale. "Aunt Elsa," Maris whispers as she pulls away to go after Jason. "Is *this* what you want?"

sixteen

IF CLIFF THINKS THINGS CAN'T get any worse, any sooner, he's dead wrong. One stop at the community bulletin board the next morning proves it. All he intended to do was post a notice advising boat owners to remove their vessels from the boat basin for the off-season. That's when he sees the violating TAG SALE notice tacked there. And he *almost* leaves it up out of some goodness in his beach-commissioner-heart, until he reads the sign's details and sees the tag sale is happening at Elsa's inn! Which is precisely when he tears down the notice and tosses it in the public trash receptacle near the bulletin board.

"Of all the cockamamy ..." he gripes while walking the beach roads back to his utilitarian office-trailer. "For crying out loud." He rubs his chin and wonders how Elsa can go through with this. "Not if I have anything to do with the matter," he decides when he suddenly notices something on nearly every telephone pole along the way. Bright cardboard signs nailed at the perfect height, the print bold and clear: *TAG SALE, One Day Only! Saturday, 9-19. Lots of Trinkets and Treasures. Everything Must Go! Early Birds Welcome.*

"We'll just see about that," Cliff says to himself as he rips off one sign after the other, thinking Elsa's leaving a veritable cardboard trail leading straight to her current location. She must be somewhere on these streets right now, manically hammering the darn notices—determined to hightail it straight out of Stony Point, straight away from her painful time here.

So he follows the signs, tearing each one off poles in front of cottages already fall-decorated with early mums and cornstalks, and cottages buttoned up tight for the oncoming winter, and others still lingering in these late-summer days—porch windows open and Adirondack chairs set in shady front yards.

Cliff finally spots Elsa near Stony Point's entrance, tacking up a sign for folks who might arrive under the train trestle. She's wearing her denim capris and a tie-front blouse while pulling a red garden wagon filled with more signs, a container of silver nails and a mini hammer. A floppy sun hat sits on her stubborn, obstinate, determined head.

"Mrs. DeLuca!" Cliff rushes to her side. "You are violating the Stony Point tag sale sign ordinance."

"Are you kidding me? A tag sale sign ordinance?"

"No, I am not kidding. Ordinance SI.02. Notices can be posted only on the day of the event, as well as *one* preceding day." He lifts a handmade sign from her wagon. "Let's see, your tag sale," he says, raising an eyebrow, "is Saturday. Today's Wednesday. So you're in a two-day violation. Compounded by the vast *number* of signs you've already hung, this is serious." With that, Cliff returns the tag sale sign—which she snatches—and pulls a ticket pad from his jacket pocket. "I have to give you a summons this time," he warns while filling in the blanks.

"A summons!" Elsa tips up her floppy hat and glares at him. "To what? Court?"

"No." Cliff continues writing. "A few board members will appear in my office—"

"You mean, your *trailer*?"

"This Saturday, around sixish. The fine this time is so large, the board will have to discuss it with you and learn your … fund preferences. Yes," he says, double-underlining his signature, "*fund* preferences."

"Fund?"

Damn it, if there's one thing this annoying, intriguing woman does, it's this: She makes him think on his toes and get crafty with his lies. "For this sizable amount," he improvises as he tears her ticket off the pad, "they will collaborate on which Stony Point *fund*, or committee, to direct your fine to."

"Clifton." Elsa grabs her summons and scans it. "Money is no object. I need to clear out my inn before I move, so I'll just pay your fine and be done with this Stony Point ordinance nonsense."

"But Mrs. DeLuca, may I remind you," Cliff says as he gently clicks off his pen and gives her a small smile. But before saying more, he lifts her darn cute floppy hat and lightly touches her cheek, where there seems to be a dried-tear stain. "The rules *are* the rules." And that is precisely when he turns and walks toward his trailer-office a block away.

It doesn't take more than a few seconds until he hears the noise. *Tap, tap, tap*, as Elsa surely nails another sign on the pole near the trestle. Then a little louder: *Tap! Tap! Tap!*

When it's come to this, when the order of breakfast pancakes Kyle flips on the griddle is for *himself*—when he stacks them three-deep on a warm plate and adds a slab of butter and sweet maple syrup before forking off a hunk—that's when his hand hovers with self-doubt, the fork dripping syrup onto the plate. "Shit," he whispers as he eats the warm pancakes, then dabs a napkin along his forehead. "Cooking only for myself? Might as well close up shop," he mutters while forking another mouthful.

As he chews, he surveys his quiet diner. Bright sunshine comes in the windows; the red-padded booths are nearly empty; one customer, a regular, sits at the counter; the parking lot is deserted. "Like a friggin' ghost town." He slathers a thick pancake piece through the buttery syrup on his plate, wiping it around and around before scooping the dripping food into his mouth. After dragging his fork across the plate to collect any soggy crumbs, he sets it all aside and gives his *empty* order carousel a spin, fearing that he'll put on ten pounds if this keeps up.

Finally, he gets around to what's really eating at him. Maybe his diner's *name* is the problem: The Driftwood Café. People could think it's some hoity-toity coffee shop, not an old-fashioned greasy-spoon diner, and so they drive right by. Maybe he should've left it Dockside Diner last year, and left well enough alone. *Ay-yai-yai.* Decisions, decisions. He fans his T-shirt beneath his apron, trying to cool off his anxiety. Another glance out at the empty booths and he considers telling his cook and former boss, Jerry, to clock out early.

First he lines up his spatulas and tongs at the stoves, suddenly optimistic when the bell over the entrance jingles.

But it's only Lauren, arriving to waitress. Her blonde hair is twisted up in a topknot, silver hoops hang from her ears, and she carries a bag of her painted driftwood pieces that folks buy as souvenirs.

Something's wrong, though. Kyle sees it, the way she doesn't even set down the bag, but instead walks straight around the counter to the kitchen area and hands him a folded piece of paper.

"Check this out," Lauren says. "Oh, I'm *so* mad."

"What is it?" Kyle wipes his hands on his chef apron before taking the paper.

"A letter from Elsa! With a check closing out my artistry work."

Kyle looks from the letter, up to Lauren. "So she *is* serious."

"Apparently. Says my services are no longer needed."

"Oh, Ell. Too bad." Kyle neatly refolds the letter and hands it back. "You were going to have lots of paying jobs with that project."

"It's all cancelled, now." Lauren heads out to the counter and drops her purse and bag of painted driftwood there. She shoves the letter in her purse, saying over her shoulder, "The barnwood inn sign, the driftwood centerpieces. Like Elsa said, sometimes I wear my artist smock," Lauren turns and lifts an apron off a wall hook, "and other times my waitress smock." She slips on the half-apron and drops an order pad and pen in the pocket.

Kyle joins her and sits on a counter stool, giving a slow spin in his deserted diner and taking long, deep breaths to calm his worried heart. He leans his elbows back on the countertop and scans the space where only two booths are occupied. "The financials took their September turn. Tourists recede like a gosh-darn wave every year at this time." He spins back toward Lauren, who is pouring herself a cup of coffee. "The outdoor patio helps, but once Labor Day hits, man, people forget about the beach. So unfortunately, we can use Elsa's check."

"Hey, that's *my* check." Lauren stirs cream into her coffee. "From painting her stair mural at the inn. And I'm putting it into our house fund."

"But business is so slow."

"Well, you said the patio helps." Lauren sips her coffee. "And I saw tiki torches on sale at that little beach shop. They've got an end-of-season clearance going on. The torches would go nice with twinkly lights on the patio. Especially this time of year, it'd look cozy."

"We can't even afford *those* right now, the way things are." Again, Kyle gives a slow spin to scope out his lackluster business.

"Kyle. We can't afford *not* to buy them," Lauren is saying behind him. "The patio is the only thing keeping us afloat. Go buy some tiki torches. They even had some bamboo ones, and a few copper."

"Now?"

"Jerry's here, he can cover for you." She motions her cup to the outside patio. "If you wait, the torches will be gone. They're probably a *great* price."

So Kyle listens to his wife, but not purely for the tiki-torch quest. He goes into his back office, lifts off his apron and hangs it on a wall hook, first. Then he peels off his damp, black T-shirt, balls it up and gives it a hook shot into the trash before pulling out a new tee from the three-pack on the shelf.

Still, the more pressing reason for making the ride to the beach shop sits in his top desk drawer. He opens it now and lifts out a pack of cigarettes. "Damn you, Barlow," he whispers, "getting me hooked again after that funeral."

Already, Kyle's calculating. If he times his tiki-torch run slowly and drives at the right pace, plus takes a longer route, he can finagle it into a three-cigarette ride, at least.

~

"Down she goes!"

Jason looks over his shoulder at the crowd assembled on the sandy beach. Some people are waving colorful pinwheels, while others hold balloons tied to long ribbons, the balloons bobbing and dipping in the sea breeze. Every now and then, random applause breaks out as Maggie Woods' old dump is about to be history. He shakes his head and turns back to his clipboard.

Here in the cottage yard overlooking the beach, it's a different story. DEMOLITION SITE signs are erected. Orange mesh fencing surrounds the work area, keeping onlookers at a safe distance. A massive payloader is parked nearby, ready to rip down walls. Windows and glass have been removed, interior walls stripped out, the place now only a dark skeleton.

Which it pretty much was, too, when old Maggie lived here, skulking in its shadows, spying on folks and ducking when neighbors passed, scurrying half bent over—thin hair falling over her panicked face—from her driveway to her weedy yard after parking her car. A car she could never manage to park straight, nor maneuver into her garage—

instead leaving it crooked and partially on the street as though she was slightly inebriated. More than one neighbor has told Jason that the Woods place put the street to shame.

Nick comes up behind him and hits his arm. "Hey, man. Ready to roll here?"

"Don't you have somewhere to be?" Jason asks without looking up from his clipboard.

"Absolutely." Nick moves closer and eyes Jason's paperwork. "Raines ordered me to oversee this demo to be sure there are no violations."

"Well, since I'm the architect *and* project manager here, I'm telling you to get busy." Jason points a pencil to an industrial hose attached to a fire hydrant on the street. "Grab the hose and spray down the demolition dust."

"Fire department notified you're taking that water line out of service?"

Jason just raises his eyebrows at Nick.

"Okay, fine."

"There's a meter on it," Jason informs him. "Be sure to tell Raines *that*, too. The general contractor is being duly billed for water usage."

Nick heads toward the hose. "Hey, your phone," he says as he picks up the nozzle.

"What?"

"Your phone!" He holds a hand to his ear, mimicking a telephone.

Jason quickly pulls his cell phone from his pocket, but is too late. A check of his caller ID tells him it was Maris, again, who he keeps missing. This time, he steps away from the demo site and calls her back.

"It's crazy in the city today," Maris tells him. "A

whirlwind of models and clothes and the press—their cameras don't stop clicking and whistling and flashing."

"Crazy here, too. It's like the whole beach is cheering on this demo."

"It's no wonder. Old Maggie never once tended that place. No pretty beach gardens, no fresh paint, no birdhouses or Adirondack chairs or flower carts or seaside lanterns. No happiness. Nothing. The cottage just rotted away."

"Listen, the countdown's about to begin to dismantle it ..." Jason glances over his shoulder.

"Wait, babe. I called because I'm worried about you. Are you feeling any better? After Elsa got you so mad yesterday?"

"I am. But I'm still ticked off at the way she's going about everything." The payloader engine starts up then. "Got to run, sweetheart," Jason says while pressing his phone close to hear her over the engine noise, and over shouts from the crew. "Love you."

"Me, too. Oh, Jason? I won't be home till late Saturday. Maybe even Sunday, depending on how the rest of Fashion Week plays out. With the shows, and a denim conference scheduled, too."

If her week plays out like the rest of Jason's day, he doubts she'll be home on Saturday. But if there's one thing Jason Barlow knows, it's that being ridiculously busy suits a purpose. From overseeing the start of the official demo today, to meeting with a client to review an application for state agency approvals, to returning to his barn studio to finalize two schematic images for a new client, to meeting with a surveyor to evaluate the site work for his Nantucket-style cottage overhaul at Sea Spray Beach, busy doesn't even begin to describe his day.

And he craves it, that busyness, to stop him from thinking about, well, about everything else.

~

But one thing Jason Barlow never sees coming in his crazy workday is a confession. After trying to keep his Stony Point friends and family together, his marriage together, his job together, his head together … the plummet is inevitable. All it takes is one hello from a neighbor at Sea Spray Beach, Jason's afternoon job site. A neighbor Jason knows all too well, as it is the same man who drove his car into him and Neil on the motorcycle nearly a decade ago. A man who had a heart attack at the wheel, and survived—while two brothers' lives diverged. A man with whom Jason formed a tenuous relationship after completing his cottage restoration this past summer.

A man Jason didn't really plan on seeing much of again.

"Got a few minutes for a beer?" Ted Sullivan calls from his cottage deck. Rays of afternoon sun warm the newly shingled beach bungalow, and on the second floor, the stained glass window of an egret in marsh reeds softly glimmers.

Jason checks his watch while walking across the sand with his job-site companion, Maddy, at his side—a stick of driftwood in the German shepherd's mouth. "Not really," Jason answers Ted. "But who's counting?"

And so for the next few minutes, which turn into an hour, Jason Barlow confesses. It's Ted's questions of *How're you doing?* and *How's everybody holding up?* and *Can't believe you two were here just over a month ago. Sal was something else, wasn't he?* that do it; that get Jason to drop his brave front. Ted's calmness—a rarity in Jason's life these days—and his accepting eyes, and wrinkled skin bearing evidence of years of wisdom, get Jason to open up.

The whole story comes out … how he took off after Sal's funeral—just packed his SUV and kept driving that night, getting as far away as he could from it all.

"From this," Jason explains, waving his beer bottle toward the beach, where the waves break and the air is heavy with salt. "From the sea, from my home. From my life, I guess. Scared the shit out of myself, feeling everything shrink smaller and smaller behind me as I clocked the miles. Everything that mattered, I was fucking ditching, man." All the while, Jason drags his father's Vietnam dog tags along the chain around his neck, feeling his morale sink the same way the soldiers' did when the war grew endless.

"It's no wonder, Jason. That was a tough day, burying Sal, and you reacted. Even my wife and I were choked up at the funeral. And you and Sal were close."

"Yeah, well. You're probably the only one who really gets it, Ted. It took you and me practically ten years to make peace over my own brother's death; to put things behind us. I don't have ten more years of that road in me."

"What about Maris?"

"Maris." Jason swigs his beer. "That beautiful woman is what brought me back. And I *am* back, but it's all different at Stony Point now." He tells Ted of Elsa's beach inn for sale; of Sal's fiancée who's since packed up and left; of Jason's own quick temper and volatility. Of a marriage he feels is just going through the motions. Jason checks his watch as the sun sets further. "I'm sorry, Ted. But I've got lots to do and have to get going."

"Next time," Ted says as he walks Jason off the deck overlooking the sea, "you stop for dinner. We'll have a steak on the grill and talk more." He glances up to the second level. "Maybe we'll eat upstairs. My wife set up a table near those windows. We never tire of the views your vision brought to our reno here."

Jason agrees, and after a quick stop at the Woods cottage-demo at the end of the day, finally it's time to go home. He checks his mailbox there, scanning the envelopes as he walks up his long driveway to the kitchen entrance around back. When he opens the slider, Madison runs in ahead and goes straight to her water bowl, lapping a sloppy mouthful as Jason tosses the mail on the counter.

Which is when he notices a familiar return address on a large envelope. He plucks it from the counter, taps it against his hand, then rips the envelope open to find a typed note from Elsa DeLuca, saying his architectural services are no longer needed for her cancelled inn renovation. She included a sizable check for all his time and efforts.

Jason reads her note, looks at the check, then takes a long, exhausted breath as he whispers, "Son of a bitch."

seventeen

ALL JASON SEES THE NEXT morning is that check. That check with its substantial dollar amount, which makes him all the more mad because it reminds him how much effort's gone into the inn's redesign. The check sits front and center on his worktable in the barn studio, and he slides it out of the way to unroll his already-completed designs for the Ocean Star Inn's turret. A balcony on the turret's second level extends out over the open-air porch roof below it. The white balusters of the balcony railing give an almost widow's-walk look to it.

Now, it's all for nothing. Jason leans his elbows on the unrolled blueprint. "You around, Neil?" he asks, staring at the design while listening for any whispers coming in on the sea breeze through the slider screen. "Elsa's in a tailspin, man." Jason turns around on his stool to face the barn-door entrance. "Throwing away a dream."

The leaves rustle outside on the tall maple tree, and a distant gull caws as it swoops low somewhere over the bluff. "Where the *hell'd* you go?" Jason asks while dragging a hand through his hair. "Could use some advice." He walks to the slider and listens for his brother's voice, or spirit, or—he can't be sure—maybe it's all just memories of their long-ago talks. "Thanks for nothing," he mutters when no whispers come to him, no foul retorts, no impatient rebuke from his brother's spirit. Just silence.

Which gets Jason even angrier. Angry enough to grab that God damn check and head to Elsa's in his golf cart, after a quick detour to the convenience store. When he pulls into Elsa's stone driveway, there are folding tables set out in the sunshine, and Elsa is carrying a small box to one. She wears an apron, and he sees why as he shuts off the golf cart. The apron pocket holds tickets of some sort, large ones, and markers, which she's reaching for now and writing on with her sweeping cursive.

As Jason walks over, he puts together what's happening here.

"You're having a *tag sale*?" he asks, looking at familiar pieces from inside Elsa's cottage. There on one table is the anchor statue used as a doorstop in Foley's back room, when the dancing moves out to the deck on hot summer nights; off to the side sit two white ceramic pitchers filled with spiky marsh grasses; and behind Elsa, an indoor-gardening table is set up, covered with those red mini sand pails that she uses for her kitchen herb pots, along with an assortment of small watering cans.

"Didn't you see the signs?" Elsa asks without looking up from a price she's writing on a ticket.

Jason glances toward the street. "Yes, I did. They're yours?"

Apparently she's too busy to do more than nod as she presses a sticky price ticket onto a platter, a platter Jason's seen plenty of vegetables heaped on while he dined at Elsa's wood-planked table this past year. When Elsa turns and goes back inside her cottage, he steps closer for a look at the other familiar items—mostly mismatched china pieces from her chipped-paint cupboard that Maris always coos over. Every cup and saucer and dish is nicely lined across the table, with small price stickers waiting to be affixed.

When Elsa emerges with another box in her arms, Jason sets down a white bag he'd been holding and takes the box from her.

"Oh! Thank you, Jason," Elsa says while tucking a loose strand of hair beneath her rolled bandana.

Jason nods, turns around and walks straight past her, toward the doorway to her cottage.

"Wait!" she calls out. "I need that box here. Over *here*!"

He finagles open the door, carries the box inside and sets it on the hallway floor. From where he stands in the foyer, Lauren's grand staircase mural is visible, the painted beachscape filling the stair risers. "*Shit*," he whispers with more disappointment at the stalled inn, before returning out into the sunshine, scooping up another box and bringing that one inside, too.

"Jason Barlow!" The door swings open and Elsa stands there, hands on hips.

Jason moves her aside and goes out to retrieve another box of her beloved inn contents that she will *not* be selling, *not* if he can get through to her.

"Ooh, you're making me *so* mad," Elsa says as she picks up a box he'd set down and brings it back outside to one of her tables.

Jason comes up behind her, and when she starts to open

the carton flaps, he presses them right back down. She pauses then, before stamping her sneakered foot and spinning around to face him. "Listen up, Mr. Barlow."

"No, *you* listen. You're already breaking a lot of hearts, Elsa. Stop this nonsense now."

"Something you folks don't seem to realize is that this is *my* inn, and *my* life." She lifts her cat-eye sunglasses to the top of her head. "To do with whatever I please!"

"Not if your *famiglia* has anything to do with it."

Elsa's eyes tear up and she quickly looks around at the several tables holding her inn's contents. "Well. Are those egg sandwiches you brought?" She walks to the far table and opens the white bag Jason left there, glances over her shoulder at him, then brings the bag to the bistro table still set on the side of her cottage, where a glimpse of the beach is visible.

"Wait." Jason drops a box onto the table and jogs over, all while pulling a piece of paper out of his shirt pocket. "Yes, damn it. They're egg sandwiches," he says while slapping the paper on the table beside the two wrapped sandwiches Elsa's already set out. "*And* your check, which I'm returning."

Using her teeth, Elsa rips open a ketchup packet. She glares at him while tugging the packet, then lifts the top of her croissant roll and squeezes a swirl of ketchup on her cheesy egg. After taking a huge bite, she wordlessly pushes the check over to his side of the table.

Jason eyes the check as he shakes salt from a paper packet. And after pressing the top back on his sandwich, he pushes the check to *her* side of the table, then bites into his sandwich. "You cannot be serious about selling this place.

Not after *everything* you did to prepare for the inn."

"But I *am* serious." Elsa nudges the check back to him. "My life's changed, and so my plans have, too." She bites into her sandwich and lifts a warning finger when he reaches to slide back the check.

Which he ignores. "But you can hold off on things without making any drastic decisions," he says while pushing the check back across the table. He takes a double bite of his sandwich, using a paper napkin to catch a drizzle of ketchup. "Fine, don't open the inn. Yet," he says around the food.

"Yet?" This time, she pushes the check quickly to him.

"Right. You don't have to open it this spring, like you planned. But *wait* to decide what exactly you'll do with this place."

Elsa lifts her sandwich and turns toward the distant beach as a breeze lifts off the water. Her eyes close briefly, then she takes a bite of her sandwich and doesn't look at Jason, not until she's silently finished that sandwich. Finally, she looks to him, first, then to the check he'd pushed back. "We're obviously at a stalemate here."

"But we don't have to be."

"No, of course not. Not if you get *your* way."

Elsa stands then, pushes in her chair, lowers her sunglasses to her face and returns to her tag sale cartons and tickets and markers, leaving her check to blow off the table in that sea breeze. So Jason picks it up, tucks it in his pocket and quietly leaves.

~

The only place he can seriously work off his anger is on the boardwalk. Once he does, somewhat, after walking its length three times, Jason sits on the boardwalk bench, watches white clouds roll across the sky over Long Island Sound, and breathes. Then again, deeper, until he's able to calmly call Maris on his cell. The problem now is that she's just arrived at a runway show, and hangs up quickly because she can't talk once the modeling begins.

A minute later, Jason's phone rings. "I thought you were at a show."

"Lily's holding my seat," Maris explains, a little breathless. "She'll fill me in."

There's a pause, then, in which there is only the sound of muffled voices and some runway broadcast announcement, followed by a slamming door and the ensuing sound of traffic on a busy New York City street. He figures Maris is outdoors on a city sidewalk now, leaning into her phone and covering her other ear in order to hear him.

"What's going on, babe?" Maris asks.

"Your aunt's out of control, I'm telling you."

"What do you mean?"

"She's having a tag sale."

"A what?"

"That's what I thought, too. A *tag* sale. Selling off *all* the contents of her cottage."

"Everything?"

"Looked it. Her own stuff, and old Foley things, too."

"Okay, I've had it. That's it, I'm coming home. This just isn't right. None of it."

"Wait, wait. It's Fashion Week, I'll take care of things

from this end. Trust me. You stay put."

"But Jason," Maris insists. "It's all wrong—poor, sweet Elsa having a breakdown, me being gone half the time, you leaving. Well, you came back, but still. It's wrong and, well, it's too much. It's just too much lately. So I'm coming home!"

Jason stands and steps off the boardwalk onto the sand. "Hold on, sweetheart. I wanted to keep you in the loop, not devastate you. To quote Kyle, don't make any rash decisions. Please. We've got enough of those going on."

"But—"

"No. Just breathe. Come on." He pauses and hears nothing. But he can picture her pacing, an arm crossed over her torso, shoulders hunched, face worried. "Take a breath, Maris. Do it with me, come on." While walking toward the water, he finds himself slowly inhaling, too, until he hears his wife give in. "Another one," he gently orders her. "Deeper." Which she does, in a soft sigh. As he nears the lazy breaking waves reaching along the beach, it's as though Maris somehow hears that peaceful seaside sound across the miles, over the cell phones, and she relaxes.

"Okay," she finally agrees. "I guess I'll stay here and let you handle things."

"That's better." Jason begins walking along the hard-packed sand below the driftline. Already the firm ground there eases the ache that kicked up in his left leg since being at Elsa's. He walks slowly, breathing, too. "Because Maris, you *cannot* come home early from the biggest fashion event of the entire year … for a tag sale."

~

Cliff's never shopped at Maritime Market before. But he's heard good things about the new grocery store, and it's advertised as all organic, so he figures he'll give it a try. Thursdays are especially popular; it's when the outdoor, tented area sells local farmers' produce. He'll supplement his bagged salad with fresh cucumber, red onion and baby tomatoes grown right here on the shore. After adding the veggies to his cart, he tries to head inside the store, but some confused guy in front of him is looking lost, reading from a list and scanning the veggies, then looking at the list again.

"Pardon me," Cliff says as he maneuvers around him.

"Hey there, Cliff."

Cliff looks back over his shoulder. "Matt? How're you doing?"

"Picking up some things to bring home." Matt waves his chicken-scratched grocery list as Cliff slowly wheels his cart toward the store entrance. "Just got out of work."

"Wait. Work?" Cliff looks back again at Matt standing there in his state police uniform, the grocery list hopelessly in hand. But it's not the wrinkled list that gets his attention. It's more the police uniform with its gold badge, and arm-patch state emblem in blue and gold, and collar pins, and holster. And, okay, the *authority* that goes with it all.

"Matthew Gallagher," Cliff says, backing up a step and shaking Matt's hand. "You might be just the guy I need."

"What's up, man?"

"Listen. You've heard about Elsa's tag sale? Pity, everything must go."

"My wife told me about it."

"Eva."

"That's right. I guess her aunt really wants out of that inn now."

"Well, that depends." Cliff inches closer to Matt. "She might change her mind if she'd give herself some time to grieve *properly*."

"I'm sure you're right. Problem is convincing Elsa of that. My wife's side of the family, I'll tell you, they're stubborn. All three generations of them: Elsa, Eva and my daughter, Taylor."

"I hear you. Set in their ways." Cliff picks up a cantaloupe and sniffs it. "Unless you might consider helping me out."

"How so?"

"Care to break some rules? Between you and me?" Cliff returns the cantaloupe to its rightful crate, steps closer to Matt and drops his voice. "Connecticut state trooper to former Connecticut judge?"

"Depends."

"What time do you get off work?"

"Right now, early morning. Working the night shift for a few weeks."

"Perfect." Cliff wheels his cart around bins of zucchini and yellow squash, then lines his cart directly beside Matt's. Without looking at him, Cliff discreetly asks, "Can you get your hands on a cruiser?"

"A cruiser? From the force?"

"Yes."

"Don't you *have* security cars?"

"Of course, but they won't do. Think you can swing by Stony Point Saturday morning in a cop cruiser, with its flashing lights? *Before* the tag sale?"

"Don't know. Stony Point's outside my jurisdiction. But

hey, you mentioned breaking rules, so I'm listening. Might be a rash decision, but what do you have in mind?"

Cliff looks back toward a skylight café right inside the gourmet grocery store. "Come on, let's have a coffee over there. I'll tell you more." He motions for Matt to follow him as he wheels his cart to the café, past tables and around potted trees growing tall in the sunshine pouring in through those skylights. Eventually, he stops at a table near the windows looking out at a sailboat-dotted harbor. "Great place this Maritime Market is, no?"

~

After talking to Matt over coffee, Cliff feels optimistic. He might be able to stop Elsa's tag sale, after all. First, though, he has to finish his grocery shopping—buying a rotisserie chicken, Monterey Jack cheese, tortillas, fresh cilantro leaves, and a few other things—before wheeling his cart outside, across the parking lot. His mind is spinning, and he almost misses a lone domino on the pavement, nothing more than a toy some poor kid must've dropped.

But to Cliff, it's a sign. He picks it up, blows it off and drops it in his pocket. He just set up one domino with Matt, but still needs to line up more. So while loading his groceries into his trunk, he calls Nick on his cell phone.

"Where are you, Nicholas?"

"On my way to the Woods cottage-demo. Been keeping my eye on things there."

"Never mind that for now." Cliff wheels his cart to the cart corral one aisle over. "Round up some of the gang, would you?"

"For what?" Nick asks.

"Important mission to accomplish. Get ahold of anyone you can find and direct them to my office. I'll be there in thirty minutes."

"Will do, boss."

"Oh, and Nick? Keep it under your hat that this is all about stopping Elsa's tag sale. So do *not*, under any circumstances, bring her in on this."

By the time Cliff stops to gas up his car and gets back to his office-trailer at Stony Point, there are two golf carts in the parking lot, alongside Nick's security cruiser. With a grocery bag in each arm, Cliff shoulders open the door, nods to Jason, Eva and Nick, and rushes to the back room of the trailer. There, he sets down the food and quietly loads his perishables into a mini-fridge before closing the pleated door between his back room and the office. Then he hurries out to his metal desk.

"Glad you all made it today," he says as he opens the desk's top drawer and drops in his lucky domino.

"What's up, guy?" Jason asks. "This better be good. Nick hauled me out of my barn studio in the middle of new plans I'm drawing up."

"Yeah, I had to bribe him." Nick nods to the doughnut Jason is raising to his mouth.

"What the heck is that?" Cliff asks, squinting from his desk.

"Sugar doughnut," Jason manages around a mouthful of food. "From the convenience store. Best around."

"For Pete's sake, you're making a mess." Cliff half stands and surveys the floor. "Look at the sugar grains dropping off that thing."

"Sorry." Jason cups the doughnut as he takes another bite.

"Get the dustpan from the utility closet, would you?" Cliff snaps his fingers and points toward the side of the room. "I'll get ants in here with that sweet trail."

Eva rushes to the closet and brushes through the clutter to find the dustpan, which she leans against Jason's chair leg.

"Okay." Cliff sits back and clasps his hands on his desk. "So, I've got all my dominoes lined up here."

As soon as he begins, Eva's cell phone rings. "Sorry, work," she says with a small smile as she takes the phone. "Gallagher Realty," she answers, then clucks, nods and calms down the caller before finally hanging up. "Three retirees," she explains to them, "having a reunion week. They rented a cottage near the beach and their toaster broke! Lovely ladies, really, but frazzled that they couldn't have frozen waffles and toast this morning." As she talks, she's typing a reminder into her cell phone. "I'll have to run out and buy a replacement toaster."

"Okay, now listen up." Cliff tries to begin again. "I'm hoping you're all free on Saturday. If not, well, if Elsa is important to you, you'll clear your schedules for this."

"Oh, wait," Eva says as she slips her phone back into her purse and lifts a watering can from the floor. "By the way, I brought this to give that shrub near your office door a drink. Poor thing is practically dead, Cliff. Maybe you should think about dressing up this place? You know, since you're the authority figure here."

"Really, Eva. This is just a modular trailer. I'm hoping to find more suitable permanent office quarters."

"Why? This trailer does have a certain charm. It suits you." She looks from Cliff, then to Jason. "Maybe you can design some type of addition to it?"

Jason shrugs to Cliff. "We can talk," Jason says, pressing the last of his doughnut in his mouth, "but only if the Board of Governors approves my fees, first."

Nick sits back in his chair. "Now that you mention it, I wouldn't mind having my own office space, boss. Even a cubicle." He turns to Jason, leans over to pick up the dustpan and hands it to him. "Think you can accomplish that in a redesign here?"

Jason takes the dustpan and sweeps up any sugar crumbs, then dumps them in the trash can beside Cliff's desk. "Anything's possible. Maybe I can remove some of the back wall and extend it to add a workroom for the guards." Jason turns toward the rear of the trailer and considers Cliff's closed accordion door.

Intentionally closed, Cliff thinks, to keep their eagle eyes off his personal space.

"That'd be sick," Nick adds. "Man, a place with a table to fill out ordinance violations, post daily logs, have lunch and chill."

When the talk veers into Eva deciding what type of curtains should be hung on the trailer windows, Cliff opens his bottom desk drawer and pulls out a beat-up gavel, which he bangs harshly on its sound block. "Order. *Order!*"

Just like in the courtrooms he presided over for many years, after a few surprised murmurs, the room goes quiet. Jason motions to Cliff that he has the floor.

"Thank you. Now the reason I summoned you all here is I need your assistance." Cliff sets his gavel on the desktop and looks to Jason. "Jason. We need as much help as possible to put this plan in place. Is Maris around?"

"No. It's Fashion Week, so she's the busiest she ever gets in New York right now. She'll maybe be back Saturday night, more likely Sunday."

"That's too late." Cliff checks his watch, then looks at his waiting crew. "So it's just us three pulling this off, plus Matt, who I talked to a little while ago."

"You talked to *Matt*? Today?" Eva asks.

"At Maritime Market."

"Oh, don't you love that place?" Eva asks. "They're all about healthy eating, and have *thee* best organic yogurt. You've got to try it, Cliff. And, oh, with their seasonal pumpkin-spice granola and fresh fruit, you've got the parfait of perfection!"

Cliff clears his throat and his hand goes to his gavel.

"Sorry," Eva whispers with a quick smile, one that she then zips closed with her fingers.

"So, anyway," Cliff continues, "Matt's in on all this, too."

"All what?" Jason asks, leaning back in his chair with his hands crossed behind his head. "What's going on?"

"The first order of business is that we need to be connected to pull this off. And cell service is too darn fickle to depend on at the beach. That's why I'm giving you all one of these." His metal desk drawer drags against the runners when he yanks it open to retrieve three walkie-talkies. "Instructions for their use are on the back. It's pretty simple—press the button and talk. I put in new batteries, and for crying out loud, leave them on the pre-set channel so we can actually communicate. But you can choose your own ringtone." He hands them each a unit. "There's a belt clip included, for easy portability."

Suddenly the trailer-office fills with squawks and static and vibrating chirps echoing off the industrial walls as the walkie-talkies are turned on and fiddled with.

Cliff talks over the racket. "This way," he yells while leaning forward over his desk, "we can stay in touch in any situation. If something goes amiss, we can get on it, right away."

"Get on *what*?" Nick asks. "This seems pretty legit just to stop Elsa."

"What? You're stopping Elsa's tag sale?" Eva asks while sampling her ringtones.

"I'm going to try, anyway." Cliff stands and walks over to a sliding window. "*We're* going to try," he corrects while gazing outside. Gray clouds are moving in, from the direction of Elsa's inn. Looks like rain. "Maybe we can keep her from packing up and leaving here."

Jason has been quiet since he took his walkie-talkie, which he shows no interest in using. "Kind of like an intervention?"

"No!" Eva exclaims, standing and pointing her walkie-talkie at Jason. "No, an *inn*-tervention!"

"I like that." Cliff turns to Eva as he says it. "An *inn*-tervention. It's all for a good cause, right?"

"Ten-four," Nick agrees as he stands and clips a walkie-talkie to his belt.

"So, okay." Cliff returns to his desk chair and sits straight with his hands clasped again. "Now, here's the plan."

eighteen

MAYBE IT'S GOOD THAT IT'S raining today. Usually Friday mornings are busy at the diner, but no one wants to go out in this dreary weather. Between the light coastal rain and fog, the damp goes right through to your bones. After watching only a few customers stop in for breakfast—jackets held over their heads, umbrellas dripping—Kyle comes to a decision. If the Italian were around, he'd find some way to drum up more business. So Kyle asks Jerry to cover the diner, then grabs his keys and jacket and makes a run for his pickup truck in the parking lot.

Because it's time to channel Salvatore DeLuca, and the only way he can try is with a book. Kyle squints past the flipping windshield wipers. Either the defroster's on the fritz in this jalopy, or his second cigarette already is clouding the windows. He gives the dashboard a whack to kick-start things, then takes a drag of his cigarette and flicks the butt out the window. "Shit, I have to quit these."

At the next traffic light, the windshield fogs even more, so he leans forward and rubs his open palm on the glass, then cranks the defroster fan after opening his window halfway. Which would be fine, except for the rain spitting in and soaking his left arm and shoulder. So he rolls up the window, squints through those slapping wipers, and continues on toward the little plaza just before the Stony Point railroad trestle.

Finally, he turns into the parking lot. Amber-colored twinkly lights line a storefront window, where colorful buoys are randomly strung around a banner reading: *The Book Buoy – We Keep Used Books Afloat.* Behind the rain-spattered window, stacks of books fan out in every direction. After parking, Kyle zigs and zags through a few puddles, opens the shop door and walks in. His wet shoes squeak on the creaky wooden floor just as an older woman steps down from a rolling ladder, two books in hand. She wears jeans and a cable-knit sweater with a gold cameo brooch. Reading glasses are perched on top of her head.

"Hi there!" she says, smiling. "Can I help you find something?"

"Hey, how're you doing?" Kyle stalls, because he knows if he can *think* like Sal, it would help him boost diner business. But how to tap into that unique Italian heritage, Wall Street smarts combo—that's the issue. He glances around the store. Simple, bell-shaped pendant lights hang from the ceiling, up and down each aisle of books. Center tables are covered with *Popular Fiction* and *Book Club Selections.* "So," Kyle begins, uncertain of what he needs. "Do you maybe have any English-to-Italian translation books?"

"Sure do." The woman motions for him to follow her. "I have just the thing for you. In our language section."

They pass the rolling ladder and a comfortable

arrangement of two upholstered chairs around a table with a coffee carafe set on it, along with paper cups. "How about books on inns, too?" Kyle asks.

"Oh! Are you travelling to Italy soon?"

"Me?" Kyle shakes his head. "No. I'm not looking for inns *in* Italy. More like an advice book on how to open an inn. Or to manage one."

"Well now," the woman muses as she pulls a couple of Italian translation books from the shelf. "Opening an inn in Italy sounds like quite the adventure!" She hands him the two books.

"Believe me," Kyle says as he looks down at the books, "I don't need any more adventures these days."

"Life is an adventure, every day sometimes, don't you think?" the woman asks as she motions to a bookshelf. "There are more language books mixed in here. And you might find books referencing running an inn in the business section." She points to the left. "Next row over."

It doesn't take long for Kyle to get lost in Italy. When he sits in one of those upholstered chairs and pours a cup of hot coffee for himself and browses his translation books, it happens. He pages through sections where word pronunciations are in italics; sections on Italian culture relating to the language; on Italian eating; popular expressions. There's something of Sal everywhere he looks, especially when he spots phrases Sal threw around. *Andiamo!* and *Che bello!* and *Va bene!*

Kyle closes the book and sips his coffee, remembering especially *Andiamo!* Let's go. The Italian was always game for a golf cart race, impromptu baseball challenge, a cold beer, fishing. To wait tables. And always with a ready smile.

Merda—shit, does he miss the guy.

But it helps, choosing a pocket translation book and a slim paperback of popular Italian phrases and philosophies. After browsing the innkeeping guidebooks, he stops at the register where he adds souvenirs for his kids: lighthouse bookmark for Evan and stuffed buoy for Hailey.

"*Perfezione*," Kyle says as he starts his pickup truck and backs out of his parking space. The rain stopped, and a sea breeze seems to be breaking up the gray clouds. "Just in time for Friday night fishing."

~

Whenever Maris takes the train home from Manhattan, the view outside the window becomes her personal meditation. The train travels along curves of lagoons and boardwalks, passing quaint seaside bungalows and beaches. With each mile of track running along the Connecticut coastline, picturesque harbors filled with boats, and shingled cottages weathered silver, become postcards of her life, her train window framing each pretty sight.

But it's different today. With her head bent low, cell phone in hand, Maris scrolls through various images on the screen. Each image is from one particular real estate listing. Each picture brings memories cherished enough that her heart hurts at the thought of losing them.

Because each flick of her finger across her phone brings a new photo of Elsa's cottage, the cottage she purchased just last year with such hope for the future. It's all here: the dining room where Elsa served so many summer dinners on her antique, chipped china plates; the infamous Foley's back room, with its jukebox and pinball machine and tattered-and-worn restaurant booths—tattered by summers of card games and talk and parties and eating and living. A booth Maris sat in with Jason two summers ago, Maris freshly returned to Stony Point after years of being away while building her fashion career.

Off the back room, there's the epic deck, strung with twinkly lights that sparkle on misty summer nights. The same deck where Jason says he fell in love with Maris fourteen *years* ago when they stood out there one night, alone, dancing to a slow jukebox song beneath an August moon.

Memories, memories. Sal's thirty-sixth birthday party in that back room, with Celia playing guitar and Lauren singing *Happy Birthday*, in Italian! The same back room where a slightly-looped Lauren once spilled the secret of her long-ago clandestine love affair with Neil. The place of summer nights like no others, filled with kisses, and looks, and whispers. The place where spirits are ever stirred up in dust particles swirling like stardust, bringing teary smiles and melancholy hearts.

The place that holds all her beach friends' history.

Now, to see the real estate listing touting the cottage as zoned for an inn, with water views, close enough to the beach for a casual lifestyle in a charming seaside village, and to imagine a new family moving in and *changing* history all because of Elsa's misguided, *rash* decision, Maris' heart breaks all over again.

But only for a moment. Only until she sits back with a quick breath and a secret smile.

Because sometimes you have to be pushed to the edge

in order to take a daring step. And that's just what Elsa's real estate listing—with its full-color photo slideshow—prompted Maris to do today.

~

"Talk to me, guy."

After he says it, Jason freezes. Every window is open in his barn studio this Friday afternoon, including the big double doors. Before, in the hiss of a light rainfall, he thought, *maybe*, there was something. A whisper, a few of his brother's murmured words. It happened while he stood at the bookshelf with one of Neil's journals in his hand. But when he turned around and tipped his head? Nothing.

"Fine, then," Jason says over his shoulder, toward the doorway where the sound of waves breaking on the bluff reaches him. "Suit yourself." When he pushes aside a stack of drawings on his desk, a scale and pencil fall to the floor, so he picks those up and throws them in a drawer before setting out paper towels. On top of those, he unwraps a ham-and-cheese grinder, loaded with lettuce, tomato, mayo and oil. Beside that, he dumps out a bag of potato chips as he grabs a working-lunch.

"But you're really pissing me off, Neil," he adds while nudging his sandwich closer. "Shit, where the hell are you, bro? No sign of you for weeks."

Then, in the quiet, he gets busy. It's either that, or stew in his sadness—which Sal was good at busting him on. So reluctantly, Jason picks up a pencil. The Nantucket-style cottage he's renovating needs a light and airy interior, anchored with strong details in the windows and moldings.

He's been loose-sketching some ideas, and it's time to bring them together in final choices for the homeowner. Grinder in one hand, pencil in the other, he decides to make one peak of the cottage stone-front rather than shingled.

"Hey, babe. I'm home!"

As Madison scrambles down the loft stairs, Jason turns around to see Maris in her cuffed ocean-star jeans with flecks of silver paint on them, from her Denim Blue Sea line. She wears a black blazer over a V-neck black tee, and, as always, her star pendant glimmers around her neck. The dog circles around her legs, sniffing at Maris' leather loafers. Jason sets down his food and grabs a napkin to wipe his mouth. "What are you doing home so early?"

"Aren't you happy to see me?" Maris breezes over, gives him a quick kiss, then picks up his half-eaten grinder and takes a big bite.

He leans his elbows back on his worktable. "Weren't you staying in New York until tomorrow? I thought you had team-meetings recapping the spring styles."

"And don't you take any time off?" She eyes his table covered with food. "Working during lunch?" As she says it, she picks up his grinder again and digs in for another bite, her eyes closing with the taste of it.

"Did you have lunch yet, or are you going to finish mine?"

She hands him what's left of his grinder. "What are you working on?" Without waiting for an answer, she bends close and brushes through his Nantucket-style sketches. "Nice," she murmurs, resting her hand on his shoulder. "Are these for the place at Sea Spray Beach?"

Jason nods as he takes a bite of the sandwich, then a long

swig from a can of soda.

Maris scoops up a handful of potato chips. "Tough choice, these sketches are all beautiful. Very coastal, very classic." She tosses a few chips in her mouth. "I'd have a hard time picking one."

Jason turns on his stool, noticing her hand reaching for what's left of his ham-and-cheese grinder. But this time, she takes a small bite, leaving a hunk still for him.

"You're looking a little shaggy. Have you shaved at all while I've been gone?" she asks around the food, all while brushing her fingers across his whiskered cheek.

"No." Jason drags his knuckles across the scar on his jaw. "I don't think so. Too busy."

"Have you heard anything from Elsa?"

"Nothing. But I *have* heard from Matt, Eva, Nick and Cliff. A plan is in place to stop the tag sale tomorrow, and hopefully it will get Elsa to rethink things." Jason opens his desk drawer and pulls out a walkie-talkie. "It's all systems go to prevent her from selling off everything."

Maris takes the walkie-talkie and turns it over in her hand. "Isn't that a little harsh, to stop the tag sale completely?" The walkie-talkie squawks when she switches it on, then off. "Maybe if she sells a *little*, she'll feel guilty and change her mind. You know, we can try reverse psychology."

"No way. We don't need to see all the stuff from Foley's back room sold to strangers tomorrow. So it was either everyone here buys all her stuff, or we stop the sale."

"I thought I'd maybe get home in time to talk her out of it?" She hands Jason the walkie-talkie, then checks her watch.

"We have it under control, sweetheart. And seriously?" He turns on his stool again to set down the walkie-talkie. "Maris, you're Saybrooks' director of women's denim, fresh out of Fashion Week." He picks up his pencil and fusses with a cottage sketch, his hand brushing back and forth over the paper. "Do you really think it's a good idea to leave your recap and strategy meetings early for, essentially, a *tag* sale?"

"I didn't leave early for a tag sale, Jason."

She goes quiet then, long enough for him to look over his shoulder at her, mid-sketch.

"I left early because I quit my job."

~

The sun came out just long enough to dry off the rocks where Kyle sets his tackle box and folded sweatshirt, along with a small cooler of pepperoni and cheese slices, and a bag of trail mix. He's not sure how many more Friday fishing nights they'll manage before the weather gets too cold. But this September night is custom-made for it: the horizon lavender, a crescent moon hanging low over Long Island Sound, the sea breeze light and the water calm. The only thing missing is Jason.

"Where you at?" he asks when he calls Jason's cell.

"Yeah, Kyle. I'm home."

"Home? I'm on the rocks, man. You fishing tonight?"

In the pause, he hears Maris, upset in the background. *I thought you'd be happy*, she's saying.

"Hey, if you're busy, Barlow—"

"No. I'm there."

And that's it. Disconnected and silenced. So Kyle baits his line and casts it over the moonlit water. First, Jason left that one night. Now, he's fighting with Maris, apparently. Kyle squints toward the beach when he sees what looks like Jason and his dog approaching, so okay ... he's obviously eager to get out of that big old house of his, too.

"Yo, bro. What's going on up on that grand bluff?" Kyle lights a cigarette. "Thought maybe you skipped town again when you didn't show up here," he says.

Jason slams his gear onto a large boulder, then tosses down his fishing rod with a clatter.

"Hey." Kyle takes a drag of the cigarette, wincing through the smoke as he watches all this unfold. "You're disturbing the fish. Cool it." He turns to the water and reels in his line a bit.

Jason settles in behind him, talking so quietly, it makes what he's saying all the more ominous. "I'm so fucking mad."

When Kyle looks over his shoulder at him, Jason's leaning against a boulder, baiting his line. Even the dog is anxious, sitting close to Jason, her ears tuned to his every move. Shit, if he's scaring the dog, God knows what went down in the Barlow house.

Suddenly there's a loud static sound.

"What the hell is that?" Kyle asks.

"Security walkie-talkie. From Cliff." Jason pulls it out of his sweatshirt pocket and raises it to his face. "Later, Cliff," he says into it.

"Hey, ten-thirty," comes back at Jason, followed by a beep.

"Ten-thirty?" Jason whispers while pulling out a cheat

sheet from his pocket and squinting at it under the illumination from his cell. "Ten-thirty." Jason's finger lands on the meaning. "Doesn't conform to FCC rules? What the hell?"

"What's that all about?" As he asks, Kyle carefully walks across the rocks to bring his trail mix and cooler of pepperoni and cheese closer to Jason.

"Cliff told me ten-thirty. So I guess he wants me to talk in FCC-approved code."

"Huh? Say again?"

"Long story. Everyone got one. A walkie-talkie." Jason tosses his on top of the tackle box. "Part of the tag sale plan."

"The what?" Kyle gives the dog a piece of cheese, then scoops up Jason's walkie-talkie. "I didn't get one."

"It's nothing, Kyle." Jason grabs the walkie-talkie back and shoves it in his pocket. "You're working tomorrow. You're not a part of it."

Gesù, Santa Maria, is Barlow cranky tonight. *Shit.* Enough to get Kyle to pick up his cooler and leave Jason to his misery, walkie-talkie and all. The night is dark, with only that sliver of moon, so Kyle's careful walking over the exposed rocks back to his waiting fishing pole. A beam of light from the Gull Island Lighthouse sweeps over the water, and the low-tide waves lap at the rocks and tidal pools nearby. After eating a few more pepperoni slices from a safe distance, he calls out, "Everything all right, man?"

"No." Jason casts his line, hard, then leans back on a boulder. He lights a cigarette, too, then exhales a long trail of smoke. "No, it's not. Maris quit her job today."

"*What?*"

"You heard me."

"Well, yeah. But. Are you *serious*?"

"Damn straight. She's done."

"And I'm taking it you did not know this was happening?"

"That's right." Jason reels in his line, tosses aside his rod and grabs the bag of trail mix. "Came completely out of the blue."

"Wow." Kyle pulls a can of beer from his cooler. "Now *that's* a rash decision if I ever heard one. What about our pact? Statistics show major life choices are skewed by grief."

Jason's quiet. Unusually so. Not a word, not a joke, not a brush-off. Nothing. Just chowing on a handful of raisins and peanuts.

"Why'd she quit?" Kyle sets down his pole and makes his way back across the rocks with a second can of beer. "I mean, *quit*? Not even a leave of absence or some bullshit like that?"

"Says it all got to be too much." Jason takes the beer Kyle hands him and snaps it open. "First Sal's death, and her aunt so upset—because Elsa's like a mother to her. Then, when I left …"

"For thirty minutes!"

"She fought damn hard for fifteen years to get where she is in that cutthroat fashion business. Director of women's denim now, travels the world. Her jeans are in catalogs, stores, online. She has this incredible customer base. *And* Saybrooks was finally giving her full design rein." Jason takes a long swallow of the beer. "I'd never have told her to leave."

"Hell, she's probably worried about you. And her aunt. You know."

"I'm not the kind of guy who needs his wife keeping an eye on him."

"Maybe she'll change her mind?"

"She says no. We've been arguing about it all afternoon. But she started the paperwork already. Going back to the city next week to finalize it."

"Damn." Kyle pulls out a cigarette from his pocket, lights it and returns to his fishing rod. "What a career she built. Making serious dough, too, I'd imagine." He casts out his line toward the sliver of moonlight falling on the dark water. "What's she going to do now?"

Jason tosses down his empty beer can and walks across the rocks to the pepperoni cooler. "Good question, Bradford." He stacks cheese on a few pepperoni pieces. "Good question."

nineteen

SOMETIMES IT FEELS LIKE ELSA'S entire life has been spent waiting. Over thirty years ago, she waited for the phone to ring in Italy. It was late in the night, and her husband was getting their son, Salvatore, ready for bed, reading him a story about sailboats and sea adventures. Elsa's sister, June, always called once a week from Connecticut, but that night she was late. Elsa tried to reach her, but there was nothing. No answer from June, or from her husband, Louis. It wasn't like June not to call. So Elsa waited. And waited.

Eventually, the phone did ring. Louis' voice reached her, bringing terrible news that June had died in a car accident that November afternoon. The car had hit black ice and skidded into a tree. June had the girls, Maris and Evangeline, with her in the back. They survived and were okay.

And then came the waiting in an airport, months later, as her flight was delayed. Though Elsa had been to Connecticut for the funeral, she was going to the States again, determined to stop Louis from putting his youngest child, Evangeline, up for adoption. Maris and Eva were sisters; their mother would never want them separated. But Elsa had no choice but to wait in the airport while a late-season New England nor'easter chipped away at her minutes. Minutes that were lost, as Elsa finally arrived in Connecticut too late. The adoption had been completed—Eva was gone. And Elsa would have to wait another three decades before reuniting with her long-lost nieces.

Back in Italy, Elsa's young son came down with strep throat. Little Salvatore was brought to the hospital when his fever wouldn't break. And Elsa waited again; her husband was alive then, squeezing her hand as they prepared to hear from the doctor. *It's called rheumatic fever*, the doctor explained. *It can damage the heart, particularly the valves. Your son needs to rest. Mr. and Mrs. DeLuca, please sit. We'll do everything we can, but we don't know how long your boy will live.*

Elsa found herself waiting more and more. Waiting to see if Sal would recover, waiting to see if his medications and monitoring would work. That waiting carried her through the calendar-years as Sal blew out his birthday candles. *Okay, he made it to sixteen. To twenty. To thirty!* she'd think with hope. All the while, she waited for the inevitable.

And it came, which brings Elsa right back to the present. With Salvatore's death, she no longer wants to spend her life waiting. She doesn't want to wait for the unbearable sadness to pass. Because it won't.

So now, Elsa is only willing to wait for two things: the sale of her beach inn, and for her first tag sale customers to arrive.

Elsa's grandniece, Taylor, is helping this Saturday morning, setting out boxed coffee and fresh cinnamon rolls. The cottage driveway is lined with folding tables, which Elsa hauled out from the small guest cottage—now used as a storage shed. Elsa stands a colorful spinning whirligig beside the food table to get folks' attention.

"These little extras help make a sale at events like this," she tells Taylor.

"Your items are too good for a tag sale, Aunt Elsa. They'd be better for your old boutique in Milan!" Having finished arranging the pastry station, Taylor sits at the cashier table and adjusts the cash drawer. "Oh, I was supposed to tell you something from my mom and dad. And even Uncle Jason."

"What's that?" Elsa asks while stacking cardboard cups.

"You're not to sell anything from their old hangout."

Oh, Lordy. How many times has Elsa heard the story since she bought this old cottage a year ago? *Back in the day, this place was called Foley's*, they've all told her in earnest. *Downstairs, the cottage was a market, stocking food and essentials for the beach community*, it's been explained. *Foley and his family lived upstairs. The old man's grandson lived there, too. The kid was rough around the edges*, they'd add, *so Foley tacked on an addition to keep an eye on him, and all us Stony Point teens, too. The rest*, the gang won't let her forget, *is history. Our history—spending summer nights of our youth by the jukebox, pinball machine and pilfered fridge stocked with beer.* Endless secrets there have been divulged to Elsa, and it's all laughs, kisses, and one-two punch near-misses. The beach friends have incessantly ordered her to preserve this Stony Point landmark-room within her inn.

When Elsa glances at her grandniece now, Taylor sits there wearing a sun visor, her long blonde hair hanging in a low ponytail down her back. She points to the cottage deck and back room, explaining, "It's their favorite place here."

With her hands on her hips, Elsa squints up at the cottage. "Believe me, I'm *very* well aware of the sanctity of that room! And they can all open their wallets and buy those relics themselves, if they want them so badly."

"Well, I can help you display these other things, since no one's here yet. Mom says visuals are important to a sale." Taylor walks to a table of small kitchen items. "She sees that when she lists a new house. That's why she loved having Celia stage them."

"Celia did a fine job," Elsa agrees. "We all miss her."

"Aunt Elsa, you're selling this? It's so pretty." Taylor holds up a beach umbrella spoon rest.

"Yes, I'm trying to downsize in order to bring as little as possible with me after I sell this place."

"Maybe I'll be able to visit you." Taylor inspects the spoon rest, then gently sets it down. "Will you move close by?"

"I'm not really sure, dear. I'll be around to settle Sal's estate. But a neighbor friend invited me to stay with her in Italy, until I get my bearings. Though that's still far off. So anyway, when will you be getting your driver's license?"

"Not for a while. My dad started taking me driving, but only in parking lots for now."

"That's good. You need your license before you head off to college one day." Elsa glances over at Taylor arranging teacups on saucers, then lining them neatly across a table. "I'm going to pay you for being my cashier today. You put that money in your college fund."

Taylor nods, then heads back to her cashiering post and takes off her denim jacket, which she drapes over her chair back. "My mom's so sad you're leaving. I heard her crying last night, telling my dad she doesn't want you to go. I'll miss you, too, Auntie."

"Oh, honey. I feel the same way." Elsa walks over and gives Taylor a quick hug. "Even though it's difficult to leave, it's simply no longer my place here." As she straightens then, two approaching women catch Elsa's eye. They're dressed in exercise garb, and Elsa gives a friendly wave.

"Hi there," one calls out, slowing to survey the tag sale items. "We're really sorry to see you selling this place."

"Will the new owners take it over as an inn?" the other asks while shielding her eyes from the sun.

"Well, now. I'm not really certain." Elsa scrutinizes her haggard-looking cottage, with its weathered shingles, and window trim needing paint. "They *could*, though. I suppose."

"My sister-in-law planned on visiting me from Rhode Island next summer, and was excited to stay in *your* new inn!" The woman takes off her sunglasses as she says it, tipping her head sadly to Elsa.

"It's nice to hear that. But unfortunately, things didn't work out for me." Elsa gestures to her tag sale tables.

The women pick up a few mementoes, holding one to the sunlight, then another, before leaving without any purchases. Elsa watches them go, then sits at her little bistro table—which is also for sale—and centers a vase of silk flowers on it, remembering the summer breakfasts she had there with Jason.

So this is it, the beginning of moving on. After a quiet moment when she notices Taylor fidgeting at the cashier table, Elsa throws her a hopeful smile. "Let the early birds arrive!"

~

Saturday morning, Matt parked his state police cruiser halfway across the beach street, leaving only one lane open at the railroad trestle. On the top of the official sedan, blue and red lights silently flash. Jason leans against the car, arms folded in front of him, as he and Matt watch Nick in action.

A car slowly turns in beneath the trestle, and Nick steps to the side of the street and waves to them to open their window. He grabs a clipboard from a sawhorse set at the curb. "Resident, or visitor?" he asks with as much authority as he can muster. For once, the new Stony Point guard uniforms are actually working to their benefit, epaulets and all.

"Probably a tag sale customer," Matt says to Jason as they watch.

Nick motions his hand for the visiting car to make a U-turn and leave. "Annual street sweeping today," he lies. "Closed to outside traffic."

"Street sweeping," Jason says, leaning close to Matt. "Whose crazy idea was that?"

"The commissioner's."

"Nice." Jason watches the car finagle a U-turn and leave. "Who wouldn't believe a beach community doesn't occasionally sweep the sand from the street?" He salutes Nick as another car pulls in beneath the trestle.

"Must be the tag sale early birds," Jason says.

"Where's Maris?" Matt asks. "At Elsa's?"

The mere mention of Maris gets Jason annoyed. He still cannot believe she quit her job. *Quit* it. It's so not like her that he doubts she won't change her mind by the end of the weekend and withdraw her notice. So he says nothing about the issue to Matt. "No, she's home. Working in her studio."

As he says it, the walkie-talkie clipped to Jason's belt gives an electronic ring.

"Jason?"

"Come in," he answers into his walkie-talkie.

"Are you there?" Eva asks back after a few seconds of static.

Jason shakes his head and glances over at Matt. "Affirmative."

"What's the 4-1-1 on TSF?" Eva asks.

TSF, Jason whispers to Matt with a shrug, to which Matt shakes his head.

"TSF?" Jason asks into the walkie-talkie then.

"Duh. Tag Sale Fail! How's it going at Elsa's?"

"It's only eight-thirty."

"Isn't that your shift?"

"No. Way too early for me. I'm at the trestle, on my way getting a coffee for Maris. She's working in the loft. So I'll be home in a few minutes, if you need me." There's a sound of static when he releases the talk button, until he lifts the walkie-talkie again. "Over."

"Roger!"

~

Maris has walked Sea View Road countless times in her life. And yet, something about the street, and the cottages, and even the sunlight glancing down from the September sky, feels unreal. It's odd, actually. The only thing she can attribute that unreal feeling to is that she's walking the sandy street with a newfound freedom today—evidenced by her faded skinnies, tee and flip-flops. So this is what it feels like to be unemployed. There's an emptiness in the view, or her thoughts. Something.

Until reality snaps right back with a blaring golf cart horn.

"I thought you were working in the loft." Jason pulls up alongside her.

"What?" Maris still walks, slowly. "Working?"

"I was hoping, anyway." He inches the golf cart forward, one hand rubbing his scruffy jaw. "Maybe you'd changed your mind about quitting your job and were designing again?"

Maris walks around the golf cart, lifts the tray of two take-out coffees from the passenger seat and climbs in, holding the coffee on her lap. "Just the opposite. I'm stopping by Elsa's. Which is something I've rarely been able to do before … take a walk on a whim."

Jason, she notices, does not move the idling cart. Instead, he folds his arms over the steering wheel and eyes her. "I have to tell you, Maris. I love you, but I'm still really mad at you."

"I wish you weren't."

"We need to talk this job thing out. Because I don't get it."

"I'm not changing my mind, Jason."

Jason starts the cart moving again, toward Elsa's place. "Please don't mention it to your aunt, okay? She's got enough going on, and maybe quitting was a rash decision you need to rethink before broadcasting it."

"Jason," Maris whispers. And damn it, her eyes tear up at the same time. Having taken that bold step of leaving her job, can't she at least not get weepy about it? So now she gets mad at *that*—at her tears!

"I'm really worried about you, too." Jason turns the golf cart onto Elsa's street. "I couldn't sleep last night."

Oh, didn't Maris know it. Up, down, in and out of the bathroom, down the stairs for a secret smoke, letting Maddy in and out. All night, Jason wordlessly made it clear that he is bothered by Maris' decision.

"Hey, listen." Jason pulls the golf cart up to the curb and nods toward Elsa's tag sale. "Taylor's here. Promise me you won't let on to anyone." He reaches over, tucks Maris' hair behind an ear and strokes her face. "Not yet."

~

Everything looks sad as Elsa waits for it to sell. Because each piece holds some memory of her son. The red-and-cream checked quilt from Sal's bed, a quilt he used all summer when he felt tired, and chilled. His bedside lamp, the one that glowed late into the night as he wrote the beach inn's extensive, detailed business plan. The cast-iron anchor statue that both Sal and Jason used as a doorstop, letting a sea breeze into the back room when the jukebox songs and dancing kicked in. The plates upon which Elsa heaped Sal's scrambled eggs all summer. She remembers how he'd breeze into the kitchen, his hair wavy in the damp sea air, his voice groggy as he said, *Hey, Ma.* And always, always, his smile.

Why won't someone, *anyone*, arrive at her tag sale and take it? That's right. Take it all, get rid of her memories that do nothing but break her heart, over and over again. Just clear these things out of her life so she can try, somehow, to move on. All this does, this detritus from one summer of living at Stony Point, is weigh her down.

She walks to the curb to see if any cars might be headed her way, checks her watch, then hears something. A golf cart, yes. Someone coming to finally get this tag sale rolling. She lifts her leopard-print reading glasses to see it's only Jason and Maris. Before Jason fully stops at the curb, Maris rushes out of the cart.

"Aunt Elsa! How are you?" Maris asks while throwing her arms around Elsa in a hug. "Sell much yet?"

"No!" She waves hello to Jason as he approaches Taylor at her cashier table, where she's been flipping through the pages of a magazine to fill the quiet time. "I drive by so many tag sales," Elsa says to Maris, "and they're mobbed. So I don't get it. Because, look!" Elsa takes Maris' hand and leads her closer to the display tables, then drops her reading glasses back on. "I put all this out, and listed nice things in my ad to draw people. You know, early birds welcome, and free coffee. And yet …" She turns up her hands.

"Maybe people missed your signs," Maris says with a worried glance at Jason. "They got washed away in yesterday's rain?"

"I don't know." Elsa squints down the empty road again. "It's strange that not *one* car has driven up."

Just then, a shrill, electronic ringtone rises from a walkie-talkie on Jason's belt. Before he has a chance to break away from his conversation with Taylor, a voice comes through the speaker. Elsa's pretty sure it's Eva, talking so rapid-fire, it's hard to keep up with what she's saying.

"Jason! The roadblock's working. Nick turned away a *ton* of cars. I just showed a house, so I'm a little late arriving.

But I'll take this shift with Nick. He needs my help, because the cars, they keep coming! If we can hang in there and keep turning them away, then we're in the clear. Having Matt's cruiser flashing the police lights was genius. Folks think serious stuff is going on."

Jason drops his face into his open hand as he shakes his head.

"Jason?" After an uncomfortable static sound, Eva speaks again, her voice lower. "Why aren't you answering me?"

Elsa walks toward Jason, slowly, waiting to see how he'll handle this bombshell.

"Jason?" another voice—this one a man's—asks over the walkie-talkie still clipped to Jason's belt. If Elsa's not mistaken, wait, can that be … *Cliff?* "We lost the connection to Jason." More static.

Then another shrill ringtone from Jason's walkie-talkie. "Jason! You there?" This time, it's Nick.

Nick, Cliff, Eva. Their *voices* all descend on Jason at the same time that Elsa does, in person. She lowers her reading glasses on her nose as she approaches, and stares over the frames at him. He doesn't flinch.

"Jason Barlow, hellooo," Eva calls out. Then comes a vibrating beep and static before she continues with, "Are we in the clear with the *inn*-tervention?"

By now, Elsa stands directly in front of Jason and holds out her hand. When he rolls his eyes and glances away, she thrusts her extended, taut hand with an unmistakable give-it-to-me-right-now shake. So he does. He unclips the walkie-talkie and drops it in her palm.

Elsa takes the little two-way radio, pushes her reading

glasses back up, eyes the controls for a moment before pressing the talk button and raising the unit to her mouth, her eyes never once, not for one *millisecond*, leaving Jason. "Oh, yes," she says into the walkie-talkie. "We're *very* much in the clear. Ten-four!"

Then? Nothing. Not for about five seconds as the bomb falls. Then comes a collective explosion of gasps from all around.

~

Jason's not sure he's ever seen Elsa this mad. By the time the others arrive at her cottage, she's retrieved plenty of cartons from inside and is throwing her tag sale items into them, all while stamping her foot, cursing beneath her breath, and—yes, he caught her—discreetly swiping at a few tears. Wisps of hair escape her bandana, random sale tickets stick out of her pockets, and she shoves her blouse sleeves up as she tosses and boxes things. Elsa doesn't even turn around when Matt's cruiser pulls in, followed by a slew of golf carts right behind it.

Maris tells Jason to calm down her aunt. So he tries, walking up beside Elsa and resting his hand on hers when she tries to pick up a small china bowl. She freezes beneath his grasp, and will not look at him.

"This is why I hid," Elsa says instead, her voice so low, it worries him. "Why I kept my decisions, yes," then she turns to him, tears lining her face, "*my* decisions, to *myself*! You people all band together and make private plans. You go behind my back," she insists while resuming packing, this time shifting over to Christmas decorations: a wreath doorknob hanger, a silver tree-star, two flocked-velvet deer.

"Elsa," Jason begins.

"You don't even *try* to understand my choices."

"Elsa, wait. That's not true." He takes her arm and pulls a deer from her hand, very much aware of the crowd gathered behind him waiting for him to fix things. "Let's talk this through, okay?" He lowers his head and tries to meet her eye. "Everyone's really worried about you. You have too much on your plate, and let's face it, this *is* all a rash decision."

When someone sobs, Jason and Elsa both turn to see Maris cupping her mouth.

"Why are *you* crying?" Elsa calls out.

"You have a For Sale sign up." Maris sweeps her arm in front of her. "You're selling everything and leaving us. You might even return to *Italy* one of these days?"

"Oh, you kids!" Elsa's glare moves from Maris, to Jason's hand on her arm, to the tables and tables of trinkets and knick-knacks and dishware, then back to Eva, and Cliff—yes, Cliff. Finally she looks at her rambling, run-down cottage at the beach. The whole time, a lump fills her throat and her eyes burn with restraint. Everything on every table should have been *sold* by now. Been sold and gone, every item a painful memory that she never wants to think of again.

"Put it away!" she orders them through her tears. "All of it." Then she snatches up a small chair from her bistro table and takes it to the cottage side yard, returns to the tag sale and picks up the second bistro chair and brings that to the yard, too. When she does, everyone there silently starts packing up boxes, clearing tables, bringing things inside, saying quiet apologies to Elsa when they pass her.

Everyone except Maris, who stands off to the side, sniffling. With a tear-streaked face, she holds a balled-up tissue.

When Elsa rounds the corner of the cottage and tries to lift the small bistro table to carry to the yard, Jason stops her.

"Elsa. Elsa, wait." He takes the table out of her grip and sets it down. "I have a question. What about Sal's rowboat?" he asks. "I saw it's still at that cottage dock, which isn't your property. Don't you think we should move it to the boat basin, after we're done here?"

"No." Elsa does not hesitate. "I have to settle some fines with the beach commissioner later." She glares past Jason to Cliff. "Although I'm sure I can now make my case to get those fines revoked, after all the ordinances you folks must have broken today, pulling a stunt like you did. Just to stop my tag sale!" She scoops up a basket of paintbrushes. "Tomorrow, Jason. Tomorrow morning. Meet me at the dock then."

Jason can see by the way she won't even look at him as she carries the basket inside that she's very hurt by their inn-tervention.

They all know, actually, because no sooner than when Elsa's out of earshot, the bickering begins. As boxes are packed, and glassware wrapped in paper, and cartons taped closed, their worry simmers with *I told you it wasn't a good idea*, and *What else could we do*? followed by *If she didn't find out, everything would've been okay*.

Jason picks up the bistro table to bring to the yard where the two chairs are, until Eva stops him.

"Jason! I thought you were having coffee at *home*! Why didn't you shut off your walkie-talkie when you knew you were coming *here*? Then Elsa wouldn't have known what we did."

Jason sets down the table. "Maris distracted me."

"Maris?" Eva asks. She turns and spots her sister near the curb, pressing that ragged tissue to her eyes. "Okay, sis," Eva says as she walks to her. "That's way too many tears. What's *really* wrong?"

Maris quickly meets Jason's gaze, then looks at her sister. Then takes a quick breath. Another glance at Jason, then her sister. "I quit my job."

"Whaaa?" Eva stops dead in her tracks.

Every jaw drops right as Matt throws his hands up in the air, Cliff slaps his forehead, and Nick gives Jason a low, you're-so-in-trouble whistle—just as Jason calls out, "Maris! What'd I say about telling everybody!"

But it doesn't matter. He can't even see Maris now, not with the way everyone is huddled around her, bent close, talking softly. For God's sake, even Nick is, who manages a look back at Jason, then steps away from the group, lifts his walkie-talkie and calls Jason on his. "Trouble in paradise, dude," Nick says after the electronic ringtone sounds. "You've got a *serious* ten-thirty-three on your hands."

"A what?" Jason asks. It's obvious Nick has memorized every damn bit of walkie-talkie jargon from Cliff's cheat sheet. "A ten-thirty-*three*?"

Nick walks closer to Jason, glances over his shoulder at Maris crying, then turns to Jason again and says calmly into the walkie-talkie. "Emergency situation."

twenty

THEY DRIVE THROUGH HARTFORD'S LITTLE Italy later that afternoon. Low golden sunlight warms the brick-front bakeries, pizzerias, boutiques and local markets selling fresh produce and homemade sausages. Beneath sloping canopies, tables spill from cafés as people dine outdoors while the warm September weather holds on.

Maris thinks of the first time Jason took her to Bella's Ristorante. It's been two years since that day, when he told her the story of the motorcycle accident that claimed half his leg, and his brother's life. More than that, it was the day she knew she was in love with him.

Heaven, she remembers saying about the warm food she was devouring.

No, he argued, such that her hand, holding a piece of buttered Italian bread, stopped halfway to her mouth. Then he leaned close, lowered his voice as his brown eyes looked at her in a way no one else's ever have, and said, *Because I'm in heaven, sitting right here with you.*

Since then, Bella's has become their *place*. The dim dining room—with its paintings of piazzas and olive orchards, with its dim lighting and aroma of fresh tomato sauce—feels like home. This is where they land during any emotional crossroads, including today's. Jason's life changed when he opened up to her two years ago, and Maris feels hers is about to change, too, opening up to him.

"What a day," Maris says when they settle in a quiet booth, the table a dark wood, the wall beside them deep gold. "I never thought Elsa would be that upset."

"I'll smooth things over with her when I move Sal's rowboat from the dock tomorrow." As Jason says it, the waitress sets down a carafe of wine and two glasses. "But tonight, I want to talk about you. I'm really worried about your decision."

"I wish you weren't. Because, listen," Maris tells him now as he pours wine into their goblets. "For years, I channeled my mother with my denim designs. What I knew of her from photographs and home movies, I worked into my fashion sketches with a casual beach essence that defined her style, and life. Especially at a time when I didn't know I had a sister, or an aunt. Denim design was my way to connect with the mother I lost when I was so young."

"I get that," Jason says, sitting back and sipping his wine. "That's why I don't understand why you'd break that deep-rooted connection by quitting the fashion business altogether."

She gives him a small smile. "Think about it."

He tips his head and turns up his hands. "Don't know."

"I'm not *searching* anymore, Jason, for my mother. For *any* family. Look at my life now. My life-long best friend turned out to be my actual sister. And Elsa, dear Aunt Elsa—my mother's sister—moved here from Italy and is in my life every day, feeling just like a mother sometimes." Maris reaches across the table and brushes the back of her hand across Jason's whiskered cheek. "And I have you," she whispers. "My family doesn't have to be sketched and imagined. It's very real now. And right here."

"Okay. But can't *that* satisfaction, or contentment, be brought to designing? Rather than abandoning your career? Maris, you worked so hard to accomplish your success. I watch your dedication to every sketch, every new denim line, every concept and wash. It's who you are."

Maris shakes her head. "Jason, I'd been secretly thinking about quitting all summer. I'd hear about the adventures of the gang. Sal, Kyle, Lauren, Eva—everyone! But I'd only hear about things on a phone call, or email, because I was alone somewhere across the world. And every story made me miss everyone and feel so sad. Then when Sal died, it hit me. The time to be present in my sister's, my aunt's and, most importantly, *your* life, is right now. Sal was always present, to everyone."

"He was."

"And I want to do the same, because we don't ever know, really, how much time we have. When I think of how I travelled to Europe and L.A. this summer for Saybrooks, I think of it with regret, not fondness." Maris looks at the candle flickering low in a red glass globe on their table, then at Jason, waiting for her words. "I've been chasing a career that's chasing my happiness away."

Jason leans across the table and tucks Maris' hair behind her ear, then touches the gold chain of her necklace. "I'm still worried that actually *quitting* your work is one of those rash decisions. Kyle says you never think it is at the time, but a year later, looking back, you'll see the decision differently. Right now, you're using Sal's death to justify your decision. But is that realistic, Maris?"

"I want to be home now, with you." She takes his hand and kisses it. "With our marriage."

"That's why something about it all feels like a sacrifice, to *be* with me. Like you maybe got spooked that night when I left you, after Sal died."

"Jason, that was for forty-five minutes." She gives him another smile while slipping off her denim cardigan and draping it on the booth seat just as their waitress sets down a basket of warm rolls covered with a red-checked cloth. "And you came back!"

"So long as you're not quitting an admirable career on my account. You know, to keep an eye on me, or keep me happy or something. Because I couldn't accept that. You've accomplished too much to give up designing for that reason." He pauses when the waitress quickly returns with their meals. When she moves on, Jason continues. "Of course, I wish you were home more. Of course, the days get lonely when you're gone. But I know I'm lucky enough to simply have you in my life."

Maris slathers a tab of butter on a warm roll. "That's so sweet, and means everything." When she takes a bite of the doughy bread, her eyes tear up at Jason's words.

Jason forks off a piece of his lasagna and raises it to his mouth, pausing halfway, the sauce and melted cheese hanging from the fork. "Just know, sweetheart, whatever you decide, it cannot be a sacrifice. I can't live with that."

"It's not a sacrifice." Maris drinks her wine, watching him closely. "It's love, babe."

"I won't argue that one," he tells her around a mouthful of lasagna. "And I love you enough to support anything you set out to do." His gaze drops to his food then as he works on scooping up another hunk of his meal. "I guess my question now is … Do you have any idea what exactly you'll do next?"

Maris slices her fork through the most tender chicken parmigiana she's ever eaten.

"You know," Jason continues, leaning close. "Will you stay with fashion? Venture out on your own? Try something new?"

"What I was thinking … was that I'd dabble for a while."

Jason raises his wineglass, pauses, then takes a long sip. "Dabble."

"Yes!" If there's one thing Maris has learned from years of designing blue jeans, it's this: Sometimes success is all in the delivery. "Yes, actually." She stops to throw in a confident smile, hoping she's summoning the right look, the right sparkle in her eyes. "Like Sal did! You know, he worked with you on job sites, pitched in at Kyle's diner, rode shotgun in the security car with Nick. So I'm going to dabble, too. I'll give myself a timeline and see what I can discover."

Then, she does it. She takes her glass and raises it over the table, silently hoping that Jason will toast her half-baked plan. Oh, he's no fool. He'll see right through her complete lack of a strategy. Her glass hovers, but yes, he does it. He takes his glass and touches it to hers, in their Italian restaurant, candlelight glowing around them.

~

Jason sees right through Maris' *dabbling* bluff—so she *doesn't* know what's next, as much as he doesn't. But she still felt compelled to walk away from one huge part of her life, into the unknown.

Into dabbling. They talk a little more over coffee and strawberry-drizzled cheesecake dessert.

"You look tired," Maris says as she snags the last bit of his cheesecake.

"I am. Between you and your aunt and work, I've had a lot on my mind."

"Oh, I hope we can convince Elsa to stay on here, even without running an inn."

When Jason helps Maris into her cardigan and walks her out of the restaurant, he tells her he'll safely get Sal's rowboat back to the boat basin in the morning. "Maybe that will help Elsa feel more settled."

"But where are we going *now*?" Maris asks as Jason drives deeper into the city after dinner.

"The place where all your troubles fade away. Where they drift off in the breeze." Because even if she's doubting herself, Jason still wants his wife to be happy. So he reaches across the seat and holds her hand in his.

They're quiet for the few minutes it takes to get there. But when the large barnlike pavilion comes into view, outlined in twinkling lights against the night sky, he glances at Maris right as she smiles and leans forward for a better look.

"The Bushnell Park Carousel," she whispers.

"You told me once about riding a horse named Shadow when you were a teenager, and how those horseback rides helped you through difficult times."

As they park and stroll across the brick walkway to the carousel, horses—rearing and charging in the night—whirl past. Jason and Maris stop just inside the pavilion and watch the majestic animals adorned in cabbage roses and blue-and-gold painted ribbons. Jason puts his arm around Maris' shoulders and waits until her big black horse approaches, its head tipped up, ears pinned back, neck gracefully arched. "Look," he says as he presses his mouth to her ear. "Shadow's waiting for you."

Maris reaches to Jason's face and kisses him, once, then again, while the carousel slows.

It's an evening she needs, Jason can tell. Heck, he needs it, too. So he takes her hand and they step up onto the carousel platform. They pass white horses, their mouths wide in whinnies, and brown stallions with manes flying, mid-jump.

But Jason ignores them all, leaving them behind in this herd of magical horses. Finally, he stops beside her lavishly decorated horse and holds Maris' hand while she sets her foot on the peg and climbs onto the saddle. But before the ride starts, before the music begins and before lights glitter as the horses spin, before Maris' worries blur away on the back of her black stallion, Jason asks her one question, one last time. He looks up at her sitting high on her horse.

"Are you *sure* you don't want to go back to your job at Saybrooks? Maybe take a leave, instead of quit?"

"Jason."

A bell clangs, and the ride starts moving then, slowly. But Jason still stands beside Maris, waiting for an answer as her horse begins to move.

"The only place I want to be now," she says, but then

stops. Instead, she leans down from her opulent saddle, slips her hand behind Jason's neck and kisses him, all while her brown hair sweeps alongside his face.

And he knows what she's about to say, just from her one kiss as the carousel moves a little faster, as the lights flicker like stardust all around them.

"The *only* place I want to be," she repeats while her leaping horse rises, "is right here with you."

~

"Boy, you two missed a crazy day at the beach," Eva tells Kyle and Lauren as they finish touring another cottage.

"Crazy? It seems so quiet here for a Saturday evening." Lauren motions to the empty street.

So after Eva fills them in on Elsa's tag sale debacle, Kyle stands at the top of the driveway and looks down its long hill. Then he turns back and considers the white one-story bungalow. A large blue awning extends over its front deck, which faces a view of the water across the street, past other cottages nestled there.

"It's perfect," he tells Eva, who is tucking the key into the lockbox now. "Just what we were looking for, and it's in good shape."

"Kyle! No rash decisions." Lauren looks down the sloping driveway. "Because I'm not sure about this one."

"But it's on the same street as Jason. The epic Sea View Road!" He puts his arm around Lauren's shoulders and kisses the top of her head. "This could be it, Ell."

"It's been on the market a long time, guys, so there might be some wiggle room in the price. Here." Eva hands them the spec sheet. "And Lauren, it has so much natural light with those front windows. Good for painting?"

"But it's only a three-bedroom. And it's *so* high on a hill, the driveway is actually dangerous. I can picture Evan cruising on his bike down that hill. He could get hit by a car, pedaling into the road so fast!"

Lauren's fading on this one, so Kyle tries to reel her back. "But that *view*," he insists. "It'll *inspire* you. Look at Long Island Sound directly across the street."

"Stop right there, so we can put this one to rest." Lauren turns to Eva, who is pulling her keys from her purse. "Eva? With that sea view, what exactly *are* the property taxes on this one?"

"I'll tell you." Kyle scans the spec sheet, running his finger down the list of dimensions and number of rooms and lot size, until, finally, he looks at Lauren—who is patiently waiting, hand on hip, eyebrow raised. "Let's just say," Kyle says, glancing down at the tax figure again, "*Gesù, Santa Maria.*"

After agreeing to keep looking and waving Eva off, he and Lauren head out to dinner. But still, while driving the road that leads to the mouth of the Connecticut River; while standing beneath the buzzing, fluorescent light of The Clam Shack and placing a take-out order; and while sitting at a stone table near the water, Kyle can't help it. He persists with his wife.

"It's the best one we've seen," he tells Lauren as he swipes a fried clam through tartar sauce. "With that awning and deck, we can entertain outdoors!"

"But all that wood inside. Knotty-pine paneling. Everywhere."

"I've been reading up on seaside décor since we started house-hunting, and paneling's making a comeback. People polish it, then do things like wallpaper the *ceiling* with a nautical stripe, to update a room's look." He grabs his tall cup of soda and takes a long drink. "Plus Jason's so close by."

Lauren reaches across the table and snags one of Kyle's clams. "With those property taxes, we'll be so broke, you'll have to use a cup and string through the windows to talk to him. *Plus*, there's not even a guest room for my parents, and they *always* watch the kids for us. Even tonight, they are!" She shakes her head. "The right cottage won't need convincing, for either one of us. You need to have—what is it Sal would say? For patience?"

"Oh, wait." Kyle whips his new Italian translation guidebook from his cargo pocket. "I bought this to channel the Italian. He was one of a kind." He pages through the book, then draws his finger down a line of text. "*Pazienza!*"

"That's it. Sorry, hon. But you need some *pazienza*."

From their outdoor table, Kyle looks toward the railing where folks lean with ice-cream cones, or drop pieces of food down below to the waiting swans floating on the dark water. "Fine," he says as he stands up. "But if I'm losing that cottage, I want a consolation prize," he adds while taking Lauren's hand. "We're getting an ice cream, instead."

~

Elsa parks her golf cart outside the white, flat-roofed modular trailer. It's still hard to believe that this industrial-looking office is home to Stony Point's own version of government. She checks her watch and walks up the few steps to the trailer's plain, steel door—still without a wreath, or welcome sign—and gives two sharp raps before sweeping it open and breezing inside.

Still, she's a little taken aback by Clifton Raines sitting at his metal, utilitarian desk and doing nothing but watch her. So she stops, tugs the sleeve of her quilted barn jacket, then marches directly to that darn desk. Where he still silently sits, with the slightest of dimples giving away some amusement at her arrival.

"This should take only five minutes, after all the ordinances you people broke today!" Elsa slaps down her tallied fines on his desk. "And you! To think you were at the helm of it."

"It might actually take longer than five minutes." Cliff thumbs through her pile of tickets.

"Oh, no it won't. Because you can throw those all out, Commissioner."

As though he doesn't even hear her, Cliff tells her to have a seat. "So we can discuss these."

But if Elsa remembers correctly, there were to be other people here to review her fines. "Where are your cohorts? I'm sure you've got every board member paid off to side with you." She looks around the sparse space, noting the empty metal desk chairs, the rickety table strewn with a few old magazines. She tugs a silk scarf off her neck and tucks it into her purse. "They're late. Isn't that a violation of some sort? It's been a long day, and I'm tired."

After all this time, Elsa still is surprised by little things Cliff does. By his reactions. Like now, the way he ignores her rant and simply stands up—wearing a denim shirt over khaki pants, and seriously? Did he pop the collar on that shirt? The way it's lifted a little, it's hard to tell.

She steps aside as he walks around his desk, drags a chair to the front of it and motions to it. "Sit, please."

So she does, while doing something else, though. While sniffing the air. "Is something ... *cooking*?"

"Cooking!" Cliff looks over his shoulder at her, then snatches up her pile of tickets off his desk. "Wait right here."

What an odd day it's been. First, the whole tag sale fiasco—from Matt's police cruiser scaring folks off, to Nick turning everyone else away with some harebrained street-sweeping lie. To Maris breaking down about quitting her job.

And now this.

Elsa watches Cliff close the accordion-style door behind him before checking her watch. So she knows that precisely eight seconds pass before she hears—if she's not mistaken—a paper shredder? She turns in her chair and tips her head. Yes, Cliff must be shredding her tickets. "Well, that's more like it," she whispers while unbuttoning her light jacket. It does get stuffy in this trailer. Nothing a little fresh sea air can't fix. So she walks to the side wall and slides open one of the windows.

But a noise has her spin around. It's a rhythmic, scratchy crackling sound. For crying out loud, is that what she thinks it is? She steps closer to that darn pleated door, listening to more of that scratching noise, before hearing what sounds like a lovely mandolin, playing a familiar tune. A step closer, her head tipped. The music is soft, and the scratchy noise is there, too, but she can make out some words, something about the moon, and pizza pie, and … oh, no. He didn't.

Another step closer, and Elsa recognizes—through the scratchy sound of, yes, a needle on a record—Dean Martin's smooth baritone voice. A voice singing about ringing hearts and playing bells, the words whirling through the room like the dance steps of a tarantella. A song getting Elsa to hum *That's Amore*, as her foot taps.

But it only taps three times before that accordion-style door clatters open and Cliff stands there, a half-apron tied around his waist, his hand extended to hers.

"Dinner is served."

Elsa places her hand in his, glances behind her at the sliding window she'd just opened, and the metal desk where fines were to be discussed, then feels a tug on her hand, and so she walks into this mysterious new room. "What are you doing?" she asks. "Cliff?"

But Elsa gets her answer when he silently steps aside to reveal a round bistro table covered in a red-and-white checked tablecloth. A toaster oven is cooking something on a nearby counter, beside a hot plate with a simmering pot on it.

All the while, Cliff pulls out a folding café chair and motions for her to have a seat.

"For heaven's sake, Commissioner Raines," Elsa says while slipping off her quilted jacket and hanging it on the back of the chair. But that's not all she's doing. She's also taking a quick look around this rear office, which is *not* an office after all! "We can just as easily, and with far less fuss, settle my fines at your desk. This really isn't necessary, to go through all this. I mean, I have food at home—"

"Would you be quiet?"

"Pardon me?"

"Please, Elsa. Don't say anything, anything at all, for five minutes. That's all I ask. Five minutes. Can you do that for me? Give me five minutes?"

"Well, I suppose …" So she draws her thumb and forefinger across her pursed lips and sits back in the surprisingly comfortable bistro chair as Dino croons about wine, and dreams, and love, while the mandolin plays on. Cliff buzzes around the room, setting candles on the small table, pulling a tray of steaming food out of the toaster oven. From where she sits, she can see melted cheese oozing from a golden-brown flatbread.

But something else gets her attention. It's off to the side of the room: the small dresser and mirror, an end table with a lamp beside what looks like an odd sofa. "Wait a minute," she says with a gasp as Cliff sets a bottle of wine on the table. "Do you … *live* here?"

"Well, Elsa, the thing of it is. You see …" he says, glancing over at his apparent sleeping space. "It's just that when I took the commissioner appointment, I got right to work. The Board of Governors was so far behind on things, there was no time to find a house. I, you know, I have a futon, a sink. I get by. I've been so busy rewriting the Stony Point rule book, but it's finally going for its print run."

If she's not mistaken then, he looks *fondly* around his small trailer space, then meets her eye again. That's when he simply nods and turns toward the toaster oven, as though realizing he just did what she usually does—prattle! So he takes a spatula and moves his toaster-oven-warmed dinner to a platter. "I hope you don't mind chicken quesadillas." He sets the dish on their table.

"Why … Why, you *lured* me here. Telling me hogwash about board members reviewing my violations. There were no fines, were there?"

"What?" Cliff asks as he unties his apron.

"You got me here under false pretenses!"

He answers her—wait, that better not be a twinkle in his darn blue eyes—while he pours their wine. "You left me no other choice, Elsa."

The aroma of the food gets to Elsa, who hasn't eaten, come to think of it, all day. Not with the turmoil of the tag sale upsetting her so, the way everyone plotted against her. So she pulls the platter closer and scoops a quesadilla onto her plate, then tries her wine. "You went to a lot of trouble, Cliff."

"Not really," he says as he sits across from her. "I did the prep work earlier, and put everything in my mini-fridge, all set on the tray. Which I didn't put into the toaster oven until I saw you arriving."

Elsa glances around the room at a framed seascape painting near his futon, and a pair of white seagull statues. All the while, Dean Martin sets a dreamy mood in the dim lighting. Elsa clasps Cliff's hand. "This was actually very nice of you," she says with a smile.

"I'm glad you like it."

"I kind of do!" She sips her wine. "Who would've thought? Me, being wined and dined … in a trailer!" As she says it, though, her heart gives a sudden, clear reminder of all she's recently been through. A painful, shooting pang of sadness tells her, lest she forget, that Sal is gone, gone, gone.

So she sets down her glass and sits back. It's not fair that she be here, enjoying herself, so soon after losing her son.

She picks up a fork and tries to eat, but can't do it. A lump forms in her throat.

"I'm sorry, Cliff," she whispers, "but what we started up, before Sal died … having lunch together, sneaking a kiss or two in that old Foley's back room, it was just a summer thing. We were caught up in a moment. It's done now." She takes a long breath and lets her words soften, hoping to sound kind. "Nobody needs to get hurt. We have some nice memories, but we can let things go."

Cliff gets a book of matches from the cabinet and returns to the table. As he lights the two candles, he tells her, "I saw what just happened, Elsa."

"What's that?" She sets down her fork and moves her plate away, waiting.

"We talked, and you actually smiled. And *laughed*."

"I did not."

"Yes, you did. Okay, it was only for a second, but you did. And then?" He returns the matches to the counter and sits with her again, pulling his chair in so close, their knees momentarily touch. "Then you shut down and turned sad. But Elsa, you cannot feel guilty for smiling. Isn't that what Salvatore said? *Sorridi?* He'd want you to smile."

Elsa scoots her chair closer. Then she picks up her fork again, slices a piece of quesadilla, lifts it up as the melted cheese hangs from the fork edge, and sets the whole mess back down on her plate. When she sits back with tear-filled eyes—*burning* tears—she listens to Cliff, and Dean, and a scratchy record needle from that old tabletop record player.

"And anyway, Elsa …" Cliff says as he scoops a spoonful of sour cream onto his dish, then dips his gooey chicken quesadilla into it. "I don't want anything from you, anything at all." He bites into his quesadilla concoction, chewing thoughtfully, then picks up a cloth—yes, *cloth*—napkin and presses it to his mouth. "Just a little smile." Cliff takes her hand across the table and kisses it lightly in the trailer's candlelight. "That's all. Just a smile. Every now and then."

twenty-one

SUNDAY MORNING, THE EASTERN SKY is still pink when Elsa crosses the dewy lawn to the dock. It's not far from her cottage, just a few sandy streets over, in the backyard of the place where Celia stayed. Like the lagoon current, her thoughts drift then. To Sal and Celia, their sweet summer romance, their collaboration on the beach inn, their rowboat rides.

Elsa removes her slip-on sneakers, sits and cuffs her jeans, then dangles her legs over the dock edge to dip her toes in the water. A pair of sandpipers flit along the muddy bank, and Sal's rowboat is moored to the post beside her. The boat gently rises and falls on the water, causing the dock to creak.

She listens closely to the noises Sal must've heard. In her stillness, what it all feels like is a quiet mass, with the peaceful sounds around her being a Sunday morning hymn: bubbling water, and whispering lagoon grasses, and creaking dock post, with the soft whistling trill of the sandpipers singing the praises of Sal's short life.

Beyond the marsh, Long Island Sound spreads out to

the distant horizon. Blue, as far as the eye can see. It's a view her own mother must have seen while crossing the ocean. This summer, Maris showed her a photograph of her grandmother—who is also Elsa's mother—arriving on a ship at Ellis Island decades ago. Her journey across the sea from a port in Naples was nearly over as she came to America to escape hardships in Europe. In the picture, Elsa's mother wore a scarf on her head to ward off the damp air on the massive steamboat.

If only Elsa could talk to her now. Instead, a gentle breeze scarcely caresses her face. On the rickety dock, Elsa leans back on her hands. She's not sure one can flee hardships. No. Life reminds her again and again that hardships of the heart are frequent, and the worst. She swishes her feet in the water and watches Sal's wooden boat. Not a steamship, just a little old rowboat that he used to escape his own private hardships, to drift on the sea beneath the starry sky. The thought occurs to her to step into the boat, to feel what he felt, alone on the water. To feel the sea move her along, the salt water lapping at the boat sides.

Sitting on the dock considering this, she's surprised to feel her shoulders shaking. It takes a few moments to realize why—to understand that she's sobbing while looking at Sal's cherished boat. And it doesn't stop; sitting alone in the early morning mist, gasps and tears and shuddering sadness rise through her body. It feels like a wave breaking over her, finally, as she fully realizes her son is gone.

When a hand clasps her shoulder, for a second she thinks it's Sal, somehow, reassuring her. But when she looks up through her tears, it is Jason standing there, his face in shadow, his dark hair wavy in the dampness. He sits beside her on the dock, puts his arm around her shoulders and takes her hand as she leans into him and simply weeps.

~

Jason doesn't talk. Doesn't try to stop Elsa, or to comfort her, or to quiet her. He just lets her cry it out. It's the only way to go on, sometimes. Otherwise, the sadness becomes an insurmountable wall. He did the same thing the night of Sal's funeral—cried it out in his SUV parked on a dark roadside, the grief feeling violent at times, the way it rose in heaves through his body. He recognizes the same in Elsa, now.

So he keeps his arm around her shoulders while she shakes with grief, her head pressed into his chest. Each sob, each breath, has her entire self shudder. Minutes pass like this. Some are quieter, while some remind him of the grip Sal's death has on them.

Finally, Elsa calms. And still, no words pass between them. The early morning sun rises in the sky, the tall marsh grasses reach up in a graceful curve, and a little sandpiper nervously paces the muddy bank while sending a random trill in their direction. Elsa reaches for her bag on the dock and finds a tissue, which she presses to her face.

"Thirty-five years ago," she whispers, "I was right here on the edge of this lagoon, with my sister, June. My sister *and* her very young daughter, Maris." Elsa takes a long, shaky breath, and Jason waits. "June rented a cottage for a September week, and I left little Sal home in Italy with my husband to come visit. It was our girls' week, together. One evening, June took Mason jars off a dusty shelf in that cottage and we went outside just as the sun set. Oh, it was magical, the way swans paddled by, and the air—it smelled of the sea! But it was the fireflies, Jason, there were hundreds of them. And they rose from the grasses looking so mystical."

Elsa leans back on her hands, then, gazing not at the lagoon, but at this memory in her thoughts. Jason can tell by her small smile that she's seeing her sister once more—young and carefree.

"So we opened our jars and caught fireflies in them. They flickered like candlelight in the night. And do you know what June said to her daughter?" She looks at Jason beside her. "To *your* Maris?"

Jason shakes his head, and when he does, Elsa points to the lagoon. "She told Maris the fireflies rising in the mist were stars, dancing in the sky. And then, Jason, the three of us joined hands and danced a circle around the twinkling fireflies, and it was one of the sweetest moments of my life."

Her tears start up again, just a little, but they fill her eyes. And with her next line, Jason knows why she shared this memory. It's where she was leading him, through the whole story.

"Sal was going to take me for a September boat ride," she says, motioning to the empty rowboat. "Past June's rented cottage, further out in the lagoon. So that I could revisit the memory of my sister. We planned it for when he returned."

"I'm sorry, Elsa."

She presses her tissue to her eyes. "I can't seem to ever,

ever get that sweet moment back."

That's when Jason does it; he stands up and takes her hand. "Come on, then."

"What?" Elsa grabs her slip-on sneakers off the dock and stands. "What are you doing?"

"Taking you on that boat ride. For Sal." He walks to the edge of the dock and looks back at her. "I'm doing it for Sal."

"What about your leg?"

"Elsa. I'm just stepping into a boat. I'm fine." He reaches for her hand again and helps her into Sal's rowboat. "*Andiamo*."

~

Jason dips the oars into the marsh water. Slowly, he sets the rowboat in motion. As he does, a few fresh tears line Elsa's face; he's sure because she's thinking that this *should* be Sal paddling her through the lagoon.

"I get it," Jason tells her as he lifts the oars and they drip, drip. "Sal was like a brother to me. Sometimes I felt as close to him as I did to Neil." When he pulls on the oars again, they creak against the oarlocks. "That night I left Maris a couple weeks ago? I was *crazy* with grief. It was awful. I couldn't even drive and she had to come and get me." The boat rounds a stand of cattails, their brown spikes rising high on the lagoon banks. "I still feel it, a sorrow, when I'm alone."

"You talk to Maris about it?" Elsa asks.

Jason shakes his head and takes a long breath of that salt air that supposedly cures what ails you, though lately, he's not so sure.

"Back when we were kids," he says to Elsa, "my brother and I paddled through these marsh inlets, reenacting our father's Vietnam war stories. This was our Southeast Asian jungle. The egrets and herons were the enemy. The blue crabs? The landmines." Jason looks toward the woods surrounding the far edge of the lagoon. "There's one story in particular that I can't stop thinking about these days. I can just picture my father sitting on his stone bench with me and Neil, out on the bluff. His voice low, the sea in front of us, his thoughts far away."

Jason tells Elsa that story now …

~

We'd been tracking a lone enemy soldier in the jungle, his father began. *Just me and one other guy. The area was heavily booby-trapped, so with each careful footstep, every damn nerve was on edge. Crude traps were planted to stop us, or at least to scare us off. Contraptions with sharpened sticks, and bamboo spikes that could kill if we walked into the tripwire. But we persisted, knowing that a lone, rogue VC kid could be worse than a whole troop. Shit, man. He's got nothing to lose.*

Right before nightfall, we saw his footprints lead into the muddy banks of a small swamp, then disappear into the water. So we circled around the swamp, but found nothing—no footprints where he'd exited, meaning he was still hunkered down in that water. Not much we could do at that point, so while my partner stood guard, I grabbed some desperate sleep in the brush on the banks. At some point, maybe an hour later, a hand woke me up when it slapped over my mouth, right as my attacker nearly fell on me. I struggled like mad until his face came within inches of mine in the pure dark, and I saw it was my partner. That's when he let up and raised his finger to his lips. I instantly understood to be quiet, but my heart beat like crazy. Someone was closing in on us and if I made a single sound, it was all over.

So instead we listened to the racket of the night bugs, and something else—some foreign tongue, repeating a line over and over again, like a mantra. It was so soft, all we heard was the low tone of voice, sounding like a hum. But it got clearer, the closer this guy got to us. He was in the water, walking so slow, the water didn't slosh. No noise, other than his murmuring, petrified voice rising through the buzz of insects.

Suddenly I looked at my partner at the same time he looked at me. He pointed to his ear as a signal to listen closely. We practically stopped breathing, trying to make out the voice. And we did. Over and over again, it said in English: Now and at the hour of our death. Now and at the hour of our death. Now and at the hour of our death.

Shit, we'd been tracking one of our own! It was a lost American who had to think that either the VC or some monster swamp snake was going to end his life that black night. It's like he was in a trance, repeatedly praying each line of the Hail Mary to save his lost-in-the-jungle soul.

And it worked. Sweet Jesus, did it work. Because it was his manic, compulsive repetition of the lines of that one prayer that brought him into our sights and saved him.

~

"Mary," Elsa says now, at the story's end. "She saved that lost soldier. *Stella Maris*, the star of the sea."

"And of the swamps, apparently." Jason points out the banks of the lagoon bordering a stand of trees. "As kids, Neil always played the poor soul in the water, slogging through the muck and reciting the prayer. When I'd round some corner in the marsh and come upon him murmuring his prayer, I'd pull him as quietly as I could up over the side of our little boat and he'd whisper *Amen! Amen!* no louder than the cicadas buzzing, so as not to be heard by the enemy." Jason nods to a great blue heron standing statue-still near the cattails.

"And what happened to the young man your father saved that night in the swamp?"

"Once they were safe, the soldier cried like a baby." Jason drags his dog tags along the chain around his neck. "Said he thought it was the end, that night. Never saw what was just around the corner, meaning my father and his partner. That guy went on to survive the war, come home and have a family of eight kids. His one night in the swamp was just that, one night."

Elsa looks long at Jason, then looks away.

"I think of that guy, and how my father was telling me something." Jason sets his oars to the water and paddles deeper into the lagoon. "It's never the end, even when we really believe it is."

~

The sun is rising higher now, and a breeze lifts off the Sound, rustling the tall, golden grasses.

"Look!" Elsa is pointing to a weathered bungalow along the lagoon.

"The cottage June rented?" Jason asks as he paddles closer.

Elsa nods. "When I visited her," she explains, her voice soft, but lighter now, "it was the first time I made a happiness jar, capturing fireflies twinkling like stars in June's dusty old Mason jars. We were so happy that magical night. Which is why Celia and I had planned on incorporating happiness jars into the inn's décor."

Jason stops paddling and the boat drifts in front of the cottage. He wants Elsa to *see* the memory that Sal had promised. Jason can almost see it, too, if he squints through the sunlight glinting through the marsh mist. There, behind the shingled bungalow: two women with a young child, jars in their outstretched hands, laughing and spinning in the moonlight, their hair flyaway, the fireflies dancing in the dark.

When he dips the paddles once more, he turns to Elsa. "Have you heard from Celia?"

"No." She slips off her jacket and folds it across her lap in the rowboat. "One day last week, I brought flowers to the tree in Addison, where my sister died in the car accident all those years ago. I wanted to go there, to tell June about losing Sal. It was late evening, and afterward, I drove down Celia's street."

"You did?"

"I parked a little before her house. It's so pretty. A yellow bungalow on a country road lined with farmhouses and small Victorians. But I didn't go to the door. Lights were on in the house, so I just watched for a minute, and then I left."

"Will you ever get in touch with her again?"

"I hope to. Someday."

Jason paddles onto a wide stream that leads to the boat marina, where they'll dock Sal's rowboat for the time being. He can't help but wonder about Celia every now and then.

Can't help but remember their dance in a dim bar beside a jukebox, her body pressed to his, their kiss urgent and deep.

"What about Maris?"

He looks quickly over at Elsa. Could Celia possibly have told her about that night?

"She was so upset about quitting her job," Elsa explains.

"Oh, that."

"What did you think I meant?" Elsa tips her head, a small smile waiting for his answer.

A smile—and question—that Jason evades. "You come over for dinner tonight. Maris doesn't have to rush off to the city tomorrow, and I know she'd love to talk with you about why she quit her job."

As he says it, Jason maneuvers Sal's rowboat into its marina slip and secures it to the dock cleats. Elsa climbs out then and stands there, waiting for him as he removes the oars from the oarlocks and sets them carefully down in the boat.

twenty-two

THE SOUNDS MARIS HEARS WORRY her. Though the sun is barely up, and Monday morning just beginning, there's a mania swirling. She listens from their bedroom. It's warm for mid-September, and the window is open. But she stays under the sheets in bed so that Jason will think she's asleep, rather than listening in on this life of his she never really witnessed. Typically, she'd be out of the house first, or even the night before, to catch a train into Saybrooks' New York City design studio.

Today, the mania starts with Jason's leg. She hears how he rolls the liner on over his knee seemingly too fast; it's obvious by the tense way he snaps and smoothes it. When he then stands and places his limb into the prosthetic leg, he quickly bounces to press his stump into it. Wasting no time, he hurries to his dresser and fusses with coins, and his keys, still occasionally bouncing and adjusting the prosthesis fit, right as his phone begins dinging and the dog paces around him.

But Maris doesn't move. This is new to her, and she's shocked at how crazy Jason's morning routine is. Still listening, she hears him rush down the stairs now, the dog's collar jangling as Maddy races him to the first floor. In a minute, the clatter of dog kibble filling a bowl rises up the stairs. Maris finds herself plotting Jason's moves by the sounds. After the dog's bowl bangs onto the floor, Jason puts his cell phone on speaker to play his voicemails as he gets his coffee ready. The drone of men's recorded voices reaches her—contractors, electricians—all while Jason fills the coffee decanter with tap water, opens and slams shut the fridge, unzips his black duffel.

It takes her a second to realize then that the few moments of silence that she *thought* would lead to Jason relaxing with breakfast, won't. No, he was dialing back contractors in that silence, and now *his* deep voice carries to her as the slider screen opens, then bangs shut, his voice still working out schedule times and stops to make in his day. When the slider opens and shuts again, he must be done and ready to eat. The microwave runs then, so he's heating something. Good. He has to eat right.

Just when Maris starts to drift back to sleep, their computer printer starts whirring and printing pages downstairs as Jason comes up to the bedroom.

"I'm off," he says while bending over her as she feigns sleep, curled on her side. He kisses her shoulder.

"Did you eat?" Maris asks softly from behind closed eyes.

"A cruller, and coffee. What are you up to on your first day of freedom?" As he asks, his fingers briefly brush her hair before he turns and walks to his dresser.

"Ah, I'm taking a two-day summer vacation," Maris says. "Because tomorrow's the last full day *of* summer, Jason."

"Really? I can't keep track of time lately. So what's on your agenda?"

"A much-needed coffee with my sister."

"That's it?"

"Oh, I'll walk the beach, and check on Elsa. But I don't know, she said Sal's friend Michael is coming to see her this week. Did she say it was today?" When he doesn't answer, Maris sneaks a peek and squints at him across the room. "Are you even listening to me?"

"Yes." He looks over his shoulder at her. "Yes, I heard you. But I've got to go, there's an early site analysis waiting. I'll take Maddy with me."

Another quick kiss and Jason's out the door, down the stairs and gone. Most worrisome to Maris is that his phone never stops dinging with texts and work emails. He's always been busy, but this extreme itinerary is something new. So she tosses back the sheet and walks to her bedroom window, leaning on the frame and pressing aside the curtain to watch her husband settle in his SUV with his bags and the dog and technical measuring gear. And with that phone pressed to his ear, giving not even a glance back at the house.

~

Later, Maris sits in one of her very favorite spots at Stony Point. This location has to be in her top three, definitely. Right after the weathered boardwalk, followed by the notorious Foley's hangout room. She cups a coffee mug while leaning back on Eva's kitchen window seat. A wide crystal vase of cut sunflowers and wisps of beach grass sits on the round table. Sunshine comes through the window behind her, where the marsh spreads out beyond Eva's yard, and so the scent of the sea also works its way through the screen.

"I bought coffee-cake muffins!" Eva grabs two potholders, opens the oven and pulls out a tray. "They're nice and warm."

"Mmm, perfect," Maris says as that aroma fills the room. Watching her sister, she notices Eva's denim shirt tucked into a white eyelet skirt—definitely one of her working outfits. "I'm not keeping you, am I?"

"No, hon." Eva puts a plate on her antique mahogany table. A tab of butter melts on a muffin there, and she nudges the dish closer to Maris. "Vacation rentals are done for the season, so that's lightened my load. But I do have a few new houses to list later." As she says it, she pulls out a chair and joins Maris over coffee. "And they could really use Celia's staging."

"Poor Celia," Maris says while setting her plate on the wide sill of the window seat, then biting into the warm muffin. "Do you think we should pop in on her? See how she's doing?"

"I don't know. Lauren thought she needed some space right now."

"Well, it seems funny how she just vanished from here. Poof! Like sand through your fingers." Maris sips her coffee. "Maybe we'll see her next month? There's lots of fall fairs there in Addison. So we'll have to set a date."

Eva nods, and there's a pause then … filled with only the late-September sea breeze puffing the lace window curtains.

"So, are your new listings here at Stony Point?" Maris asks. "Something for Kyle and Lauren to look at?"

"A couple cottages are here, and one's at Sound View Beach. That one's turnkey, but not the location they want. And hey, how about you?" Eva lifts a muffin, saying, "It's your first day unemployed. Are you sad?"

"Sad? No … It's an adjustment, but look! Here I am, with you."

"Nice," Eva answers around a mouthful of muffin. "Now we can plan your life."

"What?" Maris isn't sure how to plan her first *day* off, never mind her life. But if there's one thing she can always count on, it's her sister keeping a loving eye on her.

Like right now, when Eva hurries to the counter—still chewing—then sits again, straightening her eyelet skirt beneath her. "Here. I have a journal. Let's outline ideas for your future."

If only it were that easy. Maris moves off the window seat and sits beside Eva on a gray-cushioned mahogany chair. She folds back her blouse sleeves and tightens her turquoise cuff bracelet while watching her sister write a big heading, in all caps, across the first journal page: MARIS' LIFE PLAN.

"Eva! You can't outline a life."

"Why not? Look." She turns the pages toward Maris, then pulls the journal back. "Is Jason okay with your quitting?"

"He's coming around."

"Just give him some extra attention, sis. He's still vulnerable right now."

"Vulnerable?" Maris sits back and raises her eyebrows at

Eva. "This is the first Monday I've been home in ages, and I cannot *believe* how busy he was. I mean, something's changed. He's always been busy, but I don't know. Normally so. It was *extreme* in that house this morning."

"Maybe being busy's good for him. Keeps his thoughts occupied." Eva rests her hand on the journal page. "Have you seen Elsa since our tag sale fiasco?"

"She came for dinner last night and we talked. I think she's still hurt at how we interfered with her plans. *And* she's surprised that I left my career. But I'm hoping it might sway her to stay put, here."

"The question is, will *you* stay put here, too?" Eva counters. Which is precisely when Maris' bullet-pointed life plan begins. Pen poised, Eva eyes her. "Let's see," her sister muses. "You quit your job and will do … what? Roman numeral one."

"Seriously?"

"Partner with Jason?" As Eva says it, she writes it. "Parlay your fashion design into interior design."

Maris grabs the pen and journal and quickly scratches out that idea. "Oh, no. That's Jason's space, and I'm *not* going into it with him."

So Eva pulls the journal back across the table and numbers a few blank lines, which she then starts to fill in. "How about opening a boutique? A denim boutique with your own designs? Elsa could give you some shop pointers, I'm sure. And hey, there are lots of storefronts for sale around here. Look at that Maritime Market! They're so busy." She turns the journal to Maris, who takes it and crosses off the boutique scheme. "No?" Eva asks.

"Uh-uh." She slides the journal back. "I need a change,

Eva. No fashion. Not now, anyway." As soon as she says it, both their cell phones ding with a text message.

Eva rushes to the counter for her phone. "It's from—"

"Kyle," Maris finishes after pulling her phone from her tote. "*Talked to Cliff,* he says. *Need another Elsa meeting, pronto. But not on boardwalk—she'll see us and be onto it. Meet and Eat is here at diner, today, after hours.*" Maris scrolls back up to the top. "Jason, Matt, Nick, you, me ... Looks like everyone got the message."

"You game to go?" Eva asks.

"Absolutely, my schedule's all clear now."

Eva slides her chair over to Maris and leans very close to her.

"What are you doing?" Maris asks.

"Taking a thumbs-up, sis-pic for Kyle." Eva gives a thumbs-up with one hand, holds up her phone with the other, grins and takes a picture of the two of them. Then she studiously types a message back, *We'll be there*, and sends it with the picture attached. "Hmm, okay," she says while reaching for her journal and pen again. "Back to your life plan." Just as quickly, she throws down the pen. "I've got it! How about a SAHM?"

"Sam?" Maris stuffs the last of her coffee-cake muffin into her mouth, then dabs sweet crumbs off her plate. "Sam who?"

"No. S-A-H-M! Stay-at-home mom!"

"Oh, good one. Right." Maris pulls the journal close and doodles the letters. "Wait. You're really telling me to have a baby?"

"Well, thirty-six is not getting any younger. And maybe a baby would help Jason be happy again. He's a great guy, but so inwardly focused."

Maris scratches out her doodles. "That's not a life plan, Evangeline."

"It worked for me. Got pregnant with Tay, married my guy, and here I am."

"Way different. And you were still a teenager!" As Maris is declining her sister's ridiculous life plan, Eva pulls the journal back and is jotting a few lines of notes. "No babies," Maris warns. "Yet."

"How about a sister? Get your real estate license and go into business together?" Eva glances at her rose-gold watch, then quickly grabs her purse and keys. "Come with me? I have to photograph that new Sound View listing."

One thing Maris has to admit, she doesn't have anything else to do. While tipping back the remaining drops of her coffee as she stands, her eyes scan the last line that Eva wrote in Maris' life plan: *Sisters by the Sea Realty!*

~

That evening, Kyle flips the catalog page with such urgency, the paper rips. So he pushes the torn pieces together and, of course, sees the perfect outdoor furniture to replace the temporary, rented pieces on his diner patio. While holding the page together with one hand, he punches the purchase prices into his calculator. It takes only one glance at the total for him to open his desk drawer for a cigarette. A few quick drags, a few more calculations, and his mind is made up.

"Oh, forget it," he says, tossing the furniture catalog into the trash. "No money for extras."

"Yo, Bradford!" Nick calls from out in the diner. He

runs down the hall and swings into Kyle's back office. "You coming already?"

Kyle stands and looks out the window to see everyone gathered on the patio. On the *rented* furniture. He squints just beyond the tables near the heavy rope strung from dock post to dock post, where he sees … a fire? "What the hell's that?"

Nick comes up beside him. "Sweet, isn't it? Portable fire pit. I took an old galvanized aluminum tub from the Woods demo site." He motions to Matt adding small branches to the tub. "Toss in a few sticks and gather round the campfire."

Through the window, Kyle watches the flames reaching out of the long, silver tub. "Huh. I like that. So long as you don't torch the place, which would be on you, buddy."

"Whoa, man. Speaking of fire." Nick walks closer to the ashtray on Kyle's desk, the ashtray where his lit cigarette is propped. "Your wife know about this dirty habit?"

"Of course not." Kyle whips around, lifts the cigarette, takes a deep drag and tamps it out. "Think I tell her everything? That's not how things work. Shit, no wonder you don't have a girl."

"Just haven't gotten around to it yet. And you should quit those things."

"Eh." Kyle drops the lighter back in his desk drawer.

"Got any chow ready?" Nick is asking. "The natives are restless."

"Yeah. Grab a platter in the kitchen." Kyle glances outside once more, before lifting the fabric of his tee and fanning his gut. So he whips off that damp shirt, puts on a new one from a package on the shelf, then does a swap.

"That's right," he mutters. "Out with you," he says while tossing the sweaty tee into the trash can and at the same time retrieving the patio furniture catalog. He sets it on his desk and presses out a few wrinkles in the pages. "And in with the new."

Someone outside gives a sharp, impatient whistle that gets Kyle hurrying to the door. But he stops in front of a framed photograph hanging on the wall. Lately it's looking sweeter and sweeter, that original image of his diner from back in the day, when it was his old boss Jerry's *Dockside Diner*. It looked like a big, silver ship, and with the way those window lanterns glowed at night, you could think it was sailing out at sea.

"Salvatore," Kyle whispers while touching the frame. "Sal, man. I need more business. What should I do? Change the name back?"

But Nick clattering platters distracts him, so Kyle rushes out to the kitchen. "What, no classes tonight?" he asks Nick.

Nick balances two trays—one of crispy chicken fingers and avocado ham sandwiches, the other salted caramel bars and chocolate brownies. "Only Tuesday and Thursday nights. How many times have I told you?" He shoulders through a swinging door to the diner entrance. "Pay attention!"

Right. Problem is, if Kyle kept a list of everything needing his attention lately, he'd be too busy reading it to actually do any of it. He grabs a tray of nachos and dip before following Nick to the patio, where tonight's Meet and Eat is about to begin. The sun just set, so everyone sits illuminated by distant parking lot lights, a couple of tiki torches and Nick's newfangled fire pit.

"Thanks all, for coming." No sooner does Kyle set down the tray then hands descend on the nachos, scooping up buffalo-chicken dip and sampling the cheese spread. So he backs out of the way and swipes his arm across his forehead.

"I'll take it from here," Cliff tells him while standing and walking around a few tables. "You can relax, Kyle."

"Oh, wait! Before you begin." Kyle looks around frantically, then spots the shoebox he left on a rear patio table. "I'm taking an important poll and passing everybody one slip of paper. They're pre-made with two diner names: Dockside Diner or The Driftwood Café. There's a checkbox beside each one. Please indicate which name you prefer for this place," he explains while walking the shoebox past everyone. "It's a form of what they call beta testing, and all answers are anonymous."

"Better testing?" Eva asks.

"Beta. *Beta!*" Kyle repeats. "It's the final testing of a product or idea—in this case, my diner's name. One of those two printed names *will* be decided upon, after I test it in the field. Which is you people."

"Question," Matt says. "Why can't you just ask us which name we prefer?" He scoops a tortilla chip into the cheese, then moves his chair over to the crackling fire tub.

"Because if I ask if you like the current name," Kyle answers, "you'll all lie to my face and say yes. That's what friends do." He gives Matt a slip of paper before turning the floor over to Cliff.

Cliff checks off his poll ticket, folds it in half and drops it in Kyle's shoebox. Then he clears his throat and begins while the polling continues, pens scratching over paper scraps. "Change of plans, folks," he announces. "We need to quickly revise our *inn*-tervention. Elsa's had no solid offers on her inn, but there is some dialogue with a few buyers. So time is running out, *and* it's apparent that convincing Elsa to keep her inn and stay put is *too* big in scope. Because I'm telling you, she is one woman darn set in her ways. So what—"

"Wait!" Eva calls out. "Here comes Jason."

While finishing a cell phone conversation, Jason quickly walks through the shadowy parking lot to the patio. He shakes Kyle's hand, slaps Matt's shoulder and finally sits at a table and puts his arm around Maris, whispering something in her ear right as she slides him one of Kyle's beta-testing ballots.

Nodding to Jason, Cliff continues. "Like I was saying, we need a change of plans." Cliff paces in front of the tables, his two hands clasped behind his back.

"I hope he doesn't get out that gavel," Eva says.

"*What?*" Nick asks over his shoulder while tipping back his chair alongside the fire tub.

"His gavel! Remember at that meeting in his trailer?" Eva motions as though she's hitting a gavel on the table.

"What meeting?" Kyle asks, coming up behind Eva and holding out his shoebox for her ballot. "What'd I miss?"

Eva looks up at him standing behind her and deposits her ticket. "Where's Lauren tonight?"

"Home with the kids, *and* on the phone organizing a school bottle-and-can drive. It was her idea for this diner-name voting—"

"Folks! Please! If I can have your attention." Cliff glares

at Kyle, who gives a small bow and motions for him to go on. "Because the point of tonight's Meet and Eat is this: With a few buyers expressing some interest, we'll *never* convince Elsa to hold on to her cottage, not with our current modus operandi. For her, the thought of renovating and opening an inn *now*, after losing her son, is out of the question. It's too ambitious, so we need to downscale our plan."

"But how?" Maris asks.

"Good question." Cliff turns to Maris. "I had dinner with Elsa Saturday night, and I got an idea. We were talking, and at one point when she smiled, I realized I hadn't seen her smile since, well, since before Sal died. It was actually a beautiful thing, Elsa's smile …"

As people nod and murmur in agreement, Kyle raises an eyebrow at Jason while setting down his shoebox on the table. Then he slides two chairs closer to the fire and hitches his head to Jason to take a seat there. "So what's your plan, Commish?" Kyle asks as he sits and lifts a large stick from a pile and drops it into the aluminum tub's crackling fire.

"This. Little things are more likely to change Elsa's mind. I really believe that. Because it's the little things that make us happy … that make someone stay. So don't pressure her about opening that inn, or selling her cottage anymore. Don't nag her, or doubt her. Just, well, let's try this." He walks a few steps before continuing. "Just make her smile. That's it. Nothing else."

"*Sorridi*, man," Kyle says, saluting Cliff. "From the mouth of Sal, who was all about the smile. I like that."

"That's right, *sorridi*," Cliff assures them. "Smile. It's hard to leave a place when you're happy. And easy to leave when you're sad. So if Elsa can find happiness again, maybe she'll stay. And little smiles equal little moments of happiness."

"Ooh. I like that." Eva lifts a crispy chicken finger in a toast and pulls her chair beside Matt's at the portable fire pit. "Okay, so it's Operation—"

Maris raises half a ham sandwich in response. "Make Elsa Smile!"

When she stands, Jason grabs her chair and drags it beside the warm flames as she sets the dessert platter on a table closer to the fire.

Kyle takes another stick and nudges the burning firewood as it snaps and crackles in the tub. Beneath the dark twilight sky, after the men all load up on nachos around the fire—tendrils of smoke dancing above it, glittering sparks rising toward the stars—they raise their food in a collective toast before leaning close to the orange flames and plotting out various smiling schemes.

twenty-three

BY WEDNESDAY, MARIS FINDS HERSELF compulsively straightening the kitchen chairs, then turning to the stools at the island and aligning them just so. Because it's either fuss with the house or twiddle her thumbs. After pulling her hair back in a low ponytail, her next target is the kitchen counter: toaster cord wrapped, bread crumbs brushed away, microwave door shined, loose coins dropped into brass dish, multi-device charger plugged in and charging her cell and Jason's tablet.

From the counter, she notices that rays of sunlight not only stream in through the sliding door, they also accentuate every fingerprint and dog-nose-smear on the glass. When she scuffs over with glass cleaner and a rag, Maddy is at her heels. Maris moves around the dog and spritzes the door, all while making a mental checklist that one, she's had coffee with her sister this week; two, she's walked the beach; three, finalized resignation papers to close out her job; and four, checked up on Elsa. All keeping her busy enough to *not* think about what to do with her life now.

And what she realizes is this: Thinking is so overrated. Sometimes you just have to act.

So she quickly hurries to the counter again and lifts a nickel from the coin dish. "Heads, complete kitchen scrubdown." She bounces the coin in her cupped hands. "Tails," she says to Maddy, who is sitting now and watching her, "clean Jason's studio."

Which would require actually taking off her slippers, putting on sneakers and walking across the dew-covered lawn to the barn out back. Maris flips the nickel in the air, catches it and immediately covers it with her other hand. Slowly, she takes a peek, then squints through the clean slider doors to the dark barn. Weathered buoys hang on its outside walls.

"Tails, it is."

Later—sneakers donned, sleeves rolled up—Maris walks her cleaning cart through the barn's double doors. The first thing she notices is the comforting scent of old wood from the rough-hewn walls and floors. Jason restored the barn two years ago, not too long after his father died.

Back then, it seemed that Jason was mostly preserving memories of his father and Neil in that renovation. Once the building was restored, he spent days cleaning and displaying his father's old masonry tools. Above them, Jason hung a framed photo of Neil in his twenties, wearing jeans and a tee, hair overgrown, as he bent over a clamp while working on a wood project. Didn't she once read in one of Neil's leather journals that old buildings are more about ghosts than anything else … It's obvious in this space; their spirits are here.

Now Madison runs past her, up the stairs, and settles in

Maris' loft studio. There, the German shepherd lies down with her muzzle beneath the second-level railing to keep an eye on her master's kingdom.

But a messy kingdom, at that. "Maybe this will cheer up Jason," Maris says to the dog. "He tries to hide how he feels, but I see him out here so late at night, working, working." She straightens a few loose papers on his desk, then scans Jason's studio. "You see it, too. Right, Maddy?"

The dog's tall ears are like radar, turning to Maris' voice.

"Start at the top." Maris eyes the skylights first, then the framed pictures the sunlight reaches: a wall covered with photographs of Jason's favorite redesigned beach cottages and seaside homes. *Dusty* photographs. So she pulls a rag from her back jeans pocket and wipes along the tops of the frames, then the glass, all while admiring the bungalows and Nantuckets and shingled Dutch colonials on the edge of the sea.

Which leads her to the extensive bookshelves lined with Neil's leather journals and sketchbooks. Some are half pulled out, a couple sit on a small table, some are propped, some opened flat on the shelves. Maris goes at the journals with meticulous gusto—flattening dog-eared corners, wiping off the leather covers.

Next up? She turns and, through the dust particles floating in the space, tackles Jason's drafting table beneath the skylights. A drafting table covered with a mess of tracing paper and sketches; architectural scales; pens and markers. A swing lamp clamped to the top of the table is coated with more dust. At least now he'll be able to focus with his writing utensils arranged in a tray, papers neatly stacked, calculator returned to desk.

A ringing phone suddenly cuts through the quiet. She shrugs, hurries to Jason's big L-shaped desk and picks up the phone. "Barlow Architecture!"

"Excuse me?" a man's voice answers.

"Um. Barlow Architecture?"

"Is this Jason's line?"

"Yes! Who's calling, please?"

"Is this the answering service?"

"No, it's Jason's wife."

"Maris! Hey, I'm surprised to hear you there. Usually my calls go straight to voicemail. This is Rick, at the salvage yard."

"Rick! Yeah, I'm, well … I'm helping Jason with some office work." As she talks, the mess on Jason's desk catches her eye. "So how are you?"

"Busy as heck. Give your husband a message for me?"

"Oh, darn," she whispers while scattering invoices and contracts, looking for a pencil and notepaper. "Okay, okay." She rests a pen on the clean back side of an envelope. "Give it to me."

Once she jots down the message that several refurbished doors have arrived for Jason, she hangs up and looks at that envelope again. And then at the many other unopened envelopes on his desk. Her hand brushes across them. There must be two dozen, some postmarked from weeks ago. So she sits in Jason's comfortable, padded chair, rolls it close to the desk, finds a letter opener in the top drawer and begins ripping open the business mail, scanning the letters and clipping them to the envelopes, then neatly setting them in piles by date and priority.

After many, many envelopes have been sliced open,

emptied, assessed and sorted, Maris spins around at the sound of first, Madison scrambling down the studio stairs, and then—Jason's voice.

"What on earth are you doing?"

~

"I should ask you the same thing, hon!" Maris turns in his desk swivel chair. "I thought you had appointments all day."

"I do. I need to pick up a contract I forgot." Jason takes a cautious step into his nearly unrecognizable, spit-shined studio, then turns to Maris and sees warning signs of the free time she has on her hands. His wife wears her rarely donned cleaning threads: a button-down over a loose tee, and ripped jeans with old sneakers, her brown hair pulled back in a ponytail—revealing small gold hoop earrings and something else. Jason notices some worry in her brown eyes.

"What happened to this place?" he asks.

"I gave it the magic touch?" Still, Maris remains in the chair at his desk with her cleaning cart close by.

"But where is everything?" Jason asks while dropping his keys in his canvas blazer pocket.

"Oh, you know. A place for everything, and everything in its place!" She grabs a pile of papers and presses them into a neat pile as he heads to his spotless drafting table. "I'm pretty sure it's been proven," she goes on. "I guess Kyle would know better than me—we can check with him—that people work more effectively in an organized setting? So, well, I thought I'd straighten up. And *think*! I'm starting to think, too, about what I'll do, you know, with my life." She smiles and shrugs.

Jason lowers the swing lamp at his drafting table, angling it just so. "What about Elsa?" he asks while fussing with the light. "Aren't you supposed to be checking on her?"

"I tried." She gives him a quick smile when he glances back at her. "I went to the inn, opened the door, and guess what? A real estate agent kicked me out! Said she's got showings all day. So Eva and I are taking Elsa out to lunch tomorrow."

"Well ... Listen, sweetheart." Jason lifts more neatly stacked papers, then slides out a tray where his drafting pencils are lined by size. "This is my stuff."

"And look!" She jumps up and heads to the side wall. "I *organized* it. I even set up Neil's journals by date—"

"Date?" Jason looks to his wall of bookshelves. Normally he can pull off any journal he needs, blindfolded. "No, no. They were lined up by *theme*. Argh," he says while sliding a hefty black leather journal off the shelf, "you're making more work for me."

"No, I'm not. Look at your correspondence." She walks back to his desk. "Some of this mail's so old, and not even opened. See?"

But Jason doesn't see, because he doesn't turn to watch. He's too busy taking his brother's leather journals off the shelves and setting them in his preferred *themed* piles. He only vaguely hears his wife insisting *Here's another, and another*, as she rattles his envelopes.

"Maris," Jason finally explains. "Those are just solicitations to join architecture associations." As he says it, he heads to his desk for that forgotten contract. Except now he can't find it because everything's been clipped and noted and stapled and duly filed. Which is also when he notices that Maris has stopped talking. And he knows, not that he's especially liking it. But it's obvious his previously workaholic, career-dedicated wife doesn't know what to do with herself. What to do with countless empty days stretching before her.

"Maris," he says again while turning to her. And he sees how she gives him a small smile, but her eyes blink back tears. So he tucks a loose wisp of hair into her low ponytail, then gently rests his hand on the side of her face. "Maybe check office assistant *off* your Dabble List, would you? It is outside your area of expertise."

"You don't want me to finish up?" she asks, looking down at his desk again. "Because, wait! Wait." She grabs an envelope with a distinguished-looking letterhead clipped to it. "This is *not* a solicitation, Jason Barlow. You're winning an award! Listen." Her finger drops to the letter and drags along the lines she reads. "You are respectfully invited to the Connecticut Architecture Awards Gala." She looks up at him with the clincher. "As a *finalist*."

"Finalist?"

Maris nods, then resumes reading. "And as one of several finalists, you and a guest attend, all expenses paid. Any additional guests pay a designated fee. Please RSVP with head count and additional payment by—"

"Finalist for what?" He steps closer, his hand reaching for the paper.

"Let me see." Maris steps back, still reading. "It says on the bottom. Here. Award: Best Connecticut Coastal Architect, Jason." Her eyes meet his. "This is *big*, babe." She lifts the paper a little closer and reads more. "Property … Renovated cottage at Sea Spray Beach. Nominated by," she says, then stops and looks at him for a quiet second. "Theodore Sullivan."

"Ted?" Jason takes the invitation.

Maris moves beside him and points out Ted's name. Her voice is soft when she explains. "He wasn't sure if you'd mind."

That's all Jason needs to hear before eyeing Maris. "Now how would you know that?"

"Okay." She sits in his swivel chair again and leans back. "Ted called me. Don't be mad. We had coffee and talked. It was right before Sal died. Ted wanted to go above and beyond for you. He told me—"

"Wait." Jason holds up a hand; he has to read the letter again. So he does, walking the studio floors while taking it in, all while Maris silently waits.

But apparently she just *can't* hold this in any longer. "Ted told me," she continues, "how you said that you channel Neil in your designs, and how you couldn't do what you do today if you didn't have your brother's journals and resources, which makes Neil an intrinsic part of your work. He thought this would honor *Neil*, too, *with* you."

"Ted told you this?" Jason still walks on the wide-planked barn floor while reading the nomination and heading to Neil's journals.

Maris stands and follows him to the bookshelves. "I never knew what to make of Ted, so I *met* him for that coffee. And after sitting down and talking with him, it really helped me to understand things between you two." She reaches up and brushes a piece of lint off Jason's jacket lapel. "He knew I'd resented your taking on his cottage renovation, since he caused the accident that cost your brother's life. And so he wanted my permission before nominating you. And in a sense, nominating Neil. Which I thought was really special."

"And you gave him your permission?"

"Yes, Jason." Maris steps closer and runs the back of her fingers along his jaw before giving his scruffy cheek a kiss. "Yes. I did."

twenty-four

A DEAD TIE. AFTER ALL that beta testing, Kyle tallied the diner-name ballots and the outcome is even-steven: three votes for The Driftwood Café, three votes for Dockside Diner. So the decision rests on a tiebreaker. But is it really wise to make a life decision on seven votes? Is that rash?

He'll ponder that thought with one more cigarette as he drives his pickup to Stony Point to make a special Operation Make Elsa Smile delivery. After driving beneath the stone railroad trestle and cruising the winding beach roads, it's apparent that someone *else* made a decision, and a wise one, from the looks of it.

"Lucky dog," Kyle says to himself. A familiar FOR SALE sign now has a SALE PENDING banner pinned across it. Someone decided to buy the cottage with the blue awning on Sea View Road. Kyle still thinks that it could have worked for his family. Even though the bungalow sits high on a steep driveway, which he reconsiders while slowly driving past, they could have barricaded it for the kids.

"Doesn't matter now," he mutters through a cloud of

smoke. "Cross that one off the list."

Seems that lately he and Lauren have done more crossing off than anything else. So maybe their decision to move here is wrong. "*Merda*, now I'm sounding like Elsa," he whispers while tamping out his cigarette, then parking on the roadside a block away from her cottage. He picks up a gift basket from the passenger seat and fusses with the inn how-to books tucked inside it. Some of the books' pages are dog-eared where he found interesting tidbits for Elsa; some have his inn trivia jotted in the margins. After skimming and noting them last night, he tied the three books together with a piece of ribbon, found one of Lauren's seascape driftwood paintings, and arranged everything in a basket. Finishing touch? A scrap of fishnet edging it all.

Maybe this little Thursday morning surprise will make Elsa smile, even briefly. So Kyle gets out of his truck and treks down the beach block to her cottage front door, where he sets the basket, fusses to center it in Elsa's line of sight, rings the doorbell, then hightails it out of there.

"Shoot," he says with a quick glance over his shoulder. He didn't plan on where to hide, and so he zigs, then zags, before running behind a large tree, which he leans against while catching his breath. When he peeks out, Elsa's cottage door is just opening. She wears a robe and opens the door wider, looking around before spotting his anonymous gift basket. She picks it up and thumbs through the books, which must make her curious enough to step further outside and look down the street. It becomes the perfect photo op, so Kyle holds up his cell phone and snaps a picture of her puzzled—but smiling—face, right before she shrugs, turns and goes back inside.

Mission accomplished. Kyle checks the time on his phone, seeing that he has fifteen minutes to get back and open the diner on schedule. So he cuts across dew-covered lawns leading to where he parked his truck—anything to not be spotted by Elsa. When he climbs in the driver's seat, he looks back toward her cottage, wondering if he actually made a mistake.

Because if he hand-delivered the basket, Elsa could have cast the deciding diner-name vote for him.

~

"What I'm finding," Elsa says while holding her fork aloft later that afternoon, "is that it's becoming hard to trust people." She raises the forkful of cucumber salad to her mouth and slowly chews. "Between the tag sale fiasco when everyone I know plotted against me, to Cliff setting up a private dinner under false pretenses—"

"What?" Eva and Maris say at the exact same moment. "False pretenses?"

"You didn't tell us *that*," Maris scolds her aunt while Eva sips her tomato bisque.

"That's right. And now," Elsa continues, pointing her fork at them as she does, "my two beloved nieces taking their aunt out to lunch for girl talk and bonding? It's lies," she says while scooping more cucumber salad. "All lies!"

"But we *are* having girl talk." Maris sneaks a spoonful of Eva's soup.

"Yes. At an inn that would be my competition, *if* I went through with opening my own Ocean Star Inn."

"Really?" Eva looks around the room.

Oh, there's no kidding her; Elsa won't be fooled again. She takes in this local seaside inn's dining room. From the walls half-paneled with weathered boardwalk planks, to the Nantucket lanterns mounted on them, to the dark wicker dining chairs, it's blatantly obvious. "Your intent was clearly to sway me to open my own, *better* inn."

"Well, you do still live there. Have you even had any offers?" Maris fiddles with the gold chain of her star necklace while waiting for a reply.

"Just showings," Elsa answers. "I've been reading the feedback in the agents' emails after their clients tour my place. There's no solid interest, so you two don't have to pry and fret."

"No, Elsa. It's just bonding we're doing. Really!"

"Of course, we're doing that, *too*." Elsa sits back as the waitress delivers their dishes, setting down a loaded BLT in front of her. "Actually, this is a nice place to bring Michael for lunch." She takes a bite of her sandwich and tucks an errant piece of bacon back into the bread slices. "He'd like it."

"When's he coming?" Maris asks.

"Tomorrow, with a delivery of things from Sal's apartment. He'll be staying overnight and leaving Saturday so we have time to go through Sal's belongings."

"You'll be busy, then. Please tell him we asked about him," Eva adds, "and send our regards."

They quiet then, while digging into lobster rolls and veggie wraps. Eva and Maris cut small pieces for the other to sample.

"Ooh, Jason would love this lobster roll," Maris

exclaims after having a taste of Eva's lunch. "Scrumptious," she says as her eyes drop closed with the taste.

"Oh! Elsa!" Eva points her fork at her. "Did Maris tell you about Jason being a finalist for a big award?"

"What?" Elsa asks.

"It's true!" Maris says.

"And *very* prestigious." Eva raises her glass to Maris.

Maris toasts her sister and sips her ice water before explaining. "It's one of the few annual architect awards issued in Connecticut. Jason's been nominated for Best Connecticut Coastal Architect. And it's all because of the work he did at Ted Sullivan's place."

The irony of *that* does not escape Elsa. "The big cottage reno Jason took on last summer at Sea Spray? But isn't Ted the man who drove his car into Jason and Neil?"

Maris nods. "You just never know what good can come out of the bad. Taking on Ted's reno was really difficult for Jason at first, but he and Ted both came to terms with things in the process. You'll be there at the ceremony, right? You're not leaving that soon, are you?"

"When is it?" Elsa asks as she pulls her cell phone from her purse. "I'll note it on my calendar."

"I'm not sure of the *exact* date, but it's in a few weeks, on a Friday night. There's a dinner first, with drinks, followed by a formal award presentation. And dancing, too."

"Do you think he'll win?" Eva asks as she drizzles lemon juice on her lobster roll.

"I don't know," Maris explains while eyeing the second half of Elsa's BLT. "The competition is tough. But I'm telling you, Jason's most painful project ended up being his most beautiful." She points to Elsa's sandwich. "Can I try a piece of that?"

"Yes!" Elsa cuts off a corner of the sandwich half. "Though I must say, these are not garden tomatoes the cook used. I can tell." She places the sandwich sample on Maris' plate. "If I were, well …"

Maris bites into the BLT. "And look at the paint, over there." She points to a far wall while pressing a napkin to her mouth. "I mean, coral?"

"Never mind paint color. Aunt Elsa, check out those hydrangeas." Eva hitches her head toward a large vase of flowers on a side serving table. "They're … why, they're silk!"

Elsa whips around. "Oh, awful. Artificial flowers in a beach inn? When I think of my gorgeous hydrangeas, especially at this time of year when they have that dusty denim color. Well, of course I think of you, Maris."

Maris reaches over and clasps Elsa's arm, right above her gold mesh bracelet. "That's so sweet of you." With a quick smile, she adds, "And hey, not much personal attention here, either. I can just imagine how *you'd* ask after your guests."

Eva looks over her shoulder for their hostess. "She gave us our food and rushed off, texting away on her cell phone! And that's the last we see of her?"

Suddenly, that's all Elsa has to hear. Oh, they're good, these two sisters, the way they wheedle and distract and lead her right into their trap. "Okay," she says, pushing away her empty plate and reaching for the dessert menu. "I get what's going on. First, Kyle dropped off inn books in a secret basket."

"Kyle?" Maris asks.

"Yes, Kyle. Of course, he thinks I didn't notice him plotting and hiding. And now you two, making me compare this inn to my own possible inn, trying to get me to one-up this place."

And then nothing, Elsa notices. Her nieces simply sip their drinks and steal furtive glances at each other.

Until finally, Maris breaks the silence. "Well, Elsa." Then a pause as her voice drops to a hopeful whisper. "Is it working?"

~

The hardest part is the thinking. Cliff doesn't know how Elsa comes up with all her different chalked *inn*-spiration sayings. But most days before Sal died, a new one was written across her walkway, beside the hydrangeas, and they always got people to stop and smile beside the flowers. If he could do the same, write something uplifting, maybe she'd like that.

So then, what would make Elsa smile? Little things, little things. Little things bring the easiest smiles. So Cliff grabs a fat piece of chalk, backs up a few steps and looks up and down the street to be sure she's not on her way home, then returns to the walkway and crouches down.

And … nothing. He's got nothing. Words run through his mind while he pushes up his denim shirtsleeves. Beach, reach, peach. Ocean, motion, suntan lotion. Corny rhymes that he's sure Elsa could weave into a happy seaside lyric. But for his legally trained mind, nothing. So Cliff stands up, clasps his hands behind his neck and looks out toward the distant beach. Funny, he never noticed how, off to the side beyond the hydrangeas, there's a narrow sandy path through some dune grass. It's practically hidden by the clusters of now-golden grasses, the blades arching high with feathery seed heads shimmering in the sea breeze.

Cliff moves to the patches of scrubby dune grass and steps onto the sand between them. It's a secret entrance to the beach beyond. The golden sand unfurls like a soft carpet to the lazy lapping waves, while white puffy clouds float across the sky. Someone—maybe Elsa—left a forgotten pair of flip-flops nestled close to the grasses, maybe after heading through the sandy path for a spontaneous barefoot beach walk.

Now that's one thing he knows for sure. Elsa's walked the beach *many* times; he's spotted her when patrolling the boardwalk, or tacking a notice on the Stony Point community bulletin board. Wisps of her hair would blow across her face, a light sweater over her shoulders as she sometimes picked up a shell or stone. So this is how she gets to the beach for those leisurely walks.

Suddenly, it hits him. Cliff tosses the piece of chalk in the air, catches it and rushes back to the walkway. On his knees, he writes in a large, cursive script: *A walk across the sand, for a life simply … grand!*

Just as he dots that exclamation point with a flourish, sitting on his haunches, the sunlight on his face and shining on his happy words, it happens. A long shadow falls across it all.

"Ahem." Two legs clad in black skinnies step in front of him, with black leather sandals on the feet.

Still crouched, Cliff brushes his hands together to clean

away the chalk dust, and looks up at the rest of the ensemble: a beige silk blouse, untucked, gold mesh bracelet, and large dark sunglasses. "Elsa. I didn't expect you back so soon," he says.

"Maris dropped me off out front. We had lunch together, at that inn next town over." Elsa steps closer, moving beside Cliff. "And what do we have here?"

"Nothing." Cliff remains crouched, and props his chin on his hand as he admires his literary craftiness. "Just a few lines."

Silence, then. Enough to make him glance up at Elsa again.

"It's crooked," she says, looking from him, to the words. "Your phrase is not in a straight line. Do you see that?" She points to the walkway and twists her torso to try to read his message—which is upside down, to her. When Cliff gives another look at his inn-spiration, she continues. "Or should I say, your *graffiti* is crooked? Because this message is *not* authorized, and *certainly* not approved by me."

"Well," Cliff answers, leaning slightly back, "we just thought—"

"Wait. We?" Elsa's sandaled feet step closer, her shadow looming larger. "*We?* Okay, so this is another plotting scheme of yours."

"No, Elsa. It's nothing." Cliff cups his chin, studying his thoughtful message about walking across the sand. "Nothing at all. I'm sorry if I bothered you with this." He finally stands and brushes off his chalky hands again, then merely walks away. "Good day, Mrs. DeLuca," he calls over his shoulder, still walking.

It's important that he keep moving so that Elsa doesn't

get suspicious. He continues at a steady pace through the sunshine, past the shingled old cottage until he rounds the corner toward the street, out of view of Elsa's mistrusting eyes.

After a few moments when Elsa has to think he's gone, he peeks around the corner of the building, where random scaffolding still remains, and a rogue sawhorse leans against the cottage. He watches as Elsa carefully steps around his chalked inn-spiration message, her head tipped down, her hand holding back her thick brown hair as she looks closely.

Which is precisely when Cliff gets ready. Elsa stands directly in front of his words: *A walk across the sand, for a life simply … grand!* It's just as he'd hoped, yessiree. With her finger to her cheek as she reads his carefree lines, it can't be missed, the way her face lights up with the message. He grabs his cell phone from his pocket right as Elsa lifts her sunglasses to the top of her head, throws a quick glance to her secret sandy passageway to the beach, then reads his message again—with a warm smile on her face lighting her brown eyes … and lifting his heart.

He manages to snap one single picture before skedaddling himself out of there.

Smile? Mission accomplished.

twenty-five

EVERY NOISE, EVERY SHADOW, IS a ghost haunting her. That Thursday night, it's the rain, starting when Elsa lies awake in bed. At first, there's a random tap-tap-tapping as big raindrops hit her windowpane. She turns her head and faces the window, because the sound reminds her of late nights this past summer. She'd often read with only a bedside lamp on, the cottage dark and shadowy otherwise. But a similar tap-tap-tapping sound would rise up the stairs in the stillness; that tapping coming from Sal's fingers working at the computer keyboard as he drafted her beach inn's extensive business plan. Occasionally, there'd be a pause in the typing, and Elsa would hear papers rustle as he researched monthly maintenance schedules, and inn branding possibilities, and competitive rates.

So now, as the tapping at her window continues, it can feel like early August—and like Sal's still alive, working. Elsa throws back the sheet and goes to the window, pressing aside the curtain and looking out at the dark night. Listening. And remembering her life a few short months ago.

"*Dio ti benedica*," she whispers, her eyes tearing up when she drops the curtain and returns to bed. With the sheet drawn up and her head resting on the pillow, she closes her eyes and says the same words that end every day of her life now. "God bless you, my sweet son."

By Friday morning, the tapping has grown into a steady hiss. The sky is gray, the clouds heavy, the rain steady. On September days like this, Elsa knows just the trick to rid the dampness from the cottage. And with Sal's friend due to arrive from New York, there's no time to waste.

After a quick shower, she sets large lanterns and candles on her long, wood-planked dining room table, lighting each so that the room glows with flickering warmth. Around each candle, she scatters seashells, then sets out coffee cups and pastry dishes in front of her French country chairs. There's a box on the floor filled with spiky brown cattails and lagoon grasses; she'd cut a bunch the day Jason moved Sal's boat out of the marsh. As she arranges those cattails in large white pitchers on her chipped-paint cupboard now, the doorbell rings.

Which is when she realizes that since Sal's death, everything is about him. Everything. From the rain falling in the dark of night, to his good friends, Michael and Rachel, arriving with Sal's things from his apartment, to her pitchers of lagoon cattails—some edged with white seed fluff—Sal is at the root of every minute of her every day.

Once Michael and his wife unload the boxes from their car, Rachel leaves, taking their car to bring a care package of goodies to Michael's daughter at college.

"How is Summer liking her classes?" Elsa asks while pouring coffee in the dining room. "And being away from home?"

"Good enough," Michael says. He adjusts his chair with a quick glance toward Elsa's front door. "I'm having more separation anxiety than she is. I worry, you know."

"Sure. Every parent does."

"Lock your doors at night. Don't walk alone across campus. Be sure to keep your phone charged."

If only. If only a few routine precautions could keep our families safe. Elsa sets down a platter of pear tarts brushed with honey glaze. Beside it, lantern light flickers.

If only.

"Where will you go, Elsa? Now that you're selling this cottage of yours."

"I'm not sure. A neighbor in Milan invited me for a visit. She thought it might help clear my thoughts and let me see things with a new perspective."

Michael forks off a hunk of the warm tart. "Maybe you should hold off on selling here, then. Until your thoughts *are* cleared."

"Everyone says that." Elsa motions around her dining room, at the table that held so many summer dinners; at the mismatched china pieces on the cupboard; at the lone starfish propped in the rain-dribbled paned window. "But they don't walk these empty halls filled with ghosts."

"Ah, ghosts." He sips his coffee. "In my forty-seven years, got a few of those in my life, too."

Elsa reaches for a tart while glancing across the table at Michael. His short, dark hair, graying at the temples, can't fight the sea damp and holds a wave. And at forty-seven, he's ten years older than her son. Though Michael's face is weathered from a life outdoors, sitting here, he could look more like a fisherman back from sea than a New York mounted police officer. There are faint shadows, too, beneath the eyes of her son's friend. She recognizes those shadows; they hold Michael's own stories. Whether they're from patrolling the city streets on horseback, or from grief at losing his good friend, she can't say.

"With my daughter away at college, we have space at home in Queens. If you ever want to visit with us, where the halls and rooms aren't so quiet," Michael says, hitching his head toward the living room behind him, "you just let us know. Even if it's for a few days to settle your son's estate in the city. It's the least I can do, for Sal."

"Thank you, Michael. But I really can't. I'll let you know if I change my mind. For now, the familiarity of my own cottage suits me." She tastes a tart, chewing slowly. "Ghosts and all."

"Have you had any offers to buy this place?"

"Only one. A quick, early offer—which I've kept to myself. No sense in getting folks here worked up. The buyers lowballed me, and I declined it."

"Good. You stand your ground. Sal would want you to." Michael takes a long sip of his coffee, then wipes his mouth with a napkin. "You sure you don't want to stay put and open that inn? Wasn't Celia going to work with you?"

"She was, with the decorating. Before everything changed. But she's gone back home to Addison. To her job there, to get on with her life. And to privately grieve, I'm sure."

"Understandably. Her loss was devastating, too." Michael reaches for another pastry and takes a big bite. "Still, I'm just saying. This pear tart is amazing. You'd be doing the Connecticut shoreline a disservice, keeping recipes like this to yourself."

"Oh! That reminds me, I have something special for you. Wait right here!" Elsa says while pushing back her chair and rushing to the kitchen. She opens the refrigerator and pulls out an already-prepared plate, lifting off the plastic wrap and walking the dish into the dining room as though it holds valued jewels. "One *pomodoro* with mayo and sea salt." She sets the plate of her homegrown tomato slices beside a white pillar candle. "One with a fresh slab of mozzarella and sprinkled with basil, and a grand one drizzled with balsamic vinegar, olive oil, pepper, lemon thyme and dotted with grated Parmesan."

Michael sits back with a laugh, all while eyeing Elsa's deck-pot, pulpy red tomatoes spread out on a white dish. He brings his clustered fingertips to his mouth and kisses them with flourish. "*Perfezione!*"

Elsa smiles and nudges the plate closer to him.

"I forgot all about our tomato taste-off. But I am more than happy to have your tomatoes put mine to shame," he says with a wink. After Michael tucks a napkin into his shirt collar, he pulls a folder from a briefcase he'd brought along. "While I'm at it, now's a good time to review Sal's list with you. Because some of the items he wants to bestow are personal, and I have to be sure you're okay with them." He opens the folder and turns it toward Elsa across from him.

Setting her leopard-print reading glasses low on her nose, Elsa skims the list. "He forgot no one, did he?" she asks, looking up at Michael over the glasses' frame.

"Your son was quite the gentleman, Elsa." He motions to the list with his tomato-laden fork. "There's a gift on there for everyone who meant anything to him during his summer days here."

"Kyle, Maris, Eva. Even Nick," Elsa reads. "Jason," she whispers.

"I think Sal sensed things might not go as planned, at the end. Maybe he wasn't feeling too well. Because he gave me these items a few days before his valve surgery, right before you and Celia arrived. Sal wrote a special note for each person. It's all in a box I brought in earlier. First stop, your niece Eva's place. I've got Sal's brass bull-head sculpture for that media room Jason's working on." Michael forks another half tomato. "Like I said, everything's in that box … except for one item," he manages around the food. "One of Sal's things, intended for Maris, is still here in his room."

"For my niece?"

Michael reaches past a tall, flickering lantern, nods and clasps Elsa's hand across the table. "So I'll need to take that one with me."

~

"Put some pizazz into your handwriting," Kyle instructs the waitress. She stands in front of a chalkboard near the doorway and writes across the top: *Fall Specials*. "I read a study that said handwriting done with pressure, when the writer really presses down on the pen, or chalk," Kyle adds, motioning to the chalkboard, "communicates high energy levels. Which, in my opinion, boosts appetites."

"So, like this?" the waitress asks, pressing the chalk while writing *Foliage Filet*.

Kyle squints at it, his hand to his chin. "Yeah. Yeah, that's good." He glances at his diner, which happens to be busy this Friday lunch hour, then to headlights sweeping across the parking lot in the rain. "Keep going!" he urges his waitress. "Maybe we can sell more meals."

The waitress looks at her notepaper, then, in large cursive, chalks *Leafy Lasagna.*

If there's anything Kyle's learned during his two years of owning this place, it's to be flexible and change things up. Lauren thought this new *Specials* board would be worth trying as the weather gets cooler and more people eat inside instead of on the patio. When he walks back toward the kitchen, a familiar face comes into the diner.

"Hey, it's Michael Micelli!" Kyle says as this latest customer grabs a stool at the counter near the blueberry-muffin-lined glass pastry case.

"Kyle." Micelli extends his hand for a shake. "What's happening?"

Sometimes a handshake isn't enough, and seeing Michael Micelli in his diner, well, it's a little like seeing Sal again. So Kyle walks around the counter and gives Michael a hug, slapping his rain-slicked shoulder as he does. "Where's your horse, guy?" Kyle jokes.

"No hitching posts outside, I noticed." Michael sits again and grabs a napkin to wipe the rain from his face. "I actually came from Elsa's. She's letting me use her car today."

"That right?" Kyle gives a nervous glance to his crowded diner. Most of the red-padded booths are filled, and the windows are steaming up from the dampness outside. "Listen, I'm swamped. Really have to get to the stoves. You here for lunch?" he asks as he walks toward the kitchen.

"No." Michael eyes him for a second. "I'm here to see

you. Got a few minutes, by any chance? It won't take long."

"Oh boy." Kyle looks out at his packed diner, then over his shoulder toward the kitchen where his cooks, Jerry and Rob, are busy at the stoves. But it's the serious way Michael is watching him that does it. "Sure, man. Give me a sec to square things with my cooks, would you?"

"Go ahead," Michael says as he stands and takes off his wet jacket.

"Coffee?" Kyle asks while walking backward toward the kitchen.

"Perfect." Michael points to a far, empty booth near the diner T-shirt display hung on fishing net. "Meet me over there."

In the time that it takes Kyle to be sure that Jerry and Rob are okay with the lunch orders, then cook up a grilled cheese sandwich and pour two coffees, for the life of him, he cannot fathom what brings Sal's friend to the diner. But when Kyle joins Micelli, he does manage another idea.

"You are just the guy I need," Kyle says when he sets down Michael's grilled cheese and pickle before settling in the booth. "You, my friend, are going to break a tie in my beta-test poll." After telling him about The Driftwood Café versus Dockside Diner, Kyle pulls a slip of paper and pen from his white chef apron and slides it across the table.

"And what's this?" Micelli asks as he bites into the thick, gooey grilled cheese sandwich. "Bribery?"

"Nah," Kyle says while Micelli pours a dollop of ketchup on his plate, then dunks a corner of the sandwich into it. "It's lunch, on the house. You know," Kyle explains with a slight shrug, "any friend of Sal's is a friend of mine."

"Well, thanks." Michael takes a moment to jot a note,

check off his diner-name choice, carefully fold the ballot in half and slide it back to Kyle. "There you go, Bradford."

Kyle leans forward and slips the ballot into the back pocket of his black pants. "Appreciate it."

"Nice place you have here."

"Yeah," Kyle agrees while glancing around at the tables, and a baby in a high chair pushed to the end of a booth, and the glass fishing floats hung in each window. "I do all right."

"My pop's old paisan in the city owns a delicatessen. Sal used to have lunch there with me. We'd shoot the shit, you know."

"I miss the guy. He'd cover busy shifts here, waiting tables. Gave me some great business advice, like that patio." Kyle hitches his head to the window, where the rain is finally letting up outside.

"Not surprised," Michael says, holding his sandwich aloft. "He had that way about him."

"Without a doubt. I bought an Italian handbook," Kyle admits, then takes a long sip of his coffee. "As a way to summon him. To tap into that *Italiano*, and think like he did."

Michael wipes his mouth with a paper napkin, balls it up and puts it on his empty dish and moves the plate aside. "Sal's actually why I'm here, Kyle," he explains. "I saw him before his operation and we had a long talk about his beach friends. Man, he loved you guys."

"That right?"

Michael nods. "Also said something about that pickup truck of yours?"

"Shit, yeah." How can Kyle forget? So many times over

the summer, Sal's magic touch got that old truck purring. And the way the Italian would eye it? There was actual *desire* in his gaze. "Sal wanted that truck bad. *Swore* to me when he came back, he'd have a bank check to buy it."

Michael lifts his hands briefly.

"No." Kyle leans back, eyes locked on Micelli, who only nods. "Oh, no."

Michael pulls an envelope out of his jacket's inside pocket and slides it to Kyle. "Why don't you read this?"

When Kyle unfolds the letter, he first sees a check made out in his name. A bank check with one too many zeros on it to cover his jalopy. He lifts the check, pretty much to believe what he's seeing, then looks at Michael—who motions at him to read the letter.

A promise is a promise, my friend, and I'm good for my word. Your truck is mine now, fair and square, with this check. And what you're going to do is get a good set of wheels for that beautiful famiglia of yours. I believe there was a silver king cab you had your eye on. This check should cover it. And don't settle. Make sure it's the right one, just like I did when I saw your sweet wheels, man. Oh, and Bradford? Anything left over, you put into that house fund. –Sal

~

Maris glances up from the journals and notes and how-to books spread across the painted farm table, and looks through the arched doorway into the living room. From where she sits, the big stone fireplace is clearly visible. Off to one side of the mantel, beside a hurricane lantern, there is a framed photograph from her wedding last year: She and Jason waltz on the beach in the evening, the horizon violet over the water, tiki torches and candles throwing glimmering light on her vintage gown. They knew only happiness that night; sweet, blissful happiness.

Now she pulls her cardigan close and looks back down at her books beneath the grand lantern-chandelier in the dining room. *Harness Your Inner Light* and *Creative Careers* and *The Perfect Job: Fulfillment or Fantasy*. She picks up *Creative Careers* and thumbs to the table of contents. All the while, her fingers toy with her etched star necklace. It would be nice to find a new career that taps into her creativity somehow.

But she suddenly drops the book, looks up again into the living room and tips her head. A couple of tin stars are propped in the center of the wood mantel, with a white conch shell in front of them—the shell Jason gave her two summers ago when they started dating. A bottle of Scotch sits on the far end of the mantel, along with a short, straight glass with a thick base. If she's not mistaken, a bit of amber-colored liquor is pooled in the bottom of the glass, dregs from last night, when Jason couldn't sleep and paced the house.

Still, something's missing.

And Maris knows just what it is. She walks into the living room, straight to that mantel. Straight to her framed wedding photograph. There should be a second framed photograph beside it, one of Jason and his brother in their twenties, standing outside on Foley's deck. She picks up the wedding photo, brushes her fingers across the glass while looking at her groom in his black tux, then sets the picture down.

"Huh." She stands there, hands on hips. Her eyes search

from the sofa, to the jukebox alcove, to a few wedding gifts lining the far wall—their wrapping-paper scraps tattered—to Jason's upholstered chair in the corner beside a dark end table. "I *knew* it," Maris whispers when she hurries over. She heard Jason going out late for a walk on the beach last night, then sitting down here sneaking one of those damn cigarettes with a splash of Scotch.

And apparently bothered by something with his brother, as evidenced by the framed photograph lying facedown on the end table. She picks it up and uses the fabric of her sweater to wipe off the glass. "Oh, Neil," she says to the image. He wears jeans and a faded concert tee while standing beside Jason one long-ago summer evening. The dog-tag chain hangs around Neil's neck, his hair is a mess of waves, and his smile genuine as he stands there with his big brother. Both guys hold a beer and lean against Foley's deck railing. Young and handsome and full of themselves, the world was theirs to conquer. Beside them, twinkly lights outline windows of Foley's infamous back room, and the screen door is propped open, no doubt to let in a sea breeze on a steamy night. Was Maris in the back room that night, maybe playing cards with the gang in one of the secondhand restaurant booths, jukebox cranking, drinks flowing?

The real question is: What was *Jason* thinking last night looking at this picture? What made him toss it facedown, and pour himself a strong drink? Sometimes Maris wonders how he gets through his days lately, the way he's been sleeping less and working more.

But her worry is interrupted by a knock at the front door, so she sets the picture down and heads out to the hallway leading to the door. Hopefully, it's a delivery of more self-help books she can thumb through for job and, well, *life* ideas. She hasn't felt this adrift since high school, when she went through a long phase of missing her mother.

"Oh!" she says when she opens the door to see a familiar man standing on her porch out of the rain. He's wearing a jacket and holding a box in his arms. "Michael Micelli!"

"Maris," Michael answers. "I hope I'm not interrupting anything."

"Not at all." She sweeps open the door. "Come in out of the damp. It's really good to see you."

He steps inside and gives her a brief hug. "Is Jason home, too?"

"No. He's out on a job. Did you need to see him about something?"

"Him, *and* you. Would you happen to be free right now?"

"Sure, I actually am." Maris closes the door and leads him down the hallway. They pass the old Foley's jukebox—its glass and silver trim luminous in the alcove—on their way to the dining room. "I actually have free time for the foreseeable future."

"So I've heard." Michael sets his box on the farm table.

"You have?" she asks while brushing aside her research books.

There's a pause, then, filled with a wise look on Michael's face. "There are no secrets at Stony Point."

"Isn't that the truth!" Maris waves him off and grabs matches and two pillar candles set on wide silver candlesticks from the sideboard. "Would you mind lighting these? I'll make coffee. And a sandwich, maybe?"

"Just coffee, Maris." Michael leans over with a lit match and touches it to the wicks. "I came from The Driftwood Café, so I've been well fed."

"You saw Kyle, then?"

"I did." After hanging his jacket over a chair back, Michael sits, leaning his elbows on the tabletop. "He's got a nice operation going on there. Kyle showed me the patio Sal convinced him to install."

Maris sits beside Michael for a moment, quiet, with a small smile. "Sal loved that diner." She reaches over and clasps Michael's arm before getting up and heading into the kitchen to put on the coffee. "We all miss him so much."

Just thinking of Sal wearing his half apron and breezing through Kyle's diner—order pad and pencil in hand, charming the customers with his ready smile—has Maris' heart ache for those easy summer days again. As she fusses with the coffeepot—adding coffee grounds, filling the decanter with water—she hears Michael call out from the other room. "Sal's actually why I'm here." Maris finishes up pouring the water into the coffeepot, getting spoons from the drawer.

"I saw Sal a few days before his surgery," Michael says from the kitchen doorway now. "He needed my help tying up loose ends with his friends here, in case things didn't go well with the operation. And he had something of yours that bothered him."

That's the line that does it, that gets Maris to turn from the cupboard, a coffee mug in each hand. Which she practically drops when she sees what Michael is holding. It's the pewter hourglass Jason gave to Sal for his thirty-sixth birthday. In the soft light on this cloudy day, the aged pewter gleams, and the golden grains of sand silently fall through the glass funnel.

"Sal wanted you to have this back, Maris."

"But that was Jason's, not mine. His mother had it made special for Jason's father after his tour in Vietnam. The sand is from right here at Stony Point."

"And according to Sal, it's all *yours* now." He hitches his head toward the dining room table. "I have something for you to read. Come on," he says, turning around and disappearing into the shadowy dining room, candlelight flickering, light rain streaking the windows.

Maris hesitates, takes a step, then stops. She sets the cups on the countertop and tucks her hair behind an ear, feeling the silence in her old home on the bluff. She felt it earlier, too, worrying about Jason being so out of sorts lately. He's been quiet, the house has been quiet.

And now this. It's like the silence right when the waters quiet as the tide is about to change, the seas about to shift.

twenty-six

IF THERE'S ONE THING JASON Barlow could use at the end of this pain-in-the-ass Friday, it's a hot meal with a stiff drink. From sunup to sundown, the rain spit at him, the traffic jammed, a client cancelled, and now—he shakes his cell phone—his battery quits right while listening to his voicemail. Out of juice. Dead. The day just won't stop hounding him. Not to mention that his leg's been acting up with the damn humidity.

He tosses his good-for-nothing phone on the SUV's passenger seat and looks through the streaked window toward a narrow beach. This part of Stony Point, farthest from the main beach, is a different world. Railroad tracks run atop a sloping bank of land rising beyond a small neighborhood of older cottages. Behind those cottages, passenger and cargo trains chug past several times a day.

But the water is calm here at Back Bay, a little inlet on the remote outskirts. The secondary beach across the street, beyond some wild brush and wispy dune grass, almost makes up for those occasional rumbling trains. If he can secure the reno job here, it'll help fill in the huge gap in his schedule left by Elsa's scrapped inn renovation. And the change might do him good.

From where he's parked in front of the potential client's cottage, the bay water is in clear sight—a view of blue with which Jason can work design miracles. After another glance toward the beach, he grabs his sweatshirt and steps outside, flipping up his hood and opening the SUV's liftgate so Maddy can jump down.

"Let's go, girl. Walk out some kinks," he tells her.

And doesn't the dog bolt straight across the beach into the water in quick pursuit of a rogue seagull. To make matters worse, Maddy then swims back, lopes across the desolate beach and gives a brisk shake—standing right at Jason's feet.

"Damn it, Maddy," Jason scolds while jumping aside. "Run it off, would you? I'm not putting you in my truck soaking wet like that."

When the German shepherd takes to the beach once more—nose to sand, tail wagging—Jason looks back at the cottage across the street. He'd photographed it from every angle to reference in his initial planning, and has some rough ideas for the reno. Locking down this job would also smooth some of his contractors' ruffled feathers after Elsa's mess left them in the lurch, too.

But for now, he does what he really came out to the beach—in the rain—to do. To find his brother. Or his spirit, or memory. Something. Because it's been weeks since he's felt Neil's presence. Maybe at this more isolated corner of Stony Point, he might hear a word or two in the lapping waves. Or hear Neil's voice whispering in the hiss of the steady drizzle.

"You here, for Christ's sake?" Jason hikes his sweatshirt hood up higher and squints out at the gray sky above the dark water. The sand at the high tide line is wet and firm from the day's rain. There's not much worse for his leg than a rainy day, seaside. But walking with his prosthesis on counters the ache, right at the stump, brought on by the heavy sea dampness.

"Lining up a new job, across the street there," Jason says, hitching his head toward the old cottage behind him. "Family wants to add a second floor to grab some of this view, and I wanted to run an idea by you."

This is usually when, somehow, Jason taps into his brother's ideas, his voice. So he stops walking and simply listens. There's the slosh of small waves breaking nearby, and the hiss of the light rain hitting the bay water. And there's more—wait. He takes a step. But it's only the low moan of a distant foghorn rolling over the misty Sound.

"So you don't have an opinion on that cottage there?" Jason turns around to consider the board-and-batten bungalow nestled on a narrow cottage-lined street. And listens to nothing. "Quit dicking around, Neil. *Talk* to me, man."

When the rain picks up with a raw breeze, he throws an impatient glare at the sky, quickly crosses the beach and opens his SUV's liftgate. Maddy jumps in, spins around and jumps out again.

"Hey! Let's go," Jason orders her while pointing to the rear cargo area.

So the dog leaps in, turns twice one way, then twists the other way before giving Jason's hand a sloppy lick.

"Settle down, would you?" Jason asks, then closes the

liftgate and gets in the driver's seat, throwing one more glance toward the quiet beach where he'd hoped, maybe, Neil's voice might drift in the breeze, the tide, the rain. Instead, he's got nothing but a sopping-wet dog stinking up his truck.

So Jason can't get her home soon enough before meeting up with Kyle. Who he's sure is calling his dead cell phone to see what's keeping him. After pulling into his long driveway, Jason quickly lets out Maddy, and the dog promptly runs to the deck and gives a yip at the kitchen slider.

In the minute it takes to close the liftgate and dodge raindrops while running back to the driver's seat, there's no sign of Maris at the door. It's not like his wife has anything else to do since she quit working, so where is she? Because the last thing Jason wants is to go inside and chat about his day. Not when a burger and beer are waiting for him. So he latches his seatbelt and gives the SUV's horn a toot. Which is all it takes for Maris to show up at the slider and let in the dog, then step outside, arms folded in front of her as she squints through the shadows to wave at Jason.

"Are you fishing tonight?" she calls out, shielding her eyes from the light mist. She's got on a short black cardigan over her tee and tattered jeans. "Maybe the rain's letting up?"

"No fishing," Jason calls back through his open window. "Quick stop at The Sand Bar with Kyle. I'll grab a bite and a brew." He puts the vehicle in reverse and slowly backs up. "I'll see you tonight." But he stops when Maris steps down two of the deck stairs, holding up a hand, then tugging her sweater closed against the cool dampness.

"Wait! Did you get my message?" she asks, bending a little to eye him in his dark SUV. "I left you a voicemail."

"My phone's dead, no."

"We had a visitor today."

Jason starts to close his window just as the rain picks up again. "Go inside out of the rain, sweetheart. We'll talk later," he says with a wave before backing further down the sloping driveway and running over a good-sized stick that fell from the tall maple. "Ah, shit," he mutters, then runs a hand through his rain-damp hair before rubbing his face and wondering when's the last time he shaved. He gives his knuckles a quick swipe along his cheek. From the feel of his whiskers, has to be three days now.

~

Kyle pushes through the side door at The Sand Bar to get to the deck. He balances a heaping basket of pretzels in one hand just as he hears the question. Jason's behind him, and the question about Celia gets Kyle's attention.

"Hey! Jason, my man," the bartender calls from inside. "Been a while. Good to finally see you again."

Jason stops, half in and half out, turning back to Patrick.

"Everything okay?" Patrick asks from behind the bar. "You know, with you and that dame? The pretty little singer?"

"Yeah, it was nothing." A fluorescent light flickers over the doorway where Jason pauses. "She straightened herself out."

The odd thing Kyle notices is how Jason abruptly ends the talk right there, stepping outside into the damp night, though the rain's finally stopped. Kyle stands beneath a patio umbrella at one of the black mesh tables, sets down the pretzels and lights a smoke. "You or Maris talk to Celia since that night?"

"No." Jason pulls a lighter from his sweatshirt pocket. "You?" he asks while lighting a cigarette of his own.

"Lauren's selling her driftwood paintings at a craft fair in Addison next month. At the Apple Festival at the cove. Plans to visit Celia afterward." Kyle takes a long drag of his cigarette. "When we quitting these things?" he asks, flicking the ash. "We need to set a deadline. They're no good for our health."

"I'll get around to it." Jason squints through the smoke. "One of these days."

"Hey, there's no 'I' in teamwork. We're supposed to quit together." Kyle tosses a few pretzels in his mouth, then adjusts his *Gone Fishing* cap and eyes Jason standing against the deck railing. "Bro, you been taking care of yourself?" He brusquely rubs Jason's face. "Got that mountain-man look going on again."

Jason slaps Kyle's hand away. "Shut up, guy. Been too busy to shave."

"That right?" Kyle pulls out a chair from the mesh table, swings it around and sits with his arms over the back. Above him, strung white lights glimmer around the umbrella spokes. "What's really wrong? You seem off." He takes another long drag of his cigarette, then motions to Jason's dark, wavy hair. "And shit, you're all wet."

"Got caught in a downpour."

"That sucks. Man, that dampness today. Your leg had to feel it, no?"

"Little bit. I walked it off, Doc." Jason shifts his stance. "Been a helluva long week."

"Tell me about it. Try watching slumping September numbers and see how long the week is."

"That bad?"

"Eh." Kyle finishes his cigarette and squints through the smoke, then tosses back a few more pretzels. "So what's *your* excuse? Maybe you should buy one of those little tabletop fountains for your nightstand. Let it bubble there at night and you'll feel better."

"Seriously? A bubbling fountain will solve my problems?"

"It can help. Because I read that listening to the sound of water reduces stress hormones."

"That's just psychobabble, dude."

"No way, studies prove it. The sound of water soothes because we spent the first months of our lives peacefully in it, in the womb. And hell, you've got those waves breaking practically outside your window. So between that, and having your wife home now, you ought to be happy. But I see you're still brooding on that bluff."

"I'm just beat, Kyle. Ready to go home and take a hot shower."

"You ever do that with Maris?"

"What?"

Kyle stands and spins his chair back in place at the table. "You heard me. Shower with your wife. Works wonders, too."

All Jason does is shake his head and flick his burned-down cigarette butt, so Kyle has his doubts. Maybe Jason has, maybe not. "Try it sometime."

"Enough of that, Bradford. Let's go in," Jason tells him.

"The food's got to be ready."

"If we chow down quick, we can get in some fishing. I packed a cooler in case the rain stopped. Looks like it's our lucky night."

"Not sure I'm up for it. I've got to catch some sleep."

Kyle grabs the pretzel basket and follows him to the door. "Hey, saw Micelli today."

"That right? I knew he was stopping by Elsa's this week. What's he up to?"

"Maris didn't tell you?"

"Haven't talked to Maris today," Jason admits as he stands beneath the flashing fluorescent light and holds the door open.

"You haven't talked to your better half?" Kyle gives him a small shove inside. "After you up and left her?"

"Hell," Jason says over his shoulder. "Is anyone going to let me forget that? It was for forty-five minutes."

"You *make* the time for Maris, Barlow, after what you put her through."

They walk past the bar as the jukebox spins a slow tune, and a late-season baseball game plays on a mounted flat-screen television. Someone on a barstool calls out a greeting to Barlow as they wind their way around tables to their regular booth on the side wall.

"So apparently Micelli is making the rounds today, on behalf of Salvatore." Kyle slides into the dark booth and takes off his *Gone Fishing* cap just as the waitress sets down their order.

"What are you talking about?" Jason asks around the plates they shuffle and straighten.

"What I'm saying is that Sal had some unfinished

business he wanted settled, even after his passing. And Micelli's here checking names off a list Sal left him."

"And he saw you?"

"This morning, after seeing Eva and Matt. Said Maris was next on the list." Kyle bites into his double cheeseburger, swiping a bit of juice on his chin with the back of his hand. "He didn't catch up with you?"

"No." Jason lifts the roll of his overloaded deluxe burger and pours on a dose of ketchup. "I must not be on his list."

When the waitress sets down a pitcher of beer, Kyle lifts it and fills the two glasses on the table. "You've got to be."

"I still don't get it. What's the point of these visits?"

"It's like Micelli's granting Sal's last wishes. But this stuff's not in the will because Sal handled it just days before his death. So it's personal. Like this." Kyle pulls out his wallet and plucks a piece of paper from it. "Remember how the Italian loved my beat-up wheels?"

"Your truck? Shit, couldn't keep his hands off it."

"Promised me that when he came back from New York, he'd have a bank check ready to purchase it."

As Kyle unfolds the paper and slides a check across the table, Jason is digging in to his burger. But he nearly gags upon reading the sizable dollar amount.

"Left me a letter saying he was good for his word." Kyle takes the check back. "Told me to snag that silver king cab I've been hankering after."

"No shit." Jason takes a long swallow of the beer. "Are you really going through with it? You'll cash that?"

"What else am I going to do? I tried to give it back, but Micelli insisted he talked with Elsa. She okayed everything. Lauren and I will run it by her, but apparently Sal's closing all his deals. Must be the Wall Street in him."

"Wow." Jason takes another bite of his burger, then snags a few fries off his plate. "Unbelievable. Seems a little soon for Micelli to be making those deliveries, though. It's only been a few weeks since Sal died, and people are still emotional about it."

"Hell, it's *never* easy granting someone's last wishes … whether a few weeks or a few months go by. But Micelli's busy, too. Had a free weekend and got it done." Kyle plucks an onion ring off his plate just as the bar door opens and someone walks inside, pausing to get his bearings.

"And how do you like that," Kyle says, nodding toward the doorway. "Speak of the devil."

twenty-seven

KYLE HOOKS TWO FINGERS IN his mouth and gives a sharp whistle that cuts through the din of jukebox music and bar talk and sports announcers covering a televised game. It's enough of a whistle to elicit a sidelong look from Michael Micelli before he heads over, wearing a Yankees cap, backward, a dark jacket and jeans. Jason almost expects Sal to be following behind him; the feeling is so strong, it's uncanny. Michael sits beside Kyle, shakes hands with him and Jason, then sits back in the booth and takes in the shadowy room.

"Man, it's just like Sal described." A sudden cheer erupts from the bar, and they turn to see some crackerjack pitch from the mound replaying on the big-screen TV. "Place just like this on Long Island. Seahorse Café." Michael shakes off his jacket, pulling his arms from the sleeves. "Regular honky-tonk beach joint."

"That about nails it," Kyle agrees while motioning for the waitress to bring another glass.

"Feels good to get out of that damp air." Michael sits back and rolls his left shoulder. "It always aggravates an old injury."

"And what exactly brings you to our fine watering hole this Friday night?" Kyle asks as he lifts the beer pitcher and fills the glass the waitress brought, then slides it to Michael.

"Got some business to tend to." Michael nods to Jason across the table. "With you. Called your house, and your wife directed me here."

"That right?"

"Listen, I'm glad you showed up." Kyle pulls Sal's check from his wallet. "Because *this* business doesn't quite sit right with me," he says while giving the check to Michael beside him. "I really can't accept it."

"Sure you can," Michael counters. "Look at the date. Sal wrote it before his surgery, to keep his promise to you." He slides the check back. "He wanted it this way. You know, I was his friend for years, Kyle. And he *knew* he had health ailments from that bout with rheumatic fever, growing up as a kid in Italy."

"What's that got to do with the check?" Jason asks.

"Everything. Sal figured there might come a day when he couldn't work anymore, given his heart condition. And he invested like a boss, so he could live okay if that happened. DeLuca's net worth is shocking, boys." Michael turns to Kyle. "I assure you that 40K is a drop in the bucket. Won't make a dent in Elsa's inheritance."

"Come on, man," Kyle insists. "She can use it more than I can, I'm sure."

"No, she won't take it. I ran it all by her this morning and she gives her blessing."

Kyle eyes the check, and when Michael toasts his beer toward it, Kyle folds it in half and returns it to his wallet.

"So ... what?" Jason asks, squinting across the table at

this New Yorker sweeping into town with a bag of goodies. From the look of this city cop with a couple of faint scars on his face, and his eyes showing his forty-plus years, Jason can't really read him. "You're here to lift us up or something?"

"Come again?" Michael resettles his backward cap on his head.

"Sal made a list, and you're checking it twice? As though we can't get by without his help?"

"Hey, bro," Kyle interrupts with a wince. "Give him a chance."

"That's all right." Michael reaches for the pitcher and adds more brew to his glass. "It's also why I'm glad I finally found you, Jason. So I *can* explain."

"Okay. But I don't need to hear the bullshit." Jason downs the last of his liquor and sets his glass firmly on the table. "So let's not beat around the bush."

"And that's *my* cue. You guys can talk now." Kyle nudges Michael to let him out of the booth. "Got to use the can." As he stands, he gives Jason a warning look. "Keep it chill here, would you?"

Jason watches Kyle saunter across the room, stopping at the bar to chew the fat with the bartender, Patrick, first. But Jason's no dope. *Use the can*, like hell. His best man's giving him some space to hash it out with this arrogant dude from the city, as if Micelli knows anything about their tangled lives here.

"Sal *wanted* you there in New York, before the surgery," Michael begins. "Elsa told you that, remember? He was devastated that he couldn't reach you, couldn't explain." Michael sits back and loosens the collar of his button-down shirt, then rolls another kink in that bothersome shoulder.

"You were out of town? At a convention in Boston?"

"Don't give me that runaround," Jason says while pushing his empty dinner plate to the edge of the table. From the back of the bar comes the clatter of balls as a pool cue breaks the rack. "He had plenty of time to reach me. So cut the crap. Salvatore DeLuca chose *not* to clue me in."

"That's not how it was." Michael looks toward The Sand Bar's entrance door, then leans closer to the table. "He got really afraid at the end and tried—"

"You know something?" Jason interrupts. "Sal heard my whole story. Why I'm sitting here with half a leg, what it was like to lose my brother, how I turned my life around with his cousin Maris. He got it all out of me this summer. But he let on *nothing* about his condition? To anyone?"

"He thought he'd live. Barlow, come on. He made arrangements in *case* anything went wrong with the surgery. But in here?" Michael hits his chest, right over his heart. "He still believed he'd survive the operation and so didn't want to burden you all with unnecessary worry."

"A little selfish, the Italian was, wouldn't you say? Playing us the way he did."

"*What?* Playing you? It's not like that."

"Bullshit. We all spilled some story, every one of us, I'm sure. Kyle, Lauren, Celia. Yet, he didn't."

"You're seeing it wrong."

"Don't tell me how I'm seeing it. Because I'm seeing it for what it is. And now this load of sentimental garbage, you with your list and bearing gifts? Give me a fucking break."

Michael pours another splash of beer into his glass and downs it in one shot.

"Why don't you get out of here now," Jason tells him. His voice drops as he leans closer over the table. "You don't belong at Stony Point, and neither did Sal. There's no need to coddle Elsa and sympathize with us."

"You're wrong, Jason. Sal *did* belong here." As he says it, Michael jabs the air with a pointed finger. "He fully intended to live out the rest of his life here with Celia."

"Plans, plans. More bullshit built on one *mother* of a secret—that your friend's days were numbered. Well, that house of cards collapsed, Celia's long gone, and you can pack it up, paisan." Jason pauses, sets his arms on the table and leans even closer. "Whatever you brought for me, keep it."

"No, listen."

A motion catches Jason's eye. It's Kyle returning from the men's room and watching them from a distance. "*You* listen," Jason says while standing to leave. "Whatever you're delivering, I don't want it and said to keep it." He leans both hands on the wood table and bends low, face to face with Micelli. "Toss it, man," he whispers. "Because I don't give a shit."

When Jason heads for the door, he can't help but notice a determined Kyle making his way past guys standing around the bar. But Jason keeps walking, swiping an empty chair out of his way as he does.

"Hey, Jason!" Michael calls after him. His voice is oddly close, though; too close, actually. And suddenly his hand is clasping Jason's shoulder, turning him back.

So Jason gives him exactly what he wants. He stops, all right. Stops, spins around with a sucker punch and clips Micelli on the jaw in a way that Micelli never sees coming, losing his footing as he stumbles backward into a table.

But oh, the city slicker's quick; Jason figures those street smarts kick in when they have to. Because Michael first puts a hand to his face as he straightens and steps around a basket of pretzels knocked on the floor, then comes right back at him. He shoves his hands into Jason's chest hard enough to jostle him, muttering, "You son of a bitch."

It happens fast then. Sudden voices shout out as a handful of men leave their barstools and gather around, shifting left to right, waiting to see which way the action's going down.

It won't take long to see, not if Jason has anything to do with it. He backs up a step and pushes up his sweatshirt sleeves, noticing how Micelli works off the hit to his face by giving his head a small shake. For Jason, that's the perfect opening for a two-handed shove to Micelli's chest—a forceful push that gets Micelli stumbling back over a chair, breaking it while trying to stop his fall, and taking it crashing to the floor with him while more heated shouts rise in the shadows around them.

Figuring Micelli got the message, Jason turns to leave and walks straight into a table, but catches himself—though not before knocking the drinks to the floor in a crash of splintering glass and spilling liquor. When the couple at the bumped table jumps out of the way, he turns to them. "Sorry," he says, still walking, but backtracking to right a leaning chair. "I didn't mean … Sorry," he manages again, then shoulders himself through the riled-up men watching—some toasting Jason with their beer glasses, others slapping his back.

When Kyle calls out, "Whoa, whoa," while pushing

through the crowd, Jason keeps walking—past the bar where Patrick glares at him through customers lined up two-deep for a drink—and approaches the jukebox near the door.

One thing's for damn sure: Kyle will *never* let up on him about all this. So he figures that's who's grabbing his shoulders a moment later, and he shakes him off to try to leave. Never realizing it's Micelli on the rebound, pulling Jason's arm and spinning him around, throwing a punch at *his* jaw and connecting with Jason's face just enough to turn him sideways.

"Come on, man," Micelli yells. He whips off his hat and flings it aside, then clenches both fists in front of him as he shifts from foot to foot. "Jesus, you motherfucker," he says while taking a swipe at Jason.

"Me? *I'm* the motherfucker?" Jason sidesteps, and when Micelli moves in on him, Jason knows right where to put his shot. He lands a blow to that injured left shoulder, a blow strong enough to throw the damn New Yorker into the wall behind him. "You're going down, you prick," Jason mutters as his heart pounds and as he decides to finish off this guy, taking slow steps closer.

Which gives the bartender and Kyle the seconds they need to move in and separate the two. Kyle comes up behind Jason and hooks his arms beneath his shoulders, backing him toward the door as Patrick extends a hand to Michael and helps him to his feet.

"Shit, bro!" Kyle keeps hauling Jason to the door, even when Jason resists and loses his footing. "You hit a fucking *cop*, man. What's *wrong* with you tonight?"

Jason shoves himself back into Kyle and shakes him off.

Kyle—all six feet two of him and he makes sure Jason knows it—roughly grabs Jason and propels him toward the door. Even that enrages Jason—Kyle's forceful pressure against his back bringing a sudden flashback of Neil's body hitting his during the bike wreck years ago. Jason stumbles, then straightens and runs a hand across his sore face, looks back once over his shoulder, then pushes through the door and walks out into the night. He gasps a quick breath of the damp air, then another, while he never stops pacing.

"That's right," Kyle warns while standing in the doorway beneath the flickering fluorescent light. "Get some air and cool off!"

Jason spins around and walks slowly backward across the parking lot, throwing his open hands up in the air while watching Kyle.

"Barlow, man, what's your prob? You've got to make it right in there. With Patrick, *and* Michael," Kyle says, motioning Jason back to the bar. "Get a grip and come on, you friggin' hothead. Fix things."

Jason turns and keeps walking away, even when he hears Kyle give a sharp whistle. Nothing can stop him anymore, not when he's had his God damn fill of this eternal day, this eternal month, this life. He heads toward his SUV and feels every blessed ache in every muscle in his body with every step he takes.

~

Kyle Bradford may very well be siding with the enemy, but something about the whole night tells him otherwise. Truth be told, he never really believed Micelli would agree to a few hours of fishing here at Stony Point, now that the rain let up. Thought for sure the city boy was done with this beach's motley crew and would hightail it back to New York, bruised and fed up. With a cigarette in his mouth, Kyle leans on a boulder and baits his fishing line.

"Nice fishing hole here," Michael Micelli says from the bank of rocks. He maneuvers a few steps closer to a swirling tidal pool, then looks out over Long Island Sound. "Don't even need a flashlight."

"Not tonight, man." Kyle contemplates the view with a long drag of his smoke. The nearly full moon hangs low over the water, painting a swath of silver on the night. That silver crosses over the rippling waves of the Sound and casts seaside landmarks in distinct shadow: the big rock behind the swim raft, the pier at the far end of the beach, a slow-moving barge out past Gull Island Lighthouse. "See that moon?"

"Can't miss it."

"It's going to get better, too. In a couple of days, it'll be the super harvest blood moon."

"Come again?"

"Yup. That's what I said when I heard Leo Sterling—our local meteorologist—talk about it. The full moon that night will be the harvest moon, *and* a supermoon, one of the full moons closest to Earth and looking massive. Lunar eclipse also happening, which casts the moon in a red glow—making it a blood moon. So … a super harvest blood moon."

"Shit." Michael looks up at the heavy moon shining on the water. "You know how they say a full moon brings out something in people? Maybe *that* was your friend's problem tonight."

"Ha!" Kyle shakes his head and fidgets with his line. "I wish that's all it was." He scrutinizes a good spot to land his baited hook. "Thought I could clear the air between you and Barlow, before I head home to Eastfield and call it a day. Thanks for coming along."

"No problem. Haven't done this in years. Got a sweet little cottage right across the Sound, at Anchor Beach on Long Island. But I'm outnumbered by women there: my wife, Rachel; her daughter, Ashley; and my own daughter, Summer. They're more the *Let's go out for seafood* type, rather than the *Let's catch dinner.*"

"I hear you. And it's one of the reasons I want to buy a house here, and soon. Hoping to get my son, Evan, into fishing."

Michael climbs up over the rocky bank, finds a lure in the tackle box, sets up his line and turns toward the water. "Sal loved hanging out here, fishing with you guys," he says as he gives a few practice casts, sweeping his fishing rod in a sideways motion without releasing the line.

"I figured." With the rippling silver water spread before him, Kyle can almost see Sal sitting off to the side, tugging on his line, shooting the breeze. "He'd show up after Barlow and I were settled in. Sometimes he'd bring a basket of good grub from his ma, a few beers. Lots of times he got us betting on things. Said his friend in the city liked to wager." Kyle finally casts his line, which whistles over the sparkling water. "That'd be you, I'm guessing."

"You'd be right."

"You game for a bet? Five dollars?"

"What are we wagering on?"

Kyle tamps out his cigarette butt and reels in his line.

"Distance. See who can send their hook the farthest."

"Seriously?"

"Shit, yeah. You on?"

When Micelli resettles his backward Yankees cap and glances at Kyle, his eyes drop to Kyle's sizable arms. "You'd beat me on strength alone. I saw the way those arms hauled Barlow out of the bar."

"Casting's got more to do with technique than strength, man. But hey, if you're not up to it, that's fine."

"Like hell I'm not."

"All right, then. Send the line straight out, due south. Directly into the moonlight, so we can see where it hits. Give it a shot."

The tide is low, and small waves lap at the rocks below. Michael shifts his stance and points his rod out at the shimmering water, then pulls the rod straight up in front of him.

When Kyle nods at him to proceed, he does.

With both hands, Michael lifts his rod back over his shoulder, then swings it up and out with everything he's got, trying to get as much muscle behind the propelled line as he can.

"Tsk, tsk."

"What?" Michael asks, looking from where his hook hit the water, back to Kyle.

"Is that how you'd throw a *baseball*? All wussie, over your shoulder like that? Your fishing line went more in the air than out over the water." Kyle joggles his own fishing pole, grabs it with both hands at the base, swings it off to his side and stops. "You have to cast in a straight line from the side, just like you're on the pitcher's mound. Not arched up into the sky." With that, he flicks his fishing rod around and the line flies gracefully out over the water, beating Micelli by twenty feet, at least.

"Shit." Micelli reels in his line, sets the rod on the rocks, pulls out his wallet and plucks out a five, which he delivers to Kyle.

"Sweet, man." Kyle pockets the money. "I'll put it in the fishing kitty. End of the season, we go out for dinner. Take the wives, have a nice time."

"You do this every week?" Michael asks as he opens a bag of potato chips set near Kyle.

"Friday nights. Start up in spring, finish sometime next month, when it gets cold." There's a nibble on Kyle's line, so he tugs it, releases, and loses the catch. Good enough reason to set down the pole and snap open one of the cold cans of beer he'd brought along, holding it first to his neck before taking a swig. Then he gets the ice pack out of the small cooler. "You might want this," he says, tossing it over. "For your face."

When Michael catches it, Kyle feels for the guy. His face is weathered, and he guesses the cop's had his share of tough days on the New York City streets. On top of that now, a clobbering from Barlow.

Michael joggles the ice pack while shaking his head. "Son of a bitch," he mutters, then presses the ice pack to his jaw. "But thanks."

Now there's one for his book. Kyle whips his Italian handbook out of his back pocket, holds it to the moonlight and flips through the pages. "Or," he says, his finger finally finding the spot, "as Sal might say … *Stanna mabaych!*"

"Good one, man. You nailed it."

"Yeah, well." He tucks the book back. "Ice is crucial, to keep the swelling down. Your teeth okay?"

In the dark, Michael removes the ice pack and tests his bite, resting his open hand on his face and moving his jaw from side to side. "I'm good," he says while setting the ice pack back in place. "He just clipped me off the side."

"I'm glad you came tonight, Micelli, especially after what Jason put you through. Because the same way DeLuca knew shit about us here, knew how we lived, *you* need to know shit, too, if you're delivering the Italian's final wishes. Special people here, and I think Sal got that."

"Barlow included?"

"Absolutely. Look, the guy's got a short fuse lately, I'll give you that. But he's also kept us all together here. And in line," Kyle says as he steps to the side and snags a handful of chips. "Sal had his demon to deal with, with his heart and all. And he would want you to know about Jason, who has his own demons. Sal ever tell you about them?"

"Other than losing half his leg in an accident, not much. Said he was a great guy, like the brother he never had. The real deal. Which I'm not really seeing."

"Listen." Kyle pulls another cigarette from his pack and lights it, then leans back against his boulder. Lamplight fills the windows of the lone gray cottage close by, on the end of the beach. Some family's settled in and comfortable. Kyle hopes, wherever Jason is, he's settled down now, too. "Barlow's lived through a nightmare or two. And sometimes it's best to just leave him alone. He had a tough time in recent years, pretty bad stuff went down. And he finally came around with Maris in his life. But since Sal's funeral?"

It all runs through Kyle's mind then, images of Jason—from being stoic at the funeral, to breaking down later that night and leaving his wife. "Jason hasn't been right since that day. He hides it most of the time, but something changed with him. So what I'm trying to say is that he didn't mean anything, Micelli. Back there." Kyle motions in the vague direction of The Sand Bar, miles away from fishing, and a low, heavy moon, and a shadowy Stony Point Beach.

"Seemed it. Got me good, man. I'll be black and blue."

"Believe me." Another drag of his cigarette buys Kyle a second. "Something else is eating Jason up, and you? You got caught in his crossfire."

"From what Sal told me about Barlow being all right, I kind of figured."

"And tonight, I'm apologizing for Jason, first. Allow me that. I was his best man, after all, and he really deserves it."

Michael simply nods, then lowers the ice pack and reaches for one of Kyle's smokes.

Kyle tosses him the lighter across a few rocks. "Now let me tell you a few things about Jason Barlow."

twenty-eight

ONE THING MARIS HAS LEARNED about being unemployed is this: What day it is doesn't matter as much anymore. It used to be that her Saturdays were frantic with errands and banking and house chores. Now? Saturday, Tuesday … the days of the week are nearly indistinguishable.

Except that Jason's home on Saturdays. Though she sits with her how-to books spread out on the dining room table beneath the lantern-chandelier, Maris hears him moving about upstairs. He must be shaving at the porthole mirror over the bathroom sink. On second thought, with that bruise on his face, he might just be putting a cool cloth over it.

"I'll get it," Jason calls out when the doorbell rings. Madison races him down the stairs, eliciting a stern warning from Jason as she does. "Maddy!" he orders firmly when he reaches the bottom. "Stay, now."

Maris peeks around from her seat and sees the dog sitting, her ears straight, her haunches barely touching the floor as the German shepherd's antsy to check out their visitor. And when Maris hears the familiarity in Jason's voice when he opens the front door, she gets back to her books—three of which are dog-eared and highlighted. Noted passages advise how to change your *life*, not merely your job. Another favorite includes a pre-made Venn diagram, in which to pen rewarding moments in work and personal life. Common elements that overlap in the Venn could lead to one's inner Zen! And the next tidbit has her whip out her cell phone: Categorize your people contacts. Well, from spending over a decade in the fashion industry, her cell's directory overflows with connections.

But instead of scrolling through them, she sets her phone down. Maris *thought* Jason was talking to Matt, or Kyle, by his question: *What are you doing here?* But a sudden change in his tone nixes that. So she slowly stands, lifts her quilted denim jacket off the seat back and puts it on while listening closely to the men's voices.

"We have to talk," comes the reply from someone standing on their front porch, followed by Maddy's tense clicking paws as she paces near the door.

"Didn't you get my message last night?"

Which gets Maris to hurry down the hall, nearly tripping on a half-opened wedding box that appears to hold a silver toaster. There's only one person Jason gave a message to—a message that left Jason with a bruised jaw and bad temper since sitting with an ice pack on his face all night. Even Maris stroking the side of his cheek with a feather touch couldn't get him to calm down. The voices get louder.

"I got your message, all right."

"I guess it needs repeating. I told you then, and I'm telling you now. *Get out.*"

With one hand, Maris quickly pulls Maddy back by the

collar, at the same time slipping her other arm around Jason's waist, just as he starts to swing the door shut. "Jason, Jason," she whispers with a smile before reaching out to stop the moving door from closing on Michael Micelli. "Michael, well hello!" She looks from *his* bruised chin, to Jason, to the growling dog escaping her grip. "What's going on, fellas?"

"Your husband and I have something to work out," Michael says.

"Now?" Maris asks, squeezing Jason close to warn him to behave, all while he grabs Madison's collar, prompting a nervous whine from the dog.

"Has to be, I'm leaving today." Michael raises a white paper bag. "Egg-sandwich truce? They're nice and soft, easy to chew," he adds while stroking his own bruised jaw.

How can Maris not laugh, which she does, witnessing these two alpha egos about to duel over an egg sandwich. "I see you've been talking to Elsa," she says with a friendly wink, right before she gives Jason a small shove. "Michael, would you mind going around back?" she asks, pointing outside, around to the yard. "The deck is a perfect spot for that delicacy."

"Maris," Jason warns.

She smiles at her husband, then turns back to Michael. "Jason will meet you there in a few minutes."

When Michael nods and steps off the porch, Maris closes the front door, then follows behind Jason and an agitated Madison at Jason's heels, through the paneled hallway toward the living room.

"Jason!" she says in a hushed yell. "What's wrong with you?" When he only glares back at her, she catches up with him near the jukebox alcove, takes his hands and gives them a hard shake. "You have to stop walling yourself up. Something's upsetting you, but I'm not sure that it's just Sal's death. What's going on, babe?"

"A lot on my mind."

"But you're pushing people away again. And your leg is bothering you." She reaches up and strokes his face. "You're *fighting*," she whispers.

"He asked for it," Jason tells her as he walks into the dining room and sits in a chair at their farm table, the dog still following beside him.

"Did he? Really?"

Jason reaches down and scratches Madison's head.

"Jason! I'm *talking* to you. You're up at all hours. I *hear* you at night. You're not sleeping, you're manic with your work. You try to hide it from me that something's wrong, but I *see* it." She has her suspicions why, because Jason's done this before. So she sits beside him and takes a deep breath. "You know what I think? That you're afraid," she says softly, "beneath all that huff of yours." When Jason gives a quick laugh, she continues. "Afraid to love Sal anymore, because of the pain that came with it." She reaches to his chin and turns his head to face her. "But now Sal's friend is here, at our *home*. Give him a chance, would you? Mad or not, just hear him out."

"He annoys me."

"You don't have to *like* him. Just listen to him." Maris abruptly stands and rushes to the front coat closet. From the high shelf, she grabs the pewter hourglass she tucked in there yesterday. She was going to show it to Jason last night, but when he came home foul and bruised, she simply tended his face with cool compresses and let him explain his bar brawl.

But now? She glances over her shoulder from the closet. "If you don't want to do it for yourself, for some sort of closure with Sal, then do it for me," she says while walking the hallway back to the dining room and setting the hourglass on the table. "I listened to Michael, and I'm so glad I did." With that, she bends down and lightly kisses Jason's whiskered cheek.

It's obvious that Jason can't help himself from touching the dulled pewter. The connection to his father brought on by that one vintage piece is that overpowering "So this is what Micelli brought for me?"

"Oh, no." Maris sits and pulls the hourglass in front of her. "This is *mine*."

"Yours?"

She nods. "I have a letter from Sal. You can read it later. But I *will* tell you that he left this to me because he didn't want *you* to ever give away something so immensely valuable again. And because this is one of the finest things you have in your life, Jason, he left it in *my* care. It's mine now." She stands and takes the hourglass back to its rightful place on the mantel over the stone fireplace. Her fingers brush the pewter while the Stony Point sand begins falling through the glass funnel.

Finally, Maris turns to Jason still sitting at the table. "I listened to Michael yesterday," she says, then walks back to Jason and touches his wavy hair. "And you need to listen, today."

~

From the kitchen, Jason can see through the slider outside to the deck. The tall maple tree is showing signs of changing; some of the green leaves are tinged gold already. Another summer's come to an end. Beyond the tree, he can't miss his barn studio, its walls holding history of him, his brother and father working together long into the night. Sunlight glints off the faded red and blue and yellow buoys hung on the dark barnboard walls. For a flash of a second, he pictures his father in his old workshop out there, bent over a table beside a dingy window, sawdust on the countertop, masonry tools hung on homemade shelving on the walls.

But just for a second. Just until Jason shifts his gaze to Michael Micelli setting out egg-and-cheese sandwiches on the deck table. The patio umbrella is open and he sits in the shade. When Maris clears her throat at the kitchen counter, Jason turns to her and takes the two steaming mugs of coffee she holds. As he goes outside through the slider, it's like looking at a mirror-reflection of Elsa—or, hell, of himself—seeing how Micelli has spread out the food. Croissant sandwiches are centered on waxy paper; foil ketchup packets are lined up; paper salt packages neatly aligned; take-out napkins folded with plastic knives set on top of them. The stuff of a fast-food feast. A familiar one that Jason snuck all summer with Elsa while Maris was away on business.

Now, he takes a seat at the table, tears open a ketchup packet with his teeth, lifts his roll top and squeezes a swirl of ketchup on the thick, melted cheese before ripping open a salt packet and sprinkling his food. Then, and only then, does he bite into the gooey egg sandwich, still wordless.

It doesn't escape his notice that his adversary has been doing the same fussing.

"About last night," Michael finally says around a mouthful of egg and cheese, "I'm letting it go, Jason. I get it, everything that happened."

Jason slightly nods, then lifts his coffee and sips it, watching Micelli through the steam.

"So," Michael continues as he swirls more ketchup onto what's left of his egg sandwich. "You free this morning?"

"I can be. Why?"

"Need to take you somewhere. And heads up, your prosthesis will get wet. Maybe sandy, too, so you might want to prep for it."

"What are you talking about?"

"I'll let Sal do the talking. Here." Michael reaches into an interior pocket on his jacket and pulls out an envelope, which he slides across the table. "Read this."

Jason takes one of the thin paper napkins and wipes his mouth, then sits back and looks from Micelli—with his unshaven face, bruised jaw, backward baseball cap and tired eyes—to the envelope. He nods at Sal's New York friend who made this trip on his behalf, then opens the envelope and pulls out a folded note. The words are sparse, which is surprising. Jason expected some lengthy, overwrought message from the Italian. Not this. He reads it, looks up at Michael, then reads it again.

Jay, Your brother is very much here. Very much. There's a secluded shack, a little ways up the coast. You need to get there. –Sal

twenty-nine

JASON PADDLES SAL'S OLD ROWBOAT as far into the shallows as he can. The sun is bright at this hour, sparkling on the sea like those ocean stars Elsa always talks about, and it seems like a sign from Sal. The beach here is raw, just an untamed spit of shore with sandpipers running along the wet sand where waves break unhindered. Wild sea grass grows on a rise in the sand dunes.

"According to Sal's directions," Jason glances at the paper, "follow the coastline past Little Beach, round the bend to where the shore gets rocky. There'll be small boulders beneath the water, and continue until you notice the sloping beach grass." He looks over at the stretch of beach and dunes. "This must be it."

"I'll take the oars," Michael says, "and anchor the boat. You get out here, with your leg and all."

Jason lifts the oars, cuffs his jeans and takes off his shoes before climbing out, holding the edge of the boat to steady himself for a moment. Okay, so he'll need to spend time cleaning his prosthesis later, because there's no way to do this other than to slosh through the shallows. Once on the beach, he bends over and wipes off what seawater he can with a cloth he'd brought. As he does, the chain of his father's dog tags slips from behind his shirt and glints in the sunshine until he tucks it back around his neck. Afterward, he finds a boulder to lean up against so that he can get his hiking shoes on for whatever lies ahead.

In a few minutes, Michael Micelli leaves the rowboat moored a little further out and wades the shallows, shoes in one hand. When he gets ashore, he takes a look around the ragged beach, then quickly slips into his sneakers.

"You ready, Barlow?"

"Where the hell we going?" Jason asks while pushing off the rock.

"Beats me. Sal gave me this basic map, pointing out how to get to this shack he came across."

He hands Jason the paper with Sal's rudimentary drawings on it, each one blocked off and connected to the next with an arrow. Jason looks at the first drawing, then lowers his sunglasses and squints over the top of them toward a hilltop covered with grasses swaying in the offshore breeze. "Guess we start over there," he says while putting his sunglasses back on.

As they walk a sandy path, dune grass rustles alongside them. The grasses and wildflowers here overtake much of the higher beach. The air, too, is heavy with salt, and seagulls soar on the wind currents over the choppy water.

"You've never been here?" Micelli asks from the trail behind him.

"No. This is new to me."

"Sal insisted you get here, before the winter. Made me

promise that I'd do it, get you to this shack of some sorts. He worried that the tide might take it out in the cold months."

"Shack, shack." With a shake of his head, Jason tries to remember his brother ever saying anything about a desolate shack, but comes up with nothing.

After rounding a bend, they crest a gently sloping dune. From here, the view is incredible. Jason lifts off his sunglasses again and sees, further below, on another wild stretch of beach, a shack seemingly rising from the sand. The shack's shingles are weathered silver, and lobster buoys hang randomly from nails on the walls.

And everything about the sight in front of him is pure Neil. Jason just knows it, feels it, hears it. From the blowing dune grasses around the shack to the seaworn-smooth surface of the rope-strung buoys, to the curling paint on the white window trim—he knows. There's only one person who would have *ever* rescued and preserved this old fishing shanty.

"What is this?" Jason turns and asks Michael.

"Looks like your brother's place."

"My brother's place?" Jason hooks his sunglasses through a belt loop and turns again toward the shack, shielding his eyes from the sun. "But how'd *Sal* ever find this? How'd he know?"

Michael steps beside Jason then. "I guess Lauren knew about it. She showed it to Sal this summer."

"Lauren." When Jason says her name, it's a whisper. Of course. So this must've been some hideaway she and Neil snuck to during their surprising love affair all those years ago.

As if he read Jason's mind, Michael continues explaining. "Sal said she came here with Neil and they used it as a retreat. She painted there." He nods to the shack before adding, "And I guess your brother did some writing?"

"Holy shit. This is unbelievable." Jason squints down the sandy hill. If he looks a certain way, with the sun shining just so, can't he see a shadow of his brother walking this unpreserved beach, leather journal in hand, wavy hair blowing in the sea breeze?

"Go. Check it out." Michael motions to the shack. "I'll be on the beach. But the tide'll be changing soon, so don't be too long. I have to get back."

"You're leaving, then?"

"This afternoon. I'm actually taking Sal's Harley off Elsa's hands and catching the ferry home to Long Island." He checks his watch. "But you have some time." He hitches his head to Neil's shack. "Go."

~

Jason maneuvers the dune's sloping hillside and nearly falls while rushing down the sandy path. His hand brushes the ground and he catches his balance, but his eyes never leave the dilapidated fishing shack. The architectural history Neil attempted to preserve is apparent. Even the wood-planked door—covered with faded white paint and battered from wind-blown sea spray—would've been important to his brother. A four-paned window beside the door faces the sea; the windowpanes are opaque like sea glass. There's ropy old fishing net draped over some of the buoys hung on the shingles, and more wild dune grass grows rampantly alongside the shack, sweeping against the silvered shingles.

But it's when Jason shoves the door open and steps inside that time stops. That damn second hand doesn't move, not one bit, as he walks into Neil's secret life, his lair.

It's all here: original wood-boarded walls painted white, and a hardwood floor Neil must've installed; a beamed ceiling; hurricane lanterns and candles everywhere, the candles lined with dribbles of hardened wax; tables covered with baskets of rolled blankets and twine and eating utensils and sun visors; dusty jars of shells and sea glass.

And finally, the real surprise—shelves of Neil's leather journals stacked and leaning, bookmarked with seagull feathers and strands of seaweed. Every bit of it tells a story of his brother's life here, days Jason never knew of but can clearly decipher from these seaside relics. Tucked among the journals is Neil's dog-eared paperback of *The Stars*. Ever since he was a kid, that celestial guide went everywhere with his brother. Neil learned all the constellations in the sky, and believed you could never be lost if you knew the stars. He could find his way home from anywhere with a careful look upward.

But for some reason, the one item that brings Jason to tears is the old, manual typewriter. It's on a lower shelf, one where Neil could pull up a chair and comfortably type. Everything blurs, then. His brother, the seaside historian, never stopped recording the facts and observations of everything from the sea, to the beach, to the cottages that faced it all.

Jason walks to the typewriter and his fingers skim the keys. When they do, he can just hear the clack-clacking that must've accompanied the sound of the surf outside the weather-beaten door and window. He turns toward the still-open door when a gust of salty air blows through the shack, reaching his face.

For a long moment, Jason closes his eyes and breathes that air—the same air Neil lived for every day. *Cures what ails you*, his brother would say.

And then it abruptly happens, the way his body heaves and the emotion floods his eyes in hot, stinging tears that won't stop. He lifts one of Neil's old sweatshirts off the wall hook, presses the thick, salt-worn fabric to his face, and tries to stem the painful sobs the best he can.

When he finally does, taking a long, shaking breath of the sea air, he can't help feeling nearly ashamed. Because it's as though Sal knew; he knew Jason would be devastated by his death, by not having a chance to see Sal and say goodbye. And Sal must've known that anger would fester.

Lord help him, Jason had been so enraged at Sal on so many levels—at the man who'd been like a brother to him for only a few short months—and damn it. Sal's gone and given him Neil back.

thirty

THE SOUND ALWAYS GOT TO *me in 'Nam, that whirring thump of helicopter blades,* Jason's father had once said, his voice low in the telling of a war story. *Mostly, it broke my heart. Think of it ... filling the air. That powerful thump-thump-thump, in a steady rhythm, especially before the chopper lifted off. It was so loud, it swallowed all other sound. The insects were gone. The birds and animal calls? Gone, too. There was only that beating of the air, over and over and over, the massive blades relentless in their tempo.*

When I heard that sound, hell, it often meant I'd never see one of my comrades again. Someone was being airlifted to a hospital. And if he made it that far, he'd eventually ship out home on medical discharge. So that whirring noise had a finality that made me stop for a second; it felt almost like a death. Because I wouldn't see someone again, some pal I hunkered beside in a foxhole night after blackest of nights illuminated only by enemy fire, or a buddy I slogged behind through the swamp muck. Maybe an injured soldier we pulled off the field, dodging gunfire to keep him with us. Or maybe it was someone whose voice told me about their sweet girl back home, or about the mashed potato casserole their mom made, or about their dog—all while strange bug-buzzing filled the night, and our pant legs were tied around our ankles to keep out the monster critters. Just a regular guy would be on a stretcher, in my life until those helicopter blades spun, and then he'd be gone.

Were you lucky to be on that helicopter, maimed in some way, but safe as you were raised to the sky, soaring over the treetops, the jungle getting smaller and smaller?

Or were you lucky to be in one piece, still on the God damn ground?

Jason gets it, now. Still doesn't know who the lucky one was, but he gets it. Hearing the idling thump-thump-thump of Sal's Harley-Davidson engine, seriously, if Jason closes his eyes, it could be a helicopter starting up—its blades cutting through the air in the same rhythmic beat. Because he somehow feels the sadness his father spoke of years ago, sitting on his bench on the bluff, his mind ten thousand miles away in the Southeast Asian jungle.

It doesn't seem possible on this late-September day that it was only last month when Jason swung his leg over that same motorcycle and got on. Settled on the seat behind Sal and went cruising one hot summer afternoon. Just like the last ride he had with Neil, years ago, on a similarly hot summer afternoon. And now? They're both dead and gone.

Michael Micelli fidgets on the bike, getting acclimated to the feel of the motorcycle he's about to take back to New York. Behind him, Elsa's cottage rises up against the sky. One random piece of scaffolding lies beside it; the FOR SALE sign still stands prominently in front of it; Elsa's beloved hydrangea blossoms—a September blend of violet and tan—fill the large shrubs alongside her inn-spiration walkway.

And Michael, sitting on the seat, walks the bike forward a bit, then lifts the kickstand. Maris and Elsa step back—

Maris shielding her eyes, Elsa giving a slow wave.

But Jason does neither. He just watches Micelli adjust the silver mirrors, the bike engine still idling—thumping like one of those helicopters preparing to lift off the Vietnam ground, the sound of the blades always a swan song to his father.

Micelli lifts a booted foot to the peg, ready to return to another life awaiting him—a home life in Queens, with a wife and family and close neighbors. A city life in Manhattan, patrolling the streets on horseback as part of the NYPD's mounted unit.

A fortunate life.

Michael glances over at them before leaving.

And that's when Jason does it. He takes one step forward, breaking away from Elsa and Maris. One step, then another, in the afternoon sunshine. It's obvious that Michael sees it when he puts the Harley's kickstand back down, shuts off the engine and removes his helmet, gets off the bike and walks to Jason.

When Jason simply turns up both his hands, wordlessly, Michael hugs him close. It's a move neither could've seen coming only yesterday. But today, it's like they're both losing a comrade. It's uncertain if they'll ever see each other again. Jason feels the leather biker jacket as he slaps Micelli's back. That jacket, too, was once Sal's.

"You look after these folks," Michael says when he backs up and nods toward the two women. "And yourself, man."

"I'll try."

Jason gives him another quick hug, then steps away. When Michael Micelli mounts the motorcycle and turns on the engine, it's 'Nam all over again. It's the sound of Jason's father's voice, and helicopter blades drumming through the air.

It's sadness, mostly at not really knowing who's ever the truly lucky one.

The beach friends' journey continues in

THE BEACH INN

The next novel in The Seaside Saga from New York Times Bestselling Author

JOANNE DEMAIO

Also by Joanne DeMaio

The Seaside Saga
(In order)
1) Blue Jeans and Coffee Beans
2) The Denim Blue Sea
3) Beach Blues
4) Beach Breeze
5) The Beach Inn
6) Beach Bliss
7) Castaway Cottage
8) Night Beach
9) Little Beach Bungalow
10) Every Summer
–And More Seaside Saga Books–

Summer Standalone Novels
True Blend
Whole Latte Life

Winter Novels
Eighteen Winters
First Flurries
Cardinal Cabin
Snow Deer and Cocoa Cheer
Snowflakes and Coffee Cakes

For a complete list of books by *New York Times* bestselling author Joanne DeMaio, visit:

Joannedemaio.com

About the Author

JOANNE DEMAIO is a *New York Times* and *USA Today* bestselling author of contemporary fiction. The novels of her ongoing and groundbreaking Seaside Saga journey with a group of beach friends, much the way a TV series does, continuing with the same cast of characters from book-to-book. In addition, she writes winter novels set in a quaint New England town. Joanne lives with her family in Connecticut.

For a complete list of books and for news on upcoming releases, please visit Joanne's website. She also enjoys hearing from readers on Facebook.

Author Website:
Joannedemaio.com

Facebook:
Facebook.com/JoanneDeMaioAuthor